CW00529952

To my wonderful children, bonus children, and loving partner. All beautiful, all amazing and all mine. I love you all so much.

we are Broken

a.e. murphy

CHAPTER ONE

I WALK ALONG THE shore, my feet sinking into the soft sand with every step. Looking over my shoulder, I smile at each individual imprint my feet have left behind. Footprints are an amazing thing, even the ones you can't see. They make you wonder who's walked right where you're walking. Who's travelled this same path? What were their concerns?

Who did they love? Are they still alive?

Life is so beautiful.

Everything is good right now. No. Everything is great. It's peaceful. I'm happy.

"Can I walk with you?" An unfamiliar voice asks from two steps behind me.

I glance at the male and my heart stops.

I stare at him, at his face, at his eyes that are a shade of light brown that I can't name, one shade down from milk chocolate. I lose myself in them so easily, so quickly; the sounds all around dim and my heart seems to be beating in my head. I feel my rapid pulse thrumming throughout my entire body.

He smiles slowly and easily, his entire face lighting up with the motion. So handsome, so beautiful. The way the light hits his messy dark hair is picture perfect. It's not too long, but long enough to tuck behind his ears.

The sun catches every curve and contour of his sculpted chest. His lean body is like none I've ever seen before.

"Wow," I murmur unintentionally and my face heats.

Why did I say that out loud?

There's no denying the fact I'm probably as red as a tomato. Mortifying.

His smile widens, his eyes creasing at the corners, his amusement evident. "I'm Caleb."

"Caleb." I repeat his name; it tastes good, feels good. I want to say it again. "I'm Gwen."

"It's great to meet you, Gwen." His smile doesn't falter, not until he brings my knuckles to his mouth and plants the softest kiss upon them. He can't be older than twenty, yet he's already a gentleman.

I'm never washing this hand again.

Once he releases it, I look at the sand beneath my feet and tuck my hair behind my ear with the same hand, fighting the urge to touch the spot he just sweetly kissed.

"Can I walk with you?" He asks, his easy smile now contagious. He looks so happy and carefree. I've never met a person so seemingly happy. It oozes off him in waves, so much that I can almost see its glow coming from his body.

"Are you going to murder me?" Shut up, I yell at myself inwardly. I sound like an idiot. Why do I always do this? Am I so incapable of interacting?

"If I answer that question, will you believe me?" He has a point. "I mean, either way you won't know I'm telling the truth until I've started the sick and twisted process a murderer would probably be cooking up in their head right now." He takes a step closer, two shallow dimples appearing in his cheeks as he grins with his mouth closed. I imagine he is trying to mimic the manic grin of a crazy person but he's just too adorable to pull it off.

"Good point," I laugh, giving him a smile of my own.

"There it is!" He grins and stops me with his hands on my arms, the contact of his warm palms and fingers against my cool flesh sending tingles to places I didn't know existed until now. He turns me to face him, blocking the sun with the back of his head. I look up, almost unable to see him due to the shadow cast between us.

"There what is?" I purse my lips, trying not to smile.

"The moment you stole my heart," he announces, his eyes twinkling, his hands remaining on my shoulders.

The laughter escapes me before I can contain it. "Seriously?"

"Oh come on! That was my best chat up line."

"Sure," I snort, rolling my eyes away from him. I see a man walking his dog by the lapping waves that kiss the sand. "Is this a joke?" My eyes remain on the man and his happy, bouncing dog. My insecurities won't allow me to look at Caleb for fear of seeing rejection in his eyes.

"What arsehole made you think you weren't good enough?"

My cheeks warm. "That's not it." I turn back to face the direction in which I'm heading and start walking. Caleb keeps in step beside me.

"So, you live around here?" He asks kindly and I'm happy that he didn't push for an explanation for my insecurities.

"Since birth."

"It's nice here. We've been here a few times."

"We?" I chew on my lip, hating the disappointment I feel knowing that he doesn't live here.

"My brother, mum and dad." His bare foot kicks at a piece of dead seaweed. We both watch it fly through the air and laugh when the dog goes chasing after it, pulling his owner with him. "Do you have any siblings?"

"No, my mum isn't the most maternal person in the world."

He frowns, tilting his head so he can see my face clearly. "I don't like the sound of that."

My lips pinch together and I wish I hadn't said anything. The last thing I want to do is make myself out to be some kind of sob story. "Are you enjoying Skegness?"

"I am. It's a nice little seaside town."

"That it is." We lapse into a comfortable silence, the sound of people screaming with glee carrying to us through the air. It's from the small theme park just over a mile away. Skegness is such a small town you can hear the screams from almost everywhere if you listen closely enough, just as you can forever smell the salty air of the sea.

"So Gwen is short for...?"

"Guinevere."

"That's an interesting name."

"It matches my personality oh so well." I grin and he returns it with a simple, "That it does."

I glance at him out of the corner of my eye. "Caleb is just Caleb, right?"

The smile remains on his face. How I wish I could just smile that beautifully all of the time. "Yep. And how old are you, Gwenny?"

"Gwenny?" I snort, quirking a brow at him. I'm not sure if I like that.

"If we're going to do this whole dating thing, we're going to need pet names. So what's mine?"

Dating? Pet names? This beautiful man wants to date me? "Umm..."

He waves me off. "That doesn't matter. Those are details we can figure out another time. So... age?"

"Are you profiling? Making sure I'm the right target for your list of victims? What is it I have in common with the others? Is it my green eyes or my sparkling youth?" I jest.

He throws his head back and laughs; it's a beautiful sound. "You know, Gwenny?" His arm slides around my shoulder as casually as if we'd known each other for years. "What a glorious day this is." As he pulls me tighter to him, I smell the scent of coconut lingering on his skin. No doubt it's the scent of his sunblock, but it's delicious all the same. "But on a serious note, I'm twenty. Just turned twenty, two weeks ago."

"I'm eighteen, nineteen in five months."

"You fit the profile perfectly," he states, his smile gone and replaced with a failing psycho smile. He's just too cute to pull it off. "Is there anywhere quiet we can go so I can act out my insane plan to dismember you and throw your remains into the ocean for the sharks to eat?"

I will myself to stop giggling, but I can't help it. I feel like such a floozy.

We turn before we reach the pavement and start heading back the way we came. His arm drops from my shoulder but he remains close as we walk silently along the yellow sand. The air bites at the skin where his arm kept it sheltered moments ago.

I want his arm back.

"We're going to meet at this spot..." He stops us again after a few minutes of peaceful walking and stamps his foot on the sand before throwing his arm out to show me the area. "At the same time tomorrow." He leans in, dipping his head so his eyes catch mine. "Is that okay with you, Gwenny?"

"Don't you want my number?" I'm sure that's the normal way to do things.

He shakes his head. "I have a feeling I'll get an apologetic text. I figure if you don't have a way to let me down, you won't."

"Crafty." I grin. He seems to be good at reading people because that sounds exactly like something I would do. "I like it."

"Good, come on. Ice cream. My treat."

"You're not dressed," I announce, pointing at his dark blue, flower motif shorts and lack of shirt.

He seems to contemplate this for a moment before his mischievous eyes come back to mine. "You don't miss a beat, do you?" I shrug in response. He continues. "You have the most beautiful eyes I've ever seen."

Throb. Throb. Throb. Goes my heart.

"W... what does that have to do with you being half naked?" I stammer, trying to calm my heated self.

"If me being half naked means I get to have your eyes on me like they are now, I'll never get dressed again."

A giggle pushes up and out and I swing my face to the side, letting my hair be a partition between us. He brushes it behind my ear, his smile back. His scent is still strong and the warmth from his body is making my virginal self heat in ways that would make a nun blush.

"So... ice cream?"

"Sure."

"I know a great place just up there near the rocks; we won't even have to leave the sand." His head dips and his eyes twinkle with humour. "It's a public area of course."

"I'd like to, thank you."

He takes me for ice cream and sits across from me on the sand. Every so often he feeds me some of the chocolate treat on the end of a wafer. It's cute; he's cute. This situation is so surreal. Things like this just don't happen to me. I'm nothing special. I've always been practically invisible to the opposite sex, so this is a totally new experience. I'm not sure if it's my naivety, innocence or lack of experience that is making me fall so easily for him.

He's so sweet and charming and happy. Being around him makes me feel as he feels. His smile and laughter are contagious, his clear love for life even more so. If he asked me right now to jump out of a plane with him for the adrenaline rush, I'd do it. He's dangerous, he's addictive and every second I spend with him I lose a piece of my heart and attach it to his.

My mum would probably freak out if she knew how easily I've wandered off with a man I barely know and even accepted food from him. It's not a safe thing to do but for some reason I trust him. Even though I probably shouldn't, I do. He has yet to take me out of a public space.

He's so charming and friendly, not to mention completely gorgeous. Ridiculously so.

I've never been much of a giggler but he makes me giggle... a lot. Too much. I must look like an idiot.

Every time he gets a happy response from me he smiles wide, looking proud of himself.

"It's getting late. I'm going to walk you to your street," he states and holds out his hand for me to take. I do. "And then I'll meet you at the same place tomorrow. If you don't show, there are no hard feelings."

Oh I'll show. I'll definitely show. "Okay. And if you don't show..."

He puts his finger over my lips. "Don't speak such nonsense. I'll show."

This warms my heart to dangerous temperatures.

We walk hand in hand along the cracked pavement, finally stopping five minutes later on the corner of my street.

His hand skims up my arm and cups the back of my neck as he brings our laced fingers up to press against his chest. "Tomorrow."

"Tomorrow," I gulp and shudder as his lips touch my cheek. He releases me, much to my disappointment, and starts walking back towards the beach. I see him smile at me over his shoulder before I turn on my heel and run to my house.

***

"Mum!" I shout as I race through the door, up the stairs and throw myself on my bed. My phone, which has been charging for the day, lights up the second I swipe my finger across the screen. I'm unsurprised to see a lack of notifications. My list of friends is a short one.

"What?" She snaps and enters my room looking tired and irritated. "What is it?"

"I met a guy!" Grinning, I cross my legs beneath me and hold a pillow tight to my chest, forgetting about my phone and lack of social life. "Mum, he's absolutely gorgeous."

She rolls her eyes. "Good for you. Don't get pregnant." She slams my bedroom door behind her.

Note to self: don't wake mum up to tell her about guys after she's been on a night shift. It may piss her off.

My mum can be a bit of a bitch at times, but what mum can't? Sure she loves me, but mostly I'm an inconvenience. I know she's provided for me all of my life and I know she's proud of me for living the life she wanted but never had. She works hard for it too; it's not like I'm fending for myself. I want to go to university when I finish college. I finish in the summer and I've been accepted to a few universities nearby. The problem I have is money. I'm getting student loans but I don't want to get a high amount and put myself in a ton of debt.

As it is, my mum and I are working our butts off to save up for my time in University, not only my living expenses but my class expenses too.

I get an hour's nap, have a shower and get ready for work. Tonight I'm working at Chicago's, which is a club in town. Tomorrow I'm at a cafe for the better part of the morning and then I'll be at the beach with Caleb.

A busy night and a busy day. Brilliant.

I'm sitting on the sand enjoying the breeze when I feel him sit beside me. "You came." Why do I hear relief in his voice and an undertone of shock?

"Of course I did," I tell him, like any other option would be abhorrent. It would have been. There was no way I was standing him up, even though I know that this can't go anywhere. I don't want to miss my chance to get to know him better.

We sit in silence for a moment and watch the waves hit the shore.

His hand slowly closes over mine. "You look lost in thought."

"I'm just tired." I prove it by yawning.

"Would you like to go home?"

"No." Honestly I wouldn't. I want to stay here forever. I feel comfortable, happy. "What's your last name?"

"Are you profiling?" He jests and I tap him on the arm playfully. "Oh dear, we have an abuser! Medic! Medic."

"You're so weird," I laugh and climb to my feet. He takes my hand and stands to face me. "So, what are you doing here of all places?" I ask. "I can tell by your accent you're from out of town. Surely Skegness wasn't your first choice?"

He shrugs. "My dad's opening a store nearby. He brought me and my older brother along with him."

"A store?" I press and notice his cheeks pink slightly. "Are you in university?"

He grins and nods. "Yep. Oxford."

Impressive. "Well done, you." We start to walk along the shore. "What are you studying?"

"Law."

Very impressive. "That's pretty great."

"What about you?"

"I want to study culinary art."

"You can cook?"

I shrug. "I try to. When are you going back?"

"Never." He grins and takes my hand in his. "I just found the girl of my dreams. Why would I go back?"

I snort and roll my eyes. "Now I know you just want in my pants."

"Nuh-uh," he says like a whiny child. "I promise you I won't even attempt it. Not once. Not until you beg me to."

Great, I'm giggling again. "Be serious. When are you leaving?"

"I'm offering you my heart and already you're trying to get rid of me?" He places his hand on his chest and staggers backwards playfully as if I've shot him.

"Stop it," I scold, but my laughter takes away its effectiveness. He swings his arm around my shoulders and pulls me along. I sigh, defeated. "Fine, don't tell me."

His face sobers. "I'm serious, Gwenny. I'm never going back with them."

My palms are sweating. I've been dreading this moment all day. The sun is finally setting, even though you can't see it set here like you can over some oceans. The sky just gets darker.

"I'd love to see a real sunset, one that makes the sky look like it's on fire."

"One day I'm going to kiss you in front of a real sunset on a beach full of white sand." He promises.

I throw back my head and laugh, my worries forgotten momentarily. "You haven't even kissed me yet on this beach under the greying sky and already you're planning fiery skies and white sands?"

"Well, we'll have to rectify that." He beams and walks backwards in front of me. I stare at our footprints as we go, wishing I could make a mould of them to keep forever. Even if this does end as quickly as it started, I'll cherish the memory for eternity.

"So, what are we doing?" I ask when we stop at the spot where we met and stare out at the sea.

His grin is wicked. "I thought I was kissing you."

Blush. "Oh. Umm..."

"That's unless you don't want to."

"I do," I blurt, my face heating further. "It's just... I haven't kissed a guy since I was twelve." I hate myself. Why would I tell him that? I could have just winged it.

His eyebrows hit his hairline. "Oh."

"And he was... well he was bad at it. Or maybe I was. I just know my mouth had a bath that day and a bath is something my mouth doesn't appreciate." I'm rambling. "But I'd like to kiss you. Definitely." Somebody get me a gun so I can shoot myself. "Is that... bad?"

"No, it's just... you're so beautiful. I can't be the only man to have your lips plaguing my thoughts."

I bite my lip and shrug. "I've always been quiet, I guess. Everybody sort of overlooks me."

He cups my face with warm hands and looks directly in my eyes. "Now *that* I find impossible to believe. Maybe they just weren't as brave as me."

"I'm glad they weren't," I mumble and his face lights up further.

"I'm going to kiss you now," he states and takes a step closer.

"Okay," I breathe and lift my mouth to his. He brings his the rest of the way.

I've never been one for the theatricals, but I can honestly say time has stopped. His lips move on mine like they were made for this reason and this reason only. He takes charge, teaching me, being patient and slow. I'm glad. My body trembles with anxiety and exhilaration. His hand cups the back of my neck and a low moan echoes through his throat as he slides his tongue into my mouth to deepen the kiss. Every part of me hums, everything. I've never felt so sensitive to everything. Even the breeze makes my skin tingle.

I never believed in love at first sight, or, if I did, I never believed it would happen to me.

It has. I'm so sure it has I can feel it in my bones.

I've found the man of every woman's dreams and I'm not letting him go.

CHAPTER TWO

CALEB CHEWS ON HIS lower lip as we head up the driveway to my home. After dating for two weeks, it's time for him to meet my mum. Of course I've told her about him but not too much. We've both been too busy to have a proper conversation and then there's the fact I've been spending all of my free time with Caleb. He's perfect, so damn perfect.

I love spending time with him and, true to his word, he hasn't yet gone home. I feel guilty for taking him away from his family but it's his decision. If this is where he's happiest, I'm not complaining, although the fact that he has been avoiding me when I've tried speaking to him about it has been cause for some small amount of concern

"Nervous?" I ask with a smirk, locking my fingers with his.

"If she hates me and tells you to leave me, will you?" His light brown eyes twinkle with mischief but I also see his nervousness dimming the light that shines so brightly from him.

"Never," I promise and I'm being truthful. My mum has no reason to hate him but, if by some strange reason, she does, I'd still never leave him for that reason alone.

I'm eighteen, old enough to make my own choices, and Caleb is my choice.

"Come on." I give his hand a tug and push open the front door to my house. "Mum?"

"In the kitchen," she calls back. I give Caleb a reassuring smile and lead him through the hall. "Hello, Caleb. I'm Dawn. It's nice to meet you."

Caleb shakes her hand and gives her a nod. "You too, Dawn."

My mum sits at the small table for four and motions for us to follow suit. My palms are sweating, I'm so nervous. This is the first guy I've ever brought home, mostly because he's the first guy I've ever had as a boyfriend.

I have very good taste; this much is clear.

My mum thinks so too, if her wink in my direction is anything to go by. "So... you're studying law?"

"Yes ma'am," Caleb says, a small and nervous smile teasing the edges of his lips.

"At Oxford?"

"Yes."

"So how do you expect this to work between you and Gwen?" My mum has her stern face on. Uh-oh. She sure didn't waste any time. I don't know whether to be mortified or annoyed.

Perhaps I should be both.

"Mum," I warn.

He doesn't break or falter, only smiles wider. "I'm moving here."

"How do your parents feel about this?" My mum asks and glances at me. Why is she glancing at me?

"They'll hate it but I make my own decisions." He gives a small shrug.

My mum sighs and shakes her head. "I guess it's your choice, but throwing away a brilliant education for a girl you've known a couple of weeks is ridiculous at best."

"Mum!" I gasp.

Caleb shrugs again. "I know what's best for me and if that's ridiculous then I guess I'm guilty as charged."

"Oh you're very charming." My mum's eyes narrow, suspicious of the man before her. We watch and wait as she stands and walks to the drawers. What's she doing? What's that bag? Oh dear god no. She throws the bag on the table and a few packets of condoms fall out of its bulging belly. "Don't get her pregnant. You may be willing to give up your education for her, but..."

I fold my arms on the table and bury my face in them.

I am now simply mortified. There's no room for any other kind of emotion.

"Don't worry about it, Dawn." Caleb waves her off. "Safety first. Cross my heart."

Oh, he's enjoying this. "Caleb!"

"Just saying," he states, trying to suppress his smile but failing as it blinds me seconds later. "I promise to do everything in my power to keep Gwenny in school until she graduates."

This my mum likes; I can tell by her apparent grin. "Good." After exhaling a long breath, she continues, "So, tell me what your plans are. I hope you don't expect to move in here…"

"I've started looking at apartments near the university," he says and places his hand over mine on the table. "I have a trust fund so money isn't an issue."

A trust fund? Why am I only now learning all of this information about him? I know it has only been two weeks since we started dating but he must have known that my mum might ask him about this stuff. Wouldn't it have been better to discuss it with me beforehand?

"Okay, good." My mum nods, her lips pouting slightly as she thinks on it. "Well, you're an adult. It's your life; you'll do as you please. You, however," she gives me a pointed look, "don't take this the wrong way, but he's just a guy. Don't get distracted."

"Okay," I sigh with a roll of my eyes. I'm not stupid. I really like Caleb but I've wanted to go to University since I was little. It's important to me to get the education I require in order to become an amazing chef.

We don't have family. My mum's parents abandoned her when she fell pregnant with me and I don't think she knows who my dad is. I'm guessing I'm the result of a one night stand gone wrong and as much as I'd like to hate her for that, I don't and never will.

I suppose it's becoming more common these days for people to grow up without a father figure. I turned out okay regardless, though I won't deny the certain pangs of jealousy I get when I see other fathers with their daughters.

"Also, if you get pregnant and he leaves you, don't expect to come back here." She gives me a pointed look.

Caleb frowns at this but remains silent. I only nod. What can I say to that? I find it quite hypocritical considering the circumstances in which she found herself when pregnant with me, but hey ho. There's no use dwelling on something that is never going to happen.

"So..." She smiles warmly now, all seriousness gone. "Pizza and box office?"

"Yay!" I grin.

Caleb looks at me. "Yay? Who says yay?"

"You'll find there are a lot of things she says that nobody else would say. Good luck."

I scoff. "A lot of people say yay."

"Not normal ones," Caleb murmurs playfully and clips me on the chin. "But I don't like normal so it's all good." Then he grins, throws his arms in the air and, in a high pitched tone, he cheers, "Yay!"

"Geek."

After the initial greeting is done and Mum and Caleb are properly acquainted, we retire to the living room. Caleb and I sit side by side on the couch, with my mum sat in the chair to the right, watching some action film on TV. I'm not interested; I'm too busy playing thumb war with the guy beside me.

I wonder if all of the talk about pregnancy has him thinking about sex. It's something that I can't stop thinking about when he kisses me and makes me feel so sensual and frustrated all at once. I'm just not ready to take that step yet.

Will he think I'm frigid if I turn him down?

I have this rule that my mum taught me; she said if you can't stand in front of the person while naked and feel comfortable, to an extent, then you aren't ready for sex with them. I like Caleb, a lot, but do I feel that comfortable with him? No, probably not.

He brings my losing thumb to his mouth and wraps his lips around the knuckle. I squeal when his teeth sink in, pinching the skin and bone between them. Grinning triumphantly, he releases me and looks down just as his phone alerts him to a text. I'm curious as to why he turns the screen away. I'm not one to read over his shoulder on any normal day, or anyone's shoulder for that matter, but his secrecy worries me, especially considering the fact that he opens it with a frown. This is the second time I've seen him frown since we met and both times have been today.

<u>Nathan</u>: I can't believe you've done this to me. You ruin everything. I'm done.

"Who's Nathan?" I ask quietly so only he can hear.

He chews on his lower lip for a moment and lets out a sigh. "My older brother." I watch him place his phone in his pocket without responding.

"Is everything okay?" My ear's against his chest so I can hear his heart beating faster than it was a second ago.

"Yeah, it will be." I relax slightly until I hear him add, more to himself than to me, "He'll get over it."

"Get over what?"

"Nothing." He gives me his shining smile and kisses the bridge of my nose. "Just family stuff."

"Is it to do with you leaving?"

"Probably. Don't let it bother you. Watch the movie; you're missing the best part."

I let it lie as he asks. It's none of my business and I don't want to make him think that I'm some kind of crazy clingy girlfriend that needs to know everything. My trust in him is greater than my trust in anyone, which isn't exactly a feat since I have no one in my life that I trust. The exception is my mum, but some days I'm not even sure if I trust her. Like earlier, when she admitted to basically abandoning me if I ever made the same mistake that she made, it shook my confidence.

Mistake... is that what my life boils down to? A mistake? An accident?

As for Caleb, I know he'll tell me when he's ready and I'm sure whatever he's done isn't that bad. It's probably just normal sibling rivalry, something I know little about because I have no siblings.

"I have to go." He stretches as the ending credits roll. "My dad's expecting me and I've got a few things I need to sort out."

"Will I see you tomorrow?" I ask, missing him already and he hasn't even left yet.

"Yes, but not until the afternoon." He stands and I stand with him. It feels good to stretch my body after such a long time curled up. "Is that okay?"

No. "Course." Lies.

"Good. See me out?" The look on his face tells me I shouldn't say no, mostly because the look on his face screams of lust. There's nothing I like better than a make-out session with Caleb.

"Duh," I giggle and follow him to the front door.

As soon as I step outside and the door closes, my back is pressed up against it and Caleb's mouth is on mine. His hands grip my hips as he presses his front against me. My body immediately lights up, flames of passion licking at my skin and nerves. By the time his tongue pushes past my lips, I'm a trembling mess. My hands tangle in his hair and my underwear becomes so wet I'm surprised it doesn't dissolve.

"You're perfect," he whispers against my mouth before resting his forehead against mine. "How can one person be so perfect?"

"I have love handles," I blurt as a way to prove the fact that I'm far from perfect.

His warm hands slip under my top and slide along the waistband of my jeans. He grips the bare skin above my hips and grinds his hard bulge against me. "Every inch of you is perfection. I can't wait to see it all for myself."

Blink.

"I'm serious." He looks serious. His hand clasps mine and brings it to his chest. "You make my heart race by just looking at me."

"You too," I breathe, wanting to laugh at his words but finding myself too lost in the moment. My lips tease and kiss his soft neck. Running my nose along his slight stubble, I tug on his long hair. He grins in response and his eyes flash with wanting. "Even if this doesn't last, I'll keep hold of this forever."

He grins, his teeth glinting in the glow of the street lights. "It'll last."

"I hope so."

His hands grip my shoulders as he takes a step back. "You'll see. It will."

I mentally repeat my spoken words. I hope so.

"Until tomorrow." He kisses my pouting lips once more and walks backwards out of my driveway, not turning around until I go back inside.

"He seems nice," Mum says and my heart is even happier. "Almost too nice."

I frown. "What's that supposed to mean?"

"Have you ever heard the term 'beware of the wolf in sheep's clothing'?"

In roll my eyes heavenward and blow out a breath. "Caleb isn't a wolf, Mum. He's a nice guy."

"Whatever, just don't get pregnant."

Sigh. "I won't, Mum."

"That's what I said," she grumbles and my heart is definitely no longer happy.

"Well I'm sorry that me being born was such an inconvenience to you." I don't say it angrily; my voice is weak and defeated. I think what hurts the most is the fact that she didn't correct me. I walk solemnly and slowly to my bedroom, hoping the entire time that she will.

I have to work today but I don't mind work. I like being busy and my boss Charlie is pretty cool. He's an older guy, at least sixty, and he's fun to talk to.

We laugh a lot while we make and serve drinks for paying customers. The café is only small but we're normally quite busy. Today I'm so rushed off my feet that I don't even notice Caleb has walked in until his hands are at my hips and I'm squealing in shock.

"Don't do that," I cry but can't contain my smile.

"Best smile ever. I want you to smile at me like that every time you greet me." He dips his head and presses his lips against mine briefly.

I flush at his words and flush even more when my boss clears his throat. "Go sit," I demand and push Caleb towards an empty table. "What do you want to drink?"

"Warm milk with honey."

I quirk a brow. "Warm milk with honey?"

His eyes go slightly wider, almost defensively. "What's wrong with warm milk and honey?"

"Well, it's..."

"A girl's drink," my boss chips in with a chuckle. I'm going to pretend for a moment that that isn't totally sexist.

Caleb scowls playfully at me. "It's my family's Friday tradition. Every Friday we try to sit down together and watch a movie with a warm milk and honey."

"So why are you here and not with them?"

He grins, showing his perfect white teeth. "Because I've got a new family now and she needs to learn the tradition."

Throb. Throb. Throb. Goes my heart.

"So, take ten minutes off and drink my girly drink with me," he jests and pats the chair beside him. "Pleeeeeeeeease?"

"Go on," my boss chuckles and shoves me towards my chair. "You've hardly had a break yet. Sit."

"Yay!" Caleb cheers and pulls me onto his lap.

"Yay?" Charlie asks, his face showing his surprise.

"A lot of people say yay," I defend my boyfriend.

Ha! I have a boyfriend.

"Only you and him," Charlie chuckles and gives Caleb a pointed look. "Get out while you still can."

Caleb nips at my neck as I watch Charlie walk towards the counter. "Reckon I should get out while I still can?"

I shake my head. "No. I think you should stay."

"Well, I guess that's good because..." he lets his voice trail off before squeezing me tight and announcing, "I just enrolled."

"You enrolled?" Bloody hell. He just enrolled.

"Yep and..." He lets his voice trail off once more. "I just looked at a place. I move in next week."

Double crap. The good kind.

"Oh my god," I laugh. "That's..." And then the tears come.

"Hey," he soothes and pulls me tight to him, his hand stroking my hair. "What's the matter?"

"I thought you were going to leave me," I sniff and bury my face in his neck. I know this level of emotion is irrational but I can't seem to control myself. I wish I could explain or focus on why I feel this way but I can't. Caleb means so much to me already and I've been resolute on the fact that he'd be leaving soon. I thought we were going to be the next summer romance that ends before it really begins, so this is literally just the best news ever. "I genuinely thought you just wanted to have sex with me."

He pulls me back and wipes at my ridiculous tears with his thumb. "Well," he wags his eyebrows twice. "There's that too."

How can I laugh while I cry? That's just weird and shouldn't be possible. "Geek."

"Is it wrong of me to be excited about taking your innocence and making you mine completely?"

My breath hitches and my stomach warms in anticipation for the night that will most likely come one day soon. "I don't think so."

"Good." He bites the lobe of my ear. "Because I am really, *really* excited." I can tell by the bulge beneath my arse and I have to say, it's making me feel as though I'm out of control of my own body. I've never felt lust and desire as badly as I do with Caleb. Never.

"Milk and honey times two," Charlie says, snapping me out of my daze.

"Brilliant!" Caleb grins. "Thanks."

"Yeah," I say and sip my hot drink. "Oh my god, this is amazing."

"I know, right?" Caleb doesn't let me slide off his lap. He keeps me there and drinks his drink.

CHAPTER THREE

I CAN'T BELIEVE HE'S actually moving here! I never thought he would. I thought it was all a ruse to get into my pants, not that anybody can blame me for thinking that way. Now I feel guilt and a lot of it. He's only ever kissed me and groped me a couple of times. Never has he once tried to actually sleep with me, though, to be honest, we've never had the opportunity.

"What will your parents say about it?"

"My parents are dicks." This is his response and I'm not sure how to respond to his response. It worries me a bit.

"Tell me about them."

He seems to think about it for a moment before continuing. "They're rich and think they're entitled. Nathan and I were never allowed to do anything wrong growing up. The slightest mistake and we'd be grounded for weeks; sometimes our dad would take his belt to us. Nathan got the worst of it. He took a lot of my shit for me."

"That's sad."

His eyes seem to glitter for a moment. "It is what it is. They'll hate this; not because they care, but because they want control. That's just how they are."

"They'll blame me."

He nods. "I won't lie, they probably will but I'll keep you away from them. They're vile people and I never want that anywhere near you. You shouldn't be tainted by people like them."

"They're your parents."

"And because of that reason, I do love them deep, deep, way deep down. Also because of that reason, I know what type of people they are and they're the kind of people who you don't want to be near." I open my mouth to interject but he cuts me off with a finger to my lips. "They're the kind of people *I* don't want you to be near. Let me protect you from evil as much as I can. Okay?"

How can somebody be so seemingly sweet and so perfect all of the time? I find it hard to believe that he was single before me. I have yet to find something about him that anyone could dislike.

"Have you always been this infuriatingly perfect?"

He only smiles and responds, "I didn't used to be."

I knew it! "Why?"

"No more story time. You need to work and I have to go to the bank and sort out my funds." He stands, urging me onto my feet. "I'll pick you up when you finish." With a light kiss on my lips and one on my neck, he leaves me and my warm and aching heart behind.

Swoon.

I don't think I've ever seen a more handsome man from behind. It seems like an odd statement, but it's a true one. Caleb is sexy; he knows it but he's not arrogant about it. Even from behind you just know that when he turns around, the front is going to look so good. His back is right to promise such things, except Caleb is like nothing you could ever dream up. He's perfect. He's beautiful in the way only a man can be beautiful.

I can just tell he'll be one of those men who age well; his cheeky and charming smile will last an age. I can imagine him at the age of sixty, smiling at the women as they pass. Most likely driving me crazy but at the same time making me swoon that he's mine. I seem to do a lot of swooning around him. I need to get a grip of myself.

When work finishes, Caleb picks me up. He's not in a good mood but it's not aimed at me, nor do I suffer for it beyond feeling his mood shift to grumpy whenever he looks away from me. He's not very good at hiding how he feels. I wish he would talk to me about it but no matter how hard I push he keeps his lips sealed.

We're currently sat in his car outside my house because it's raining, meaning we can't go to our special spot on the beach, the spot where we first kissed.

He rests his head between his hands on the steering wheel, his leg bouncing up and down. I see his bottom lip disappear under his top row of teeth as he worries it.

"Hey," I say softly and place my hand on his back. "What's the matter?"

"My parents cut me off."

"W...what?" What does that mean?

"They emptied my trust fund and said I can't have it back until I graduate."

Oh shit. "That's not so bad."

"Trust me," he grimaces, turning his head so his temple is on the wheel and his eyes are on me. "It is. I don't graduate for two years. How the fuck did they find out I wasn't going back?"

"They've done this to get you to go back with them?" Oh no, he's going to leave me.

"Yep."

Thump. Thump.... Thump. My heart just skipped a beat and not because of something good. "That's..."

"It's fucking bullshit," he shouts, startling me when he sits upright and punches the steering wheel.

"Hey," I say softly and run my fingers through his hair. "It'll be okay, you'll see. You can just go back and do what you need to do."

"No," he blurts, his eyes on me. The desperation behind them startles me. "I can't do that."

"It's just two years."

"To some people," I think he says, but I can't be sure because it was as quiet as his breath. He sighs and grips his hair with both hands. "It doesn't matter. I have about ten grand in my other account and they can't touch that. Oxford will surely transfer the course money so I won't have to worry about that. I'll just get a job here. At least my deposit is down on our place, along with the first few months' rent. That will give me enough time to get a job."

I can't believe my ears. My heart skips a beat for a good reason this time. "You're still moving here?"

"Fuck yeah!" He grins and brings my hand to his lips. "It'll be great. Who needs money?"

My lips twitch. "Everybody?"

"True that," he remarks and leans over to kiss me. "Let's just forget about them for now. Let's just forget about everything. How about we go for a long drive, pull over somewhere and you let me kiss you until our lips are sore?"

"Kay," I breathe and in seconds the car is running and we're driving to location unknown. I hate to ask but I do anyway. "How *did* they find out? I haven't told anyone but my..."

"She wouldn't. She doesn't even know who my parents are." His eyes suddenly widen as realisation dawns. "That bastard. That absolute fucking bastard."

"What?"

"My brother." He roughly handles the gearstick. I want to ask what the gearstick ever did to him, but I don't think that it would be appreciated right now. "Damn it! I'm going to fucking kill him!" He pauses and smirks a little. "Nope, I'm going to throw eggs at him."

Eggs? "Eggs?"

"Yeah."

"Why eggs?"

"My brother..." As we're turning down a wooded lane there's a pop followed by a hissing sound and then the car starts to wobble as we pull to a stop. "NO! NO! NO! NO!" Caleb shouts and climbs out of the now prone car. I follow and watch as he kicks the flat tyre over and over again. "This is not my fucking day. Fuck!"

"Caleb!" I rush to him and grab his arm. "Calm down; it's just a tyre. We'll fit the spare."

He chews on his lower lip and looks at me apologetically.

"Bloody hell. You don't have a spare." This isn't a question; the look on his face has already told me the answer. I'm just voicing his thought. "Great." I lean against the rain splattered bonnet and watch him pace backwards and forwards in front of the car. He mumbles to himself for a while, looks at the tyre, turns back around to continue cursing and mumbling, before finally coming over to me, grabbing me by the back of my neck and slamming his lips down on mine.

The force of it makes me squeal in surprise but it doesn't hurt. Not even a little bit. His tongue plunges into my mouth. He devours me, leaving no part of my mouth untouched. I do the same.

This feels amazing; it feels primal and possessive and seems to be his way of relieving a lot of stress right now. I'm not complaining.

His hands grip my jacket and slide it down my shoulders. I shiver as the cool droplets of water tap against the bare skin of my arms and, without detaching his mouth from mine, he throws my jacket through the open door and onto the seat. We separate for a moment as he tugs my vest over my head and throws that in too, but his mouth is back on mine when he fumbles to pull the back door open and slowly slides me onto the back seats. The rain no longer serves as an aid to cool my heated skin and my arousal seems to multiply in seconds.

I'm in a bra and jeans in front of a guy in the back of a car in the middle of nowhere, but it feels so good I don't want to stop.

Tingles erupt through my body as he works the button on my jeans, popping it open with one hand before tugging them down my legs and also throwing those to the side. The sound of them hitting the steering wheel is the last thing I hear, as his mouth is on me over my thong.

"Oh god," I say, wanting to push him away at the same time as wanting to pull him closer. The sensation is foreign but beautiful. I'm going to explode; I can feel it.

His breath curves around the juncture to my thighs, making my legs shake and quiver. I cry out in a way that I should feel shame for but don't.

"Caleb," I pant, watching him as he hooks his fingers around the narrow fabric and pulls it to the side. "No... not tha...ah. Oh god." My head falls back, hitting the window button which makes it descend with a hum and a squeak. Who cares? This is amazing.

His warm and wet tongue traces me before dipping inside and hitting me in exactly the right place. I want to be filled. I want to feel every inch of him inside of me. That's all this is missing; the tingles in my core ache to clench around something warm and thick.

"I want you so bad," he says, peppering kisses over the top of my mound. "You have no idea."

I really do.

He goes back to what he was doing before. This time his tongue circles lower and lower, his mouth sucking on all of the right places, his hands gripping my thighs to hold me in place. "I want to get lost in you."

"Okay," I respond in a whisper of passion.

The tingles still remain as he stands and tugs down his jeans. I hesitate and stiffen when I see that he's wearing no underwear and his erect length falls out of its denim confines looking angry and swollen. My eyes widen. Is he going to take me with that? Because I'm certain it won't fit. Not only that, but I'm not sure this is how I imagined this to happen.

"Touch yourself," he orders softly, his hooded eyes on me.

"What?"

He grasps his solid cock in his hand and strokes it slowly up and down. "Touch yourself," he repeats and his free hand rests over my core, his thumb beginning to slowly circle over the sensitive nub. That feels nice. Really nice. "Actually don't. This is so much better." Leaning forward, I feel the throbbing head of his shaft prod against my entrance and squeal at the feel of it. He sees the panic in my eyes and kisses me softly. "Don't worry. I'm just going to do this." The head finds my clit and starts circling. "I want to make you come like this. I want to make you scream using this only."

Shiver.

His hands still rub his length up and down, twisting gently as his palm reaches the head. I want to do it but I know he wants control this time, so I let him have it. I trust him not to hurt me or push me too far.

"You're so beautiful," he murmurs as his nose pushes the cup of my bra out of the way and his mouth envelopes my hard, pointed nipple. "Put your legs together."

"Huh?"

"Legs together... please, baby." He shifts so I can manage this and climbs up my torso a little. His hand goes to the back of my neck and I feel my face moving up, only stopping when his cock is an inch from my lips. "Need you to wet me."

"W... what?" In my mouth?

"Open up." He grins, his back bent awkwardly due to the lack of space between me and the roof. "Please."

My mouth opens slowly, but I have no idea what I'm doing.

I glare when he taps the end on my lips a few times before running it around them like one would do with a tube of lipstick, but he only smiles wider. The hand that's gripping my neck starts stroking me softly, soothingly. "Ready?"

I nod and open my mouth when he slides the tip onto my tongue and lets out a long and loud groan. This isn't that bad actually.

"Close your lips around the head. No teeth." I do as I'm told and instinct kicks in. He trembles and curses. "Do that again." I do so. "Ah. Again. Keep doing that." My tongue swirls and flicks before he slides it deeper and deeper. Before I realise it we have a rhythm going. He thrusts slowly, in and out, in and out, the tip never leaving my mouth. "Suck." It's almost at the back of my tongue; is it possible to suck? "Suck really hard, like you're drinking a Krushem and there's chocolate lodged in the straw."

I suck as hard as possible, which is difficult to do when I'm laughing at his comment. My cheeks hollow and begin to ache. He pulls out slowly, his face scrunched and contorted with ecstasy, his lips parted half an inch. The moans he releases really set me on fire. I've never been so turned on before and I'm shocked that it's from doing something I always said I'd never do.

He's either very persuasive or I'm very weak minded.

"Brilliant," he pants and pushes to the back of my throat, almost making me gag but not quite.

My jaw aches.

Suddenly he's gone, leaving my mouth feeling empty. Situating himself so his torso is pressed to mine, I feel his length slide between my closed thighs and gasp when the smooth surface of it rubs against me. The burning begins again and spreads, almost too much to bear. Our combined juices create a slick passage as he slowly thrusts between my tightly shut thighs.

My fingers tangle in his hair and I'm happy when he kisses me. I'd be offended if he didn't.

He's rubbing all of the right places. I've never felt anything like it. Our breaths mingle as I thrust my hips in time with his, making sure that he reaches exactly where I want him to.

The tingles intensify and spread upwards, rising until I feel my nipples harden further. The ripples slowly move out and spread down my sides, to my thighs, burning in the most pleasing way.

I've never... I can't...

I inhale a sharp breath as he picks up speed, his forehead against mine.

Moments ago I was worried a car would drive by; now I don't care at all. The need to orgasm consumes me.

I've gone from virgin to virgin-exhibitionist-slut in one hour.

"I'm going to come," he announces in a strangled moan, the muscles in his arms bulging as he thrusts faster and faster. The sound of him slipping between my thighs, coated with our juices, is so erotic. The sound of his moans make the burning inside of me so much worse. "Nearly... there."

My stomach clenches. I can't breathe; I can't speak; I can't cry out. My head seems to explode as my eyelids flutter closed of their own accord. I can't control it; my body is no longer my own. My soul seems to expand and wrap around his as we both throb together, pulse together, orgasm together. I cling to him desperately as I reach my peak and he reaches his. I want him inside me, filling me. If I'd been at the right angle I'd have forced it too. I've never found myself so lost to pleasure before.

I want to go again and we aren't even done yet.

The tingles slowly retreat and my blurred vision focuses as his thrusts slow to an occasional sharp jerk of his body.

I'm crushed against the seat when he collapses on top of me, breathing heavily. "Amazing."

"Yeah," I agree, trying to regulate my breathing by taking a few large gulps of air. "Can we do that again?"

He laughs and nods against my neck. "Yeah, but not here. We've been lucky this time."

Or so we think, until we hear an engine as a car drives our way. The car in question beeps three times and somebody cheers, "GET IN!" before driving away. The entire time my cheeks get warmer and warmer and Caleb covers me with his body, so tight he almost absorbs me. I am mortified.

"Stay here," he whispers and kisses my lips.

Hastily I bring my knees to my chest, covering my nudity, and stare at the greying sky through the window.

Caleb quickly tugs on his clothes, leaving his shirt off. I shy away when he cleans the mess between my thighs, but it soon turns to laughter when I see the wet stain in the middle of the seats. He crinkles his nose playfully and nips at my lips before helping me to pull my clothes on.

"Come on," he instructs and guides me into the passenger seat. "I'll call for help."

Oh right, the flat tyre. I completely forgot about that. Not that anyone can blame me.

"Is that the first time you've had an orgasm?" He asks me as the sky gets darker.

We're still sat in the car, waiting to be fixed. The company he called said they'd be an hour and it has only been thirty minutes.

His question shocks me and I choke a little on air. "Umm... no. Obviously I've... you know?"

His smile widens to one of cockiness and eagerness. "Do tell."

"Everybody masturbates," I mutter, nervously tucking my hair behind my ear.

"Fuck me, you're cute."

"Sorry."

"Hey..." He places his finger under my chin and finds my eyes with his. The way they stare directly into mine with such softness makes me feel like he's caressing my soul. Parts of me I've never felt before want to detach and wrap around him, keep him locked to me forever. "Don't ever apologise to me. You're precious."

"Precious?" My brows hit my hairline.

"Perfect." He leans forward and kisses the corner of my mouth. "Cute and sexy and so bloody pretty I just want to eat you."

"You just did," I mumble aloud and hang my head in shame the second I realise my error.

He throws his head back and laughs. His arms hook around my neck and he pulls me to him over the console. Kissing my hair, he leans back and makes eye contact once more. "Did I tell you I'm fucking ecstatic I gave my heart to you on the beach that day?"

"You might have mentioned it."

"Good, because it's true."

"I believe you," I admit because I do believe him.

I get that the dating phase is the best phase but something tells me that this is real and this will last. Maybe I'm naïve, but I don't care. I'm just lucky to feel like this. I'm lucky to have Caleb even for a few minutes, let alone for as long as I have already.

Chapter Four

"**Y**ou've got paint on your nose." Caleb grins.

"What?" I rub my nose on my sleeve, perplexed when it comes back clear. "Where?"

"Here." His thumb rubs across the bridge between my eyes, making them cross to watch his thumb. "Gone."

I step back and admire my work. I've painted his bedroom in three different pastel shades, green, blue and lilac. It sounds weird but it looks amazing. Caleb and my mum both gagged at the idea but now it's done I'm sure they'll love it. Each colour blends into the next. It's bright, it's airy and it's perfect.

"I love it." He gives an impressed nod, admiring it with me. I want to stick out my tongue and chant like a child, 'told you so, told you so.'

"How are the shelves coming along?" He's been downstairs for a while trying to set up a bookcase while I've been painting.

He lowers his head in embarrassment. "Not too good actually."

I laugh and wrap my arms around his waist. "It's okay. We'll do it together in a minute. Go put the kettle on. I need to finish up here."

Caleb is extremely talented with everything academic, but is entirely hopeless when it comes to building, skating and even biking. Football too. Pretty much anything that involves any kind of coordination with his body or the use of his hands. That doesn't include when his hands are slipping between my legs, because his hands really know how to work magic in this area.

It's one of the things I love about him.

He's also not the best dancer in the world, not unless he's dancing with me and then it's like we're making love on the dance floor.

I place all of the paint trays and rollers in the bath and get to work on cleaning them. Once those are done, I head downstairs and immediately laugh when I see the state of the room. There are planks of wood all over the place, none of them organized, none of them labelled.

"You're hopeless," I snort and squeal when he starts tickling my ribs.

It's been a week since our car tyre blew on us and I still can't believe he's actually staying. I'm actually standing in his new house, covered in paint with my heart hammering a mile a minute. I feel on top of the world.

We have somewhere to play and by play I mean make out properly. And by make out properly I mean have sex.

Caleb isn't a virgin. He lost his innocence when he was only fourteen years of age. Apparently it was messy, awkward and uncomfortable.

Also he came in about three seconds.

I laughed at that part of the story.

He knows what he's doing now though and has promised me that when the time comes he'll take it slow and make it as painless and as beautiful as possible.

Just being with him will be beautiful.

Even if I'm terrified.

It seems silly to be scared of the real thing when we've pretty much done everything else over the past week. Every day he's made me climax, either with his hand, his mouth, his cock or, at one point, his thigh. All were amazing, all were mind blowing and all left me feeling sated and tired.

"You look lost in thought," he says softly and blows on the shell of my ear.

I shrug him off, giggling, and start putting the wood in the right order. "I don't hear the kettle boiling."

"Yes, Miss Bossy."

"Still not boiling," I comment dryly, marking off each plank.

"I haven't even left the room yet. I'm too busy admiring this." He pokes my arse with his pinkie finger. I threaten to hit him with a board and he soon vanishes.

After the shelves are up, which were so much easier than Caleb made them out to be, we shower together. This is an odd experience for me. I've never been fully naked like this with him. We've always been in his car or at my house when exploring each other.

When we fornicated at home, even though my mum was at work, I was terrified of her coming home early and getting caught. Caleb never managed to do more than get me to grind on his thigh, which was amazing, albeit a little embarrassing. I felt like a dog humping someone's leg, but no matter how mortified I felt by my actions I couldn't stop myself. It felt too good. I lost all sense of reason and pride.

Caleb said it was the hottest thing he'd ever witnessed, having a normally shy and composed woman, whom he's severely attracted to, lose all of her inhibitions for a few marvellous minutes because of him.

Things are unfortunately going pretty badly with his parents. I still haven't met them but I've heard them shouting at him on the phone. Last time he hung up on them, but I could see the pain in his eyes. I don't know what they said to make him so miserable but it took me a while to break him out of it.

I gave him a blowjob. I've actually discovered I enjoy giving blowjobs. Maybe it's just the way Caleb responds to them that triggers my enjoyment. There is nothing more erotic than pleasuring a man. Nothing. Even thinking about the way he moans and grips my head as I please him is making me hot inside.

Shiver.

His parents have returned home and, as far as I'm aware, his brother has too. I hope they leave him alone now. Of course I'm all for having your family around you but I never want to see him miserable again. It breaks my heart.

My mum is being a bit off with me as well. I had to work at the club Chicago's last night and when I got home I tripped on a shoe (which was my mum's) and woke her up. She was pretty pissed off with me. The night wasn't a complete disaster, though. I put in a good word for Caleb and he starts next weekend, which we're both pleased about.

He has a job and I can lay claim to him in front of everyone.

As it is, right now I'm out of the shower and getting dressed and Caleb is lying on his mattress, completely naked save for his tight, black boxers which make his sun kissed skin seem to glow in contrast. He doesn't have a bed frame yet. He doesn't have much; the stuff he does have are some bits he picked up throughout the week and kept at mine, ready to move into his new place.

"Can I ask you something?" He snaps me from my thoughts. I roll my eyes when he adjusts himself.

"No."

"You don't even know what I'm going to ask." He pretends to look affronted while his hand slowly rubs his growing bulge.

"I'm busy," I giggle and try to dart out of the way when he jumps off the mattress and lunges for me. I don't get far but I don't want to get far. He's too delicious to avoid and his skin is so warm. "What?"

"Move in with me."

Choke. Splutter.

He pats me on the back, laughing. "I'm serious. I want you to move in with me."

"W... when?"

"Today."

Bloody hell, he *is* serious! I can see it in his eyes. "I... but I've just..."

His finger rests over my lips, effectively silencing me. His eyes search mine, a handsome smile in place. "Please?"

"It's... I don't know what to say."

"Say yes."

"Okay," I blurt and inwardly curse.

"Really?" His smile widens further as he turns me in his arms and presses my back up against the wall. "Seriously?"

I nod quickly. "Yeah. I don't see why not."

"Fucking brilliant." He beams and picks me up so my thighs are around his hips. His lips crash down on mine and I don't refuse them. I'd be crazy if I did. "I was worried you'd say no." Me too, but seeing as he's left his hometown and his family and he's chosen me over an unknown amount of money, there's no way I can say no. Besides, it's not like I don't have a job and can't afford to live here. Money will be tight but it'll be worth it. "Really? You won't back out?"

"I can't wait," I admit eagerly and suck on his lower lip, making him groan. "Thank you."

"Let's celebrate," he whispers, his eyes twinkling. "I'm hungry."

"You want to go out for food?"

His eyes narrow with mischief. "I was thinking of something sweeter, something south." South?

Oh. My mouth forms the shape of the word. He laughs a little and throws me onto his mattress. "Lay back and relax, baby."

"Okay," I breathe and allow him to slide my trousers off. I even help him by raising my hips a little. Brilliant.

My legs are still jelly and it's been two hours since I climaxed all over his face.

I hope my mum doesn't see how weak I am and put two and two together. It's a silly thought; there's no way she'll know or even be thinking of that, but I can't stop. I'm so paranoid. She's sitting in the living room with a cup of tea in her hands watching some reality show on TV when we get inside. I pause it and sit on the couch with Caleb by my side.

"Oh dear," she says, noticing my need to talk. Her elbows rest on her knees as she looks at us both. "Go on. Spit it out."

Okay. "I'm moving out."

"No," she says with a firm shake of her head. "You can't afford to get distracted."

"Mum," I hiss and squeeze Caleb's hand. "I'm eighteen. I've finished college. All that's left is University and I promise I'm not going to mess up. It means a lot to me. You know that."

She shakes her head. "It's not happening."

"Mum." I warn, wondering why she's being so difficult.

"Come on, Dawn." Caleb pouts, his eyes wide like a puppy's. "Think about it - we're not far and you'll get privacy and one less mouth to feed."

"I don't think you two realise how serious this is, what with your university classes and expenses."

"Trust me, Dawn, I do know how serious this is. I've never been more serious in my life." I can tell by the stern expression on his face. My breath catches at the intensity of his eyes. "I want her with me, all of the time. I promise I won't let her fail and I'll send you her grades every month. If they drop to the point where you're worried, I'll bring her back here myself." He looks at me apologetically before turning back to my mum. "Please?"

She chews her lower lip, seeming to contemplate this for a moment. "On one condition."

"What's that?" I inquire, my excitement rising, my heart fluttering.

"You go on the injection or the implant or something," she demands, giving me a pointed look.

I nod eagerly. "I'm already on the pill. You know how vigilant I am with it." Caleb quirks a brow at me, making my face heat at the awkwardness of this conversation. "What?"

"Nothing." His face becomes a mask of cheekiness and I suddenly know where his trail of thoughts are leading.

"Okay." My mum relents and places her palms flat on her knees, rubbing them a little. "I guess it's okay that you move in with him."

"Yay," Caleb and I both say together. He laughs, I crinkle my nose playfully and my mum rolls her eyes.

"Well, you are a match made in heaven, I'll give you that," she adds jokingly and stands. "Are you staying for lunch or do you have things to do?"

"I'm going to pack."

"I'm going to help." Caleb grins and chases me up the stairs to my room. "Okay, you take that section." He waves to the entire room. "And I'll take this section." He opens the top drawer of my chest of drawers and pulls out a pair of lacy pink French knickers.

Snatching them from his hand, I hand him a suitcase and place the lace inside. "Stop being a pervert."

"Yes, ma'am!" He grins over his shoulder as I start putting everything I want to take onto the bed. Out of the corner of my eye I see him picking up my underwear with less speed than necessary and slowly placing them in the suitcase.

I grab a tennis ball off the shelf by my bed and throw it at his head.

"Ouch," he laughs, dropping the thong. "What was that...?" I grab another and take aim. He laughs and holds his hands up. "Okay, okay I'll be good." I place the tennis balls on the bed, looking perplexed and feeling perplexed when he puts them back on the shelf. "I think we'll leave these behind. You have a good aim."

"Yep. Be warned."

"Oh I'm thoroughly warned. If I go against your warning, will you spank me?"

"You're such a geek!" I giggle and go back to my job. "Hey, Caleb."

"Yes, Princess?"

"Thank you."

His brows furrow. "For what?"

"For getting me out of here."

He walks over to where I'm sat and I have to tip my head all the way back to see his face. His body dips as he places his soft lips against the bridge of my nose. "No problem, Gwenny."

Swoon.

***

We spend the evening unpacking my things after spending the afternoon boxing them up and fitting them in the car. We go through bills and utilities and figure out a way to pay for them until he finds a job.

My boss Derrick, who owns Chicago's, tells me to bring him in and we'll give him a trial.

It's safe to say he picks it up easily enough and works here most nights. I only work weekends as I work at the café during the week and, as much as I love working with my boyfriend, I also hate it because I have to watch girls fawn all over him. When I see him smiling or laughing with them, I turn a dark shade of green. I trust him, though. He announces to everyone that I'm his girlfriend and is always touching me when we cross paths. Most girls don't care, though. There's one girl in particular who I want to feed to rabid wolves.

She's stunningly beautiful and she lets him know she's interested by showing up every Friday night and sometimes Saturday, in a different outfit to the one before. Each outfit is more revealing than the last.

I see her before he goes to her table. She pulls her dress down and pushes her boobs out. Slut.

Fortunately my boyfriend can see straight through her and we laugh about her after every night. Her desperation is astounding. Whenever he's taking her order and listening to her flirt shamelessly, he looks at me and pulls a face or winks. He doesn't let her know he finds her severely unattractive, though, because he's got a job to do and because of her obsession she's spending a hell of a lot of money.

It's the following Monday when Caleb takes me back to the place we met and sits by me just silently watching the waves flow across the sand. He's holding my hand firmly, his thumb circling my palm.

I smile at his profile and his eyes meet mine. He looks at me with so much love in his eyes I can't resist leaning in to kiss his perfect lips.

He smiles back at me and lowers me onto my back, his body hovering over mine as the kiss deepens.

It only lasts a few minutes and I'm so relaxed due to his fingers stroking my cheek that I barely register his words at first. "I'm falling in love with you, Gwenny." The way he says it is quiet but so sincere that tears come to my eyes. "No," he amends and runs his nose along mine. "I am in love with you. You're now the very reason I exist."

My breath hitches and my eyes flutter closed as his words warm every cell of my body. Opening my eyes, they connect with his. "I'm in love with you too, Caleb."

His easy smile returns and I notice his hands shaking as they stroke my skin. "I want you tonight. I want all of you. Will you give me all of you?"

I blink a few times, shocked by his question. There's only one answer though. Gulp. "Yes."

"Thank you," he whispers and slants his lips over mine. I relish the sensation of his usual stubble scratching at my skin. It reminds me that he's real, that this is real.

***

"You know I'm completely in love with you, right?" Caleb whispers as we fall onto the bed. He rolls me onto my back and situates himself between my thighs. "I'd never do anything to hurt you."

"I know," I breathe and press my lips to his. "I love you too."

He smiles and moves his lips to my neck. I press my hips up, my core aching for something it's never felt but wants to feel. Badly.

My skin becomes sensitive and produces a layer of goose pimples.

Caleb leans back onto his knees and pulls me to a sitting position with his hand behind my neck. His other hand slides around to cup my arse, pulling me slowly onto his lap.

In seconds my long, thick black hair is tumbling down my back and Caleb's mouth is on my neck, his lips sucking and teasing as his fingers slowly unbutton the front of my beige cotton dress.

Feeling his mouth on me as his hands slowly slide the dress up my thighs and over my head almost makes me explode. The tingling and aching between my thighs feels so much worse but oh so much better all at once.

Next my bra goes and I try not to shy away. He's seen my breasts before but never has he stared at them like he is now, his eyes dark and intense. Leaning back, his lips parted, he brings his hands up to cup each one, causing me to shiver. His fingers softly squeeze and roll the nipples, making them harden into small pebbles.

"Beautiful," he whispers and takes a nipple into his mouth. The suddenness of it makes me cry out, not in pain but in pleasure. Bolts and bolts of pleasure spiral through my body before filling my womb, causing it to clench and simmer. "Lie back, baby."

I lie back, watching him pull his t-shirt over his head and throw it on the ground. I try not to frown but if he starts making a habit out of that, we're going to have problems.

He sees my frown and smiles. "I'll pick it up later, Miss Clean Freak."

His long and talented fingers rid his jeans of his belt, and moments later he's completely naked and hovering over me. I'm only wearing my French knickers and I'm wondering why there is anything between us.

"Just lie there and relax, baby," he tells me and kisses his way down my torso.

Every touch of his lips makes me want to squeeze my thighs together, every nibble of his teeth makes my back arch and every whisper of his breath makes me moan.

His lips stop just below the button on my navel, his fingers hooking into the side of my underwear, and as his lips slowly descend his hands do too until his mouth is there and my pants are off.

I groan and grab the bed sheet when his tongue slides between my lips and finds my sensitive nub. It's a sensation I never want to stop feeling.

He bends my legs and flattens his tongue against me, swiping it up and down slowly and torturously. I'm a mess of feeling and emotion. My hands have pulled on the sheet so much it's come off the top corners of the bed.

Then his finger enters me and I freeze. It hurts a little but not too much; he's gentle and only probing a tiny fraction. He's never penetrated me before so the feeling is entirely foreign and I'm not sure that I like it.

Something builds deep down. I've had orgasms before but I have a feeling this is going to be so much bigger than the rest. My embarrassment soon leaves the building as my hands grip his head and my hips bucks desperately against his face. It's his finger inside, giving me something to clench around, that is making this experience so much better than the rest.

I explode with a loud cry. I barely register the fact he slides up my body and poises himself at my entrance.

As my orgasm continues, he slowly pushes inside. I wince with the pain mingling with the pulsing pleasure.

"Ready, Gwenny?" He asks, his eyes on mine.

I nod slightly. I'm ready.

"This is going to hurt, baby, but I'll make it better I promise," he explains and there's a tearing sensation deep inside as he thrusts his hips forward. It knocks the wind out of me and brings tears to my eyes. I cry out and try to move away, but he sinks in deeper and holds me in place with his hips and his chest. "You feel so good, Gwenny."

The initial pain fades but there's still a deep and dull ache that won't seem to shift despite the pleasure.

"I'll go slowly, but I'll make it quick," he promises and kisses my mouth languidly. "Then we can go again in a couple of hours and I swear it will feel better than this."

I look into his amazing brown eyes full of love and concern and nod slowly. It feels good to be connected to him.

He moves slowly, in and out, never going too deep for fear of hurting me. Watching his face as my body pleasures him makes me tingle all over. It's an amazing sight, one I'll cherish forever.

"You feel so good," he whispers and kisses my neck. "Honestly, babe. I've never felt anything so good." His head comes up, his lips slightly smiling. "I love you."

"I love you too." I hold his shoulders as he picks up the pace. The dull ache is still there but not as intense. I know I'm not going to finish. He knows it too and it's why he gave me the orgasm before and will probably give me another one after.

His hips slide slowly back and forth, his long, thick and hard member moving in and out.

I was made for him.

The looks of wonder as his pleasure builds, the smiles when I moan, the scrunching of the eyes and shudders when he feels particularly sensitive, all of these I burn onto my brain. All of them. I'll never forget and I want to see them again and again.

When he orgasms, he thrusts in deep; it's a little too deep but I don't care. I wrap my legs around the back of his thighs and hold him as tightly to me as possible. His member thickens and grows inside me, heating and throbbing. I feel it all. I hear his moans and groans before finally releasing my name with his pleasure on a choked cry.

As he collapses on top of me, I feel him softening inside. It's not uncomfortable but it is definitely a new feeling.

"Are you okay?" I ask and trail my fingers up his back.

"Give me a second, I need to find my way back from heaven," he pants, his chest heaving against mine as he tries to catch his breath.

I laugh and cringe as he slips out, leaving me feeling empty and hollow but blissfully happy.

"Ewww," I remark and feel his body begin to shake. "Don't laugh at me! That's kind of gross."

He only laughs harder. "I'll clean you up. Stay there."

"Kay," I respond and keep perfectly still, not liking the feel of the wetness between my thighs.

When he finally cleans me up, the smile on his face is huge. He even holds up the damp cloth to show me my red blood mixed with the other bodily fluids. "Stop giving me that face. It's beautiful."

"I think we have different opinions on beauty," I state and roll out of bed, glaring at the pink stain in the centre. "Damn it. These are Egyptian cotton."

"Oops, I never thought about that," he apologizes and strips the sheet off the bed. "Sit. I'll deal with this."

And deal with it he does.

Finally we curl up in bed together and I'm exhausted. It doesn't stop him from bringing me to orgasm once more though. He would've done it twice but I was too sated and sore to go again.

My head rests on his chest, his arms holding me tightly, and after a few sweetly whispered words and gentle caresses, we finally fall asleep. Best night of my life.

CHAPTER FIVE

THE WEEKS FLY BY and our relationship only gets stronger. I begin my advanced culinary and baking and even make two new friends. Sasha is a stunning blonde with startling blue eyes, and Tommy, who's extremely handsome with mousy brown hair and brown eyes.

At first when I told Caleb about him he got jealous.

I remember just striking up conversation on how Tommy had taken myself and Sasha for coffee.

He was less than pleased.

No... he freaked.

"What do you mean he took you for coffee?" He frowns, looking impossibly cute.

I slide onto his lap and roll my eyes. "It's just coffee. He's a nice guy. You'll like him."

"No I won't." He pouts but his smile is slowly returning.

"Why's that?"

"Because he gets your attention when I don't."

I giggle and slap his arm.

"Abuser! Abuser!"

"Stop it!" I slam my lips onto his, still laughing. "Quickie before class?"

"No." He's pouting again.

"Since when don't you want a quickie?"

"Since you started dating another man."

I laugh harder, my entire body shaking with it. "Then you'd better mark me where he can see and cover me in your scent. Just in case."

His grin is wicked and alluring. I want to lick the seam of his lips. "Hell yeah." I'm up over his shoulder before I have a chance to blink. He slaps my arse and carries me, kicking and screaming with glee, up the stairs. "By the time I'm done you aren't even going to remember his name."

"Whose?"

"Good girl." He smiles, pushing inside me after moving my pants to the side. "That's better."

"Mm."

A year goes by. I'm officially twenty and Caleb has thrown me a party. I feel bad because he looks a bit peaky, but he insists he's okay. He's been suffering with migraines a lot recently but his mood seems to pick up when he's ill, rather than get worse. It's weird. I'm a raging bitch when I'm poorly or hungry.

I've never known a person be so happy about being ill. Maybe it's because of the way I slave over him.

I decide that that's probably it. I spoil him too much.

"Over here!" Sasha screeches from the stage. We've hired out a bar for my birthday bash and I'm happy to see all of my friends have come. "You look absolutely gorgeous."

I look down at my tight, gold dress and nod my agreement. "I know, right?"

"SHOTS!" I hear Tommy shout from somewhere near the bar.

I dance with my girl and wave at Caleb, who is stood by Tommy. He winks at me, throws his head back and cringes as the fluid burns his throat. Tommy laughs and slaps him on the back. They turn away from us. I can't hear what they're saying but I can see them talking about something. Hm. What's that all about?

"Oh my god, Stacey just fell on her face!" Sasha starts pointing and laughing along with the rest of our group. That's kind of funny.

"You're such a bitch," Stacey jests and elbows Sasha in the ribs. "I'm getting another round."

"Can you handle it?" I giggle, which earns me a glare from our friend.

We climb down from the stage and head to the bar. As soon as I make it to Caleb's side, Caleb walks away and Tommy wraps his arm around my neck.

"What's up with Caleb?" I ask, trying to crane my neck to see him, but Tommy's arm is too tight. "You can let go now."

"Nope." Tommy says and sways a little. Sigh.

Sasha hands me a pink cocktail. I sip it sparingly, not wanting to get too drunk. It's my birthday. I want kinky birthday sex. I can't have kinky birthday sex if I'm half unconscious.

Speaking of birthday sex, where is my partner?

"Okay, so... ha, I almost fell." Oh god, what's he doing on the stage? "So, well... It's her birthday... Gwen's I mean." He scratches his head. Tommy actually releases me so I assume I'm allowed to watch this. "And for her birthday I got her a gift." He looks me straight in the eyes. "Come here, Gwenny."

I shake my head and take a step back. There's no way in hell I'm going up there.

Seconds later Tommy has my arm and forces me towards the stage. Oh god.

My palms are sweating. What's he doing? "Are you crazy?" I hiss as Caleb tugs me up to his side.

"For you," he responds into the microphone and a collective 'aww' can be heard.

I'm in hell. "Stop it."

"She hates being the centre of attention," Caleb tells everyone, like this trait is adorable. I'm mortified. "So I'll do this as quickly as possible."

"No sex on the stage," Tommy shouts, making everyone laugh and me blush further.

"Shut up," Caleb responds and looks at me. He turns me to face him and grips my hands in his. His lips move but I'm too anxious and nauseous to catch what he says. I manage to refocus just as Sasha begins to make a scene.

"Are you fucking kidding me?" Sasha shrieks and my eyes go to her. "All of the planning, all of the preparation and that's how you're going to ask her? You're hopeless."

Ask me what?

Caleb's eyes go wide and the room goes silent. Did I miss something?

"Fuck," he says and takes a step back, looking panicked and dejected. "Seriously?"

I blink in astonishment. "What? Do I have something on my face?"

"I ask you to marry me and that's all you have to say?"

Oh.

I mean... *what*?

He wants me to marry him?

"You want me to marry you?" I cry and take my own step back. "But..."

"You didn't hear me? How could you not hear me? I was standing right here."

"I was too busy thinking you wanted to have sex on the stage," I mumble so only he hears me. He laughs and pulls me into his arms.

"So, will you?"

I chew on my lip and nod slightly. "Only if you let me off this stage."

He smiles; it's wide and brilliant and his eyes glitter with happiness. "She said yes."

There's a roar of sound as everyone screams together. Caleb lifts me and kisses me deeply. I return it before pushing him away, heat bubbling in my cheeks.

"Where's the ring?" Tommy shouts.

"Fucking hell!" Caleb curses and sways a bit. "I have it, one second." He pulls a small box from his pocket and falls to one knee before me. Oh dear god.

"Will you marry me?" He asks again. Why is he asking again?

"I've already said yes," I laugh and watch as he places the ring on my slender finger. It's beautiful, gold with a single diamond. We can't afford much but if we were able to afford the most expensive of rings, they wouldn't even rival the beauty of this one. "I love it."

"And I love you."

"Ugh, cliché, I hope you know you ruined this night for me." Sasha pouts, slaps Caleb upside the head and stomps away, leaving us laughing in each other's arms.

"I did mess it up a bit," Caleb admits, his body swaying again. "Dance with me, Precious."

"Kay," I agree. We don't dance, however we do kiss... a lot.

I'm engaged.

Oh my god. I'm engaged!

I'm marrying the man of my dreams.

Three shots later I stand on a wobbly chair and announce this to the entire room.

Caleb gives me two more shots and an hour later I'm announcing it around his dick... in the privacy of our bedroom.

I pace back and forth, my teeth nibbling on my fingers. This isn't happening. This can't happen.

I'm scheduled, I'm on time and everything I own has a place. Caleb always says my body doesn't know how to be late for anything. He's not wrong.

"I'm back." Caleb charges through the door, panting like a dog.

I don't hesitate to snatch the plastic carrier bag from his hand and race him up the stairs, shedding the bag and the box on the way. When I make it to the toilet, all I hold is the stick.

"You're seriously going to stand there and watch?" I quirk a brow at Caleb.

He closes the door and leans against it. "Yep. I'm not missing this. I should take pictures."

"Why the hell would you want pictures?" I gape at him in disbelief.

"Because then we'll be able to show our son or daughter the moment we found out about them."

"Son or daughter?" I choke and sit on the toilet. Once that's done, I rest the stick on the side of the bath and wash my hands. "What do you mean son or daughter?"

He shrugs. "Well, what else does a pregnancy lead to?"

My jaw hits the floor. "I don't want it to lead to anything."

He freezes, his eyes on the stick as the pee starts slowly moving across the white paper behind the little window. Gross. "You don't want kids?"

"Not right now," I cry and run my fingers through my hair. "It's... we can't afford a kid. We're both in University. I don't want to give up my education." How did this even happen? "I haven't missed a pill. Not one. I haven't been sick, I haven't had any kind of medication that can mess with it and I haven't suddenly changed my eating habits. I don't get it." I look at him, directing my anger at him because it needs to go somewhere. "You know how vigilant I am. *You know.*"

"We'll figure it out." He looks way too happy about this. Way too happy. He picks up the stick after a few more moments and compares it to the back of the box that I dropped on my way in. His smile widens. "It's positive."

Sob.

His arms wrap around me. "It'll be fine. We'll figure it out, I promise. I love you so much, Gwenny."

This only makes me sob harder. I don't want a baby right now. I want to finish school and get married and all of the other stuff that comes with growing up.

"We're still kids," I sniff and wipe my nose on a piece of tissue. "We need to deal with this. I can't be more than a couple of weeks. I've only missed one period."

His eyes darken to an intensity I've never seen before. I wish I hadn't blurted that out so callously. "Deal with it? What do you mean deal with it?"

I tread cautiously, my words soft and hopefully convincing. "The doctor can have it solved in no time. It's just a minor problem and then, as soon as I finish University and we have our own house and jobs, we can try again. Obviously we'll be married then too."

He stares at me, his mouth hanging open in shock.

I continue. "It's what's best, Caleb."

Pain flits through his beautiful brown eyes, his hands fisting on the counter in front of him.

"It sucks, if it's... look," I sigh, hating that I've put this look on his face. "We'll talk about it later. I have to get to class."

I throw my bag over my shoulder and lean down to touch my lips to his unresponsive ones. He doesn't look at me and of course this worries me, but I have a test in twenty minutes. I need to go.

On the way to class I meet up with my closest friend Sasha. I admire her hair choice of the day; it hangs in loose, blonde waves to her shoulders and a black clip holds her fringe out of her eyes. "Hey!" She grins and links her arm through mine. "How's tricks?"

"Same old," I lie but she doesn't see through it. "I'm so not looking forward to this test. Have you got a placement sorted yet?"

"Me too and nope. We aren't all as fortunate or as smart as you," she jokes and elbows me in the ribs playfully. "How's the husband?"

"He's fine." I lie again and again she doesn't see through it. "He's got a placement at Anderson's firm. He'll finish his remaining year there."

She shakes her head. "I'm so jealous."

"Of?"

"Your life, it's so organised and you know what you're doing. Not to mention the fact you have the best guy in the world and he worships you."

HA! How wrong she is right now. Still, I reassure her as a good friend does. "You'll get sorted, babe. You'll see; it'll all work out in the end."

"Hey, Tommy!" She calls to our classmate. He races over to us, breaks our link and shoves himself in the middle. His arms curl around our necks. "How are the two most beautiful females on campus this morning?"

"Fabulous," Sasha responds and smiles up at him. "Where's your woman?" He met a very nice girl called Maci at my birthday party two months ago and they've been dating steadily ever since. I'm happy for him; they're a good match.

"Over there." He points to a group heading into the building. "Hey, sexy!" His girlfriend rolls her eyes but I see her smile and know all is well. "Got to go if I want to get me a little somethin' somethin' before my next lecture."

"Your next lecture is in three hours," I laugh, knowing my friend's schedules by heart. That's just how organised I am.

"Exactly. It's just not long enough." He races away and waves over his shoulder.

"That lucky, lucky girl," Sasha sighs wistfully and pushes her way past a group of people loitering by the door. "Come on, we're nearly late."

The test went well and even though my mind was on other things, I have no doubts that I've passed. I've studied my arse off for this test. If I fail it's not a huge deal, but it counts towards a percentage of my overall grade that I'd like to keep.

My culinary course is going great, mostly because there are only twelve of us in the class. It's my English Literacy class that has me constantly studying. I'm not sure why I took this as an extra. It seemed like a good idea at the time and I do love to write.

Now, to solve my current problem... I tell Sasha I'm going home for lunch when in reality I'm going to call my doctor to book an appointment and then I'm going home.

As expected Caleb is inside. He's sat in the living room drinking tea and eating biscuits while thumbing through his phone.

"Hey," I announce and his head tips back so he can see me.

"Hey," he responds, his eyes dead and his easy smile non-existent. It makes my heart hurt.

"The test went well." I sit on the arm of the chair and run my fingers through his hair.

He manages to smile but it's too sad to be put in the happy smile category. "That's great news, babe. Proud of you."

"I also booked an appointment at the doctor's for tomorrow." I say it cautiously, not wanting to sadden him further. He needs to see this from my point.

His eyes darken dangerously. I've never seen him look so... angry. "Just do what you have to do, but don't expect me there if you do it."

What? "Are you serious?"

His eyes go back to his phone. "Yep."

"I'm doing this alone?"

"Uh-huh." He sips his drink, his face firm and unrelenting.

My heart breaks. "You're not going to support me? Hold my hand?"

"No."

"Well... okay then," I struggle to say because I'm fighting back tears that seemed to be lodged in my throat. "I'm going upstairs."

"Whatever," he says, seeming unaffected by my obvious distress. He's always supported me, always. He hates to see me cry. Whenever I cry he tells me it breaks his heart.

Once we argued so badly he ended up throwing a plate against the wall and it scared me. I thought he was leaving me. I cried. I remember how much pain I felt when he said he couldn't deal with it anymore and threw his plate of food across the kitchen.

It wasn't long after we got engaged that it happened. My mum isn't being supportive in the slightest. She thinks I'm a young and naïve girl with her head in the clouds. She'll see just how happy and stable we are when I finish university and get married and all is well.

He was pissed off because his parents refused to give him his trust fund, even though he's doing amazingly well in university. I told him it'd all be okay and he just looked at me and shouted, "You don't get it; you'll never get it."

He was angry at them, not at me, and it was the first time he's ever raised his voice so it scared the hell out of me. Angry Caleb is not a good Caleb.

What couldn't he deal with anymore? His parents? Me? Us? The house? The lack of money? He never did tell me; he just told me to drop it, which was totally unlike him.

I started crying and instantly he sobered. He stopped being angry and just held me, begging me not to cry. He told me it breaks his heart when I cry.

And now he sees my anguish but does nothing. Screw him.

I stomp up the stairs, my eyes burning even though my tears are spilling over. I try not to think about it too much. He'll forgive me; I know he will. At least... I hope he will. Now is not the right time for a baby.

I'm shocked when I hear him follow me up the stairs. Clearly he has something on his mind that wants out. Maybe we can resolve this.

I sit on the bed and wait for him to reach me. When he does, he stands in the doorframe just staring at me, his eyes blank. I can't read him at all.

"Why are you doing this?" He asks suddenly, his brows scrunching.

"Because it's the wrong time. I'd like it if you came with me," I say, my sorrow clear.

"No." He bites out through clenched teeth. "I won't."

"Babe..."

"If you do this..." He stops speaking and straightens abruptly while his fingers run through his hair. He looks devastated. It hurts me deeply. Too deeply.

"Yes?" I prompt, not wanting him to finish his sentence but knowing he should.

"I'll never forgive you." My chest constricts at his words. "Never."

"Caleb," I gasp, my hand going to my chest, as if trying to shield it from his emotional blows. "You don't mean that."

"It's ours," he shouts. "It's half mine. I should get to decide."

"We're not ready," I shout back. "I want to finish my education and buy a house first."

"We'll figure it out," he says, his voice almost pleading. "Together we'll figure it out. I'll ask my parents to help with childcare."

I laugh coldly. "You mean the parents that disowned you for staying with me? Why would they help?"

He winces. "They'll help. I'll just go into work for my dad."

"The reason you left home in the first place was to avoid working with your dad. How is this a better option? You'll end up resenting us." I reach for him, but he steps away. "We have a lot of student loans to pay off and the first year of work neither of us will be bringing in much money. They're just placements. There's no guarantee they'll keep us and they definitely won't keep me if I'm pregnant."

"We'll make it work. You'll see. It'll all be fine."

"You're living in a dream world. We have no money, no family. It's just us." I say this firmly.

"I'll drop out. I'll go back to University in a couple of years." He grips my arms. "We'll make it work."

"It'll be too hard."

"I want this baby. I want a baby with you."

I scoff. "You don't think I want that? Of course I do. Just not now!"

"So you've made up your mind then?" He spits, his face a mask of anger and hurt. "Without even listening to what I want?"

"What about what I want? What I need?"

"Fine," he snarls. I've never seen him so angry. He's even angrier than the time he smashed the plate. He rages past me, his body tense and trembling. My heart stops when I see him packing his things into a large suitcase that he's just pulled from under the bed.

"W...what are you doing Caleb?" My heavy heart stops entirely when he looks at me and replies, "I can't stay here."

"Why?" Panic at full throttle, I think I'm dying. My body hurts.

"I can't watch you kill our baby." That stings.

I blink in horror. "You're leaving me?"

"Yes." My chest tingles and my stomach heaves.

"Is this an ultimatum?" I breathe, not believing my ears or eyes. My tears spill over; I can't control them. He doesn't respond. "Caleb, please don't do this."

He freezes, his hands gripping the open case that lays on the bed.

"Please," I sob and grab his arm. "Please, Caleb. Don't make me go through this alone."

"Keep it." He demands, his body still tense.

"Why can't you just wait?" I half shout, half sob. "Why can't you just fucking wait?"

"You're murdering my child."

I jerk away from him, his words burned on my brain. "Don't see it that way. Please."

"How can I see it any other way?"

No. He can't do this. He can't.

But he is.

I watch him pack up his bags, his face set and his steps sure. He leaves, taking the car, and all night he doesn't come back.

I sit in the doctor's office and explain my situation, relieved when she understands. She gives me a test just to be sure. When it comes out positive, she books me an appointment at the clinic. I have two choices of termination, one where they put me to sleep and get it all out, or one where they give me a tablet and I sit for six hours waiting for it to leave my body.

I opt for option one. Call me a coward.

My appointment is in four weeks. They give you a gap to change your mind. The gap is too long; I want it done now.

In class Sasha notices that something is wrong but I don't tell her. I don't tell anyone. Right now I can't. Nobody needs to know about this. Nobody.

Even I don't want to know about it.

When I make it home, I curl up in bed and cry. He's not home. Why isn't he home?

Can I honestly do this to him? Can I honestly look him in the eye and tell him I'm going to murder his child? Because that's what it is. I'm giving him no choice and it's half of him. He was right.

I roll onto my back and close my eyes, letting my woes sink into me like an anchor into the sea. My hand rests on my flat belly and I try to imagine what it would be like to stay pregnant, to carry Caleb's baby in my stomach for nine months, to bring him or her into the world.

What would he or she look like?

Would they have his hair? His eyes?

I let out a long breath coupled with a sob and turn back on my side. Curling into the foetal position, I weep. My sorrows and sadness are too heavy to bear, my conscience too plagued with indecision.

"I can't do it," I say out loud to nobody. I can't do it.

Who am I kidding? There's no way I can kill it. No way.

But if I don't, my university experience will be ruined. No more drinking, not that I drink much anyway, no more just going out to the cinema or to a club. I'll be studying my arse off and then coming home to diapers, poop and vomit.

One of us will have to quit school because there's no way we'll be able to afford childcare. Maybe there's something to help students in this situation?

I'm lost so deeply in my thoughts I don't hear the door open, so when someone touches my shoulder and the bed dips, I scream bloody murder and fall from the bed.

"Christ." He's laughing. Laughing? How can he laugh right now? What an arsehole. "Are you okay?

Oh my god. Caleb's here. "I'm fine." I climb back onto the bed, nursing my wounded pride. "You're here."

His laughter stops and his smile vanishes. "Yeah. I should never have left. I hate it when you cry. It breaks my heart. I'm so sorry." His arms close around me and soon I'm on his lap. His heat sinks into me through his warm embrace.

I welcome it.

"Forgive me?" He whispers and kisses my neck. I bury my face in his chest, relieved that he's here. "I should have handled that better. It's just..." He sighs long and heavy.

"What?"

"Do you ever feel like it doesn't matter what we do or who we are, we never really leave anything behind?"

And again... "What?"

He pulls back and rests against the headboard, propping the pillows up behind him. "Kids are our only legacy."

"I don't know what you mean."

He rubs his face with his hands and pulls me to his chest. "I mean, I want a child with you. This child, right now. Sure the timing isn't great, but it's a situation we'll deal with together." Warm hands grip mine and his eyes implore me to see his side of things. "Please, Gwenny. Don't destroy it."

"Okay," I sigh and my head falls forward. "If this is what you want, then okay. We'll do this."

He beams and pulls me to him. "Gwenny, honestly, it'll be great. You'll see."

I press my lips to his and murmur against them, "I believe you."

Something flashes in his eyes, something that makes me uneasy. I can't be certain what it is, I just know I won't forget it.

"Thank you," he whispers and presses his lips to mine. "I love you."

"Me too."

"Hey," he gives me a squeeze and frowns. "If you're going to say it, make sure you say it properly."

Eye roll. "I love you too."

He releases me and climbs from the bed. "I'm going to make you some tea and whatever else you want."

"Okay." I smile sweetly at him and watch him leave the room with a heavy heart.

He reappears seconds later. "I almost forgot." Crawling onto the bed, he lifts my shirt over my navel and kisses just above the waistband of my trousers. "Love you, baby Weston."

Oh god.

I just melted.

"I'm sure he loves you too."

He kisses my navel once more, covers me up and rushes down the stairs.

I definitely just melted.

CHAPTER SIX

"You're six weeks and three days." She puts a circle around the foetus so we can see it more clearly. "This flicker is its heartbeat; this will be his head eventually." I stare mesmerised at the screen.

I hear a choke next to me and turn my head towards Caleb.

"Are you crying?" I ask him, my lips twitching.

"No." He pouts, his hand holding tight to mine and his eyes on the screen.

The room is dark, only lit by the black and green glow of the screen. The dim shine catches a tear trail on his cheek. I wipe at it with my thumb and my smile widens.

"Soppy."

"I'm not crying," he protests with a smile. "I have something in my eye."

"Both of them?" The scan lady remarks and I burst into a fit of giggles.

Caleb leans forward and presses his lips against mine. "Love you, Gwenny."

"Love you too," I whisper back and deepen the kiss for a moment.

"I'll just print off some pictures," the woman says, giving us some privacy.

I look into the eyes of my fiancé and run my fingers through his longish hair. "Are you sure about this, Caleb?"

A panicked gaze comes to mine. "Aren't you?"

"I am. That's why I'm asking you, because if you back out now I'll be on my own."

His shoulders sag, his thumb stroking my cheek as his beautiful brown eyes meet mine. "I'll never leave you on your own, Gwenny. Never. I want this more than you know."

What's that supposed to mean? Why do I feel like something isn't right about this? Of course I'm happy, what expectant mother isn't when she finally wraps her head around it? It's just... I can't help but feel like Caleb is hiding something.

I'm probably being stupid. Maybe it's my extra hormones making me read into something that isn't there.

"Your mum is going to kill me," Caleb says, piercing my erratic thoughts and making them pop into a million more.

"Oh shit." I never even thought of that. "We just won't tell her until I start to show."

"I'm sure she'll get over it." I can tell he doesn't believe his own words any more than I do.

My mum, though I love her, has always provided me with what I need but I've never been more than an inconvenience to her. When she finds out about this, she'll never talk to me again. Part of me doesn't care. The child in me still wishes for her approval and is still eager to make her proud.

"You've got me." Caleb's reassuring words do just that. He's right; I have got him and my friends. They are all I need.

"Forever," I murmur, my eyes on my sparkly ring.

"For all of eternity." His lips slant over mine but quickly pull back when the woman walks back in with our scan picture.

When we get home, Caleb frames it and puts it on the wall in the hallway. "This will be our timeline. Our wedding photo will be in the middle. Tomorrow I'm going to put our first ever picture right here."

"You're such a romantic," I laugh and kiss his stubble. "I'll put dinner on."

"Brilliant, chicken wraps?"

I nod and walk away, my hand pressed against my belly.

"Hey, almost forgot..." I'm spun in a second and Caleb is down on his knees, pulling my top over my midriff. He presses his hands on my navel and then kisses in between them. "Love you, baby Weston."

I just melted again. He has that effect on me.

***

I cling to the seat, my forehead on my arms. Caleb ties my hair back from my face and rubs slow circles on my back. "Finished?"

Hurl.

"I guess not," he says around a yawn and wipes my forehead and then my mouth with a cool cloth. That feels nice. "Poor baby."

"I hate this. You've done this," I joke and sit back on the cool tiled floor. "Ugh. If I'm never sick again it'll be too soon."

"It's a good sign; he's growing well." Caleb is insistent that it's a boy. He really, really wants a boy but he'll still be happy if we get a girl. "Caleb Weston," he says with his hand on my stomach, "has a nice ring to it."

I laugh and slap his arm before climbing to my feet. "That's your name."

"Exactly." His arms snake around my waist as I quickly brush my teeth, eager to get the putrid taste of vomit from my mouth and rid my teeth of that gritty feeling. "Fourteen weeks and three days. Can we start telling people now?"

"Don't give me that," I say, my mouth full of minty foam. Spit. "I know you've told everyone already. Even Sasha knows, though she's pretending she doesn't."

He has the decency to look ashamed. "I couldn't help it."

"You're incorrigible," I snort and rinse out my mouth, squirming when Caleb's hand cups my sex through my pyjama shorts. Shiver. "Right now? Really? My stomach is still doing somersaults."

"Let me take your mind off it," he breathes against my neck and pushes his hardened length against my arse cheek.

A banging sounds at the door downstairs and both of our heads whip around. "Who's that? It's like," I check my watch. "Six fifteen."

"No idea, sounds urgent," Caleb says and releases me. "Stay here."

I nod and follow him into the room and then the hall. I wait at the top of the stairs and listen as Caleb opens the door.

I don't recognize the male voice that starts speaking over Caleb's, but I soon know who it is when Caleb asks him, "What do you want, Nathan?"

"I can't let you do this," Nathan responds, his voice deep and low. Do what?

I descend the stairs and my curiosity increases tenfold with every step as their voices become hushed. Did Caleb just say, "I love her, I swear?" Because I can't be certain.

When I make it to the last step, two sets of matching eyes come to me. Nathan is a couple of inches taller than Caleb and although they look alike, Nathan's face is much sharper than Caleb's and there isn't a hint of stubble. He's wearing a suit and he looks good. I always did appreciate a man in a suit, though the gloves that cover his hands perplex me. What's up with the black leather gloves? It's warm outside. Does he have a motorbike?

His eyes scan my body, a dark look on his face. My hand goes to my belly almost protectively.

"I told you to stay upstairs," Caleb hisses with a frown.

"I'm Gwen," I say to Nathan and hold out my hand. "It's nice to meet you."

Nathan looks at my hand for a few seconds before turning back to his brother. "Are you crazy?"

"At least say hello to my *pregnant* fiancée, Nathan. Where're your manners?" Caleb bites out through clenched teeth. Why did he say pregnant like that?

Nathan looks at me again, but his eyes are focused on my stomach. "I can't believe you."

"Nathan," Caleb warns, his hands raised and his eyes wide. Nathan's scowl is scary and even I'm shrinking fast. "Please." Nathan seems to think about whatever the hell they're talking about for a moment. His eyes narrow, so I'm guessing the conclusion he's drawn isn't a good one.

It happens so fast, too fast. Nathan's fist strikes out and connects with Caleb's cheekbone. Caleb flies backwards, tripping on a shoe before falling to his arse. My hand goes to my mouth in shock.

"You'll do well to get rid of that before it's too late," Nathan says, pointing at my stomach. I watch him whip his glove off and start squirting some kind of sterilising fluid onto his hand. He turns and leaves, still rubbing the lotion around his fingers with his gloved hand. That's weird. What an arsehole.

"Are you okay?" I ignore Nathan's comment. As much as I want to scratch his eyes out right now, Caleb needs me.

He rolls his jaw and touches his cheekbone with a finger. We both wince. I can already see it swelling and have no doubt it's painful to touch. "I'll get some ice and then you're going to tell me what the hell just happened."

"My brother's a dickhead, that's what just happened," he snaps and pulls his arm free of my hands before stomping into the kitchen. "Fuck, he's got a good right hook."

I stand in the doorway and watch him grab a bag of frozen peas from the freezer before wrapping them in a tea towel and placing them on his face. "Is that all you're going to say on the matter then?"

"I don't want to talk about it," he sighs and rests his head back. "I'm sorry you had to see that."

"Me too. Especially since I don't know what I've seen exactly."

He shakes his head. "He's pissed that I left him to deal with our parents and even more pissed that I got someone pregnant before marriage. My brother is weird."

"So why'd you tell him I'm pregnant?"

Caleb shrugs. "Seemed like a good idea at the time."

"He told me to get rid of the baby. That doesn't seem like normal behaviour."

He laughs coldly and I've never heard such a laugh from him before. It's kind of scary. "My brother isn't normal. Stay away from him, Gwen. Okay?"

I nod, not wanting to argue over something I'm in complete agreement with. There's no way in hell I'll be going near him again. "Maybe you should report it."

"No, he's my brother. He punched me and he left. It's done." Caleb says and now he looks sad.

I slide onto his lap and wrap my arms around his neck. "I'm sorry, Caleb."

Kissing his mouth gently, I press my body against his, wanting to absorb his pain.

"I love you, Gwenny. Don't ever," he pulls back and looks me in the eyes, "forget that. No matter what. Okay?"

I frown, nodding. "What's gotten into you lately? You seem on edge and you're always coming out with weird things that you wouldn't normally say."

He shrugs. "It's probably the excitement of becoming a dad. Sorry if I've seemed..." Now he's smiling. "Weird? Is that the right word?"

"You're always weird. Maybe it's because for once you've actually been acting normal."

"Cheeky," he chuckles and forces me to straddle his lap on the high stool. "Let me take you to bed and remind you how weird I am."

"I don't think I need reminding, but I'll gladly play along and pretend I do."

***

Two weeks go by and I've finally told my boss I'm pregnant now that I'm starting to get a bump. I show up for work late due to Caleb being ill. His migraine has him stuck in bed, his face under the covers. I feel bad for him and want to stay at home to look after him, but I can't. We need all of the money we can get.

My boss, Derrick of Chicago's, is really understanding thankfully. He even gives me a hug and congratulates me which is nice.

Work is boring and I'm sick of everyone asking me where Caleb is. He's at home! Obviously. Why is it anyone's business? If it was me that was off they wouldn't be panicking, they'd be trying it on with my fiancée. I know this because Sasha comes in with a group of girls every Wednesday. I don't work Wednesday nights. She tells me about the group of women who constantly surround him, but he brushes them off as much as he can.

You'd think the news of our engagement and the pregnancy would warn them off, but some of them try even harder than they did before. It drives me around the bend.

Fortunately I have complete trust in Caleb so I'm not worried at all. It's just irritating. It stresses him out too.

When I finally make it home, I climb into the shower and afterwards I snuggle up with my poorly, soon to be husband in bed. He instantly wraps himself around me, bringing my face to his neck.

"Marry me," he whispers as I place my hands against his feverish skin.

"You're burning up." I try and pull away so I can get his medicine.

He doesn't let me. He just looks in my eyes in the dark; they're serious, extremely serious. "I want to marry you on Wednesday."

"What?"

"Please. Just do this for me. I've already made the appointment. Two PM on Wednesday. I wanted tomorrow, but tomorrow was taken. We're going to Gretna Green; it'll be a road trip."

"That's impossible! It takes time. We have things to post and declare. You can't just get married in two days. What's wrong with you?" I snap and pull myself free of his arms. "Let me get you something to bring down that fever."

"You're not fucking listening!" He exclaims suddenly and sits bolt upright in bed. He winces and presses his hands to his head. "I need you to marry me, please. It's simple. We can have a party in a couple of months but I want to make you my wife. I already did everything. I already posted everything. I started the day you agreed to marry me. I'm sure I did."

Damn it. This is crazy. He's delirious.

"Promise me!" He sounds out of breath.

I nod, not saying the words but sort of meaning them. "Okay."

He sags back, his body too heavy for his lack of energy right now. I take this chance to rush into the bathroom and wet a lot of towels. When I place them over his skin, he cries out. My panic increases. "What's wrong? What is it? I think I should call an ambulance."

"No!" He almost shouts and his hand wraps around my wrist. "I'll be fine in the morning; it's just the flu or something."

"I don't know, Caleb," I whisper and place a wet flannel on his forehead.

His eyes come to mine. "Please, Gwenny. No hospitals."

I sigh and agree. He's right, it's probably nothing. I'll just have to keep a close eye on him.

"I almost forgot," he whispers and motions me closer. "Bring him here."

Giggling, I move up the bed and bring my navel up to his face.

"Love you, baby Weston," he says and I feel his lips press against my stomach. Seconds later he's fast asleep and I'm changing the towels. His temperature is so high the water in the towels is now lukewarm. That's crazy. Now I'm really worried.

The morning comes and Caleb is much better. His fever broke in the night and I know this because I didn't sleep at all. I don't want him to go to class and I'm shocked when he so easily agrees and spends the day with me in bed, watching movies and eating junk.

Then he reminds me of what he said last night and my heart starts racing. "We're getting married on Wednesday."

I roll him onto his back. "What's the rush?"

"You're pregnant with my son. I want to do this properly."

I frown and think on it for a moment. I want to walk down an aisle in a stunning white dress. I want the after party and the confetti. I don't want to get married at a registry office just for the sake of getting married.

He sees my thoughts churning and gives me a little shake. "I hate to pull this card..."

"What card?"

He rubs his hands over his face and flips us over so I'm on my back. "If you don't marry me then I'll think you don't love me."

Drama. "Stop being an idiot."

His face falls and I see the desperation in his eyes. "Please, Gwenny. Please."

Now I'm really panicked. "What's going on Caleb?"

"Nothing..."

"Don't lie to me."

"I had a dream," he blurts and pecks me on the lips. "I had a really bad dream and I can't remember it, but I know I want to marry you and I don't want to waste another minute."

"Damn it," I groan and turn my head. "Fine. Fine. Wednesday we'll get married."

"You swear?"

"Ugh."

"Swear it, Gwenny, or I'm never eating you again."

My mouth falls open in horror. "You bastard."

"Swear it."

"Okay, okay, I swear it!"

The smile that lights up his face is mesmerising. He kisses me deeply before rolling back onto his back and pulling me tightly to him. "Love you, Gwenny."

"Love you too." Even though we've agreed, something in my gut just isn't right. There's something going on here and I want to ask him but I'll give him time to get better first. He looks exhausted, sounds exhausted and is clearly unwell, even if his temperature has broken.

"Let's just stay in bed until we get married," he murmurs, his lids hooded and sleepy looking. "How does that sound?"

I nod. "I still have to work your shift though."

"Ask someone to cover it. Don't leave my side for a second."

I'm about to ask what he's talking about, but I'm distracted by a strange thumping sensation in my stomach. My heart accelerates along with my excitement. "He's kicking," I whisper and press Caleb's hand to my stomach.

We wait and, just when I think it's not going to happen, I feel him tap. "Really?" Caleb laughs and looks at my stomach in wonder. "That's..." he moves down the bed and rests his cheek on my navel. "I wish I could feel him."

"Me too."

Tears fill Caleb's eyes, his lips pinching together as if suppressing them. He looks up at me, his eyes full of hurt and sorrow.

"What's wrong, baby?" I ask and hug him as tight as possible. His body starts to shake and a sob escapes him. Now he's crying, it's almost like I can feel his pain and my own eyes begin to tingle and burn. "Talk to me."

He shakes his head. "I'm happy."

"That's a lie. I know you and I know these aren't happy tears."

"I'm so sorry, Gwenny."

"Sorry?"

"Oh god," he chokes out and sobs tear through him. I've never heard such mournful sounds. They torture my very soul.

His arms hold me tighter with each second and my chest becomes wet from his tears. My own tears stain my face as I try to figure out what's wrong with him, but nothing comes to mind.

"Talk to me," I beg, closing my eyes to push out another tear. "Please, baby. Talk to me."

"Don't ever lose yourself, okay?" He whispers. "Promise me."

"What are you talking about? You're scaring me."

"You're perfect the way you are. Don't ever change. Never leave me. Never. I know it's selfish, but I..."

"Hey," I soothe him and stroke my fingers through his hair. "I'll never leave you. I swear it."

***

Sasha and Tommy have agreed to be our witnesses for the wedding tomorrow. I'm nervous and excited and nervous and even more excited. Caleb hasn't brought up last night and I daren't. Seeing him so tortured has killed me. Maybe everything has just gotten on top of him at last. He wasn't bothered when his parents disowned him, or maybe he was and he just bottled it up. He's always so happy. To see him so devastated... it makes me sick just thinking about it.

I never want to see him like that again. My heart can't stand it. It's because of this that I don't get angry at him for planning our wedding without me. I want to be hurt and angry that he'd rush me into this and do it behind my back, but right now just isn't the time. What does it matter when or how we get married? I love him, that's all that marriage should be about.

Now I know what he means when he says seeing me cry breaks his heart.

He looks happy enough, although I know he has a headache because he's wearing sunglasses indoors and he's going through painkillers like they're sweets. I keep telling him to go to the doctor but he won't listen. He assures me it's nothing, but this can't be normal. Can't he sense how worried I am?

As promised, I haven't been to work or classes. I'm yet again curled up with Caleb watching crappy TV with Sasha and Tommy, who are insisting they drink in front of me seeing as I can't join in. Caleb isn't drinking either; he says he wants to suffer with me. I love him even more for it.

"I can't believe you're getting married," Sasha sighs wistfully and downs the rest of her glass. Tommy leans over and fills it with white wine. "You two were meant to be."

"You're so soppy," I joke, throwing a scatter cushion at her.

"I'm serious. I've been single for a year. I'm sick of it now. I want what you have." She wags her eyebrows at Caleb. "Sure you don't want me instead? I'll teach you things you didn't know were physically possible."

We all start laughing when she tries to hook her ankle behind her head, fails and falls to the ground with an 'oomph'.

"I'm sure you're hot, Sasha, but Gwenny blows my mind."

"I'm sure she blows something," Tommy mumbles, earning a glare from me and a cackle from Sasha.

"Oh my god, I only just got that. That's funny," Caleb starts laughing a few seconds later, earning a glare from me and a cackle from Sasha and a high five from Tommy.

Caleb starts drifting asleep on my shoulder after a few more minutes. This concerns me because he's not normally this tired by nine at night. I say my apologies to Tommy and Sasha and take him up to bed, even more worried when he leans on me the entire way. My panic is overloading when I have to help him get undressed.

"I just need to shut my eyes for a while," he says softly as I kiss his cheek. "Hey, I almost forgot." I lift my shirt and smile when he kisses my small bump. "I love you, baby Weston."

"Caleb," I whisper and sit beside him. "Are you okay?"

He looks me straight in the eyes and nods. "Yeah, Gwenny. Hurry up and come to bed. I want to hold you until..." His voice trails off as he drifts to the land of nod.

I rush to say goodbye to the others and hurry back to bed. I'm getting married tomorrow and that's the furthest thing from my mind. What's wrong with Caleb? Is this a lasting effect of his illness?

He pulls me into him so my head rests on his chest and my thigh across his legs, while my hand teases the hairs that travel from his navel to below his boxers. Normally he'd jerk and laugh, but this time he remains peacefully sleeping. Sigh.

"I love you, baby," I say and kiss his lips.

"Love you too, Gwenny," He murmurs and tightens his arms around me. I thought he was sleeping. I guess not.

Nuzzling into his chest, I stop playing with his trail of hair and instead I hold him as tight to me as possible.

***

The sun hasn't risen yet. Why am I awake? Ugh, morning sickness. Nausea roils my stomach.

Leaning over Caleb, I check the clock. Five fifteen in the morning. Great. I'll never get back to sleep now. I'm one of those people who, when they wake, they're awake and that's it.

I can feel the smile cross my lips as a myriad thoughts flit through my sleepy mind. Today's my wedding day. I'm marrying the man I'm truly, madly in love with. I'm pregnant with his child. I'm going to be a mother.

Mrs Guinevere Weston.

Life is so perfect.

With a happy sigh, I stretch out my arms and legs. The wonderful relaxing feeling is interrupted when I feel a dampness with my toes, near Caleb's knees. Slowly I sit up. I instinctively know something is wrong. The bed feels cooler and there is a sweet sickly smell that hits the back of my throat and aggravates the nausea I already feel.

Caleb's still, sleeping form lies next to me. Looking at him, he looks peaceful, but I look more closely and my throat catches. I can't see his chest rise and fall. No wait, there's a twitch in his arm. I let out a sigh. Of course I'm being silly. I touch his arm to wake him and tell him about my stupid thoughts.

When I touch his hand, it's cold, not like ice, but cold like we have been for a walk down the beach in winter and need to wrap our hands round a cup of hot chocolate to warm them. His skin has an almost pearlescent look to it. It's too pale.

"Caleb," I whisper and push myself off his chest. "Caleb?" I notice his arms by his sides rather than holding me, which is odd for him. "Caleb," I say louder this time and push his chest.

He doesn't stir. That's odd. Maybe he's still sick.

"Caleb!" I say even louder and tap his cheek. His head rolls to the side, but he doesn't make a noise. My heart hits my ribs and sharp tingles spread through my chest. "Caleb!" I shake him violently this time and switch on the lamp.

"No." I whisper and place my hand an inch from his mouth, staring at his chest. This isn't happening. He's not... "CALEB!" I grab both of his shoulders and shake him vigorously. "CALEB! Please. This isn't funny!" His eyelids don't even flutter.

Oh my god.

He's not breathing.

I place my trembling fingers to his neck.

"NO!" I scream, my eyes burning and my lungs constricting. "Baby, please, wake up now." No. No. No.

I kick the blanket from the bed and cry out at the mess on the sheets. A choked sob sticks in my throat and my body trembles as I try to comprehend what I'm seeing.

I pull at his body. He still feels warm but he is a dead weight in my arms. No this can't be happening.

'You can't be dead. We have to get married today. You have to see your child be born. I'm going to be all alone.'

"Wake up!" I scream, ignoring the pain it brings to my throat.

Ambulance. I need to phone an ambulance, but I'm torn. I don't want to leave him but I need to get my phone from my bag. My legs feel leaden as I stumble downstairs. It's going to be fine. They will help him. They can bring him back. I dial the number, my fingers quick and clumsy on the small buttons.

"He's not breathing! I can't wake him," I sob to the woman on the phone, but she isn't understanding me. She tells me to stop, take a breath, think about what I want to say and repeat it slowly.

"What happened?" She asks me. What do I tell her? I tell her whatever it is I'm seeing, my address and his name. She's still talking but I can't hear her. I need to do something.

He's... no... he's not dead. "You're not dead! Wake up. Wake up right now. This isn't funny." I breathe into his mouth while pinching his nose. I throw my phone and start doing chest compressions. Come on, baby. Come on. "Please, Caleb. Please."

His lifeless face doesn't twitch and my heart shatters. He's not dead. He'll wake up and start laughing.

Minutes pass before I hear sirens and rush down stairs to open the door. I don't wait for them to come in before I run back upstairs and continue forcing him to breathe.

I peel open an eyelid and a glassy lifeless pupil stares back at me, the iris bigger than I've ever seen it. My lips tremble and a cry escapes me.

My body burns. "Please, Caleb, don't leave me!"

The paramedics come inside and I'm pulled gently out of the way. I watch them work on him and I'm escorted to the side as they begin CPR and defibrillation. I look on helplessly as they pass electric currents through his heart. They work for what seems like only seconds instead of the minutes that actually pass.

"I'm so sorry," a woman says as they call his death.

They call it.

They just call it.

"NO! Keep going!" I yell at them, but no one listens to me. Time just keeps flying in a blur. I feel as though I'm falling through reality, every second melting into the next. I'm unaware of everything, yet more aware than I've ever been.

The Police arrive and one of them tries to take me out of the room. "He wouldn't leave me! He's fine! People just don't die in their sleep!"

"Please, Miss," the officer says in my ear, trying to get me to move. "I'm so sorry."

"There's nothing we can do. He's gone."

"No." I fall to my knees as they surround the bed. "No! Please. Don't stop trying. You can't stop."

I can't hear anything they say after this. I see the men start to lift him.

"No," I cry and throw myself towards his body. "No you can't take him."

The tears that trickled at first begin to cascade down my face. I can't stop them and I don't want to.

It's not fair! Why him? Why? There are others out there with less to live for. Why couldn't they have died instead?

"We'll let you have a few minutes, sweetheart." I don't know who says it and I don't care.

A few minutes? I was meant to have a lifetime with this man. We were going to grow old together.

Everything is so surreal and the fast erratic thoughts on why this is happening soon slow and turn to an empty numbness. My whole world feels like it has just collapsed. Nothing seems to matter apart from the fact he has gone.

Nothing.

I'm left looking over his body.

I have heard people describe a dead body as a shell of the person they once knew. This isn't even a shell of the man I've lost. Gone is the warmth of his almost chocolate gaze and the vibrancy this body once held. Even in his sleep he was captivating. Now all of that essence has left. He's left and I'm left with nothing.

I look at the most beautiful man I've ever seen as he's placed on a stretcher and covered with a sheet. They cover his face. I don't want them to cover his face. Why won't they listen?

They keep asking me questions. Who are my family and friends? Who are his family and friends? I can't answer. I can't do anything but sob.

"Where are they taking him?"

I'm surrounded by people, police officers and strangers, as I tear out of my house. I have no sense of time or place, my eyes on his lifeless body.

"Stop!" I scream, but they keep going.

Someone grabs me around the waist and holds me tight. Tommy's here. When did he get here?

"We should sedate her," someone says.

"She's pregnant. Be careful."

"Why are they taking him? They need to help him!"

"Hey," Tommy says softly in my ear and pulls me towards an ambulance.

I try to pull free but my energy levels are non-existent. I'm non-existent. This isn't happening to me, it's happening to somebody else.

Twenty three year old males don't just die in their sleep the night before their wedding.

"What happened, does anybody know?" Tommy asks whoever is here.

"They think it may have been a heart attack, but they won't know for sure until they get him to the hospital."

Numbness overcomes me. I turn in Tommy's arms and cling to him, my body shaking like a leaf, my mouth emitting noises I've never made before.

He's not gone. He's not. They'll get him to the hospital and they'll see.

"Don't let them stop trying, Tommy." I beg, my fists gripping the shirt of my friend.

Everything goes black. I'm not sure how or why, I just drift.

I wake up in an unfamiliar bed. I'm in the hospital. Why am I here?

"Hey you," Tommy says and I see Sasha beside him.

I open my mouth but nothing comes out. Tears spill and the sobs that plagued my body once already come back immediately. Sasha rushes to my side and envelops me in her arms. "I'm so sorry," she whispers and I feel her own tears fall onto my hair.

No. "No. No. He's not... they were supposed to save him."

"I know," she sniffs, still rocking me and stroking my hair. "They couldn't do anything. I'm sorry."

"Why? What happened?"

Tommy and Sasha look at each other. "They won't tell us anything. His parents got here as quickly as they could and they won't permit you to know anything."

"I'm his fiancée!" I shriek. "We're getting married today."

"The nurse told us all she knows is that his heart failed and it couldn't be prevented."

"I have to see him," I shout and climb from the bed. "Why am I even here?" They're about to answer but I cut them off and push the door open. "It doesn't matter. Where is he?" There's a nurse doing her rounds and I stop her before she has a chance to enter the room by mine. "Where is he? I need to see him."

She blinks in shock. "You shouldn't be out of bed."

"Please, I need to see Caleb. Where's Caleb?"

"Maybe I should..." She glances around nervously but I place myself in her line of sight. "I can't help you. I'm sorry."

"No, you don't understand," I huff, my eyes burning. "I have to see him!"

"What's going on?" A doctor in a white shirt and black trousers walks over to us from the nurses' station.

I immediately turn to him. "Please, I need to find Caleb. Caleb Weston."

He glances at the nurse and then at Tommy and Sasha, who are close behind me. Letting out a breath I see him relent. "Come with me."

I want to hug him, but I don't. We follow him down a few hallways before he stops and speaks to a porter. "Please escort these three to the morgue."

A choked cry escapes me as I realise just how real this is. No.

Tommy takes my arm as Sasha takes the other. My legs are unsteady but I manage to follow the porter.

The hallways are long and they all look the same. It takes a while but we finally get there and when we do I'm not happy to see his parents stood outside in the hall. Caleb's mum looks dishevelled and there are tears falling from her eyes.

"What are they doing here?" I screech, my anger rising. "They disowned him." I point at his parents. "You disowned him. You didn't want him!"

"Is there a problem?" The doctor who they were speaking to asks and glances down at my stomach.

"She's not family," Caleb's father spits, his narrowed eyes shooting daggers at me.

"She's his pregnant fiancée," Sasha snarls and holds up my hand to show the doctor the ring that sits there.

"So she says. I've never met this woman in my life," his mother hisses, her hate for me clear.

"Because they disowned him," I shout and plead with the doctor with my eyes. "Please. I just need to see him."

"She was the one he was brought in with. She was with him when he died," Tommy explains, his voice calm and collected. "She just wants to know how he died and to see him for a few minutes."

He's not dead, he isn't. This is all a bad dream, some sick joke. "Please. Let me just have a few minutes with him."

His mother steps closer. "If she even steps foot in that room, I will sue."

My mouth drops open. "How can you be so evil?"

"At least tell us how he died," Tommy pleads. "It's not right, a perfectly healthy twenty three year old just dying in his sleep without warning."

Nathan steps through the heavy doors leading to the morgue. "Heart failure. Caleb was born with a hole in his heart. We thought it was fixed... it wasn't. Until the autopsy is complete we won't know for sure, but if there were any other factors leading to his death, which is unlikely, I'll notify you personally." I notice his parents look at him, their scowls faltering. They almost look as confused as I feel. "Let her have a few minutes with him, Father. He loved her. He chose her and he'd never forgive you if you didn't."

"Two minutes. That's all."

I'm immediately led into the room. I expected him to be in one of those drawers that you see on TV, but he's not. He's on his own in a large room, a sheet pulled over his waist, his arms by his side. He looks so beautiful, so peaceful. He doesn't look dead on first glance.

I reach forward, realising it's just me and the doctor. My hand touches his cheek. He's so cold.

"Wake up," I beg quietly, praying for his chest to start moving and his eyes to flicker open. I want to see his sleepy smile. I want him to grab me and drag me under the sheet with him to warm him up. "Please, Caleb."

Still no movement. This isn't right. He wouldn't leave me. He wouldn't.

I stand and stare at him, burning his image on my brain, relishing the feel of his skin beneath my fingers. None of it makes a difference. He's gone.

"One day I'm going to kiss you in front of a real sunset on a beach full of white sand. That's what you promised me. Why would you make that promise?" I want to be angry. I want to shout at him but I can't. I'm just so tired, so lost right now. "Why didn't you tell me? Maybe I could have stopped this." My body aches to wrap itself around him and hold him until there is no longer a breath in my body. I don't. I just stare at him, stare at the shell that was once the love of my life.

The burning ache in my chest expands and my lungs constrict. I'm not sure how I feel; there's no word to describe it. Devastation isn't enough. This isn't devastation, this is so many things that I don't want to feel, all rolling into one giant mess of an emotion.

"You broke your promise," I say softly. "You broke all of them."

I half expected to walk in here and some strange paranormal force to bring him back to me. It would happen in a movie. He'd wake up and we'd live happily ever after. Realising it's not going to happen, I shrink back into my pit of despair and weep silently by his side. I never want to leave his body.

"Time's up," the doctor says softly and places his hand on my shoulder. "I'm very sorry for your loss."

The sobs tear through me as he leads me away from the love of my life. So lifeless and cold and pale. He's never been pale. His skin is like liquid gold. It almost sparkles when the sun hits it.

Sasha holds me tight as I exit. I sob into her shoulder and the cries tearing through me are so painful I almost lose my footing.

"I want to go home," I demand, tears still falling. This pain is unbearable.

"Sure."

When I'm in the car, I stare out of the window. My mind can't seem to grasp onto the reality of this. It's not possible. None of this is possible. Caleb isn't dead. He didn't die last night. He's going to die when we're both old and grey and he's going to let me die first like he promised.

Sasha and Tommy speak quietly but I don't care what they're saying.

The journey home seems to last forever. I rush inside. I know he's not here but I can't stop hoping this is some sort of elaborate joke. They're fucking with me, I just know it.

But they aren't.

I race up the stairs and look at the blanket on the floor. It hurts. It hurts so badly. I've never felt pain so potent, so thick and so powerful. The bed sheet has been stripped and the mattress has been cleaned.

"Babe," Sasha says softly. I feel her hand on my shoulder.

"He wouldn't leave me. He wouldn't." I snap, but I know this isn't true. He's left me. He's gone.

He's dead.

I break. I completely break.

I'm a mess. I'm a crying heap on the ground. She holds me but it brings me no comfort.

My world just ended.

Caleb... he's gone. He's gone and he's not coming back.

I scream. I shout. I blame everyone. I blame myself.

Sasha cries with me. She calls my mum despite the fact that she's on holiday.

"I don't want you." I cry at them both. Tommy and Sasha both try to comfort me but I won't allow it. "I want him! I need him!"

"We know, baby," Sasha says on a choked breath and reaches for me. I move away.

"Please," I beg. "Please, I just need to be alone."

"We'll be downstairs." Tommy looks devastated, so does Sasha, but they don't get it.

They'll never get it because they'll never have a Caleb. Caleb was one of a kind. Caleb was mine.

He's my world and I was his.
They don't get it.
They'll never get it.
I hate them for that.

CHAPTER SEVEN

THE BLANKET STILL SMELLS like him, so I wrap it around my face and inhale deeply. He always did smell good. My hand goes to my belly. We find out if it's a boy or a girl in just three weeks. Caleb was so excited.

We were supposed to get married today.

We were both so excited.

Why would God give me such an amazing man, such an amazing gift, and then just rip it away? Why can't he take me too? Why Caleb?

Is this some sort of punishment? Did I do something to offend him? I'm sorry! Now send him back! Please, just send him back.

"You need to eat," I hear Sasha say.

Eat? How can I eat? Why are they even here? Just let me be.

"If you don't eat..."

"I'll die."

"You have a baby to think about."

Tears spill from my eyes. One of them trickles over the bridge of my nose but I make no move to wipe it away. He died in this spot. I want him to feel it. I want him to feel my sorrow.

"Come on." Tommy sits me up and kneels beside the bed. Sasha holds a tray of food. "You need to eat something."

"It all tastes the same," I whimper as she feeds me yoghurt. "It all tastes like ash."

Tommy rubs the back of my neck, his eyes swollen and his face showing his pain. "I know, but you still need to eat it. Please."

I nod. He's right. "And then can I sleep?"

"Sure," he whispers and squeezes my hand.

They leave the room when I'm done. I feel like throwing it back up. It stays down somehow and my stomach settles long enough for me to close my eyes.

It's such an empty feeling, knowing he's not coming back. You see it happen to other people and you cry but you never truly feel what they feel. I know this because I've never felt this. Never.

"You need a shower, sweetie," Sasha whispers and slides the cover from over my head. "It's been three days nearly. It's time to start moving." Her words are soft but her demands still hit me deep. I don't want to move. "Come on."

"I'm tired," I say and reach for the blanket. It's tugged away completely, much to my annoyance.

"No, you need to get up and shower," Sasha says more forcefully this time. I sigh and climb out of bed. She leads me out of the room and into the bathroom. "And you're not sleeping in that bed another night."

Where the hell am I supposed to sleep then?

"Tommy is bringing over some new bed sheets after class." She answers my inner monologue. She's psychic as well as a nuisance. Brilliant. "Don't look at me like that. I'm only trying to help."

"I don't need help," I whisper.

She sighs and hugs me from behind. "His funeral is in two days. You need to pull yourself together."

"I don't want to," I admit. I just want to sleep and waste away.

"I know." She unbuttons my shirt, knowing I barely have the energy to do it myself. "But you need to. Because of this." Her hand rests on my protruding stomach. "And for Caleb. But mostly, you need to do it for you. Before you sink into a darkness so final you probably won't be able to find your way back."

My lower lip trembles. I don't think it's stopped trembling since that night. "I'm sorry, Sasha."

"Hey," she turns the shower on after releasing me and gives me a smile. "It's okay. It's not your fault. Come on, get undressed and get in."

I nod and peel off the rest of my clothes after she leaves the room.

My reflection in the mirror stares back at me. She looks tired, heartbroken and hideously unkempt. She looks broken. A mirror doesn't show you the opposite of everything. Sure it looks like everything is on the opposite side to what it actually is, but everything inside is still exactly the same. In mirror land I'm still a mess and Caleb is still dead.

How does a twenty three year old die from heart failure? It makes no sense! He was healthy.

I knew I should've taken him to the doctors. If I'd rung that ambulance when he had the fever, he'd still be here now!

This is all my fault.

The water does its job but I don't feel it. The hot spray cleans away the dirt but it'll never clean my soul. I want it to. I want it to wash away the pain and leave the girl I once was in its wake, but it won't. It'll only cleanse my skin and leave me feeling more awake than I was before I got in.

Which is bad because I just want to sleep. I don't want to feel this.

My tears blend with the water as it falls down my body. I know they're there, I can feel them leaking from my eyes. So many tears. Do we ever run out? Has anybody ever truly run out of tears? Does their body dehydrate and wither or do they merely fall asleep?

If Caleb were here, we'd Google it together on his phone.

I don't feel any better after my shower, especially not when I see the bed. It's been completely stripped. My body can't muster the right emotion for it though, so I just stare blankly at the naked mattress and try not to picture his lifeless body lying on it. Naked bed or not, the image is still there.

My tear bank is empty.

"I don't feel anything," I say to no one and make my way to my closet. It doesn't take me long to find something black. It's one of Caleb's hoodies that I insisted he stopped wearing. It's too big on me. It buries me. It's perfect. It even smells of him. I wear my own jeans and a pair of socks before slowly descending the stairs.

Sasha is on the phone to her mum. I know she's worried but no advice can be given. I'd say I feel bad for putting this on my friend, for loading my grief onto her and being ungrateful about it, but I don't feel anything.

There isn't a day that doesn't rain in one's grieving mind.

"Mum, I'll call you back," Sasha says when she sees me stood in the doorway. She places her phone on the side and smiles softly. "Come on, let's go for a walk."

I shake my head. "I can't face the outside world yet, Sash. Please don't make me."

She frowns slightly, so slightly I barely see it. "Sure. Let's play a board game then."

"No thanks." I sit on the stool, my head resting on my hands. "You can leave if you have to. You have classes and a job."

Sasha quirks a brow at me. "I have been leaving. Have you been getting out of bed at all while I've been gone?"

She's been gone? "Sorry."

"I'm worried about you." This is said in kindness, her tone screaming of sincerity and concern.

"Me too," I mutter and stare out of the window. "Why'd he leave me, Sasha?"

"He didn't."

I shake my head. "Spare me the spiritual bullshit." If anyone even tries to tell me that he's with me in spirit, I will hurt them.

"Shall we cook something?" I shake my head in response. "I'm going to cook us something."

"I'm going back to bed," I whisper and climb back off the stool.

"I'm just trying to help."

I nod, my face as blank as my soul. "I know, babe, and I'm sorry your efforts are lost on me."

"It'll get better." She clasps my hand with her own and gazes at me with warm eyes. "I promise it'll get better."

No it won't. I don't say this though. I just retreat back to my naked bed and pull a pillow over my head. I lie here in darkness waiting for it to consume me. Then I realise... it already has.

***

We have to drive for three and a half hours to get to the funeral. So do all of our friends from town, which is irritating. The journey doesn't end quickly enough and when we get there, I keep my eyes on my shoes until I'm seated. I don't absorb anything, I daren't.

I do scan the room though. I want to see how many people Caleb touched in his short life.

I'm grateful when no one talks to me from his side, although I doubt they even know who I am. I'm just some knocked up woman in a navy blue dress. There was no way I was going to wear black. Caleb wouldn't have wanted me to.

His family sit on the opposite side of the room and they don't look at me. Not that I care.

I'm watching the coffin be carried by people I don't know. I glance around at faces I've never seen and then glance at the ones I have. They're all sad, all of them. I don't get it. It's almost like his life has been split in half. On one side of the room, the side I'm sitting on, is everyone from my town that knew him. On the other is everyone from his old life, before I knew him. They're all formal and distant with each other. On my side everyone clings to each other. It's strange. I could never imagine Caleb on the opposite side. I can't imagine him ever being distant and aloof, especially not during such a traumatic time.

His picture sits on top of his casket, baby blue flowers spelling his name along the sides. It hurts. I can't look at his picture; it slices me too deep.

His mother cries, his dad sheds a tear, his brother doesn't. His brother sits with a stern expression on his face looking more bored than anything. Why are they even here? They disowned him! Sure I know that they sorted this funeral out and the wake, because Caleb and I aren't married, therefore I'm apparently lucky to even be here, according to a harsh whisper from his mother to his brother.

Lucky?

How can anybody be lucky to be at a funeral? What a warped mind she must have.

I don't care. I don't care about any of them.

It's emotional but I contain my emotion and the urge to cry uncontrollably by focusing my thoughts on other people in the room, the flowers and the vicar, and only the odd tear falls. The pain is indescribable but it's also shadowed by a numbness I've never felt before. I feel like I'm on the outside looking in, my soul scratching at the surface, wanting to leave my body and go with him. It's an almost desperate feeling of loneliness and nothingness, almost as if there's no longer a heart in my chest and only a gaping pit of despair. My skin tingles and my eyes blink away the tears that blur my vision. I don't want to miss this. I'm sadistic but I need to see it. I need to feel it.

Until the moment the curtains close and the coffin goes on the conveyor into the furnace, only small tears fall, tears that aren't sure what emotion it is they carry in their watery depths. Grief, pain, sorrow, anger... I feel it all and yet I feel nothing.

Confusion?

Why is this happening? I shouldn't be here. We should be at home feeling my bump and talking about what colours to paint the nursery.

I realise this is it, this is real; he's leaving me. I will never see Caleb's face or hear him talk again. I want to jump onto the conveyor, make them stop and beg the funeral director to take the body back so I can have a few more days looking at him and talking to him, but I know it's not possible. The dam breaks and the tears fall, tears of sorrow, tears of loss and grief and every emotion that solidifies just how lonely and distraught I feel.

I can't even say goodbye. I'm scared if I try to connect with him in the slightest way, I'll start screaming and I won't stop. The sobs are already bad enough. Will this pain ever end?

He goes up in flames and that's it. It's time for the wake but I don't go to that. Instead I travel back home with all of my friends and go to our local. We sit and chat about memories while I sip an orange juice and try to join in. After a few long minutes of forcing conversation, I find a quiet corner and slowly die inside.

I had the man every woman wants.

And now I don't.

It feels like the end.

Just... The End.

I wish I could drink my sorrows away. This isn't getting easier. Sasha and Tommy have left to go back to University and their lives. I know I should move, but I can't. The most I can do is lie in bed and pretend I'm somebody else. Pretend he's here beside me.

They can't stay any longer, plus they feel like they're not helping.

I'm a lost cause. I have nobody.

Well... I have nobody I want. I only want him. His family haven't called and I don't want them too. I have enough to deal with. I have bills to pay that I can't afford and I'm having a baby in twenty-one weeks.

TWENTY-ONE WEEKS!

It's been a week since the funeral and my mum still hasn't been in touch. What's worse is that Caleb's bank account was emptied by his parents (I assume) so there's no way for me to pay the bills. I should go to work but what's the point? I still won't be making enough to cover everything.

I'm stuck in a rut and I don't want to claw my way out.

Sasha was right - if you let yourself spiral into darkness, you'll never find your way back.

"Why'd you leave me, Caleb?"

I can't cope. I'm going to lose everything. I'm going to have to give up the house.

So I do the one thing I never thought I'd do.

I call his parents. I beg them for help with the rent, to help with something. It takes every ounce of pride I have left but I can't do this alone. Babies cost money and they have money. I don't.

His father slams the phone down and when his mother calls back, she tells me, "It's your fault he's dead. If he hadn't met you, this never would have happened." What's worse is... she's right.

Everything goes to shit. I can't pay the bills. I can't even afford bread. Sasha gave me a hundred pounds but it's not enough to cover the electricity bills. My pay cheque came in yesterday and that's barely enough to cover the gas.

Chicago's gave me five hundred pounds to help. They collected the money from staff and customers to put towards expenses. I put it all in the bank and pray for help. For strength. For courage.

It doesn't come.

Even if I use this five hundred to pay the bills, I'm still going to lose the house. I refuse to go on benefits yet and, even if I did, there wouldn't be enough to cover the rent and utilities. But this is our house. We decorated it together!

I don't want to lose it.

But I do.

Two weeks go by and I lose the house. Fortunately, considering the circumstances, they don't sell my things. They put them in a warehouse for me to collect when I get a new place, so I go to my mum's, thinking she'll take me in considering the circumstances, even though she hasn't so much as texted me since she found out I was pregnant.

The door opens, my mum takes one look at me and then sneers in disgust, "He's left you."

"What?" I gasp, tears pooling in my eyes. "No... mum, he's dead." How has she not heard?

She looks shocked but it doesn't last. "And now you want to come home?"

"We had a house, jobs, school... I can't do it on my own." I admit, my tears spilling over. "I need you."

"I warned you. You swore you wouldn't get pregnant. We worked our arses off, we worked day and night to get you into University."

I look into her cold, cruel eyes. "This wasn't my fault. I can still go back. I just need help."

"I never wanted this for you," she says with a frown. "I can't help you, Gwen. This is your mess. I dealt with my mess and now you need to deal with yours. I'm disappointed in you."

"I can't help what happened!" I shout, my hand pressed to my belly. "Please, mum, I don't have anywhere to stay."

She takes a step back and just as I think she's going to invite me inside, she shakes her head and says, "I'm sorry. I can't help you."

I bang on the door and I keep banging until my fists hurt. She doesn't answer. She doesn't even glance. How can she be so cruel? None of this is my fault.

"Mum! Please! Please!" I sink to the ground and bury my face in my hands. My sobs tear through me like a chainsaw through paper.

I've lost everything. I have no home, no family and no Caleb.

After a few more minutes of accepting my fate, I head to my car and drive until I can't anymore.

Even Sasha can't have me; she lives in a hall of residence. I'd be allowed there for one night. Just one.

I'm stuck, completely stuck.

I have to drop out of university. It's already paid so I can go back and finish my course in the future, which is a relief. What's not a relief is the fact I have to quit my placement that I worked so hard to get, but the café I used to work at have given me my job back. The problem is, I'm going to be huge soon.

I'm pregnant and I have nowhere to live and no money. There are no spaces at the closest women's refuge shelters, plus I don't want to go to one of those. Not that they're bad, I just want what's familiar.

So here I sit, a sob story, in the front of my car outside of my old house, photos and clothes and other bits and pieces sitting on the back seat in huge boxes.

At least I still have the car... for now.

I rest my head on the steering wheel and cry. It's been a while since I've cried, but now I've started I can't stop. It hurts... it hurts so bad.

I'm never going to see him again.

I'll never get to feel him again.

Why did you leave me, Caleb?

I should move but I can't bring myself to do it. My hands won't move to the ignition and gear stick. If I leave I can't come back. This house will no longer be mine. The last few memories I have of Caleb will be just that... memories. I won't be able to walk into the hall and recall the time he put his bare foot straight onto the paint tray by mistake when we were decorating the hall. He painted the wall with his foot, making me laugh so hard I ended up choking on my own saliva.

I won't be able to lie on the bed and remember him resting his head on my flat stomach and promising me and our baby an eternity of love and loyalty.

I won't be able to look in the bathroom and recall the time he had a bad curry and ended up sitting there all day. Seriously. I brought him his laptop and put on YouTube so he could watch funny videos of cats. Every time he laughed he'd release a noise from his nether regions so disturbing it sounded almost demonic. It was so funny.

Sob.

My life is over.

It's over and I'm scared.

There's a knock on the window. Great. Who wants to bother me now? What the fuck?

I wipe my eyes and slowly roll it down. "Nathan?"

"Gwen," he says in a clipped tone.

My hands tremble on the steering wheel. Why is he here? "Y... yes?"

"Why aren't you inside? You shouldn't be sat out here crying," he bites out, his jaw clenched.

It hurts to look at him. He looks like an older, sterner version of Caleb but he's just as handsome. His eyes are the same shape and colour, his hair too, although Nathan's jaw is wider and stronger and his cheekbones more pronounced. He also doesn't have a hint of stubble, not like Caleb used to fashion on a daily basis because he couldn't be arsed to shave.

I miss that stubble.

"We don't live there anymore," I murmur.

He sighs. "I can't hear you if you don't speak properly." What an arsehole.

"I don't live there anymore, okay?" I say, louder this time, and the words make me cry again.

"So maybe you should go to where you do live," he snaps.

Why is he here? "You're looking at it."

"What?"

"Are you deaf? I said you're looking at it! This is everything I have left."

His harsh eyes soften slightly, his face seeming to slacken. "Oh."

"Yeah," I agree. "Oh." Then I sigh, sick of his presence. He's too tall and it has to be hurting his back bending over like that. "Why are you here, Nathan?"

He looks at the house, to the back of my car and then to me. "I don't know."

"Right. Well then maybe you should leave."

"Yes," he agrees and stands. I watch him via the wing mirror returning to his large and flashy black car that's parked behind my crappy metal box on wheels. I didn't see it pull up but I'm seeing it now. It's huge. He climbs in and two seconds later he pulls away, leaving me once again to my own thoughts.

Was he wearing a suit? He was wearing a suit.

Who wears a suit during a casual visit?

Caleb would rip the shit out of him for it, I have no doubt about that. But Caleb isn't here and he isn't coming back.

I turn on the ignition, giving one last lingering look at the house that was mine. Then, with tear filled eyes, I head to work.

My boss lets me park directly outside of the doors, due to my car being full of my things, and he winces when he sees me. "Go into the back, wash your face, have a few minutes and come back out."

I don't argue with him. I need it as much as he thinks I do. Probably even more.

My stomach aches as I work, and my ankles are swollen but I'm determined to keep going. I keep getting large tips because people see my stomach and how young I am and take pity on me. Right now I'll take that pity. Their pity is what's keeping me fed.

The ones who know about my circumstances don't make eye contact with me. I'm unsure why this is. Maybe it's a guilt thing because they have a house and a support unit. Knowing I don't have either probably makes them feel bad to be in my presence. These people give me tips too.

"Hey," Sasha says as she comes in with a few of her friends. "How are you doing?"

I shrug. "I'm fine."

"Are you okay... to be working?" Honestly no, I'm in agony and everything hurts but it helps me get through the day. I don't say this though.

"I'm fine, I promise," I respond and lower my eyes from her concerned stare. "What can I get you?"

She orders their drinks and I scribble it down on my notepad, my mind on where I'm going to go tonight. Then my boss swaps places with me, taking orders and serving. I just make the drinks. I'm relieved for this change; my back ache is becoming too much.

"Do you want to call it a day?" Sasha asks me as I potter about behind the counter, filling drink orders and toasting croissants. "I can take over your shift."

I shake my head. "No. I..." have nowhere to go and I don't want to sit in the car for another minute. "Thank you, though. You're a good friend, Sasha."

She touches my hand gently. "I wish I could do more."

We share a sad smile before she leaves and it's only then I notice she's left two twenties and a ten on the counter. Is this what I've become? A charity case?

I know she wouldn't think of me like that, but it still hurts to take hand-outs. I've sunk so low.

"Why'd you leave me, Caleb?" I whisper and turn away from the customers to reassemble myself.

I imagine him up there, outraged that he's been taken. I imagine him banging his fists on the pearly gates, watching me with tears of his own. He hates it when I cry; it breaks his heart.

So I need to stop.

For him I need to find my strength and get my shit together.

"You shouldn't be working in your condition." I wince at the sound of his voice and turn to face him, two cups of coffee in my hands. "You look exhausted."

I stare at Nathan and then I look away. "Why are you here?" Please leave, you look too much like him.

I place the drinks on a tray and slide them towards my boss.

"I followed you," he states without hesitation. "How far along are you?" His familiar brown eyes flick to my protruding stomach. It's not as though I have a huge bump or anything as I'm still early. It's the weightloss that has made me look bigger than I should be.

"I didn't realise you cared," I say and it's supposed to sound snappy but my voice sounds dead and flat. Exactly how I feel inside.

Nathan leans on the counter, chewing his lip like his brother did. It makes my eyes burn. "Where are you staying?"

"Why are you here?" My life isn't his business. He didn't care about his brother so why should he care about me? Not to mention the fact he assaulted Caleb the last time we saw him. "You live hours away don't you? What do you want?"

"I asked you a question." A muscle in his jaw jumps, his eyes narrowing with irritation.

"And I asked you three."

"If you don't want my help then fine. It's on you, not me."

My mouth drops open. "I never asked for your help and no, you're right. I don't want it!"

He shakes his head and stalks away. I don't realise all eyes are on me until the moment he leaves and I stop thinking about how much he looks like Caleb from behind.

"He's such an arsehole," I say to my boss, who frowns at the door where Nathan just exited. "I've met the guy once before and he just swans into town... what a bastard."

"Who is he?" My boss asks with raised brows.

"Caleb's older brother by two years."

"Maybe you should've accepted his offer."

I laugh once and stare at my boss incredulously. "He didn't offer to help. He just asked me where I was staying. And this was after he'd already walked away once."

"It sounded like he was offering to help then." He gives a small shrug. "But I only heard half of the conversation."

I relent. "He did, in a strange way, but... he's infuriating and mean."

"He's also the only option you have right now. Hear him out. See what he has to say. Not many people would care about their family members' woes and you're technically not family."

I want to slap him. I know I'm hormonal but he doesn't have a clue what I'm going through right now. He doesn't understand the complexity that is Caleb's childhood. He doesn't get it, so maybe he should just let me work, sign my cheques and stay the hell out of it.

Work goes slowly and I'm glad for this as my night is still uncertain. When I'm done here, I have no idea what I'm supposed to be doing. I'll go to Sasha's for the night. I know she won't mind. I just don't like putting on people, but either way I need to stay somewhere.

I text her to let her know and, as suspected, she agrees.

What have you done to me, Caleb? Why am I doing this alone?

I'm thinking about it again. I need to stop thinking about him.

Every time that I do my body trembles, my hands especially shaking.

It's tough but I'll get through this. I have to for our baby's sake.

Is it wrong that I'm hoping for a boy? I want him to be a boy so I can look into his eyes every day and see his father smiling back at me.

What kind of a life can I give him now, though? I have nothing to offer him.

Deep breaths, Gwen, deep breaths.

After half an hour of driving aimlessly, I fill up the tank and head to Sasha's. As I'm taking the turn towards campus, I notice a large black car following me. It's definitely him. Christ this is becoming irritating.

"What does he want now?" I say out loud and pull over when he flashes his lights twice.

His body moves with ease and grace as he climbs out of his vehicle and strolls towards me. After a few attempts, I finally manage to stand by the door of my own vehicle. I still have to tip my head back to look at him. Much like I did with... no I won't go there. I focus on the brisk chill in the air instead.

"Problem?" I ask, trying not to sound as exasperated as I feel.

"You shouldn't be getting in and out of a car that low," he remarks and already I want to hit him.

"Well it's not like I have another option is it?"

He frowns. "Follow me. We need to talk."

"I don't have anything to say to you." I try to get back in the car, but his hand closes around my arm and effortlessly tugs me away. "What?"

"Please?" He grits out and I can see just that one little word takes a whole lot of effort for him to say.

"Fine," I relent. It's not like my day can get any worse. "What's this about?"

"Follow me and you'll find out." He places his hand on my back and the other under my arm to support me as I sit. I'm not sure whether to be irritated that he touched me, or relieved that my arse didn't hit the car seat as hard as it usually does.

I wait for him to drive ahead before following directly behind him. He leads me quite a distance; I'm lucky I stopped for petrol.

We finally pull into a swanky hotel set on the edge of town, one I've never even been inside before. It's not my thing. I like simple and basic beauty, not elegance and fine china.

After parking beside him, he climbs out and this time helps me up and out of my vehicle. I didn't realise how hard it was until he started assisting me. He's right, the car is low.

"Come," he orders and leads me inside with his hand gripping my arm. I'm nervous as to what he wants. Does he want to help me or is this some kind of ruse? Is it a way for his family to ensure that they get the child I'll be birthing soon? The thought makes me nauseous.

I almost want to turn around and run.

When we enter, we go straight to the desk. The woman takes a look at me and my stomach before training her eyes on Nathan. There's no small amount of admiration and lust there, that's for sure.

Ewww.

"Send up some tea and something to eat that's safe for pregnant women."

Seriously? I give him a look, but he ignores it and propels me towards the elevator.

It's awkward, quiet and uncomfortable as we ascend. I find myself wanting to rock on my heels or whistle just to disturb the silence.

As soon as the doors open he takes my arm again and leads me through the patterned beige hallway. I huff, sick of being led around in silence. Again he ignores me.

Once inside his fabulous room, he takes my coat and hangs it by the door before leading me to a large and expensive looking couch. It's black, pure black, with silver scatter cushions. It looks amazing. "Sit."

I guess I'll sit then.

He doesn't. He shrugs off his jacket and hangs it by mine, undoes his buttoned shirt sleeves and rolls them up to his elbows. Is he planning on delivering the baby? This thought almost makes me smile. Not quite but nearly.

"Okay." He rubs his hands together, drawing my attention to the black leather gloves that cover them, and sits on the coffee table only four feet away from me. He's wearing gloves again. Was he wearing them earlier? I can't recall. "You have nowhere to live. I have space."

"Come again?"

"I think it's appropriate that at this point in time you stay with me. I live only a few hours away in a very nice and quiet village only an hour's drive from London. Just until you get back on your feet. I think you'll find my home to be of good taste," he says calmly and I can't help but note that he talks weird.

"W... what?"

He sighs. "You do speak English, correct?"

"Correct."

"Then listen to what I'm saying."

"I am listening, I just don't get it."

He pinches the bridge of his nose. "I'm missing work to be here right now. I don't appreciate your blatant lack of respect."

Scoff. "I don't know you well enough to respect you and so far you've been nothing but rude to me. Not to mention the fact the last time I saw you with Caleb, your fist was connecting with his cheek. Forgive me for not wanting to be all smiles to such an arsehole at such a difficult period of my life."

His glare is open and cold. "I understand you're hormonal, but I never want to hear such language. It's improper for a female to curse."

"Fuck you," I murmur, feeling even more irate.

"You're carrying my brother's child." His hands fist between his open knees, his cold brown eyes staring into mine. "I'll not have his child or should be wife wandering aimlessly around town. Whatever transpired between my brother and I isn't your concern. Siblings fight. We would have made up eventually. As it is, I don't have that chance right now so instead I'm going to assist you and your child until I feel you're established. Are we agreed?"

"I..."

"Good," he clips, not giving me a chance to protest, and checks his shiny large watch that probably cost more than my car. Caleb's car. "Rest here. We'll leave in the morning. Do you have any perishables in your vehicle?"

"No," I respond to his question, the rest of his words still sinking in. "What do you mean leave? I'm not leaving. Everything I own is here."

"Which is apparently very little. I've spoken to your previous landlord and I've settled your debt with them. Your furnishings that are locked away will be moved for you when you have yourself situated in viable accommodation." He states, glancing at his watch one more time. "Is there anything else I need to know?"

"Yes!" I gasp and clamber to my feet after he stands to leave. "I can't and I won't leave here."

"You're being difficult."

I laugh once. "I don't know you and your brother hated you. Why should I trust you?"

He doesn't even blink at my words but for some reason I know I've struck the wrong chord. "You will leave with me tomorrow. There's no doubt about that." He rubs his eyes with his gloved fingers. "I have somewhere I need to be, as enjoyable as this has been. Good night, Guinevere."

"It's Gwen."

He rolls his eyes. "I have your car keys and the staff have specific instructions to call me if you try to leave. Good night."

"You can't just force me to stay." I grab his arm, my eyes blurry from unshed tears. He looks at my fingers tightly gripping his forearm before looking at my face. "Please. I don't want to leave."

"It appears you don't have any other options," he states and pulls himself free. "Be ready at seven. We'll leave then." The door shuts behind him. I want to kick it.

Who does he think he is, speaking to me like that? He doesn't know me. He barely even knew his brother.

But he's helping me, a niggling voice tells me. Nobody else is and damn it if I don't need help. I think that maybe I'm being too harsh. Or am I? I don't know how to feel about anything anymore.

I'm resigned to my fate right now. He's right; what other options do I have? He could at least be kind to me and maybe discuss it with me first.

And I'll curse all I fucking want.
Shit, fuck, twat. Arsehole.

CHAPTER EIGHT

A S INSTRUCTED, SOMEONE DOES in fact bring me tea and a healthy looking mixed leaf salad with boiled chicken and a natural yoghurt for dessert. I don't hesitate to wolf it down almost angrily. That's how hungry I
am.

Next I flick on the television, sipping my hot tea. My mind wanders as it usually does. I don't know what to do. The thought of leaving this town behind, this town where I met Caleb, this town where we made love, where we conceived our child and where he died, it's all too much to bear.

I don't want to leave but something keeps prodding me, telling me to do it. Part of me wonders if it's him, throwing tomatoes at me until he gets his own way. He used to do that sometimes. Never hard, only enough to irritate me and normally we'd roll around afterwards.

He said my angry sex was the best sex. I was angry often. This makes me almost smile.

What's the deal with Nathan? I never really spoke to Caleb about it much, so all I know is that he and Nathan never got on. Nathan stayed behind and Caleb left. Why so much animosity? And if Nathan hated Caleb as much as Caleb hated Nathan, then why is he helping me now?

Guilt?

It's possible and it's Nathan's explanation, but it doesn't add up right to me.

While pondering on this I call Sasha and let her know my day of events. She doesn't like the fact I'm leaving any more than I do, but even she agrees

I don't really have any other options. Sigh. I'm too tired to keep tormenting my mind with all of these questions that seem to have no answer. I'm not in a place where I can freely discuss things with Nathan. He seems to hate me so I doubt he'll want to answer me.

After a few minutes of exploring the hotel room and finding a glass for some water, I decide to bathe in their luxurious bath. I even go all out and add bubbles. Maybe too many, because when I climb in the only thing visible is the hill that is my stomach poking out of the water and through the foam. I love this; it's relaxing.

Caleb would tell me to relax in the bath and, on the odd occasion that he was too busy to join me, I'd leave the door open and splash a little, pulling his thoughts to the naked female in his tub. He'd give in and five minutes later he'd climb in behind me. Every single time.

After my bath I pull on my nightgown and climb into the large bed. I have no clean clothes and I'm not putting back on the ones I wore just to sleep in. This'll have to do.

Shoving a pillow between my thighs, I turn off the lamp above my head and try to sleep. Sleep doesn't come easily, but eventually it does come.

***

My arm is being shaken and words are being spoken rather loudly. "Wake up. Guinevere." Someone clicks in front of my face. "Guinevere."

"Five more minutes," I grumble, my eyes burning. So comfy... need sleep.

"Guinevere!" This time my name is being shouted and my eyes instantly open. Caleb?

My heart sinks when I realise it's Nathan. Why do they have to look so much alike? "Yeah?"

"Your alarm has been going off for the past thirty minutes," he snaps and shoves my phone in my hand. "I could hear it from my room next door."

"Oh, sorry." I sit up, making sure my nightgown is covering my assets. "I sleep heavily. It's the pregnancy."

He only frowns and moves away from the bed to the curtains. With a swift move, he tugs one side open before the other. "Get up. We leave in twenty minutes."

"Uh-huh," I say and stretch my arms. Damn, I'm hungry. "Is there anything to eat?"

"We'll eat when we get there."

I don't say anything, mostly because I want him gone. He leaves after a minute of making sure I'm awake and returns ten minutes later with a bag from my car.

"I've moved your things into my vehicle." This is all he says before leaving again.

I quickly get dressed in a loose fitting T-shirt and jeans that barely fit me anymore. My long black hair is sitting okay considering I slept in it and haven't brushed it, so I leave it how it is. After brushing my teeth, I step outside with my things ready to go.

Nathan doesn't talk, he just leads me out the same way he led me in, a hand on my arm tugging me along. Sigh.

"What about my car?" I ask, seeing it sitting in the parking lot looking all lonely.

"I'll provide you with a car."

"But I..."

"It's too early to argue. I'm exhausted."

"Nath..."

"Enough, Guinevere!" He snaps and my mouth instantly clamps shut.

I look out of the window, silent tears falling down my cheeks. "It's Caleb's car."

I see him wince out of the corner of my eye but he says nothing. We continue driving and more than anything I just want to go home. The problem is that I don't have a home.

After twenty minutes my stomach starts growling, reminding me how hungry I am. The baby does nothing to help, although I can barely feel him move and I'm not too far along. It's still uncomfortable trying to bend in any way. I used to be able to touch my toes and now I can only lean forward enough to pat my knees. I roll my seat back so my stomach isn't so crushed and pat my bump affectionately.

We drive past a service stop on the motorway. I almost salivate at the thought of food.

"So, the plan is," I'm startled by the sudden sound of his voice. "You're to stay with me for the foreseeable future. I'll handle any expenses you may have."

"I don't want to be a burden."

"Yes, well..." His voice trails off and his top teeth sink into his lower lip. "I'm rarely home for more than sleep and I can afford it, so it's not the cost that's the burden." Just me and the baby then. Ouch. "I have plenty of room for you and your child. All I ask is that you don't invade my privacy and you don't bring narcotics into my house."

"Well obviously." I point at my stomach with a roll of my eyes. "I've never done narcotics in my life. I don't plan to start now."

"Good. And lastly, don't make noise when I am home and stay out of my way."

With pleasure. I don't say this. Instead I say, "I appreciate your help, Nathan." When I go to place my hand on his to get my thanks across, he pulls away abruptly almost like I've burned him before I even have a chance to touch him.

"And don't touch my hands. Ever. Is that understood?"

I blink in astonishment. "Loud and clear."

"Good."

What an arsehole. It's hard to think he and Caleb were related. They're both extremely different.

"Anything else?" I enquire, wanting to know all of the rules now so I don't get chastised again in the future.

"No. Eat what's available when you want. I have a cleaner come in every morning, not including the weekends, so try to be out of your room by eleven. As for luxuries, anything you need, just speak to the cleaner or ask me if I'm home. If I'm not available, call me."

I nod slowly. "Okay. Thanks."

"How long have you got left?"

"Nineteen weeks." I rub my belly once more whilst staring at the bump.

"You look further along than that."

"So I've been told." Which sucks.

He keeps his eyes forward but his body seems relaxed. "I'll book you in with an appropriate doctor when we arrive."

Well that's one thing I can cross off my list of things to worry about.

"Now please, I'd appreciate quiet," he says firmly, so I plug my headphones in and listen to music on my phone instead.

After an hour my stomach is churning even more than before. I'm so hungry I could eat a raw carrot and I hate raw carrot. Suddenly I'm craving raw carrot. We pass another service stop but we don't pull in.

I'm also desperate for a wee. My bladder is fit to burst.

I hold it and hold it, but now I'm just putting myself at risk of infection. That and I may pee myself.

Carefully pulling my headphones off, I glance at Nathan and contemplate whether or not I should speak. Fuck it. "I have to go to the bathroom."

"Hold it." He orders, not even glancing my way.

"I'm pregnant, I can't hold it anymore. I've been holding it." I try to say it calmly, not wanting to piss him off. "Please? I wouldn't ask if I wasn't desperate."

He sighs and checks the signs for another service station. "There's another in fifty miles, give or take. We can be there in about forty minutes. How's that?"

"Brilliant," I sigh with relief and sink into my seat. "Can we get food while we're there?" My stomach agrees loudly.

"We don't have time." His jaw is set and his demeanour says, 'don't mess with me.'

"Please?" I beg. "I'll grab something to go."

"No food in the car." Yet another ridiculous rule.

I scowl at him. "I get that we have to be quick, but look at it this way: I have low blood pressure. If I don't eat, I'll faint and that'll be a long trip to the hospital that you really do not want."

"Fine," he bites out, finally seeing reason. "We'll stop for food."

***

Ah, sweet bladder releasing bliss. That feels good. It also has to be the longest one I've ever had in my life.

After washing my hands, I head back out to the food court and look around for my brother in law. I don't see him immediately, mostly because I don't think to check the salad bar where nobody usually frequents. My first thought is to check the fast food joints.

Sigh. Another salad. I need red meat and junk and burgers. This is the only time in my life where I can eat what I want (within reason) and not feel guilty about it.

"Hey." I announce my presence and watch him fill two salad tubs. The selection isn't so bad. They have boiled eggs and slices of nice looking ham and a decent selection of dressings. "So, how long until we arrive?"

"Just under two hours after we leave here and that's if the traffic's good," he says, being careful to watch what he's doing.

"Which one's mine?"

He nods at the top one. Brilliant. I add a whole lot of ham to it and three boiled eggs.

"Eggs aren't something you'll be eating in my company and neither are processed meats. This ham has about as much real meat in it as this lettuce does." Why does he have to argue with everything?

"I want the eggs and I want the ham." I'm putting my foot down. "It's my body."

"And it's my brother's baby..."

"It's my baby too," I hiss, being mindful of the people nearby. "And your brother let me eat whatever and whenever I wanted. If I craved something we didn't have, he'd go out in the middle of the night just to get it for me and he didn't care if I had fallen asleep by the time he got back. Which happened more often than not."

"You're not having the ham."

Should I cry? I feel like I should cry to make him feel bad.

I don't. If I start crying again, I won't stop.

"Fine, but just a bowl full of lettuce isn't going to fill me up."

"It'll be fine until we get home," he bites out and slams the lids shut on the salads. "Now, hurry up. I don't have all day."

I shake my head, my stomach disappointed that it's being treated like a rabbit. Making my way to the newsagents, I pick out a couple of magazines, shocked when Nathan doesn't protest and even buys them for me. I guess he's not all bad.

"Thank you," I say softly, keeping my head down and walking along beside him.

"You're welcome," he responds, his voice also soft. It doesn't match his handsome yet stern face. "Quickly."

And the soft voice has left the building.

"When we get back, I'm afraid I'll have to leave you for an uncertain amount of time," he explains and, with a hand to my elbow and another to my back, he helps me into his car. He barely pays attention to his gentlemanly ways and I wonder if he even notices he's doing it.

"Do you mean like an uncertain amount of hours, days or weeks?"

He doesn't answer until he's in the driver's seat. "Days."

"Can I ask why?"

"No." He states. "I like my privacy."

"Okey dokey." I clear my throat and take the salad pot eagerly. Even though this is closer to rabbit food than it is to human food, I eat as much as I can manage, which is the whole pot. "What's going to happen to my car?"

"I'll have someone collect it and store it. It's too low for you to be driving in your condition and I'm shocked my brother would allow you to do so." His hands tighten on the wheel. I see now he's wearing black leather gloves. I don't remember him wearing them earlier but, if memory recalls, he was wearing them while dishing out the salad.

"He didn't have a choice."

"May I ask what happened to his trust fund?"

I shrug. "Your parents took it all from him when he moved."

His mood seems to darken further. "He's an idiot."

"Hey," I cry. "Don't call him that."

"Well he was and always has been." His hands squeeze the wheel, making his gloves squeak against the rubber. "His life choices were selfish and preposterous at best."

I shake my head, wanting to ignore him for insulting my Caleb.

After a long sigh, he glances at me. "Don't get worked up. Caleb would have just laughed at my seemingly harsh words. I mean them in jest more than I mean them in distaste."

"But you do mean them in distaste. You shouldn't speak ill of the... the..."

"Dead," he finishes for me when he sees that I can't finish it myself. "Calm yourself. If I know Caleb, he'd hate to know how much stress you're feeling." Why does he seem to say this like the words taste sour? "It's not good for the child."

I don't respond. He's right, obviously, but it's not like I have a stress switch I can just flick on and off. Not as much as I'd like. Stress is a part of this life unfortunately and, considering the circumstances, it's no surprise I have a rather unhealthy dose of it.

Staring at his profile hurts and I wonder if that feeling will ever stop. He's not a clone of Caleb, not at all. Their differences are significant in looks and personality, but there's enough of Caleb in his face to make me ache.

It's all still fresh. It's only been a month since he died. That's not enough time to truly get over someone and this is Caleb. My Caleb. My first love, the first man I gave myself too.

I'll never get over that.

"Why are you staring at me?" I see his lips thin to a white line. I'm irritating him.

"Sorry," I mumble and stare out of the window. I just can't decide whether it's painful or strangely soothing to look at him, knowing that the life in my womb isn't the only piece of Caleb left in the world.

There's a gentle tapping sensation under the surface of my skin. I gasp and sit up, placing my hand over the bump.

"What is it? Is it the baby?"

"He just kicked me a little harder than usual," I explain, still rubbing my abdomen. "It's not a big deal. It just shocked me. I've never felt him move so obviously before. It's usually just little taps and fluttering, but this was more prominent."

He nods, seemingly appeased.

Time for silence.

He was right when he said I'd find his house to be of good taste. It's really not what I expected, not in the slightest. This is a family home. It's large and spacious, with a lot of land surrounding it. We're atop of a cliff but about three miles from the edge.

I noticed other homes as we ascended the steep incline, but not one of them were as pretty as this one. Caleb grew up in the city nearby with his parents; it was the place he escaped. Not liking the hustle and bustle of a busy place, from a young age, he searched for a smaller town and found mine.

I'm wondering why Nathan lives so far out of the way. Sure it's only an hour drive from London, but it seems like an unnecessary one. This man is complex, I see that now.

"The fridge is full of food suitable for your condition," he explains as he guides me into the entrance hall.

Condition? I'm pregnant. This isn't a condition.

Sigh.

I take off my coat and watch him hang it inside a closet to my right. There are wide stairs to the left against the wall. Before those is an archway leading to what looks to be the living area, which is huge, very old fashioned and quite cosy if I'm being completely honest.

I've always been into modern and quirky furnishings but this place is all antique and comfort. The walls could do with brightening up from their deep browns and oranges. The hallway is beige with a wooden border to make up the bottom half.

"These lights are cool," I remark and point at the candle shaped wall lights.

"If you get cold the thermostat is here and there's another one upstairs in the hallway. Just press the plus button until you get to the desired temperature and press this button." He moves on to the next thing, showing me how to work the oven and the water purifier. "I need to leave now. Make yourself at home. My number is by the phone in the kitchen. Call me if you need anything." He goes to leave, stops and turns back. "Your room is up the stairs, take a right and go up the three steps. It's down that hall, two doors on the right. My room is on the next floor. Respect my privacy and stay out."

"Okay." I watch him leave, his body perfectly poised, his legs carrying him with a grace that shouldn't be possible for his height. He's a couple of inches taller than Caleb, now that I think about it. It's the hair that's driving me nuts when I view him from behind. He needs to have it cut. Soon he'll be tucking it behind his ears like Caleb had to. I loved it on

Caleb. I won't be able to handle it if I see it on the brother who looks so much like him.

The wind is powerful up here. I discover this fact when I wander outside into the garden and the wind blows me back a few steps. The house is along a secluded path with nothing but a narrow road leading to it, between rows and rows of trees. This area is private. I know this because I just passed a 'Trespassers Beware' sign.

I don't wander far, mostly because the sky's grey with thick clouds and my ankles are aching with each step. The farthest I go is a mile before heading back. It's beautiful out here. I want to go to the cliff edge at some point, not too close because my fear of heights will paralyse me, but close enough to look over the countryside. There's no sea here, which is sad as I'll miss the sounds and smells, but the air is fresh and the views are stunning so I don't mind too much.

I'm back at the house and it's a little bit cold so I fiddle around with the thermostat until I hear the hum of the radiators heating up. Next I explore. This place is big and beautiful and way too clean. My nesting instincts don't kick in like they usually do.

His cleaner is obviously brilliant. I bet she gets paid well. I can't see a speck of dirt anywhere and the scent of bleach lingers in every single room. It's irritating. I need to get rid of that. I wish I'd opened the windows upon my arrival to get rid of the smell.

I keep away from his room and also his study when I discover it on the first floor. As soon as the door opened, I almost gagged on the strong scent of bleach. It's burning my nose. The room is spotless. I doubt there's even a speck of dust in the air.

I back away slowly and move on to the next room.

Three hours later I've managed to give the house a little bit of air, but now it's freezing again so I shut all the windows and turn the heating back up. That's the extent of what I do for the day, not including raiding the fridge and finding nothing but organic fruit, veg and fresh meat.

I can live with this.

Food is food and organic food certainly has a nice taste to it when prepared correctly for consumption.

Heading up to my room, which is large and actually quite feminine and beautiful in a floral sense, I sit on the padded window seat, my phone in my hand. For a while I skim through a book that I'm not actually focusing on. It's raining, rather badly now. Every drop hits the window like a tiny baseball. It sounds like I'm in a greenhouse, that's how heavy the droplets are on the window. The rattling sounds like it's coming from every direction.

It's depressing.

I give up on the book and climb into my temporary bed instead.

My bed is comfy but it doesn't smell like Caleb, though it still offers me the security I need at present. Burying my face under the covers, I close my eyes and shut off my thoughts. Back into the abyss I go.

***

Waking at nine, I have time to call my boss and quit. I apologize for not giving him notice, but he's completely fine with it considering the circumstances and wishes me the best of luck.

After getting dressed and brushing my teeth, I don't want to go downstairs. I want to stay in bed but my stomach is eating itself. No matter how sad I am, I need to put the baby first. He didn't ask for this.

I have breakfast, which consists of toasted brown bread and beans.

What Nathan doesn't know won't hurt. I would've preferred eggs, but I can't see any in the fridge or anywhere else. My thoughts go back to what he said yesterday. Does he think they're bad for the baby or does he just have a problem with eggs in general? Do I honestly care?

I'm certain it's raw eggs that aren't brilliant for pregnant women and not cooked eggs, so his concerns don't worry me. Not that I can actually call his concerns 'concerns'. He doesn't seem bothered; he just seems like the type that likes to be in control and this is a shitty situation, so those urges are kicking in, in all of the wrong places.

I'm sure he means well.

I wonder what he's doing. Maybe he's at a business conference or something.

I know Caleb's father owns a chain of jewellery stores spread across the country and it's forever expanding. He owns the company that finds the gems and the company that finds the metal. I'm not sure how rich this makes him or how rich this makes Nathan, or if they're even rich at all.

Obviously they probably are and this house certainly screams 'wealthy', but it doesn't scream 'Bill Gates'. Not that I care. It's just something to think about to keep my mind off the other issues I have to deal with.

Like the fact I'm technically a widow. Oh my god. I'm a widow... sort of.

That's something you read about, or hear about, or see in older people. It's not something you experience at the age of twenty one.

Well, twenty one as of seven weeks ago.

I know it is something people experience at this age. I'm not stupid. You hear about it, but you never think it's going to happen to you. I wish we'd taken out life insurance, safeguarded our future.

It should've been the first thing we did when I fell pregnant. At least then I wouldn't be here. I'd have been able to afford the rent and everything the baby needs for a while until I finished university and got a job.

Gah. It's no use thinking about any of this. Why am I torturing myself with ridiculous what ifs?

"Morning," a cheery sounding female voice calls as the main entrance door opens and then closes. "Anybody home?" She enters the kitchen, sees me and smiles. I'd smile back, but I haven't gotten to the point of my grief yet where I can feel emotion enough to change my facial expression from blank or tortured. "Well look at you."

"Hi," I say politely.

She's a mid-forties woman with a soft smile. Her eyes are deep blue and you know just by looking into them that she's lived. It's odd how you can just tell that with some people. I wonder if you can tell that by looking at me.

"You must be Mr Weston's guest, Guinevere, right? It's a pleasure to meet you. I'm Jeanine." She opens her arms and gives me a firm hug. Her hand rubs my back a couple of times before she holds me at arm's length, her smile still certain. "You are absolutely gorgeous, and look at this bump. May I?"

"Sure," I say, my fingers tucking my hair behind my ears.

She instantly places her hands over the small swell. "My, my, my. You're going to have an eight pounder, easy."

"Great," I murmur solemnly and try to picture my future. All I see is a whale with my face.

"A healthy one too." Her smile gets brighter. "You sit. I'll make us some tea. How are you feeling?"

"Fine," I respond, but her eyes tell me she knows the truth.

Fortunately she doesn't comment, she only sets about her business, a bounce in each step. "It's wonderful to have you here. I'm sure Nathan thinks so too."

"Ha," I let out unintentionally.

If this woman smiles any wider, she's going to lose the top of her head. "He gets awfully lonely up here, even though he denies it. He rarely gets to leave, what with work." Oh, so he's a work from home kind of guy. That explains the distance from the city thing. "It'll be nice having you here and of course the baby." I watch as her smile falls, pity and concern replacing it. "I'm very sorry for your loss. I was told not to mention it, but it wouldn't be right if I didn't offer my sincerest condolences."

"That's okay, thank you. No point avoiding the obvious." I say this with a sigh.

It's true, though. There's no point tiptoeing around something so huge or the people dealing with it will never fully learn how to face it. As much as I don't want to face it and it hurts to be reminded that he's gone, he is in fact gone and I have to deal with that, for my sake and the baby's.

"Well, have you eaten?"

"Yes."

"I'm sorry about the food. Nathan insisted I buy only organic for his niece or nephew. But..." she smiles wickedly and places a finger to her lips before beckoning me to the pantry. "If you look back here, there's a large plastic container. I filled it with goodies." Goodies? People still say this? And I highly doubt he referred to my unborn as his niece or nephew. Or maybe he did. I don't know him well enough to assume.

I want to hug her again. "Thank you. I've been desperate for chocolate."

"I didn't get you anything with peanuts but what I got is still bloody brilliant." She wanders away, leaving me to raid the container. I find a Twix and almost cry from the relief. "How do you like your room?"

I shrug. "It's very..."

"Old fashioned?"

"You could say that. It's beautiful though." It's just a room with a bed where I can bury my head. I don't care about the décor.

She grins again. "Redecorate. We'll do the nursery too. How I do love decorating a nursery, although it's been a long time since I had this joy. My youngest just left home last month."

"I'm sorry to hear that."

She lets out a short cackle. "Oh I'm not. It's about bloody time he figured out his place in the world like his older siblings." I want to laugh, the feeling is there, but I just can't. She doesn't take offence. Her eyes yet again are knowing. She does touch my shoulder gently and add on a quiet whisper, "It'll get easier, my darling. You will smile again."

With a nod I sit back down and watch her potter around the kitchen. She natters away about her kids and life and how she came to work for Nathan three years ago. The story isn't interesting. He put an ad in the local newspaper and she was interviewed. So were two other younger and slimmer women, but she kicked their arses. Again I wanted to smile but couldn't. She laughed and smiled enough for both of us, so that's okay.

After half an hour and a cup of tea, she leaves me in the kitchen and goes about her business.

Now what do I do? I guess I could see what's on the TV. Hopefully something interesting.

CHAPTER NINE

TWO DAYS SLOWLY PASS by and I get no word from Nathan. Not that I want or need word from him. I'm absolutely exhausted. Today I walked two miles out instead of just the one and almost got lost on my way back. Tomorrow I'm going to take a piece of chalk and mark the trees as I go so I don't get lost. My skills at exploring are definitely below par.

I also need some walking boots and some more clothes. All of my things are still in Nathan's car, which is irritating. The only thing I brought in is my rucksack. I wonder what made him in such a rush that he couldn't spend twenty minutes bringing in my things.

Sigh.

It's late and I'm currently curled up on the couch in a robe which Jeanine brought for me this morning. I'm wearing the matching nightgown beneath, which is satin and feels amazing against my oversensitive skin, especially my belly. It fits perfectly, snug around the breasts but floats over my belly and back like a silky cloud.

Caleb loved satin. He tried to make me buy satin bed sheets but they're irritating when it's warm and the quilt never stays in place inside the cover.

My eyes burn. I refuse to cry. But sometimes, even though you tell yourself not to cry, you can't help it.

I miss him so much and the baby's kicking. Every time I thought that I could feel a flutter, Caleb would instantly put his hands or his head there if he was nearby. Even though he couldn't feel it, he liked sharing the experience with me.

He's never even going to get to hold him, never going to see his first smile.

I can't stop the tears as they flow down my cheeks. This time I don't try. I cry so much exhaustion sweeps through me. My eyes drift shut, but I don't feel like moving so I don't go to bed. There's no point.

Something is sliding under my legs. That tickles. "Hmm," I murmur, my eyes still shut. My arms go around the neck of whoever is lifting me as a strong arm snakes around my back. I press my forehead to his neck and inhale deeply. He smells like fresh linen and a cologne I don't know the name of. It smells wonderful. Kind of spicy but also sweet. Manly. "I'm heavy," I mumble but get no response.

From his scent alone I know he's not Caleb, but part of me can't help wishing.

"Go back to sleep," he whispers and begins walking.

"Uh-huh," I say, my lids still shut. This earns me a gentle squeeze.

I wake to the sound of curtains being pulled open. Ugh. "Morning. It's almost eleven twenty. Somebody must have been tired!"

"Hello, Jeanine." I say around a yawn and stretch. In shock, my hands go to my bare shoulders. My night dress is still on my body but my gown isn't. When did I take that off?

I think back... I didn't take it off. So who did?

"Is Nathan back?" I squeak and Jeanine nods with her usual smile. "Where is he?"

"He's making breakfast."

"I'm surprised he didn't wake me. He told me to be up by eleven every morning."

She quirks a brow. "Well he gave me specific orders to let you rest, but I figured you wouldn't want to sleep all day and that baby needs to eat." She hands me two spoons that feel like they've been in the freezer. "Put the curved part on the bags under your eyes. It'll get rid of the swelling."

I groan but do as I'm told. "Do I look like hell?"

She smiles sadly. "No, my darling, you look like a woman who's just lost the father of her child." I lean into her hand when she strokes my cheek, needing the comfort. "Now come on, up, up. Get dressed, I'll be back in ten."

As I walk into the kitchen my nose is assaulted by the scent of mushrooms and butter. My mouth waters.

Dumping the spoons in the sink, I spy Nathan sitting at the dining table in the next room, a book in one hand as he eats with the other. He's wearing glasses and I feel like sniggering but still haven't reached the point of that emotion yet. He looks older than his time but he also looks too young to look old. I'm not sure if this makes sense, but it also sort of does.

At least he's not wearing a suit this time. It's good to see him looking human in a plain white T-shirt and dark blue jeans. It suits him, although I have to admit that the suit looks better on him. The suit is now the image I associate him with.

Without looking up, he motions to the space beside him and I see my plate of food and frown. "Why don't I get fried mushrooms?"

He looks over his book at me from the end of the table as I take my seat beside him.

"Oh come on. If I don't get any fat in my system, I'm going to lose weight."

"Fried mushrooms aren't on the list for a healthy pregnancy."

"If your concerns were real then nobody would have a healthy pregnancy." I spy his full plate, sausages, bacon, toast, beans, mushrooms, the whole shebang, but no eggs. Then I stare at mine. "Grilled tomato and brown toast with margarine? You're kidding me."

"Eat." He snaps, his eyes skimming through his book.

I do and it tastes bland and awful. "Has this been cooked with sunflower oil?"

"Organic."

"Ewww. Can't I just have a piece of bacon?"

He flips the page. "No."

"Just a bite?"

"No."

I let out a growl and so does my stomach. "You're killing me here."

He looks at me again, his brows raised like a parent does to a child when they're being naughty. "Eat, Guinevere."

I have a forkful of my chopped and grilled tomatoes and cringe. He's looking at his book. He won't notice if I sneak a mushroom from his plate. They smell too good to resist.

It's the bacon my heart is set on, though. He has four slices. Four. That's just greedy. Nobody needs that much bacon.

Very slowly and carefully I slide my hand along the table, using my other one to eat the food I have so it doesn't look like I'm doing anything suspicious. He can't see. The book is in the way of his eyesight.

Almost there... smack.

I gasp and pull my stinging hand back, my mouth open in shock. He looks over the top of his glasses at me, his closed book now on the table.

"Did you just hit my hand with your book?" I ask, my shock still evident as I rub the back of my hand with my other one. It didn't hurt it just shocked me.

"I said no."

"You just hit my hand with your book," I say, my voice lower and more dangerous this time. "I can't believe you just did that."

"Are you an animal?" He scowls, his palms flat on the table. "Because only animals steal food from another's plate."

"Are you an animal?" I scowl back, repeating his words. "Because only animals hit pregnant women."

He sighs and rolls his eyes. "So dramatic, it was just your hand."

"It's still assault."

"My food. Don't touch." He glares and picks his book back up.

Why do I have this insane feeling that I want to do it again? If he hits me again I swear I'll hit him back. I'm prepared.

So when he looks back to his book, slowly chewing the food in his mouth I slowly slide my hand over. YES! I got the bacon.

"Put it back," he states, his eyes not leaving the book. How did he see me?

"But..."

His eyes still don't leave the book. "Put it back."

"You don't control me or my body. I'll eat what I like."

"As long as you're staying here, you'll look after your body and your unborn child the way you're supposed to." His book is now down and his eyes are on me.

"It's just bacon, you freakin' pig Nazi. I can't live on organic. I still need a bit of junk food," I snap, my voice sounding as exasperated as I feel and I feel extremely exasperated.

"Do as you're told," he half shouts.

"No." I bring the bacon to my mouth, take a bite and chew.

He's up in an instant. His sudden move startles me so I'm up faster than I've been able to get up for the past three months. We stare at each other, his eyes full of warning, my body now shaking. I'm a little bit scared to be honest.

I just want the bacon. I take another bite and he stalks towards me. I step backwards with each step he takes.

"What are you doing?" I ask, paralysed by my fear. I shouldn't have pushed him. I hardly know him. What if he slaps me or chains me up in my room?

What if he takes my bacon?

"Give me the bacon."

I blink when my back hits the wall. "It's just one slice of bacon."

"You deliberately disobeyed me," he snaps and holds a napkin out. "Give me the bacon."

"Fine, fucking have it," I shout and place it on the napkin, my temper rising.

Suddenly he's in my face, his hand slamming into the wall beside my head. I whimper as he comes closer until his nose is only an inch from mine. "Curse again and you'll regret it."

"What does that mean?"

"Curse again and find out." He threatens and pulls away, the bacon and napkin crushed in his fist.

I slide down the wall after he leaves the room, taking our plates with him. If I could wrap my hands around my knees I would. Suddenly I don't want to be here anymore.

Before anyone sees me, I race up the stairs and hide in my room, my mind running through idea after idea. He's clearly unstable. He has serious control issues that I'm not sure I want to deal with.

Maybe I should just stay out of his way. Maybe I should just leave.

Where will I go, though? I need to be realistic here.

I climb into my bed after kicking off my shoes and bury my head under the covers. This is my safety; this is where I feel the most comfortable so this is where I'm staying. Why do I have to deal with this? I don't deserve this.

My heart and my breathing are the only sounds I can hear as I shut out the world. My breath is thick as it's hard to breathe under a quilt, but it's okay. At least I'm not crying. I'm so sick of needing to cry.

"I'm leaving now, poppet," Jeanine calls through the door. "Make sure you eat. You didn't touch your breakfast."

I bury myself further under the quilt after saying, "Okay." I'm so tired. So darn tired.

Does this ever get easier?

There's a knock at the door after the sun makes its descent. "Guinevere?" It's Gwen. The knocking becomes more insistent. "Guinevere, open the door."

"Go away," I say quietly but I know he hears me.

The door opens. I pull the blanket tighter around my head.

"Stop moping and come and eat." He demands, his tone showing his annoyance.

I don't respond. I don't want to eat with him. He needs to leave me in my cave of woe in peace.

He sighs and I hear his footsteps get closer. "Gwen."

"I'm tired."

I squeal when the blanket is ripped away from my body and Nathan looms over me, looking every bit as pissed off as I now feel. "This isn't healthy."

I try to bury my head under the pillow but he takes that too.

After a moment of squeezing my eyes shut and burying my face under my arms, I'm airborne. "Put me down," I order, not daring to wiggle as he cradles me to his chest for fear of him dropping me. "Now."

"Eat and then you can wallow all you want," he says calmly and carries me from my room. My arms automatically wrap around his shoulders. "You're very light for someone who's pregnant."

"Didn't realise you made a habit of carrying pregnant women," I remark.

"You're also extremely frustrating."

"I am not." Maybe only a little bit, but who can blame me?

He lets out a breath and begins to walk carefully down the stairs. "I apologize for upsetting you this morning. Jeanine was rather insistent that I should never take food from a pregnant woman. I'll try to be more reasonable in the future."

What the hell should I say to that? "Okay."

He doesn't speak, only takes me into the dining room and places me gently on the chair beside his. My nose picks up the aroma of garlic and beef before I even see my plate and my mouth waters at the sight of the stew.

"You cooked this?" I question, impressed with the food.

He gives a little shrug. "It's just stew."

"Caleb could barely cook a frozen pizza," I point out and dip a piece of fresh bread into the broth. Oh my god. "This is better than mine. Thank you."

His eyes wander over my face for a moment before he begins to eat his own. "I see you're not religious."

"Did you want to pray?"

"No."

"So..."

"It was just an observation."

I quirk a brow at him. "You observe strange things."

"Is it wrong of me to want to know the woman who now lives with me a little better?" His eyes fall to his food and his lower lip slips beneath his teeth.

"I suppose not." I swirl my spoon around the wonderful mixture and pick out a piece of beef and potato. "Well I'm not religious. I wasn't raised religious but I do believe in God."

He nods slowly but doesn't seem all that interested. His face is a mask of indifference and we fall into silence. It's an uncomfortable one.

I clear the table, just to have something to do while he sits and speaks loudly to somebody on his mobile. My ears perk up when he starts talking about his dad so I wash the dishes in the kitchen, giving me a reason to linger. All I hear is, "Yes, well, what my father says clearly goes." And then he moves onto talking about stocks and shares and other boring things.

When he's finished, he steps into the kitchen and loosens the blue tie around his neck. "Thank you for doing the dishes."

"No problem." My nesting instinct wouldn't let me leave them anyway.

"Can I trust you to be present for breakfast in the morning?" I shrug in response. "I'll take that as a yes."

"Okay."

"Goodnight, Guinevere."

"It's Gwen and it's only seven. You're going to bed already?"

I hear him take a few steps closer. "What I do isn't your business... Gwen. Remember that."

Wow. Seriously? He's going to be that rude? "I was just making an observation."

"Don't. You won't like what you observe," he states coldly and stalks out of the room. The entire time I didn't look at him and felt no desire to either, until his parting comment. Now I can't take my eyes off his back as he walks away.

What the hell did he mean by that? What won't I like? Not that I'm trying to like anything or looking for something to like.

I wake up in the morning earlier than usual. Stupid morning sickness should have stopped by now. It hasn't. I race to the bathroom and fall to my knees in front of the toilet. Yuck. Luckily the sickness subsides after the first emptying of my stomach, unlike the past few months where it has lingered deep in my midriff, unrelenting for hours, sometimes making me feel so ill I've cried.

Once that's over with, I have a long shower. It's needed. I'm ashamed of myself for going for so long without one, especially when there's a bathroom right next to my room and it has a gorgeous walk in shower and a huge tub. They're old fashioned but they work brilliantly.

When I finally make it downstairs I have to breathe deeply when I smell bacon. It's odd because yesterday I wanted bacon and now the thought of it makes my stomach roll. I tentatively make my way into the dining area where I find Nathan sat much like he was yesterday morning, only this time he holds a different book and no glasses are perched on his nose. His hair is styled differently too, or maybe he just hasn't combed it yet.

He looks far more casual than yesterday in a blue shirt and dark jeans. This makes me wonder why he was wearing a suit last night. I don't remember him going anywhere to make him feel the need to change into something so formal.

"You're staring at me," he comments as I lower myself into my seat.

"Sorry," I mumble and look down at my plate. I can hear Jeanine in the background singing to herself, although I'm not entirely sure which direction her voice is coming from. "I was wondering..."

"Jeanine!" His hand smacks the table making me jump and gasp. "Enough!"

I'm shocked when I hear her laugh loudly before falling silent. He rubs his eyes with his gloved hands and places the book down on the placemat across from me.

"You were wondering...?" he prompts me to finish my earlier sentence.

"Oh, umm... I can't remember now."

He gives me a pointed look and I have to fight against my need to shy away from his dark gaze. "Don't play with me. Spit it out."

Snort. I haven't felt the need to laugh in a really long time, but this almost pushes me over.

He thinks on it for a moment before rolling his eyes when he figures out the reason for my unattractive snort. "Honestly, how old are you?"

"Twenty one."

"It was a rhetorical question aimed at your level of maturity."

I keep my eyes down and pick at the bacon on my plate.

He sighs loudly. "Yesterday you wanted bacon and now that you have it, you aren't happy. Typical."

"No," I shake my head. "It's great. Thank you." I slowly move a piece toward my mouth, my eyes flickering to him. "Smoked. I love smoked bacon." My stomach makes a loud churning noise and I stand slowly. "Excuse me." With my hand over my mouth, I rush from the room and back upstairs. Hurl. Gross.

Jeanine joins me a few minutes later with a cup of ginger flavoured tea and a ginger biscuit. Why do all older people think ginger is the cure for all sickness? It doesn't work. Well, it doesn't for me. I can't stand ginger.

I head back to my room seeking solitude.

There's a light tapping at the door after twenty minutes of my being in here but I don't respond. I sit on the window seat and stare solemnly through the glass. The trees look so thick and vibrant when you try to look through the leaves, but if you're walking through them they don't look nearly so thick. They're actually quite spaced out. It's all of the bushes and twigs that make the forest difficult to walk through. I bet if you flew above this particular patch of trees and looked down, it would look like a blanket of leaves covering the cliff.

The tapping turns to knocking. I still don't respond.

The door opens anyway. Great.

I don't turn to look at whoever it is, but I feel them enter and I can sense his domineering presence. I know who it is as soon as he steps through the door.

"You're sick?"

"Morning sickness, which comes on randomly throughout the day," I explain and tuck my hair behind my ears, my eyes still staring off into the distance.

"You're sad," he observes and I want to gape at him.

"How can I not be?"

"It's been nearly a month," he says quietly, almost as if trying to comfort me with his tone.

This time I do look at him. "Please tell me you're kidding."

He looks at me for a moment longer, his blank eyes giving nothing away. "You have a doctor's appointment in thirty minutes. He's travelled to the village to see you. Don't be late."

"And how exactly am I expected to get there?" I ask, my voice casual, my body tense.

"Jeanine will drop you off on her way home and I'll pick you up when it's finished." He closes the door on his way out. I rush around getting ready, making sure to put on trousers so the doctor won't get a glimpse of my 'mini' if he has to do an ultrasound. Unfortunately I have only one set of clean clothes left due to the fact my things are still in Nathan's car and I've used all the clothes in my rucksack. I pull these on with a sigh, thankful the brown T-shirt matches my beige jeans and boots. I don't look a total disaster. They fit too, which is an even bigger relief.

Nathan is nowhere in sight when I leave and I'm glad for it. I'm not sure how to react to him right now. The guy has issues I don't want to deal with. You'd think he'd be a little more sympathetic towards me right now. You'd think he'd be a bit more emotional too. Caleb was his brother and yet he shows no signs of grief. He shows no signs of any emotion whatsoever. I've never met a more robotic person in my life.

Why is part of me screaming to be grateful? He's messing up his privacy, his home, just to accommodate me and my baby.

But another part of me is saying he should. It's his niece or nephew that is growing inside me. He should make sure he or she has everything that his brother would've given. Well, not everything, but he should help.

It still doesn't dismiss his demeanour towards me.

"Be patient," Jeanine tells me as we pull up to the curb after a long and quiet ride here. "He'll calm down. He's just not used to company."

"What do you mean by that?" I mean, it's obvious she means he lives alone but I can't help but feel that there's more meaning to her statement.

"Would you like me to come in with you?" Ah, a subject changer. She must be sworn to secrecy because Jeanine doesn't come across as the type who likes secrets.

I shake my head. "No, it wouldn't feel right. It was our thing... you know?"

She gives my hand a squeeze and nods, her eyes misting over with understanding. "I know, pet."

The doctor sees me immediately. He informs me his name is Dr Meadow and he'll be delivering my child privately. I guess I'm not getting baby care on the NHS. What the hell is wrong with Nathan? What's wrong with the NHS?

He does an ultrasound to see how far along I am, even though I already told him two seconds ago. I find no enjoyment in it. I hardly look and refuse to know the sex of it yet. It was for Caleb and I to discover together. It doesn't feel right doing this on my own. He takes far more measurements than the people back at home did, which concerns me. He assures me it's so he can monitor every single aspect of my pregnancy from now until the end.

Apparently I'm perfectly healthy as far as he can tell and my baby is going to be a big one. He wants to take my bloods to test me for diabetes and other illnesses, mainly gestational diabetes because apparently people with gestational diabetes have large babies.

This makes me want to slap him, even if he is being nice about it. I'm large, pregnant and hormonal and I don't need a doctor telling me I shouldn't be so large.

Fortunately I haven't put much weight on anywhere else. My breasts are massive and I hope they never deflate. The rest of me, however, is still a good size.

I also tell him to give me a list of all the foods I can't eat so I can prove to Nathan that he's being unreasonable. Then I come to the conclusion that all I have to do is get up earlier than Nathan and raid his fridge. What he doesn't know won't hurt.

It's when the doctor tells me he'll be putting me in to see a therapist that I decide I want to leave and I want to leave now. He thinks I need to talk to someone about what happened or there's a possibility I won't bond with the baby at birth. Finding your lover dead is, according to him, a terrible tragedy that needs dealing with appropriately. I disagree. Sure it's a terrible tragedy, but I believe it needs leaving where it belongs. Locked away until my last breath. I'm not ready to rehash the tale and I'm not sure I ever will be.

So far since Caleb died, all I've thought about is the fact that he's gone. I haven't thought about the night in question. I'm secretly praying I'll suppress it forever because if I even get a glimpse of his lifeless body lying on our bed ever again, I'll die inside and I'll never be revivable.

He assures me that I'm at a higher risk of postnatal depression due to the events and he's concerned for my mental state when the baby is born, which is a ridiculous notion because it's half of Caleb. If anything, I'll love him or her even more than I would have done if Caleb was beside me. I refuse the help and thank him anyway.

Nathan is on time, which I like. I'm never late for anything. Caleb used to joke and say I'd probably go into labour exactly at midnight on my due date. The funny thing is, I don't disagree with him. I don't think I've ever been late for anything in my life. Poor time keeping is not a good trait to have.

I don't say hi as I climb into the car. He looks ticked off that I don't wait for him to help me in, but who cares? Not me.

I place the scan picture in my bag and tilt my seat back a little.

"I took all of your things inside," he says. "I apologize for not doing it sooner."

"Thanks."

He spares me a glance. "Did your appointment go well?"

"Isn't the private doctor just going to call and inform you of the developments later?"

He sighs. "I'm just trying to give you a good level of healthcare so everything goes as smoothly as possible."

"I'm not complaining," I admit honestly and look at his profile. "I just think we should have discussed it first."

His tongue runs along his bottom lip. "Guinevere, am I okay to assume you'd like private healthcare?"

"If you're offering then I won't decline," I say, wanting to smile but it won't come.

"Good. So how did it go?" I open my mouth to repeat my earlier statement but he cuts me off. "Contrary to your beliefs, I'm big on privacy and I wouldn't invade yours in such a way. If you don't feel like telling me then fine, I won't ask again."

That's actually kind of sweet in a strange way. "It went great. He's checking me for gestational diabetes because apparently people with diabetes have bigger babies, but he's sure I'm fine. I don't have any of the symptoms."

"Your baby is too big?"

"He's guessing it'll be about nine pounds." I wince, not wanting to push out something that large.

Nathan's lips twitch and it's the first time I've ever seen him smile. Well, slightly smile. I wonder if his lack of humour has been because of grief too. "Caleb was eight pounds twelve."

"I didn't know that. What about you?"

He looks at me in shock but only for a second, as if me being interested in his birth weight is a ridiculous notion. Have I been that much of a bitch?

No.

He's been just as unapproachable, if not even more so than me.

"I was nine five." He says it quietly and twists his fists on the wheel.

"Yay. My baby is going to destroy me," I mumble.

His hand goes to my knee and he gives it a soft squeeze. "You'll be fine." Now I'm the one gaping in shock and I'm doing it for a lot longer than a second. Even though his hand only stayed there for a brief and comforting squeeze, I still feel his touch linger. What the hell was that?

I'm even more shocked when we don't go home immediately. We make a stop at a clothing store. He leads me inside and puts me at the mercy of two women with tape measures.

"This one," he says and points to a row of clothing. "These and these. Have them ready by next Monday and I'll pick them up by eleven."

I'm annoyed he's choosing my clothes but I don't say anything. I do need new clothes and the ones he's picked are actually quite nice, even if they are mostly black and white.

"I'm shocked," he announces and runs his hands over a row of stretchy denim jeans.

"About?"

"You're not arguing with me. I thought for sure I'd have a Guinevere induced migraine by now."

Scowl. "I don't give you migraines."

"I've never had so many migraines in my life."

I'm about to snap but I realise this is his way of teasing. It's the first time I've ever seen any emotion other than irritation in his eyes. He leads me out of the shop and helps me back into the car, but we don't pull out immediately. He sits, staring ahead aimlessly. I can see he wants to say something but I don't prompt him; I only wait. "Look, Guinevere. I know this move hasn't been easy." You can say that again. "And I know what you're going through is a grief like none I can imagine." You can definitely say that again. "I think things have been tense for both of us and I'd like it if we could try to get along. This stress isn't good for you and it's irritating me greatly. My home shouldn't be a place of war. I want you to feel comfortable."

"Stop stealing my bacon then."

He lets out a choked laugh but covers it up with a cough. "If you recall, I gave you bacon this morning but you found the toilet to be greater company than I."

"For future reference." I look at his profile and think that he should smile more often. He doesn't have any of those little crinkles around his eyes that tell you you're in the presence of a happy person. Something about this makes my chest ache. Caleb had the lines, but he was always smiling. How can his brother seem so different? "And me too. I think it'll be good if we at least try to tolerate each other," I say and hold out my hand. "Shake on it?"

He stares at my hand like it's a foreign object. "Oh, right, the no touching of the hands thing. Sorry, I forgot."

He falls silent for a moment. I see the cogs working in his head as if he's making a decision. He pulls out onto the street and finally talks. "I don't like germs."

"Come again?"

"I have an issue with germs. It's a real condition." He adds when he sees the look of shock on my face.

I nod slowly. "Yeah, I've heard of it."

"Good. Don't bring it up, it only aggravates me. Just ignore it."

I nod, appreciating his honesty and wanting to respect his request. "I won't mention it."

He seems to let out a breath but I can't be sure as I only saw his chest deflate slower than before with no sound to accompany it.

We fall silent once more. This time it's comfortable.

It's dinner time and I'm starving. After searching the fridge and cupboards, I decide on spaghetti. I make a mean spaghetti Bolognese according to friends and it's been forever since I cooked. I want to go up to my room and bury my head, but I need to start taking better care of myself. I've lost six pounds, putting me one pound under my recommended weight for my height and size. In reality, that means I'm about four pounds underweight because the baby obviously weighs something.

It scares me. Caleb would never let me go more than a few hours without food. He'd done nothing but force me into the kitchen throughout my entire pregnancy. I knew if he could cook he would have, but after a while of trying and failing on so many different dishes, he just started putting me in there and helping in every way he could.

Caleb... just... I...

Sigh.

Nathan went upstairs as soon as we arrived home three hours ago and hasn't been back since. Maybe he's hungry. I should make some for him too.

Oooh, I'll even be able to make some homemade garlic bread. Brilliant.

I tug the apron on, groaning with frustration when it only just reaches around me enough so I can tie the very ends of the strings together, and set about making dinner. I'm one of those people who cleans as I go along, so even though what I'm doing is quite messy, there isn't a huge mess left when I'm done.

It smells delicious as it simmers in the pot and even more delicious when the bread begins to rise in the oven. With a glass of juice in my hand, I sit on the counter at the corner and stir the simmering Bolognese. My mouth is watering, I'm so hungry.

Once it's served, I set the table and contemplate whether I should shout for Nathan or go upstairs and knock for him. I don't want to piss him off by invading his space so I shout for him first. Unfortunately I get no response, so I shout again.

I make my way up the stairs and shout once more. He's either being extremely ignorant or he's not here.

I'll just knock on his study door.

"Nathan?" I call and knock on the door. "Nathan? Hello?" My hand clasps the handle and I'm about to push the door open when I change my mind. He could be sleeping at his desk or listening to music through his headphones and I don't want to disturb him, or anger him by invading his space. This is his house. He asked me not to do certain things so I'll respect that.

I wrap up his plate in foil before placing it in the oven, and pack the leftovers away before putting them in the fridge. I'm mostly doing this just in case Nathan comes down. It's like I'm delaying so I can eat in his company.

Sitting down at last, I bite into my food and moan. This is so good. I don't remember when food stopped tasting like ash in my mouth, but I'm grateful I have this one joy back in my life. It's like a tiny bit of colour poking through all of the grey that is my consciousness.

I'm so glad I chose to be a chef.

It's lonely here. Too lonely.

I decide to call Sasha but she doesn't answer. I text her telling her I miss her and to keep me updated on everything. She doesn't text back. I'm guessing she's busy so it doesn't upset me too much. Sasha would never purposefully ignore me.

At least I have all of my things now. The first thing I do is place a photo of me and Caleb at the beach on my nightstand and then I get to work on the rest.

The best part about falling asleep tonight is falling asleep seeing my fiancés face.

The worst part is that when I wake up, his face is still just a picture.

It's been two whole days and the only person I've spoken to is Sasha. She's fine, worried about me and my sudden decision to up and leave but she understands. Jeanine has been busy and has said hello and goodbye but that has been the extent of our conversations.

I'm going stir crazy. Nathan is here but he's keeping out of my way completely. When I wake up, breakfast is ready for me. He skips lunch but has eaten every dinner I've made and left in the oven. I don't know how he's avoided me so well. Are there hidden tunnels in this house?

I'm losing it.

I need to get out but the rain and the wind are relentless and I have no car. There's never anything on the TV, I don't have a computer and my phone won't connect to the Wi-Fi so I can't do much on that.

I feel like camping out in the kitchen and waiting for Nathan to collect his dinner, but that would be weird and boring. Also, what would I say to him? "Oh, umm, let's talk?" We have nothing in common. What would we talk about?

Why's he ignoring me though?

My boredom has reached new levels. I'm currently sat on the cold wood floor in my bedroom doing a thousand piece jigsaw puzzle. The problem is that I can't reach the top end of it because my belly won't let me bend that far forward. I have to bum shuffle around it on the ground like a dog.

When the doorbell rings I almost cry with relief, even though I know it isn't for me. I feel like a puppy when its owners come home. In my mind I'm screaming, 'PEOPLE,' and wagging my tail.

I'm a freak, it's simple.

I need conversation. I need distraction. If I don't have it, my mind wanders and I can't control the direction in which it wanders. Caleb is becoming a more prominent thought in my mind and each day seems to be getting slower and harder. I genuinely thought I was finally in a good place, not because I'm happy or even content but because I have the strength to keep myself out of bed throughout the day.

Pulling open the door I look at the red haired, plump woman holding up a huge tray of what looks to be lasagne. "I'm a friend of Jeanine's. She told me there was someone new in town." She glances at my belly. "Someone new and pregnant. I couldn't help but be nosy."

"Hi," I say with a nod.

"Oops, I forget my manners sometimes. My name's Paula. I live three houses down from here with my two dogs and my husband Michael." She reaches out to shake my hand. "I brought you lasagne."

I'm about to take it from her when I feel him right at my back. "Hello, Paula." I feel his heat; he must only be an inch or so away.

"Hello, Weston," she greets him coolly. I wonder what's going on with her calling him by his last name, but I don't ask. "I was just greeting your new lodger here and offering her some of my famous lasagne."

"How kind," he says, but he sounds far from sincere. "Allow me to take that."

She passes him the dish. "So, I was thinking that I've not seen you out and about."

"Mrs Harris is always out and about," he says close to my ear, his warm breath making the strands at the side tickle the back of the shell and I feel my lips twitch. Mostly at his words but also at the ticklish feeling.

She scowls at him but her eyes soften when they come to me. "I wondered if maybe you'd join me tomorrow at noon. We could go for lunch. I'll take you on a tour around town. I've heard you've only seen the inside of the doctor's office and Darla's Elegance." I assume she means the clothing store. I didn't pay attention to the name. I knew it wasn't a cheap place though.

That would be better than finishing the puzzle I have no interest in. I nudge Nathan with my elbow and he sighs dramatically. "If you want to go then go. You can take my car."

"That's okay, I can pick her up." Even better.

"She'll not be getting in a car that resembles a lunch box with wheels. It's not good for the baby," he says, his voice holding not only an air of authority but an underlying tone that I recognise to be possessive. What's that about?

He's also being rude. "Thank you, Mrs Harris, I'd love to come. If it's all the same I'll take his car, just in case I feel the need to leave before you do. I tire easily."

She smiles widely and nods eagerly. "Just Paula, dear. Such good manners for such a young woman. I'll leave you both to your afternoon."

"Have a nice day." Nathan's farewell is as snide as his hello was.

"Don't worry about the dish, dear. Bring it back when you're done," she calls over her shoulder.

I don't get to wave as Nathan has closed the door.

Lasagne.

I follow him into the kitchen and watch as goes to tip the contents of the dish into the bin. "NO!" I scream like my life depends on it and grab the plate. "My lasagne."

He blinks in shock. "You're not eating this. You don't know what she's put in it, what meat she's used."

"So?" I retort and tug on the dish.

"Fine!" He snaps and lets go. Unfortunately, due to the extra hundred pounds in my stomach, I fall backwards.

Quick hands snag my wrists to stop my descent, but in doing so the lasagne dish tips and smashes against his front.

"Oops," I say and slowly step back, assessing the damage. "I am so, so sorry."

He stares down at the mess on his chest and abdomen. The red sauce clings to him as the small clumps of minced meat slide to the floor with the pasta sheets. He looks pale. Extremely pale.

"Are you okay?" I ask and take a step towards him. His hands are trembling.

He shakes his head. "Germs."

Oh right, the germ thing.

"Nathan," I say softly. "What do you want me to do?"

"Nothing." He takes a step and dry heaves, his entire body bending over with it. Holy shit. "I can feel it on my skin."

"Okay, okay, just stand there." I grab a cloth from the cupboard under the sink and soak it with warm water from the tap.

I see sweat bead on his brow as he stands perfectly still waiting for me to help him. His eyes are lowered and his lips are pinched together. Shit. This *is* a real condition. I should have Googled it but I don't have anything to Google it on. Maybe he has books on it that I can study. It seems like something I need to learn about if I'm going to be staying under the same roof as him.

"I'm going to take these off," I say cautiously and start undoing the buttons on his jacket. He doesn't move an inch as I slide it from his shoulders and place it on the side. "You know?" I try to make him feel better as I slowly and carefully untuck his shirt from his trousers. "I have a horrible phobia of rats. It doesn't seem much compared to this, but it's a deep one. It comes from when I was little." I slowly start unbuttoning his shirt from the top, revealing a light spray of dark hair over his sternum. "My mum took me on holiday to my grandpa's dairy farm and we all got to camp outside for the night. It was brilliant at first." I slowly undo the last two buttons and step behind him so I can peel it from his body without getting the sauce anywhere else. "While I was sleeping, I felt something running across my legs."

"What happened?" Finally he speaks. Relief.

"Wait there," I say and walk over to the sink and warm the cloth once more, all the while still talking. "Well, I woke up obviously but I couldn't see anything. It was dark and I was on my own. My mum was in the tent next to mine with her then boyfriend." Swiping the wet cloth across his front, I take my time. I'm not sure why I do it so slowly, maybe because it's a connection. I'm close to somebody. And his torso is delectable; it's golden and smooth and powerful. Every dip and groove is muscled perfection. He shudders as I sweep it over his pebbled nipples, so I move away from that area. "All I could see were these two red eyes in the dark moving around my tent. I screamed and screamed. Eventually my mom came. Her boyfriend killed the rat and she made me stay in my tent. I was petrified. I was five and I didn't know what a rat was." I look at his clean chest and go to pull my hand away.

In a quick move, his gloved hand presses it back to his abdomen, his fingers clasping my wrist rather than my hand itself. "Don't stop." His eyes come to mine. "I can still feel it."

I nod and continue slowly wiping at his smooth skin, watching as the dark trail leading from his navel to places unknown shines with droplets of water. "I don't think I'd have been as affected as I was if she hadn't made me stay in there, you know?"

He nods. "Was she a good mother?"

"As good as she could be. She was good to me, but she was also selfish. She helped me pay for University as much as she could. She just wanted me to have a good life but didn't know how to do that. She wanted herself to have a good life and forgot about me whilst getting that sometimes," I say, running the cloth over the rim of his trousers, being extra careful not to touch where I shouldn't.

His throat bobs as he gulps, his body no longer trembling. "Thank you."

"Better?"

He nods and I slowly remove my hand before throwing the cloth in the sink.

"I'm going to have a shower... could you?" He motions to the ground where the lasagne has splattered. "If it's too much, leave it and I'll deal with it."

"I'll do it, you go," I reassure him, my eyes lowered again, and allow him to pass. Once he's left the room I squat and clean. It's not easy and it's not comfortable but it takes my mind off what just happened.

What did just happen?

Chapter Ten

Nathan didn't come out of his room again last night. I don't mind. He's probably embarrassed, even though he shouldn't be. Maybe it's after what I did with the cloth. I shouldn't have been so... sensual and slow about it. Maybe he read into it wrong. I was just trying to comfort him, but I can see why he'd think I wasn't.

Nah, I'm being ridiculous. He didn't read into it at all. I'm the one reading into it too much.

Unfortunately, due to the heavy rain and strong winds, Paula reschedules our lunch date for Friday. It's aggravating but also a relief. I'm not ready to socialise with the outside world yet, as ridiculous as that sounds.

It hurts me to see other people happy.

Maybe I should see a therapist.

No. I need to just keep myself busy to keep my mind off it.

Stupid knots in my stupid hair. Comb through, damn you.

There's a knock at my door. "Come in," I call, still trying to get the tangles out of my hair.

Nathan steps inside. "I'm sure I don't have to remind you," he begins and I look at his reflection in the mirror, "that anything that happens between us, anything you see that relates to me, is confidential." Anything that happens between us? That could be misconstrued, so I choose to read into it in the safest possible way and assume he's referring to conversations and other daily things.

"Duh." I roll my eyes and place the brush handle in my mouth as I use both hands to pull my thick hair atop of my head.

"That's disgusting. You've..." He clears his throat and looks away for a moment.

I quickly drop the brush from between my teeth and it lands softly on my thighs. "Better?"

"Yes." He takes another step into the room and his brow quirks. "You're very tidy."

"Always have been. I like everything to have its place."

"OCD?" He asks politely.

I shake my head. "No, I'm just organised. How are you feeling?"

He runs his tongue over his bottom lip, his face becoming a hard mask. "I'd appreciate it if you didn't mention yesterday."

"Of course." I stand and make my way back to my not even nearly finished jigsaw puzzle. Crossing my legs, I sit on a scatter cushion and finger the pieces until one jumps out at me.

He's still here. Why's he still here?

"I'm serious. If I hear whispers of it pass over even Jeanine's lips, I won't be happy," he snaps, shocking me.

I blink up at him. "I won't say a word."

"Make sure you don't."

His eyes burn into mine for a moment longer, imploring me to soak up his words, before he turns on his heel and leaves my room.

I can't believe how... cold he can be at times. I get that what happened isn't something he wants to talk about, but can't he at least speak to me with a little more respect? I feel like a naughty child.

He's so back and forth with his demeanour towards me. I can't tell if he hates me being here or not. If I'm such a burden, why not just rent me a place? From what I can tell he has enough money to house me somewhere else and at least then he wouldn't have to deal with me on a daily basis. None of this makes sense.

Or maybe I'm just over-analysing it like I do everything.

Sitting back on the floor, I continue on with the jigsaw. It's boring to say the least, but there's nothing more to do around here. My eyes linger on the bed where I long to just curl up and forget everything in a world of darkness. It takes everything I have to stand and leave the room. The baby gives me a few kicks and I'm assuming it's because he or she is grateful that I've chosen to be more active.

I can't go outside; the rain and the wind are too strong. It looks tempting though. I want to run through the winds and the heavy droplets of water that fall from the sky. Imagine how freeing it would feel.

"I'm bored," I say to my bump as I descend the stairs. "I can only imagine how you feel."

The room is dark due to the thick grey clouds covering the sun and the shadow from the nearby trees cast over the bay window. I blow out a frustrated breath and switch on the TV. It's new and so is the equipment beneath it, but there's nothing on. DVDs are nowhere to be found either so I can't even watch a movie.

I call Sasha but she doesn't answer, neither does Tommy. I'll try again later.

After twiddling my thumbs for all of twenty minutes, I enter the kitchen and decide to have a snack. I'm not feeling too hungry after a lonely breakfast this morning but I should eat, so I do.

At the table I sit with a persimmon fruit between my hands. I use a plate to catch the sticky juice and cringe when it begins to dry on my fingers. This is the highlight of my next hour. Eating fruit and washing my hands. I don't remember ever being this lonely or bored at home, but that's probably because I always knew Caleb would be home soon and I wasn't forever trying to keep my mind busy.

A cracking noise shakes the house, making my hands automatically grip the worktop for support. The cracking noise is soon followed by a deep rumbling. It's a good thing I'm not scared of thunder and lightning, or this would be awkward.

I'm not sure how I feel about all of the lights flickering off. I can still see, it's not dark, but it's still eerie and I'm now completely convinced there's some kind of ghost breathing down my neck.

I scramble off the stool, not daring to look behind me for fear of seeing something there that I've imagined in my strange mind. My footsteps hammer the stairs as my heart hammers in my chest. I just need to get back to bed and everything will be fine.

Crack! The hall lights up, casting strange shadows along the walls. I'm too frantic to try and rationalise it.

Feeling like a child I race into my room, dive onto the bed and pull the blanket over my head. All the while my mind chants, "It's not real, it's not real."

The rumbling follows. It's louder and more ominous than before and it's freaking me the hell out.

The rain seems to get heavier and the wind more powerful. Shaking hands clutch the blanket tight to me. I curl my body into a ball, not daring to even poke a toe out from beneath the covers.

My ears pick up footsteps above. It's Nathan. It's got to be Nathan. But if that's Nathan, then what just opened the door to my room?

Oh my god. Ghosts are real. I think I'm going to cry.

The blanket is whipped from over my head and I scream.

"Guinevere!" Nathan shouts and seizes my flailing arms by gripping my wrists.

"Huh?" I blink open my eyes and look up at the shadowed male who looks like Caleb. Seeking comfort, I latch onto him, my arms around his waist and my head squished to his chest.

"You're trembling," he says, not returning the hug but I refuse to let go right now.

"If you're down here then who's upstairs?" I whisper when I hear more footsteps from above, though they sound like they're now coming from the staircase.

His hand rests on the top of my head as his other unwinds my arms from around him. I peek up at him through my lashes. "I have company."

"Company?"

"Yes," he responds and peels himself away from me. "What happened?"

"You didn't see the power cut out?" How could he not have noticed that?

"I was occupied," he states and I see a female step into the bedroom. She's beautiful, with thick golden hair and no clothes. Why's she walking around in just a robe?

"Oh." Why is he fully dressed when she isn't? Why is it any of my business? "Sorry." I scoot back on the bed, looking between him and the female.

"I told you to wait upstairs," he snaps at the girl, who immediately lowers her eyes.

"I heard her scream. I got worried and thought you might need help." She murmurs and takes a step backwards.

I glance between her and Nathan's burning eyes aimed at her. He doesn't look happy and her excuse seems legitimate, so I'm not sure if she warrants his anger.

Nathan's eyes come to me as if waiting for me to react in some way.

"Thanks but I'm fine," I explain to the female, who can't be more than five years older than myself. "That was kind of you, though. I'm not a fan of the dark."

"Yeah, this house is pretty creepy when it's dark," she giggles, but immediately stops when Nathan glares at her again. "I should go," she whispers and gives me a small smile.

"Yes. I believe you should," Nathan bites out and her face falls.

"Tomorrow?" She looks confused and a little bit hurt.

"I'll call you. Escort yourself out. I have to see to the fuse box." Nathan's tone is stern and unyielding. I want to slap him for her.

Shockingly she says nothing. She just scarpers away with her metaphorical tail between her legs.

"Do you have to be so mean?" I snap at my kind of brother in law. His eyes come to me but he only looks bored. "She was only trying to help."

"She was trying to be nosy when she had no right to be." He takes my arm in his hand and leads me out of the room, back onto the creepy landing.

"I don't want to go back downstairs."

"Tough. I need you to hold the torch while I check the box."

"Can't blondie do it? She was eager to help."

"No."

"But..."

"I'm not leaving you on your own for another second. I don't trust you not to start making that awful noise again."

"Noise? You mean my screaming? You ripped the blanket off my head! I thought you were upstairs!" I defend myself but he doesn't care.

"You were screaming before then, Guinevere. What do you think made me come downstairs in the first place?"

I stop in my tracks. "I wasn't screaming."

"Yes you were."

"No I wasn't." I know with one hundred percent certainty that I wasn't screaming. Why is he lying? "And I didn't hear any screaming from anywhere else. Maybe it was blondie."

"Her name is Lorna and yes you're right, maybe it was." Ewww. It doesn't take a genius to figure out what he's referring to. Even though I referred to it first, it's only natural that I feel grossed out by his confirmation.

"Nobody was screaming." I return to my previous argument as he leads me into the kitchen and searches under the sink for something. "Why did you come downstairs?"

He doesn't respond. He does, however, find a large torch. "Come."

"Oh no. No way... no... not a chance." I back away from the door leading to the basement. "This is exactly what they do in horror movies."

"The basement isn't like basements in horror movies. It's a gym. Come on," he sighs and guides me towards the narrow steps. I inhale a deep breath and allow him to lead me down the staircase. The torch lights the way well enough but I'm still freaking out.

He's right, this basement isn't creepy like horror films. It holds a treadmill, some weights and a load of other workout equipment that I don't know the name of. I follow close behind Nathan, my hand on his shoulder as he guides me to the far corner.

"Hold this," he says and hands me the torch. I shine it on the box as he opens it and watch him flick a few switches. After a moment he sighs and takes a step back. "It's a local power cut. We'll just have to wait it out."

"Can't we go somewhere else?" I plead, handing him back the torch.

Another loud crack lights up the sky, followed by the hideous rumbling.

In the glow from the torch I see him run his tongue over his lower lip and then he seems to relent. "Fine. Come on."

We rush up the stairs and quickly pull on our coats. He holds an umbrella up before taking me out into the harsh rain and helps me into his car. I rub my hands together in front of the heater as soon as he turns the key in the ignition, grateful he has a decent car that takes only seconds to heat up rather than the fifteen minutes it took in Caleb's.

"Movie or food?" He asks and carefully reverses before setting the car straight and heading down the narrow drive.

"Movie?" I ask and another thought comes to mind. "Where's blondie?"

"Her car has gone. She left while we were in the basement."

"Oh. You were mean to her."

His face gets tight and his eyes narrow. "It's none of your business. Don't try and make it so."

"Sorry," I mumble because he's right. Still, it doesn't feel great knowing how rude he was and not being able to say anything about it.

"Accepted."

Christ, he's such an arsehole sometimes.

The cinema is empty when we arrive. I'm shocked it's even open. We had to drive for nearly an hour to get here and the rain is still pelting it down. We argue for a while over seeing an action movie versus a psychological thriller. He wins and we have to watch the thriller because he can't stand action movies. Whatever. It does look good to be fair.

Apparently popcorn is a big no-no. Who goes to the cinema and doesn't have popcorn? The only thing I'm allowed is a bottle of water. He's paying so it's not like I can complain. It's awkward enough that I can't afford things for myself and I feel guilty because of that. I do have some money in my account, but I'm scared to spend it. I might need it. Who knows how long his generosity will last?

We don't speak throughout the movie for obvious reasons. We also don't speak as we leave, for not so obvious reasons. When we get outside I'm relieved to see the lack of rain. Nathan seems to think it'll be okay to go back home and I hope he's correct in his assumption because blondie was right, the house is freaky in the dark. I'll never look at it the same way again and I'll be damned if I ever walk around at night after this.

"You're a good cook." His voice startles me.

"Thanks." I think.

"I have to say, though, the spaghetti was my favourite. Very rich."

"It's sort of my speciality I guess."

He glances at me out of the corner of his eye. "Where did you learn to cook like that?"

Does he genuinely not know? "It's what I studied in University. I want to open up my own restaurant and bakery one day."

He seems surprised and I wonder why. "That's a good endeavour. I'm guessing you've had to drop out due to the recent events?"

"Yes. Caleb was going to drop out and stay at home with the baby."

I see him shake his head as he mutters, "I bet he was."

"What's that supposed to mean?" I notice his gloved hands twisting on the steering wheel, the leather squeaking against the rubber. "If you have something to say, then by all means say it."

"I don't." I wait for him to explain his strange muttered outburst further but he doesn't. A large part of me wants to press him for more but I'm afraid to create more drama between us. "Will you be cooking this evening?"

"If you like." I shrug and stare at the passing trees. "It's beautiful out here. I wish I could enjoy it more."

"Meaning?"

"Meaning I wish Caleb were still alive and then everything wouldn't seem so bland and tasteless, and I'm not just talking about food."

He lets out a sigh and chews on his lower lip for a moment. "Caleb hated the countryside."

"He did?"

"Yes. He preferred the beach."

"Oh." I didn't know this. My eyes burn slightly, but I'm not sure why. Maybe it's because I've just realised I'm never going to know a lot of things about him now, only what I already know and what I'm told by others.

The rain starts up again but it's only a light drizzle in comparison to how it was before. I seek refuge in the kitchen, surrounded by bubbling pots and a warming oven, as Nathan left me as soon as we arrived home. I'm grateful for this. The darkness that I've tried so hard to keep away has come back again and right now I just need to be left to my thoughts.

I refuse to go to bed and wallow this time. I'm going to cook. I need to do something. I don't want Caleb shouting at me from up there, telling me to get a hold of myself, which I know he's probably doing.

Or maybe he's stood right beside me, brushing the hair from my shoulder in preparation for his lips. Maybe he's whispering in my ear, telling me it's all going to be okay.

"It's not, Caleb," I respond to nobody, my bottom lip quivering as I try to swallow the lump in my throat and relieve the burning behind my eyes. "It's never going to be okay again."

There's no response, not like I was hoping, so I knuckle down and continue making dinner.

It must be the smell that has drawn Nathan from his room because he's sitting at the dining table right as I finish serving. He inhales deeply and looks at me. "This looks amazing."

Sitting beside him, I sip my water and take a bite of my own. It tastes like ash again. "Thanks."

"It tastes amazing too."

"I would've made something different but there isn't much in." I explain my reasons for making spaghetti again and take another bite.

"Is everything okay?" He asks, his eyes concerned rather than full of their usual irritation.

I shrug. "Fine."

He opens his mouth to speak but shuts it again and shakes his head. I'm grateful he doesn't ask, but part of me also wants him to. I want to spill everything that's in my soul.

Although even if he did ask, I doubt I'd tell.

I continue picking at my food until he finishes his and then set about clearing up. He helps me carry things from the dining area and into the kitchen.

"I won't be available tomorrow. I have to go to the city. I doubt I'll be back until Tuesday morning." He licks his lower lip and dries the pots as I pass them to him, his gloves still firmly on his hands.

"Okay." Great, another lonely day.

"I've arranged for a laptop for you. It should arrive in the morning after I've left. I'll write down the password for the WI-FI and pin it to the fridge before I leave."

Oh. Well I wasn't expecting that. "That's brilliant, thank you."

"No problem." I pass him a small bowl and gasp when it shatters on the ground after our fingers connect ever so slightly. "I'm so sorry. I should've been more careful with my hand." I immediately crouch and start picking up the shards.

Nathan whips off his gloves and immediately goes to the sink to wash his hands. He does realise I didn't actually touch his skin, right? "It just shocked me. I should have been more careful," he says calmly but I can see the stress in his eyes. "Leave that. You'll cut yourself. I'll get the sweeping brush."

I stand and search for the dustpan and brush as he sweeps the entire area into one small pile. After scooping them up, I tip them in the bin and watch him wash his hands again.

Placing a napkin over his fingertips, he opens a nearby drawer and pulls out another pair of the same style gloves. He really has a problem.

"We good?" I ask, tilting my head to the side.

He nods, flexing his fingers inside the leather. "I apologize for startling you."

I'm shocked. He sounds genuinely apologetic. I go to place my hand on his arm as a way to comfort him but think better of it and take a step back. "It was an accident. Could have happened to anyone."

His eyes linger on my face for a long while and I look away, unwilling to decipher the emotion in them.

"Gwen..." He lets out a breath and stalks from the room.

What was he going to say? Probably apologize again or maybe a thank you.

My thoughts don't linger on this as I get back to the cleaning. My stomach rolls and turns as the baby tries to get comfortable. I pat my swollen belly affectionately and retire for the night.

***

Nathan has left before breakfast, leaving me to deal with the delivery of my new laptop. I set it up immediately, eager to play. I have to admit that it's a very good laptop and obviously expensive. This makes me feel even worse about my opinion of Nathan. Sure he may be moody and a bit of an introvert and sometimes rude, not to mention the fact he can be mean and tactless, but he's trying to help. Whether that's due to guilt or loyalty to his brother, I don't know. Either way, he's still helping and he's still providing me with anything I require.

When collecting the password from the fridge, I notice Nathan's mobile number underneath the pin. I set up the WI-FI and contemplate for a while whether or not I should text him.

I decide yes.

Gwen: Thank you for the laptop. It's great. G x

He doesn't respond but I don't expect or need him to.

I sit and have a cup of tea with Jeanine before she leaves and watch videos on YouTube. They're funny videos that should crack even the coldest of souls, yet none of them even draw a smile from me.

I wonder if I'll ever feel the same but then I realise I don't think I ever want to. Gone is the bubbly girl who smiled at everything and in her place is the girl who found her fiancé dead beside her only five months before the arrival of their baby.

I keep reminding myself that it has hardly been any time at all and grief takes time to settle. It'll always be there but it will settle eventually. I'm still grieving... aren't I?

Sure I get sad when I think about Caleb, but other than that I don't feel anything at all. I'm in a constant state of numbness.

***

"I don't agree," I add to the conversation between myself, Paula and her friend Daisy who has met us for lunch. "The best unscripted ingredients are a dash of cinnamon and a spoonful of mayonnaise."

"Codswallop." Paula waves me off. "Everybody knows if you warm the batter first and add nutmeg it tastes divine."

Daisy chuckles. "Let's agree to disagree."

It feels good to be talking about food again. It feels like it's been years since I last attended University. In reality it has been a little over four weeks. It's only been a little over five weeks since the love of my life died and I'm feeling something other than numb.

It's not happiness or contentedness, but it's something above the darkness that I've succumbed to of late.

It makes me feel guilty.

I was happy over food. If anything could spark an emotion after Caleb's death, food would be it. Food has always been my passion. Cooking, baking, frying, stewing...the list is endless.

Caleb used to love how excited I became when I successfully made a dish. Any kind. As soon as it was done, I'd practically jump for joy, force it down his throat and pant at his feet until he told me how good it was. Sometimes I wondered if he just told me it was good so I wouldn't get disappointed.

Caleb wouldn't do that. He knew how important honesty was to me, especially when it came to my craft. I'd only learn by trial and error when experimenting.

"What do you think?" Daisy asks me.

I blink a few times and shake my head. "Sorry, I was miles away."

"We were talking about Nathan. Paula was just informing me of his rude behaviour towards her the other day. Is he like that with you?" Daisy asks.

I shake my head. "He mostly just keeps to himself."

"It's nice that he's taken you in after Caleb's unfortunate demise," she says quietly and I want to walk away from this conversation. Like now. "It's almost unheard of in this day and age. It's very gallant of him."

"Especially considering his parents. Ugh. I had the pleasure of meeting his mother once. Foul woman, absolutely foul." Paula adds with a cluck of disgust. "She used to be awful to those boys. They weren't allowed to do anything wrong."

"They grew up in the city," I say, but it's more of a question than anything else. "How'd you know this?"

Daisy leans in, eager to tell the gossip. "They did but Nathan also spent a lot of time here. The house you're in now is the family home. It's Caleb's grandfather's home. They came back and forth quite a bit. She usually dropped Nathan off when she'd had enough, which was more often than not."

"Yes," Paula agrees, also leaning forward. "Nathan was unruly. He was a menace. Always causing trouble, always speaking badly to his grandfather. Caleb however, now he was the happy one although we didn't see too much of him growing up. Always daydreaming, always smiling and playing. Such a lovely boy, he didn't spend nearly as much time with his grandfather as Nathan did though."

"If Nathan hated his grandfather so much, why'd he claim his house?" Daisy asks the question I was thinking but wasn't going to ask.

Paula shrugs. "I've no idea. What's it like inside? Are there still portraits on the walls?" I think about it for a moment. Now that I am, I realise I haven't seen a single picture anywhere. How odd.

"Hmm," I agree and sip my decaf latte. "So, what is there to do around here?"

"Not much." And just like that the conversation changes to better things.

CHAPTER ELEVEN

IT'S THE MORNING AFTER my outing with Paula. I haven't seen Nathan for a few days. He came back on the Tuesday morning as he said he would and I borrowed his car to go out, but that's the extent of our conversation. I'm not sure what's wrong with me right now. I'm in such a bad mood. I have been since I woke up thirty minutes ago. Even the fact that I can eat whatever I want for breakfast again without throwing it up doesn't cheer me up.

My movements are heavy because even my body is angry.

I stomp into the kitchen and slam cupboards as I prepare food. Even the mushrooms are pissing me off. Stupid food. Stupid house. Why is everything hurting? I don't mean my body, I mean my mind.

"Morning," Nathan says cautiously. I'm ignoring him. I'm ignoring everybody. "This looks good."

It tastes like ash and brimstone. What would he know?

"Seriously good." He moans a little and takes another bite.

Why is he talking to me?

I eat another mouthful of ash flavoured food. Huh, Jeanine is here. I didn't notice. She eyes me warily but I barely glance at her as I pick up my plate and walk past. I do notice them both exchange a look of concern, which just makes me worse.

They don't know me, but I guarantee when my back is turned they'll have quiet words and Nathan will probably blame me and say its hormones. I'm not hormonal. I'm tired, my back's hurting, I can't get comfortable... and oh yeah. Caleb is dead!

"Hey, my darling," Jeanine says and stands by the counter as I wash the dishes. "I think that plate's clean now."

What would she know? Are her hands in the water? No. It'll be clean when I say it's clean.

"Are you okay?"

I nod and scrub the plate some more. Jeanine reaches into the hot water and takes the plate from my hand. "I'll do this. Why don't you go and rest?"

"I don't want to," I snap, instantly feeling guilt but also not caring much.

"Okay, why don't you bake or something?" Her warm eyes search my profile and I feel her concern piercing my bubble of fury.

"I just want to be alone," I say quietly and brush past her. "Sorry."

Their hushed tones follow me up the stairs. I can't hear what they're saying and honestly I don't care. As soon as I enter my room, I put the photo frame face down without even looking at it. I can't deal with your smile today, Caleb. Life isn't always a fucking joy. Clearly.

Look at me. I'm a mess. Pining for a man that's ash on his mother's mantelpiece.

Not to mention that I'm in a house that doesn't belong to me, using money that I didn't earn, with a man who practically hates me, because of reasons I don't fucking know.

There's a knock at my door.

"Go away."

"Is this mood due to something I've done?" Nathan starts but I'm not in the mood to hear him.

I open the door, my eyes narrowed and hopefully shooting daggers. "Not everything is about you. Leave me alone." The door slams with a little more force than I intended.

I take my usual spot by the window, only leaving my room to have a quiet lunch and an even quieter dinner alone.

I wake up in the same mood and sleep in the same mood again and again for the next few days. Fortunately everybody avoids me for these days. When Nathan leaves my new clothes outside my bedroom, he only knocks and walks away. I should thank him but I don't know how.

The clothes are great, all of them warm and fitting my swollen belly to perfection. They cheer me up a fraction, I won't deny.

I even have some new walking boots which I'm grateful for, but I'm also curious as to how he knew I needed some. Maybe he's been paying closer attention to me than I thought.

Sucking a long breath in, I shake my body loose and make my way downstairs.

Nathan is sat in his usual spot at the end of the table, a bowl of cereal in front of him and one where I sit. He looks up, gives me a nod and turns back to his book. "I didn't think you were coming down."

"Me neither." I sit and stir my spoon around the milk before taking a bite. "Where's Jeanine?"

"No idea, she didn't show up for work this morning," he responds but he doesn't seem to care.

"She's probably sick."

"Either that or she's about to stage an intervention."

"What?" I look up as he places his book down and his eyes come to mine.

"You need to see a therapist."

My voice is shrill this time. "What?"

"We're concerned for your mental health. You haven't left your room in three days except to eat and use the facilities."

"So?" I gawp at him, my earlier anger returning with force.

He leans back in his seat. "It's not healthy."

"You do it all of the time," I snap and push away from the table. "I don't want to hear this."

"Go and get dressed. You're coming into the city with me today," he states and his tone tells me there's no argument.

"I don't want to." I argue anyway.

"Either go upstairs and make yourself presentable or I'll drag you to the city looking the way you do now."

"What's wrong with how I look?" Arrogant arsehole!

"You look like you've just rolled out of bed."

Well... I have. Who cares?

He gives me another pointed look. I groan with exasperation and leave the room muttering, "I'm going, I'm going."

"Oh, and Gwen?"

"What?" I call from my place at the bottom of the stairs.

"You're welcome."

Damn it. The clothes.

I forgot to thank him. I rush back inside the dining room and his eyes go wide when he sees me charging at him.

Gripping his wrist in one hand and his shoulder in the other, I press my lips to his cheek, say, "Thanks," and leave the room. I want to snigger at his shocked face but I don't have the energy to do it, so I sit and wait for him to wash his cheek. After counting down from ten, I spy him rushing into the kitchen to scrub at his cheek with a clean cloth.

I definitely wish I could laugh. This is hilarious. Okay, so I'm evil for playing with a man's mental issues. Who cares?

"Why do we need to go to the city?" I ask as we pull out of the long driveway, shocked that he hasn't chastised me for my earlier antics.

"I need to go into the office to deal with a few things. You can keep my father's secretary company."

"You're dragging me out of the house just so your father's secretary can babysit me? That seems a bit extreme. I haven't been that bad."

He doesn't respond, which makes me huff.

"I really don't fancy meeting your parents," I admit after a few minutes of silence. "I mean... your mum blames me and your dad hung up on me."

"What?" He seems to be astonished by my revelation. "When?"

"I called them, asking them for financial support from Caleb's trust fund. They refused. Your mum specifically told me it was all my fault. She called me back just to tell me."

"That..." His hands twist on the steering wheel. He does that a lot. "Don't worry, my parents aren't here this week. They're abroad."

"Abroad?" I gasp in horror. "How can they be abroad?"

Nathan shrugs. "My parents aren't good people, Gwen. I would never introduce them to you."

Caleb said the same thing.

It takes almost two hours to get to the city, due to traffic being horrendous and the distance we live from it. When we make it to the office building where he works, I'm relieved to see he has a designated parking space. The parking situation is worse than the traffic around here.

I'm guided in through an entrance at the back of the building and straight into an elevator. We get off at the fifth floor.

"Come on," he says and pulls me toward a large round desk. I instantly spot a young woman, not too far from my age, with huge brown eyes and short brown hair. "This is... umm..."

"Sophie," she sighs with a roll of her eyes, but I can see her heart has been crushed.

"Great." Nathan pushes me into a chair and walks through a door across from us.

"How many times have you told him your name now?" I ask, noticing Sophie's lingering look.

She purses her lips and sighs heavily. "About a million and one."

"That sucks."

"He will never notice me," she whines and taps away at her computer. "You're Gwen, right? The pregnant heathen who stole Mr Weston's son away?"

"That's me, although I prefer the term 'slut', if you wouldn't mind."

She laughs loudly and her sparkling brown eyes come to mine. "Ignore them, they were very protective of..."

"Sammy!" Nathan shouts from the doorway. I didn't notice him come back out.

"It's Sophie," she bites out.

"Know your place!" He snaps and slams the door. I see her face pale and wonder what the hell that was all about.

"Coffee?" She asks and stands abruptly.

"No thank you. I'm not allowed caffeine." I clear my throat and watch her smooth down her skirt. "What were you going to say?"

"I'll get you a tea." She doesn't meet my eyes as she scarpers through the door to my left. What on earth was that all about?

She brings me my tea, which tastes foul but I sip it anyway. She clicks away on her computer and answers the phone on occasion, all the while chatting animatedly to me about the baby and how her sister was when she was in labour. I listen politely but otherwise lose myself in my own world.

More time passes and I become more bored by the second. A few people come and go, requesting to speak to Mr Weston. All of them are denied. There's still no sign of Nathan. Now I'm just irritated.

I've been sat here for two hours and the company I'm in isn't great. She reminds me too much of Sasha and that hurts.

Before Caleb died I had lots of friends, but none of them have called or texted since I left. Now I'm wondering if they were ever friends at all.

"Nathan wants you to go to him," Sophie says, breaking me from my thoughts.

I sigh and head towards the door he vanished behind two hours ago. Giving it a tap, I push it open and blink when I see him sat at the desk with his head cradled in his hands.

"What is it?" I ask and walk over to him.

He looks up at me, his eyes tired. "Keep me company."

"W... what?"

He pulls the closest chair next to his and pats the seat. I sit, wondering what's going on. "We're going to have to stay in a hotel tonight. There's too much to be done and I won't be finished until late."

Groan.

"Is that okay?"

I shrug. "I guess it'll have to be, but be warned - I'm never coming here with you again."

He smirks and I'm shocked at the motion. He never smiles or smirks. It suits him. "If you like I can have somebody take you to the hotel now? I'm sure you'll find it more comfortable."

I'm about to say yes but then I see how drained he looks and reject his offer. "No. I'll just hang out here with you, if that's okay?"

He turns his face to his computer. I swear I just saw him smile but I can't be certain. He turned too quickly. "As you wish."

I lean back in my seat and snag his phone from the desk. His eyes question my actions.

"I want to play a game."

His gloved finger taps at the screen. I watch it unlock and start downloading games when I realise he doesn't even have Angry Birds. His phone is extremely cool. Who doesn't have Angry Birds when they have an extremely cool phone?

"Do you need any help with anything?" I ask after a few minutes of failing to tear down a building with a bird.

"No, you play your game."

"It's lost my interest. That's a really pretty necklace." I point at the screen, where a golden circle with a tiny red gem shines back at me. "Really pretty."

"You think so?" He asks as I admire the spiralling pattern engraved on the flat disk, leading to the tiny red gem.

"Yes." Obviously, or I wouldn't have said it.

"Why do you like it?"

I shrug. "It's different. I like the fact the disk isn't prominent. It makes the gem stand out, even though it's small."

"Huh." He licks his lower lip and flicks through a few more images. "Would you like one?"

Umm... yes. "No. You've given me enough."

"It's one of a kind," he states, his eyes now on me. "It would suit you well."

I'm not sure what to make of what he just said, or the way his gaze seems to be burning into me in a way it never has before. I'm reading into things. "Why do you say that?"

He turns back to the computer and crosses off the screen. I hide my disappointment by looking at the sheets of paper spread out along the desk. I have no idea what they are.

We order in food as he's still not done and it's now five. I have to admit that his company hasn't been terrible. He's made conversation when necessary and asked me whether or not I like some of the jewellery he shows me. Some of it isn't my style but some of it is beautiful. I make sure to give him my honest opinion on every one and my reasons behind it.

After a while he seems to get aggravated, almost like he doesn't like my answers. I can't help what I like and what I don't like.

"This one?" He snaps and shows me a picture of a single loop charm with a purple disk in the centre that can be flipped over showing a mint green colour on the other side.

"It's great, a necklace for two outfits."

"You've been in my office haven't you?" His question startles me.

"What? No!" I gape at him, my heart hammering. There hasn't been a single time I've gone in there, apart from the first time when I opened the door and immediately shut it when I realised it was his study.

His eyes narrow. "I only gave you two rules. Stay out of my way and don't invade my privacy."

"I swear, I haven't!" I gulp and implore him with my eyes to believe me.

"Then how is it you like every single piece of jewellery I've designed, but nothing that my father has?"

I laugh a little, but it's humourless and nervous. "Even if I had been snooping, which I haven't, I didn't even know you designed jewellery. How the hell would I remember them all and why the hell would I like them all? You're making zero sense." I climb from my seat to put some distance between us. "Maybe your designs are actually really good and maybe that's why I like them."

"If I find out you've been in my office, Guinevere..."

"Oh save it." I snarl and stomp to the door. "I'll take that ride to the hotel now, if you don't mind."

"Don't walk away from me, Guinevere."

"Fuck you," I shout and reach for the handle.

A hand comes from behind and slams against the door, keeping it shut no matter how hard I tug. "I'll accept that I've upset you and that's the reason you just spoke to me with such a lack of respect, but next time you swear I will make it so that you never even dare to swear in my presence again. Are we clear?"

His whispered threat hits me straight in the chest and no small amount of fear overcomes me. I have no idea what he means to do and I don't care to find out.

"Now sit down. You're right, I probably have jumped to conclusions and now I feel guilty because of your honesty over my jewellery. I shouldn't have been so quick to judge your motives." His hand comes to my wrist and circles it tightly, but not so tightly that it would leave a mark or hurt me in any way. "Please, come and sit and we'll eat when the food arrives."

"Let go of me," I whisper, my lower lip vanishing under my teeth. He doesn't move away and my trembling gets worse. It's not from fear but from my attempts at keeping the tears away. No matter how hard I try they fall seconds later, spilling silently down my cheeks. I hate that I'm so emotional but these days the slightest trigger sets me off.

He spins me so my back is against the door, his eyes following the shiny, wet trails that mar my face. "Gwen, I..." His eyes roam over me, from my eyes to my nose, before finally settling on my mouth. "Don't cry. I didn't mean to frighten you."

"Let me go," I tell him again and lower my eyes. "Please."

He slowly nods and takes a step back. I pull open the door and keep my head down as I pass the large desk.

"Lock up," I hear Nathan order. "Guinevere, wait."

I stop as I reach the elevator we came up in. "What?"

"I'll take you to the hotel," he says and presses the button with his gloved pinkie finger.

He doesn't speak until we reach the car, for which I'm grateful. "You're correct in thinking I've been completely irrational."

Scoff.

"You're right. You have no reason to lie to me about liking them. It was just a shock because my father and Caleb hated them."

"Caleb hated them?" I blink at this announcement. "Caleb would love them."

"He told me so himself." He shrugs like it doesn't bother him, but part of me knows it does.

A thought flashes across my mind. Does Nathan secretly seek acceptance from people? He seems so hard and so unaffected by everything. Is it all just a façade?

"Well I think they're great. If I were to buy something, that first disk with the red gem would be the first thing to catch my eye." I'm not saying it as a hint for him to get me one either, although that would be nice. "Why don't you put them on the market?"

"It's my father's company. What he says goes."

"Your father is an idiot," I grumble and relax in my seat. "You're very talented. I imagine your father was once. He still is but his style is older, more elegant. Yours are modern and eye catching. I know obviously your father's jewellery sells well, but I bet yours would sell better."

"I doubt that but it's kind of you to say so." He smiles gently at me, his eyes seeming to see me in a whole new light. "You're not actually that bad when you lose the attitude. I'm starting to see what my brother saw in you."

My mouth drops open at his teasing words. "I'd say the same to you but..." I tap my chin in thought. "I really shouldn't lie."

His laughter sounds through the car and my heart almost stops. He has a nice laugh. Very nice. It's deep and throaty and full of joy. His smile brightens his entire face and those hard and stern lines completely vanish. He looks his age and he looks more like Caleb, but this time it doesn't hurt so much to see the similarities. For once I welcome it and find my lips curving up with it.

CHAPTER TWELVE

W E ARRIVE AT THE hotel. It's fancier than the one we stayed in before leaving my home town. I wonder vaguely about what happened to the food we ordered, but that thought vanishes when I see the huge tub in the en-suite bathroom.

"Dibs," I announce and close the door behind me.

It's been a while since I've had a soak. There's a nice enough bath at Nathan's, but this is a hotel tub. You can't go to a fancy hotel and not use half of their bubble products. It wouldn't be right. I'm certain there is a law against forgetting to test their wares and if there's not, there should be.

Once the bath has reached capacity and the heat is as I desire, I step into the foamy water and sigh as it heats my body perfectly.

"What do you want to eat?" Nathan calls through the door.

"Something greasy."

"Salad."

"Something extra greasy."

"Lots of salad."

"You're an arse."

"Even more salad."

I smile to myself, my hands rubbing over the bump poking out of the water. "Whatever. Surprise me."

"Salad."

My breath comes out in a rush as I let out a small giggle. I'm happy when guilt doesn't follow immediately afterwards. "Thanks."

He stops speaking through the door, leaving me to soak and wash my hair.

By the time I'm done, the food is here and I'm relieved to see proper food, not salad.

There is some salad but it's with chicken wings and ribs and steak. Oh my god, I'm so hungry. There's peppercorn sauce. I almost cry. You can't have steak without peppercorn sauce.

Another thing that should be illegal.

"Come sit," Nathan says and points to the seat beside him. Why does he like me sitting beside him? Every breakfast, lunch and dinner we've shared, he's pulled me next to him. When I went into his office, he had me sit next to him. I don't get it. I can still talk to him from across the way. What's up with that?

I completely ignore the chair he holds out and sit in the space next to it. Nathan pulls out the chair a little bit more and pats the seat.

Why am I winding him up?

"I'm okay here," I say and gauge his reaction.

"Is there a reason you don't want to sit beside me?" He asks, his features carefully blank as I slide my plate to my new spot.

I shrug. "No reason."

"Okay." He elongates the word and looks down at his food. I start cutting into mine, happy to see it's not pink in the middle.

I watch him out of the corner of my eye as he begins to eat, his eyes drifting up to me every so often. This makes my lips twitch. "So, how long will you have to work tomorrow?"

"I should be done by noon," he says after a moment's thought. "Would you like to join me?"

I eye him warily and tease, "Are you going to accuse me and shout at me?"

His eyes soften and I can see he's sorry for his actions before he even says it. "No and I apologise profusely for reacting that way."

I wave him off and flip my braid over one shoulder. "It's fine."

"No," he says sternly. "It's not fine. You shouldn't be subjected to that by anyone. Even me." His lips curve up at the ends. "Well, not including when you annoy me."

Scoff. "I don't annoy you."

"No, you're right," he says, his voice soft and quiet. "You don't."

My breath hitches. I'm not sure why and I don't get a chance to think on it as he's changing the subject.

"I thought we could go out tomorrow when I've finished." I continue to chew on a piece of steak as he speaks. "Have you ever been to the city?"

"No, but there are a lot of places I want to see," I admit, keeping my fingers crossed that he'll let me see them. I should just ask him but I don't want to impose too much on his generosity, despite the fact that I've promised myself that I will one day pay him back.

"Brilliant. We'll spend a few hours wandering around if the weather is agreeable and then I'll bring you back in a few weeks. We'll see a show."

"A show?"

"Theatre." His eyes search my face. "Unless you don't find the theatre enjoyable?"

I shrug, a smile teasing my lips. "I've never been, so I'd love to."

"Great." He blinks, seeming surprised that I've agreed. I see a spark of excitement in the depths of his brown eyes and feel a twinge of happiness because he's happy. It's not much but it's there. "I'll make the arrangements."

"Thanks." I take another bite and fail to stifle a moan. My eyes close and my belly tingles with appreciation. Everything tastes better when pregnant and hungry. *Everything.* "Damn this steak is amazing."

I catch his eyes on me but they flicker away the second I fully refocus on my surroundings.

Quick, gloved hands skilfully slice through his food using the fancy cutlery. I notice how he only eats the food on his plate, not even touching the ribs or the chicken wings. How odd. I don't comment, though, I just eat as much as my stomach will allow. The way he eats is none of my business, although I can't deny that it fascinates me as much as a grieving person can be fascinated.

"So, where am I sleeping?" I ask after washing my hands and face. There is only one bed and a large couch. I wonder why we didn't get separate rooms but I figure money might be a bit tighter now that I'm living with him and he's paying for my private healthcare. "I don't mind taking the couch."

He frowns and leads me over to the bed. "You sleep here. I'll take the couch. I'm going to have a shower, so use this time to get ready."

"In what? I have no clothes here."

He hands me an empty plastic bag. "Put your clothes in here. I'll send them to be washed and dried with my own."

"Okay," I say and take the bag from his hands. "What about for the night?"

"Here," he says and I almost stumble backwards when he starts removing his jacket and shirt.

"I could just sleep in the gown…" He turns his back towards me, pulls his white vest over his head and passes it to me. I take it. "Thanks."

"No problem."

"What about you?"

"I'll be fine," he says and pads into the bathroom, still only half dressed. I should cover my eyes or look away but I can't. He has a very nice back. Very nice. I find myself tracing the patterns and lines of his sculpted muscles and golden skin in my mind. I can't help myself, regardless of the fact that it makes me hate myself. I'm human and I appreciate things that I find pleasant to look at. Nathan's back just happens to be on that list.

During the time he showers, I call down to reception and ask them to bring up some bed sheets and a blanket. They do so in record time and I manage to set up his bed for the night before he exits the bathroom. I also manage to strip off and pull his vest on, which would probably reach to mid-thigh if I didn't have a huge bump in the way.

I bag up my clothes and place them by the bathroom door before climbing into bed.

Nathan leaves the bathroom but I feign sleep to give him the privacy he deserves. Okay so I'm a liar. I peek through one eye and I'm shocked to see him in nothing but a towel, his golden skin damp and glistening in the dim light from the lamp by the couch. My eye quickly shuts again and I mentally scream, "OH MY GOD!"

I've never been this close to a naked man other than Caleb and it's making my heart race. I try to steady my breathing but my constricting lungs are making it difficult.

I peek again and almost gasp when I realise he's looking at me over my shoulder. He's checking to see if I'm looking.

I'm not. Totally not.

His tongue peeks out and runs over his lower lip. I almost copy his action but fortunately refrain as he's still looking at me. The muscles on his back tense as he pads over to the door, opens it and grabs something from outside after placing the bag of our discarded clothing in the hall. He walks back towards the couch, pulling a cotton, white robe on and tying it at the front. The towel drops to the floor. I can't see anything because of the robe, but my heart lurches again at the thought of his nudity. My mouth goes dry, as do my lips. I wish I'd moistened them moments earlier when I had the chance.

To make my sleeping state more believable, I snuggle further into the bed and tighten my legs around the pillow between them, careful to keep my features lax. He seems to freeze and look over at me. I close my eyes completely as being a creeper is making me feel like a... well a creep.

I finally begin to doze not long after he turns the TV on low and pours himself a drink from the mini fridge. Of course he did all of this after putting on his gloves and rinsing the glass out about six times. The rinsing of the glass was the perfect opportunity to wake up 'involuntarily' but I don't want to impose on his quiet time.

He really should see somebody about his germ issue. If he hasn't already, that is.

We arrive at his office at no later than seven fifteen, which annoys me because I was hoping to sleep in until at least nine. Plus the way he woke me up wasn't exactly nice.

He stood over the bed and shouted, "GWEN!" Louder than was necessary. I almost peed myself during the flailing that tangled me in the bedding. He thought it was hilarious. It's nice to see him laugh. I can't deny that his laugh is wonderful; it's contagious and I found myself wanting to laugh with him.

"Why can't you do this at home?" I ask, my chin resting on my hands as I sleepily watch him work on the computer in his dad's office.

"Because I can only access certain files from my home computer and these need to be done today."

"Do you want a drink?" I ask, eager to change the subject from files just in case he decides to give me a lesson in exports, imports and stocks.

"I'll ask Sammy."

"It's Sophie," I correct and shake my head. "She has a crush on you."

His cheeks seem to pink slightly. "Huh. I didn't notice."

"Yep." I spin in my seat, stopping as I face him. "She was devastated when you forgot her name yesterday."

"Huh," he murmurs and places his leather clad hand on the phone.

"I want to make the drinks. I'm bored."

"I'd rather you didn't." He frowns and glances down at my stomach.

Well that makes no sense. "I'm pregnant, not an invalid. Besides, I cook for you at home all the time."

I watch as defeat falls over his face. "Do as you wish." He waves his hand flippantly in the air. "I'll take a coffee, bla..."

"Black, one sugar, got it. I'll even rinse the cup out six times just for you," I remark and waddle towards the door.

"You have a mean streak, joking about a real condition," he teases and flexes his hands in an apparently subconscious gesture.

I grin at him. It's real, it's mischievous, it's old Gwen. He winks at me, noticing my shift in mood, no matter how temporary.

Then it's ruined as the second I place my hand on the door it swings wide open. My body lurches backwards as it connects with my arm, narrowly missing my swollen navel.

Ouch.

Before I lose my balance entirely, I manage to right myself and Nathan rushes to my side.

"Are you alright?" He asks, scanning me from head to toe with worried eyes. After I nod he turns to the intruder. I see his body visibly tense and I peek around him to see who it is. Familiar scowls shadowed by dark hair come into view. Their faces are the same masks of disgust that have taunted me since our first meeting.

His parents.

Both Nathan and Caleb share their mother's eyes but everything else belongs to their father. It's strange to look at. He's one of those people that age well, like George Clooney or Richard Gere. Still handsome after they passed their prime.

I gulp when his mother's cold eyes narrow on me. Nathan closes the door, his eyes still on his father who's staring at me with shock and disgust. "Explain." He barks at Nathan, who just stands silently, his jaw tense, his eyes slightly wide.

"Why is *she* here?" His mother hisses and I wince at the bitterness to her tone.

"She's my guest," Nathan responds, his tongue marking his lower lip.

"Your *guest*?" His mother shrieks and looks back at me. "How can you even think of having that... that... slut as your guest?"

My mouth drops open and Nathan's body tenses further. I remain behind him, my heart racing with fear. "She's carrying Caleb's child," Nathan says and shifts on the spot.

"So she says," his father adds and my temper rises. How dare he?

"Why are you still standing there?" His mother shouts at me and my hands instantly go to my stomach. How do I react to this? "Leave!"

Nathan steps to the right, blocking them from view. "She'll stay as long as she desires. She's my guest."

"She's nothing but a whore," his mother adds, trying to lean around Nathan so she can see me and spit her venomous words at my face.

"Mother." Mother? Why not mum? "Watch your language."

"You'll get rid of her," his father snaps and walks towards us. "Send her back. That's an order." Well I see where Nathan gets his controlling tendencies from.

Now I'm really freaking out. My skin feels warm. I feel nauseous and dizzy. I want to leave but I'm stunned into stillness.

His words plague me and twist my fears into a knot that rests at the base of my tongue.

Get rid of me? Where will I go?

"She's carrying your grandchild," Nathan bites out, his body turning so his hand can wrap around my bicep and bring me closer. I'm grateful for the support.

"That's no grandchild of mine," his mother sneers, her eyes now on me. Damn it, if I wasn't pregnant I'd be cursing at her right now. How dare she? "Don't you care that she ripped our Caleb from us?" My lips part with horror. I did no such thing.

"He's doing this to spite us," his father laughs, nodding at Nathan, but there's no humour to it. "Forever the disappointment."

"What?" I gasp and look up at Nathan. He glances at me out of the corner of his eye, warning me to be quiet. I won't. Not anymore. "How can you say that?"

"Listen to her, she sounds so... common," his mother spits, her mouth curling in disgust. "You make me want to spit." Oooh, big words...

"What did I do to you?" I try to take a step forward but Nathan holds me in place.

"You took him from me!" His mother shouts, her distress evident in the tears pooling in her eyes. For some reason my heart goes out to her. A mother has lost her child and she needs someone to blame. That doesn't make this right, though. "His last moments were with you. Not with us."

"See what this is doing to your mother?" His father shouts at Nathan, whose entire body is rigid. "Look at her!"

"Come on," Nathan says to me and begins to lead me to the door. "Those files still need printing and faxing. I've done the majority."

"You can return once she's gone," his father snarls, and swings open the door. "If she's not gone by the end of the week, you won't have a job here, boy. Make the right choice, your family or your brother's whore."

Nathan pulls me out as I give a long and lingering look of hatred towards his father. My body trembles and I struggle to put one foot in front of the other as we leave.

As soon as we enter the elevator after avoiding Sophie's eyes, my heart breaks. I'm going to lose Nathan and his home. It shouldn't be so devastating, but it is. I don't want to be alone. I don't want to do this alone.

"Nathan," I say softly, my legs barely keeping up with his long strides towards his car. We climb in and buckle up before hightailing it out of there. Just like the elevator ride, the car journey back towards the hotel is silent.

"Stay here," he snaps, his tone angry and clipped. I do as I'm told and wait in the car as he rushes into the hotel. He doesn't take long, only fifteen minutes before he's climbing back into the driver's seat.

We race along the streets, breaking more traffic laws than I'd care to admit. He pulls up outside a bank and orders me to wait here again.

This time I'm waiting for an hour, my mind working overtime, my hands still trembling from the adrenaline that was released during the heated argument. What am I going to do?

Nathan storms out of the bank and stands beside the car for a moment. I watch him pace a few times, his gloved fingers ripping through his hair before he finally climbs into the driver's seat.

"What's wrong?" I ask, concerned for my friend.

He chews on his lower lip for a moment before swearing a few times and hitting the steering wheel with the side of his fist. This brings back memories of Caleb, the time he gave me an orgasm in his car after we lost a tyre.

"Hey," I soothe and place my hand on his wrist, careful to not touch his skin. "What is it?"

"He's cut me off." He snarls and I blink in shock.

"How can he cut you off? You work there. Surely you get your own pay cheque?"

"I do, but it's all in stocks and shares." I shudder at the thought. "I've been living off my trust fund, hoping to gain enough revenue to... Damn it!"

I rub his wrist with my thumb, wanting to stroke his hair or hug him to make him feel better. "You'll be okay. You'll figure it out."

"I know, I have money to get by, it's just the principle," he snaps, like I should know this. "I'm sick to death of... of..."

"Being controlled?"

He glares at me. "Mind your own business."

I shrink back at the tone of his voice. I've never heard it so venomous. For a moment there I could see his mum in him and it's not an attractive thing to behold.

"I should have just set you up in an apartment, but no. I had to take you home," He rants, mostly to himself. "I had to get involved. Stupid. Stupid. Stupid."

"I'm sorry," I whimper, wishing he'd just shut up now. "I didn't ask you..."

"Honestly? You didn't ask? Didn't you call my parents begging for help?"

"I was..."

"Desperate, I know," he shouts, pulling the car out into the road. My eyes burn; I don't deserve this. "I was there when you called."

Then he's a bloody good liar because I specifically remember his shock when I told him about that call.

"I never should have gone to you. You've ruined everything." He hits the steering wheel again, causing the horn to go off.

I don't say anything. I want to get out of the car but I doubt he'll stop in order for me to do so and, even if he does, where would I go? I don't have any money. I don't even have my phone with me.

"This isn't my problem; that kid isn't my problem," he continues. I try to mentally shut him out but the masochist in me keeps listening, absorbing and storing his words so I can use them against myself at a later date. "Why did he pick you? Out of every single female that was available to him, he chose you. Why? He could have picked a female who had her own money, someone who could provide for herself in this situation." It's not like Caleb knew he'd be abandoning me, so his rhetorical questions make no sense. "Why did it have to be you?"

I ask myself the same thing on a daily basis. Trust me, I don't get it either.

"Sure you're good company, but you're nothing special." He grits out and my heart breaks further. Even the masochist in me has finally had enough. I felt my resolve crumbling with each verbal punch and now it's non-existent. "Nothing special."

"You can stop now," I sniff and wipe my eyes with the inside of my sleeve. "You've said enough."

His breath seems to catch in his throat and his hands tighten on the wheel. I stare out of the window, watching the scenery blur by as a heavy silence lingers between us. He says nothing else. I don't want him to say anything. I just want to leave.

I've had enough now.

I don't deserve this.

We drive home in total silence, the tension as thick as syrup lingering in the air leaving a bad taste in my mouth. The urge to vomit is prominent. As soon as we pull over outside the house, I climb from the car and walk towards the door. Nathan swiftly follows and unlocks it, his strides longer and more confident than my own so he beats me easily.

I'm not about to try and outrun him. I don't have the energy.

"Gwen," he says, his tone a lot softer than it was. I ignore him and immediately ascend the stairs. He follows, hot on my heels. "Gwen." His tone is more urgent this time.

Stomping into my bedroom I try to slam the door behind me, but it doesn't slam as he catches it with one hand.

"Gwen." his voice is quiet, softer than I've ever heard it. I hear the remorse there, I feel the remorse there, but it's too late.

Grabbing my suitcase, I throw it on the bed and begin yanking clothes out of my closet.

"Gwen," he repeats, ducking as a shoe flies by his head.

When he sees I have no more shoes to throw out of the closet, he steps towards me, his hand circling my wrist. I don't look up at him. I stare straight ahead at the row of clothes, ironed and hanging on the single rail.

"I shouldn't have taken my anger out on you." He steps even closer, his chest now only two inches from my arm. "I'm sorry. Forgive me."

"Forgive you?" I laugh once and angrily wipe the tears from my eyes. "What's to forgive?"

"Gwen." He turns me to face him.

"I envy you," I whisper, staring at his tie as my lip trembles and my body is overcome with grief. "I envy your inability to feel a thing. I envy how cold you are. I envy how mean and unfeeling you are."

"I didn't mean it; I was angry." His free hand reaches up to cup my cheek. I look him dead in the eyes and see his guilt and sorrow, but it doesn't penetrate the walls I've pulled up. "I'm not a nice person when I'm angry. You were close by and... I took it out on you."

"Let go of me." I tug myself free and continue gathering my things. My shoulder hits his chest as I shove past, my arms filled with clothes.

As I bend over my suitcase he waits by the door, his tongue once again teasing his lower lip. "I don't have to help you, Gwen, but I am. I'm here. You have somewhere to live and you have everything you need. I promised you I'd provide for you and that's what I'm doing."

"You don't want me here. I'm here because of the guilt you feel."

"Guilt over what?" He scoffs, spinning me around again. I'm sick of being spun.

"I don't know!" I shout, looking into his broken eyes and feeling my heart stammer. "I don't know what guilt you feel. Why else am I here?" He doesn't respond but I see a shadow of emotion flicker in his eyes. It's almost like he has an answer to that question but refuses to say it aloud. Christ, I don't even care right now about his secrets. "Let me go."

"And where will you go? What will you do?"

"I don't know." I sniff unattractively. "I don't care."

"You're not leaving. I've apologised, now put it behind you. It's not worth it."

"Christ, you are such an..." I don't swear, I don't want make him angrier than he already is. "I don't know... I just... move out of my bloody way."

"I'm sorry, okay? I'm sorry. Is that what you want to hear?"

"I don't want anything from you."

"Whether you want it or not," he snaps, giving my arm a shake to bring my eyes to his. I remain strong, despite the urge to cower at the anger and darkness swirling in his light brown irises. "You need it. If you leave, where are you going to go? You have nobody to turn to."

"I'll figure it out." I continue throwing things in my case.

A blur of colour and black passes my line of sight. My suitcase is gone from the bed and has just clattered against the wall with a loud and heavy thud. The contents spill out all over the ground.

He did not just do that.

Nathan stands to the side, his chest heaving. "You're not leaving. Do you understand?"

"You can't hold me here." My fists tighten by my sides, making my nails bite into my palms.

"I will if I have to. I made a mistake. I got angry and I've apologised. I'll say it a thousand times if I have to. I'm sorry. I'm fucking sorry." He glares down at me, his breath coming out in shallow pants. "I will lock you in this room. Don't test me."

My mouth drops open and I take a step back. He wouldn't dare... he couldn't. There's no way he'd do that.

"Shout at me, get angry with me, do something. Just don't leave." I'm startled by the desperation in his voice but it does nothing to deter me.

"I would, but you're not that special," I hiss as venomously as he hissed it at me.

"You're right," he says without blinking. Long, cautious steps draw him closer. "I'm not. I don't pretend to be. But you are." His hand grips me by the back of my neck. "You are. Caleb didn't deserve you, Gwen. I'll never deserve you."

What?

What does that even mean?

Who is he to judge?

"Stay." He dips his head to look me directly in the eye. His head is now only an inch from mine. "I'm sorry. Believe me." His hand wraps around mine and it's soon pressed against his chest. I feel his rapid pulse beneath my fingers and mine speeds up with it, shocked at his... well... this entire situation. I know how difficult it must be for him to touch my hand and the fact he hasn't yet pulled away seems to startle us both. "I've never been sorrier in my life."

Another tear falls from my eye, wetting a path behind it.

"I'll stay out of your way, I promise."

Closing my eyes for a moment, I listen to his ragged breathing while his heart beats under my hand. What options do I have? I don't have any. It's either stay here and figure out a way to get money to move on with my life, or leave now and struggle.

My confused thoughts and feelings don't relent and the fog that is my mind only thickens with each passing second.

Guilt encompasses me in a relentless embrace as I realise I like having my hand there. I like being in Nathan's company. I'm not sure if it's because of some strange attachment issues now his brother's gone, but I feel it all the same. The broken look in his eyes seems to spark a whole new feeling, a feeling that I want to get to the depth of his brokenness and put the pieces back together.

I'm going against Caleb's wishes being here. I promised him I'd stay away from Nathan but I had no other choice... or did I? Am I just making excuses so I can be close to the man that looks like my dead lover?

Nathan presses his lips to my forehead and takes a step back. "Get some rest and think on it. If you still want to leave in the morning, I'll arrange accommodation for you."

I nod. This is a good bargain to agree to. "Okay."

"Gwen," he says before leaving the room. I look up, his broken eyes tearing into my soul. "I am truly sorry."

"I know."

He dips his head and leaves the room, closing the door behind him.

What am I doing?

What am I doing here?

Chapter Thirteen

I GO TO MY next doctor's appointment. Jeanine drops me off and waits for me to finish. I'm not diabetic, I'm perfectly healthy but my baby is going to be huge. The doctor hasn't confirmed this, it's just obvious. I'm measuring bigger than I should be. It should cheer me up that the baby is alright, but it doesn't. My mind is still in a funk over yesterday's events. I want to go to Mr and Mrs Weston and claw at their faces, hissing and spitting like a cat. I want to scream at them for being so cold and cruel.

I wonder, if like Nathan, they're taking their grief out on me. Maybe one day we'll reconcile and my baby can have at least one set of grandparents in his life. It's such a farfetched thought. They're awful people. Awful. I mentally berate myself for even hoping for such a thing. If only happy endings existed.

There's one thing I know for sure - when they realise this is Caleb's baby, they can kiss their rights as grandparents goodbye if they don't change.

Jeanine notices my silence and tries to get me talking but I can't. I just don't feel like it. She soon gives up but I know she doesn't hold it against me. I need silence. I'm sure there have been times where she has needed silence too.

Thoughts of Caleb are once again prominent in my mind. It's hard to deal with. I miss him so much and he should've been there for the doctor's appointment. He should have been there with me, holding my hand and getting excited and reassuring me about how fat I'm not getting, even though we'd both know that I am.

Nothing about this excites me anymore.

I don't understand any of this. I don't understand his parent's hate and anger toward me. This isn't something I've brought to Nathan's attention before. It's not something I've asked him, but I can't deny the temptation to. What have I done that's made two clearly well raised people hate me so damn much?

Why would they cut Nathan off like they did Caleb? Is it truly because of what their mother said? Because Caleb spent his last moments with me?

How is that my fault? Neither of us knew he was going to die.

Maybe it's the guilt they feel for shunning him and now that they've lost him, they wish they could have that time back.

I don't know.

None of this makes sense.

I feel as though there's a void in my reasoning. I need closure but I'm not sure what from. Will I always feel this way?

When I finally get back to Nathan's I'm relieved to see he's absent, much like he was this morning. I don't know where he is and I don't really care. He's a grown man, he can do what he wants.

As I'm sat at the counter in the kitchen, there's a knock at the door. I don't want to answer it but I do anyway and I'm shocked to see blondie standing there, shifting nervously on her feet.

"Hi," I say as she realises I'm not Nathan and her shoulders sag. "I don't know where he is."

"Did he tell you to say that?" Her disbelief is warranted I guess.

I shake my head. "No. I haven't seen him since yesterday."

"Oh..." She twists her hands in front of her. "If you see him, please tell him to call me."

"Sure." I go to close the door but she calls out once more, stopping me halfway.

"Is he... are you? I mean... is he seeing someone else?"

Is he? "Honestly, I have no idea. I promised him I wouldn't invade his privacy so I haven't. I didn't even know about you until the other day when we first met." I give her an apologetic smile and look her up and down. She looks cold. Where's her car? "Where's your car?"

"I walked."

"From the village?" Is she crazy? That's a four mile walk, not including our long driveway.

"Yeah." She takes a step back. "Thanks... umm..."

"It's Gwen."

"Right, I'm Lorna. It was nice to meet you." She nervously tucks her hair behind her ear and descends the two steps leading from the door. "Take care."

I close the door, worried for the woman's welfare but figuring she got herself here so she can get back. I should have offered her a drink and rest but it isn't my house.

Her relationship with Nathan must be more serious than I thought. Should I have invited her in?

My head hurts.

Oh well, it's not my business. I just hope she doesn't think I'm out to steal her man because I'm totally not. I don't want a reputation as boyfriend stealer.

The village is small; word travels.

I pad into the room and fire up my laptop. There's nothing much I can think of doing that I'd enjoy, so moments later I switch it off and blow out a breath of air. I hate how grey the skies are up here. I daren't venture through the trees when the sky is so dark, even though it's two in the afternoon. I might get lost, even if I do follow the markings I placed on trees.

My geography never was very good and I never could figure out how to work a compass. It points north, that's great. But even if it points north, I won't know which direction will take me back to the village. Although I do have GPS on my phone, I'm lucky if I can get a signal long enough to receive a text message, let alone an internet connection.

I miss my friends. I miss being close to people I know.

Part of me even misses my mum, even if I do hate her guts right now.

Picking up my phone, I scroll through my contacts until I find Tommy's number. It rings a few times before he answers, which brings me joy I haven't felt in a while.

"Hey you," he says softly. "It's been a while."

"Yeah," I say and move into the kitchen. Reception is better in here. "I miss you."

"Miss you too. Maybe I can come out and see you soon."

"I'd love that." Seriously I would. "What have you been doing?"

"Not much." He pauses for a moment. "I passed."

"Oh my god." Blink. "Oh my god! Tommy, that's brilliant. I'm so pleased for you."

"Thanks, Gwen. University isn't the same without you though."

My joy flickers to sorrow. "Yeah. I miss it."

"You'll go back one day. Until then, keep making delicious food and send me pictures. When I come down, I'm never leaving your place and you're never leaving the kitchen. I want a feast fit for a king," he demands playfully. "Sasha misses you."

"I miss her too."

"How are things with Nathan? I bet it's weird, isn't it?"

You have no idea. "Just a tad. He mostly stays out of my way though. I don't even know where he is today."

"Are you getting on?"

Are we? "Yes. There have been a few disagreements," understatement of the century, "but we've moved past them."

"Why do I feel like you're not telling me something?"

I just can't be bothered to go into full details of the tale that is Nathan and Guinevere. It's too complicated and I wouldn't even know where to begin. "I'm telling you everything."

"Okay." He doesn't believe me. "I have to go. I'm meeting Zoe in twenty minutes. Keep in touch." Zoe?

"You too."

I hang up the phone and walk over to the fridge. I hope he can come down. If he does, I'll definitely make him a feast fit for a king.

My mind drifts to Nathan and although I'm still angry at him, I'm wondering if he'll be back for dinner. I text him and ask him, but after an hour I still have no reply.

The fridge is bare and needs restocking urgently. There's not much in the way of good meal food but what is there is edible.

I'm desperate to do the shopping but Nathan still isn't back and the sun has finally started to descend. Leaning back, I pick at my meal and casually rub my stomach. Today has been a better day, not a great one, but with the anger I've felt it's helped to keep my mind from the things it seems to like clinging to, such as Caleb and how much I ache for him.

I hate how much easier it's becoming. It's still hard, really fucking hard, but it's not as hard.

The days don't move as slowly and the pain in my chest isn't constant. It only comes when I think of him or when I'm reminded of him. The pain is welcome. It reminds me that my life with him was real.

The door opens and shuts with a bang causing me to jump in my seat. Nathan strolls into the room, his tongue teasing his lower lip. He stops in the middle of the room and watches as I uncurl my legs from beneath me. "Get ready, I'm taking you out."

"What?"

"You heard me. Get ready."

"Where?" I ask, eyeing him as he turns back into the hall and grabs my jacket off the end of the banister.

"There's a... just get ready."

"Fine," I sigh and allow him to help me with my coat. In seconds we're outside and I'm being lifted into his car. "Now I'm intrigued."

He smiles slightly as he climbs into the driver's seat. "You'll enjoy it... I hope."

"Blondie came to see you today," I announce as the engine starts up.

"Who?"

"Lorna, your girlfriend."

His smile vanishes, only to be replaced with a frown. "She's not my girlfriend."

"Does she know that?"

"Yes."

"She walked all the way from the village."

His frown deepens. "Where was her car?"

Shrug. "I asked her the same thing. She didn't give me an explanation." I eye him warily for a moment. "Girls only do something like that if they feel more for you than whatever it is you think she feels."

"She's just a... we just... she's not my girlfriend."

"If you say so."

"I insist it," he responds, his tone clipped. "Can we stop talking about her now? How was your day?"

"It was uneventful. We need to go shopping. There is zero food in."

He sighs and glances at me. "Have you eaten?"

"Yes."

He chews on his lip for a moment, his eyes nervous. "Does this mean you're staying?"

Does it? "I... do you want me to?"

His head turns towards me, his eyes determined and set on mine. "Yes."

"I can't..." I look away an exhale a long breath. "I can't keep dealing with your mood swings. Things are..."

"I know. I'll do my best to stop being the way I'm being. I'm just not used to this." He gives me a sad smile before looking back to the road. "I'm glad you're staying."

Melting a little, I smile to myself. Fingers crossed things get better and stay that way. "Although I don't know how much longer I'll last without food."

"Okay, I'll do the shopping in the morning."

Now's my chance. "Can I come? I'd like to start cooking and baking again. If that's okay?"

"Sure. But if I say no to something, don't argue with me on it."

"Whatever." My mood just soared a little. "Thank you."

"How's the baby? I'm sorry I missed your appointment."

"I'm not diabetic or anything, thankfully."

"That's good then." He reaches over and places his hand on my bump, shocking the hell out of me. It spreads a warmth across and through me. "Does it kick yet?"

I wet my lips that suddenly dried. "Sometimes, but it mostly just feels like fluttering." I stare down at his hand. It feels weird and I'm uncertain how to react. It's not like Nathan to just casually touch me like he's done it a million times. He pulls back, sensing my discomfort most likely.

"If he starts again, tell me." He clears his throat and rubs his hand on his thigh. "If that's okay?"

"Sure." It's an unusual request from him but I don't have a problem with it. "Have your parents been in touch?"

"No and I don't want you to worry about them. They're my problem, not yours." He says this softly, regret evident in his features. "I'm sorry for everything that happened yesterday. I should have protected you. They weren't supposed to be back for another week."

I blink in shock at his apology. He's already apologized. Is that what this is about? "It's okay, I get it. We all do shitty things when we're mad."

His body tenses. "I hate it when you swear."

Oops. "Sorry," I mumble and look out of the window. "I didn't realise until I'd already said it."

"Try to. It doesn't suit you."

Okay then. "Where have you been today? You didn't respond to my text."

"Out," he says and that's all he says. Why does he have to be so cryptic and closed off? It only makes me even more curious as to what he's thinking and doing and everything else he could possibly hide in that closed off mind of his.

"Out?"

"As in not in the house."

"As in the location known as…"

He chuckles, his eyes sparkling in the dark. "Out."

"You're so weird."

His smile widens. "Yes. Probably."

"Where are we going?"

"Out."

"Grr," I growl, wanting to nipple twist him. "You're so frustrating."

"As are you."

"I am not."

He quirks a brow at me, his eyes still twinkling in a way they never have before. "Are too."

"Are we seriously doing this?" I giggle, my body shaking with it. "Let's just agree to disagree."

"I'm not agreeing to anything until you agree that you're frustrating."

"Tell me where we're going and I'll agree."

He throws his head back and laughs loudly. "That's the same as agreeing."

"See?" I prod him in the chest. "You're frustrating."

"I never denied it." Good point.

Still… "You're really not going to tell me where we're going?"

"No."

"Not even a clue?" I stick out my lower lip and clasp my hands under my chin.

"Not the puppy dog eyes, anything but the puppy dog eyes," He jokes, pretending to shield his face with his hand.

"Is it working?"

He instantly sobers. "No."

"Damn."

"Nice try."

"I thought so."

We've been driving now for the better part of an hour and I have no idea where we are. Too many trees guard the roads. It's when we reach a clearing that my heart starts beating with excitement.

"No way!" I grin and press my face against the glass. "A theme park?"

"It's a night festival, only here for two weeks," he says as I take in the lit up Ferris Wheel in the distance and a few other rides I can just barely make out. "I can't go on any of the rides."

"I know, but there's more than just rides."

"This is great!" Seriously and utterly great. "I want candy floss."

He opens his mouth and I know it's to protest but he soon relaxes and instead he says, "You can have whatever you want."

"Brilliant. You rock."

It takes another ten minutes before we finally find the car park, which is mostly just a field with lots of cars. The place is packed and people are still arriving. At least I won't have to queue for rides, definite bonus.

There's a huge archway of flashing lights and balloons as we enter. I look up at it, smiling. Nathan seems unimpressed but I don't care. He leads me to the side and exchanges money for tokens. I get to keep the tokens.

We soon realise that the tokens are for the rides and not the games. The games cost even more money.

Nathan doesn't seem to mind though and lets me drag him to a game where you have to throw a ball in a bucket which rests on its side. It looks so easy. It's not. I fail every time.

"Let me try," Nathan laughs and hands the man behind the counter a note. He throws and fails the first time but the second time the ball stays put. On the final try the ball bounces off the ball already in the tub and onto the ground. "Huh."

"Next time." I shrug and pull him towards the candy floss stall. He doesn't want to budge. Instead he quietly hands me a note and waves me away. Laughing, I head over to get candy floss and donuts on my own.

Nathan is clearly occupied. He won't win. I'll let him figure that out on his own.

As the donuts flip in the fryer, something soft brushes my cheek. I turn and blink in shock at the brown teddy dressed as Superman. "You won."

Nathan grins, clearly proud. "Of course I did."

"Is that for me?" I go to take the bear but he tugs it back.

"No."

My mouth drops open. "What happened to being a gentleman?" The sugared donuts are placed on the counter in a paper bag. I scoop them up and follow the man who won't give me the bear that looks like Superman.

"I never claimed to be a gentleman," he says haughtily.

"I want the bear."

"You got candy floss."

I pout like a petulant child. "It's not the same."

His smile comes back and it almost blinds me. "You can have the bear." I reach for it but again he snatches it back. "When you've finished your food."

"Want some?" I wave the floss near his face. He shudders and shakes his head. "More for me." Then I hold the bag open that contains the donuts. "Donut?"

The look that flashes over his eyes shows me that he does want the donuts, but I'm guessing they're too messy for him to want to hold. Suddenly I see him in a whole new light. How frustrating it must be to not want anything on your hands, the two things you use most throughout the day.

"Take this for a second." I hold the candyfloss out to him. He holds the stick with the tips of his fingers, shuddering once more. My fingers grip the sugary snack and pull it from the bag. "Here."

"You're touching it," he says with a small shake of his head.

Sigh. "I haven't touched that side." I move it close to his face. "Come on. You know you want to."

He leans forward and wraps his teeth and lips around one side, sighing slightly. "I forgot how good they were."

"More?" I bite into the one he's already broken into and groan in delight. "Best donuts ever."

"More," he says, so I hold the same one up to his mouth. He bites the half of the broken ring that I haven't bitten. "Definitely the best donuts ever."

I click my tongue and shake my head. "Wait until you try mine."

"You make donuts?"

"Sure, it's actually really easy," I say but my attention immediately becomes distracted. "Oooh, look!"

"It's a ring toss."

"I'm aware of what it is, Sherlock. Come on."

"I hate ring toss."

"That's because you suck at it."

He pretends to be insulted. "I do not." Determination comes across his features. "I guarantee I'll beat you."

"You couldn't beat a rug."

"Why would I want to?"

Good point. "Ring toss."

"Dispose of the cloud of sugar." He holds the pink candyfloss out to me. I take it, have another bite and throw the rest into a nearby rubbish bin. "Donut."

"I'm not throwing away the donuts," I gasp in feigned horror that he could even think about doing that. Donuts are the king food of carnivals. Well, it's either donuts or hotdogs.

"No." He taps his mouth.

"Oh." I pick another from the bag and hold it to his mouth. He takes a bite, his eyes on mine.

"Thanks."

"No problem." I close the bag after giving him two more bites and popping the last piece into my mouth. He cringes so I give him a pointed look. "What?"

"My mouth has touched that, yet you still eat it."

I shrug and tuck the bag of donuts into my jacket pocket. "Do you have some kind of horrific virus I might contract?"

"No." He pulls a face to show how genuinely disgusted he is at the thought.

"Then I'm sure I'll survive. Now stop delaying the inevitable and watch me kick your arse at ring toss."

He lets out a snort that makes me snort and to the ring toss we go.

***

"I had the disadvantage," I grumble, glaring at the ground as I walk.

"Oh yeah? What's that?" Nathan smiles, looking far too proud of himself.

"The belly." I pat my swollen stomach. "I can't swing my hips during the toss like I used to."

"Excuses."

My mouth drops open. I refuse to take that. "It is a legitimate excuse."

"In your world I believe it is." He slides his hand down my arm, his hand stopping to circle my wrist. That's strange. Not uncomfortable, but definitely strange. Is this his version of holding hands? Or is his arm aching from the ring toss, meaning he can't be bothered to hold onto my bicep? "Ferris Wheel?"

"Will I be allowed?"

He shrugs. "Only one way to find out."

We stand in the queue for fifteen minutes before we make it to the front. The guy looks at me, looks at my belly and opens the chain to let me through. Yay.

We sit in the not too sturdy looking metal seat and click the bar in place. I laugh when Nathan wipes at it with a napkin after squirting the metal with his hand sanitizer.

With us both in one car the fit is tight, or at least this is how I rationalise his arm around my shoulder. We start ascending slowly. The chill gets cooler the higher we get, but I don't mind. The arm around my shoulders is serving a purpose other than making me feel uncomfortable.

"I like the direction they've faced this. It's beautiful, even in the dark," I comment, looking out over the large fields that curve on the horizon. It's not amazingly high, only sixty feet at best, but it's high enough for me to truly appreciate everything within viewing distance.

"I feel like a child up here." He doesn't say it with disdain, more like awe.

"Me too. Everything just vanished."

"What vanished?" He turns to look at me as we finally reach the top.

I look into his beautiful light brown eyes, for once not recognising them as Caleb's but recognising them as Nathan's. "Everything that we left down there."

His eyes sparkle and his lips twitch. "You're so strange."

"Shut up." The seat rocks slightly as I turn away from him and rest my head back against his shoulder. "Let's just stay up here for an hour."

"Too late, we're descending," he whispers and rests his chin on top of my head.

"Actually, that's not such a bad thing. My bladder is chewing on itself."

"Nice."

"I thought so."

He helps me off as soon as we reach the platform. By this point I'm bouncing continuously on the spot.

"I'll just be over here," Nathan says and points towards the main area. Whatever, too full in the bladder to care.

The ladies queuing push me to the front which is a relief. By the time I'd made it to the toilet I would have peed myself. Gross but true.

Now... where is he? Ah... what's that he's tucking into his jacket? Where's my Superman bear?

"Where's my bear?" I frown.

"Right, wait here," he says and paces back to the Ferris wheel. I'm relieved to see him return with the bear. I don't remember him leaving it there when we took our turn, but to be honest I was far too excited to pay attention. "Here." He shoves the thing in my arms and grips my wrist again. "Let's go."

"But..."

"It's late."

"We've only been here for an hour."

He pinches the bridge of his nose and I know he's had enough.

"Okay, let's go."

His soft eyes come to mine. "I'm sorry. I'm exhausted, I've been awake since midnight."

"Why midnight?"

"I went out."

Gasp. "That's what time you left? Are you crazy?"

He gives me a look that instantly makes me shut my mouth. None of my business, I keep forgetting.

"Ready?" He diverts the subject which I'm grateful for and leads me away from the fun.

"Aww, photo booth, Caleb loved those. We went to a place called Pleasure Island once and went crazy in a photo booth. Ended up with more strips of photos than walls to cover." I smile fondly at the memory.

"Do you want to?" He motions to the small booth with a wave of his hand.

Do I? "No, that's okay." It wouldn't be right.

"Are you sure?"

"Yes." I nod because I am definitely sure. "I'm actually kind of tired now that you mention it."

My eyes close and stay closed before we even make it out of the car park.

***

It's morning when I wake and the curtains have been pulled wide open. "It burns."

"Come on, up," Jeanine says and pulls the covers from my 'could be' naked body. My superman teddy almost falls from the bed. I snatch him back to me and rub my face in his silky fur.

"Why?"

"It's eleven fifteen," she says in a singsong voice. "And the skies are no longer grey. Can't stay in bed when the sun is shining, dear."

"Okay," I say around a yawn and sit up with my legs crossed, the bear nestling in the dip. "I can't get changed with you here."

"I'm leaving." And leave she does.

As I decide what to wear, I can see all of my clothes have been neatly hung up again. I make a mental note to thank Jeanine later.

Wait...

I'm in my vest and knickers.

Gasp.

Nathan has seen me in my vest and knickers. Nathan undressed me!

Be calm. It's all good. He's seen plenty of women naked before... I think. Why am I obsessing over this?

I get dressed, pushing the ridiculous thoughts from my mind and quickly brush my teeth after washing my face. Finally I feel refreshed and my eyes aren't sticking together.

"Knock, knock," Nathan says instead of actually knocking. Although the door is open so I can understand this logic. I think. "Any plans today?"

"I was going to call Paula."

"Do you need the car?"

"Umm," I shrug and start running the brush through my hair. "Can I?"

"Yes, I don't need it." His eyes look me up and down as I sit at the desk turned vanity table. His light brown eyes linger over certain spots but I pretend not to notice. I shouldn't notice.

"Thank you." I wind the bobble around my hair to hold it in place and stand to face him, trying not to meet his eyes due to the awkwardness of knowing he's the second man to ever see me in my underwear. "How do I look?"

"Pregnant," he teases. I waddle past him, punching his arm as I go. "Oh and one more thing..." He throws me his car keys and I catch them clumsily. "No food or drink in the car."

"Okay." I start towards the stairs.

"Another thing." I look over my shoulder and see him strolling towards me, so I turn to face him. "Go grocery shopping, buy what you want... within reason. No peanuts, no liver, nothing that's damaging."

"Really?" I smile. Oh my god I'm smiling. He notices too and his eyes go to my mouth, his face softening.

"Really." He holds out his wallet.

"You want me to take your wallet?"

"It only has notes in it," he responds with a shrug.

My smile gets wider. "I should say no but I'm too excited for cake." The moment gets better when he smiles too. "Thank you, Nathan. I thought you wanted to come?"

"And deny the house cook her chance to shine?" I like this Nathan; he's all friendly and teasing. It suits him, oddly enough.

"Have fun, drive safe."

"Promise," I say and descend the stairs. "Do you want anything while I'm out?"

"No." I start to move again. Then I halt because he calls my name.

"Yes?" I add extra emphasis on the S, my eyes narrowed suspiciously. He's stalling... but why?

"You don't just look pregnant." He takes a step down, his eyes coming to mine.

"I don't?"

"No." He shakes his head, his breath leaving him. "You look beautiful."

My breath leaves me too. *I... it's... they... but...*

"See you soon," I shout quickly as my hand closes around the handle and pulls it open and close the door behind me. What the fuck was that? Maybe I shouldn't swear but that was cause for cursing.

You look beautiful.

You look beautiful.

You look beautiful.

Is this a platonic compliment? Surely he wouldn't... couldn't even think about such a thing. I've only just lost Caleb. It's only been a month since his funeral.

This is so messed up.

I'm reading into it. All I ever do is overanalyse things.

Nathan is aloof and mean but he's also not. In fact, I'm wondering now if the Nathan I knew is even the real Nathan at all. Which leads me to wonder why such a clearly sweet, kind, generous and handsome man would ever put on such a horrid mask.

His desperation to have me stay clearly runs deeper into him than I realised. Or maybe it doesn't. I don't know him well enough to make that judgement, but I also saw a broken man in his eyes. Is that because he lost his brother or is that because of something deeper?

Why am I overanalysing everything again? Is my mind really that desperate to think of anything but Caleb and what I've lost?

Am I trying to find someone more broken than myself?

***

Even though I said she didn't have to, Paula also escorts me around the supermarket after three hours of traipsing mindlessly through the village. It's a few miles out of town but it's big enough and has everything we need. I'm grateful that she pushes the trolley. My back is killing me.

"So what are your plans now that you're here?" She asks as I throw a variety of sauces into the trolley. A home isn't a home if you don't have condiments.

"To have the baby. That's all I've figured out so far," I admit and wince when she smiles with pity.

"How long do you have left, dear?"

"About seventeen weeks, if the baby waits that long."

I turn down the bakery aisle and instantly start grabbing things from the shelves. Paula continues light conversation, asking if I have everything I need, nursery wise.

I don't have everything I need. I don't even have bottles or nappies. Damn, I really need to get my head together. Will the baby be in my room or will they be in a nursery? Where's he or she going to sleep?

I should ask Nathan but he's already giving so much. I'll just have to use what little money I have left to prepare. This is my baby and my responsibility. Part of me wants to get a job, but I'm not stupid enough to try. Nobody is going to hire me in this condition and I'd be a fool to think otherwise.

My phone begins to ring and I check the screen before answering. His voice and angry tone are immediate. "Where are you?"

"Not even a hello?" I quip.

"Hello." He barks. "Where are you?"

"I'm just getting groceries," I explain, moving away from Paula so I can have some semblance of privacy. "Is everything okay?"

"It's almost five."

"And?" I'm confused as to why that's an issue.

I hear him exhale out an exasperated breath. "And it'll be dark soon. You've been gone for hours."

"Okay, I'll be there in about an hour." I grab a couple of bags of flour and throw them in the trolley, coughing a little when a tiny poof of powder hits me in the face. It's not enough to cover my skin but enough to make my lungs constrict for a moment.

"You're getting sick. I'm coming to get you."

"It was a bag of flour," I groan, almost stomping my foot on the ground. "I'm going stir crazy at the house. I haven't been food shopping in forever. Let me have this."

He hangs up without responding. I get my arse into gear, get the things I want and need, pay for them and say goodbye to Paula.

Nathan was right about it getting dark soon. I'm half way home and it's pitch black. Fortunately I don't mind driving in the dark so it's not too difficult. I just hope he isn't having some kind of mental breakdown.

He has no right to give me a curfew.

Or does he?

It is his house.

Damn this is so confusing and annoying and... gah. I'm going to go home, have a cake, a decaf cappuccino and curl up on my window seat with my headphones on.

When I park outside the large house, I smile. It looks like a postcard. Most of the lights are switched on inside making it glow in the midst of the trees.

My picture perfect image is ruined when the front door flies open and Nathan storms out. He starts shouting before he even makes it to the car. "You left at noon!" I climb out on a sigh.

"I'm fine, Nathan." Opening the boot, I start grabbing bags. Nathan snatches them from my hands. "No lifting. I'm extremely disappointed in you, Guinevere."

"For lifting?"

He shoots me a look that makes me pinch my lips together in an effort to not give him the same look back. "For driving home in the dark. You don't know these roads."

"I'm a good driver."

"What would Caleb say?" He hisses. A whimper escapes me. I don't want to think about that. I don't want to talk about that. "I'm not trying to make you miserable..."

"I don't want to talk about this anymore," I say quietly, my tone warning.

I move towards the house, my heart thudding and my face burning as my anger cooks. Who does he think he is? I'm twenty one, not five.

Nathan follows me in, his hands full. "You're acting like I'm the bad guy here."

"Aren't you?" I bite back and start putting away the shopping. "What the hell is wrong with you? You seem to want to control everything I do."

He runs the tip of his tongue over his bottom lip, his annoyance barely concealed. "I'm just trying to help you, Guinevere."

"Help me?" I scoff and spin to face him. "Well thank you, Nathan, for putting a roof over my head and buying me food, but that doesn't mean you get to control my actions or what I do. I'm an adult. You need to remember that."

"And you need to control yourself and your own actions before you end up harming yourself or that baby!"

I gape at him. He did not just go there.

"You're grieving. Your thoughts aren't your own. Especially if you think it's acceptable for a pregnant woman to be carrying heavy things and driving at night."

I laugh once. "You're kidding, right? How many pregnant women in the world have done both of those things and have lived to tell the tale? You're being dramatic and completely intolerable."

"Where are you going?"

"Away from you." I make my way to the stairs.

"I'm not done talking to you."

"I don't get it," I spin on this shout, my hands on my hips. "Honestly, I genuinely don't get it. I thought after yesterday we were friends."

He cringes. "What about yesterday?"

"The Ferris wheel, the donuts, everything." I half shout, my anger bubbling to intolerable levels.

"Just because I decided to be kind doesn't mean you can put yourself or that baby in unnecessary danger."

"Oh my god," I laugh, seriously not believing this. I could scream right now. "What the hell is wrong with you?"

He shakes his head, a frown on his face. "Nothing is wrong with me. You're my brother's fiancée; I'm just trying to do right by you."

"Stop bringing up Caleb!"

"It's true."

"And completely irrelevant!"

"But still true."

I throw my hands up and turn away. I've had enough of this. "You're impossible."

"Don't walk away from me."

"If I could run, I would."

"We're not done talking."

"Oh we are." I look at him over my shoulder, my eyes connecting with his. He looks as angry as I feel. "We are so done. The sooner I get out of here the better."

"And where will you go? What will you do?" He follows me up the stairs. "I asked you a question."

Stopping outside my door, I place my hand on the handle and my forehead against the wood. "Do you know what is bad for a baby? Stress. And you are piling it on. I feel like I'm walking on eggshells. You clearly can't make up your mind on whether or not you like me. It's best if I leave."

Something seems to have struck a chord in his system because his face has softened. "You're right. I apologize for causing you stress."

"Your apology isn't accepted. I get he was your brother, but he was also the love of my life." A flash of pain swims through his light brown eyes. It's gone in an instant and I wonder why it came in the first place. So far he's showed no signs of grief over the death of his brother. Has he been hiding it? "I only put him to rest five weeks ago. I should still be a grieving mess, but for you, to make you feel more comfortable, I've been trying to perk up a bit. I haven't had time to grieve properly. You of all people should be the main one to show me compassion right now."

"I apologized."

"It was insincere and I don't want it anyway. Just leave me alone." I open my door and step inside, making sure to lock it behind me.

I rest my back against the door and listen to him sigh. "It's not a good idea." What? "This, you and me, the whole 'being friends' thing. I was stupid to try." Ouch.

His footsteps disappear from earshot after another minute and I let out the breath I didn't realise I'd been holding.

Lying on my bed I touch my sweet Caleb's face, my fingertips hating the cold feel of the glass that protects the photo. A tear slides from my eye.

"I'm scared, Caleb," I admit and hug a pillow tight to my chest. "I'm so damn scared of doing this alone."

His easy smile shines back at me and, for once, it doesn't comfort me in the slightest. I want to throw it across my room but my conscience tells me I'll later regret this, so I refrain.

CHAPTER FOURTEEN

"YOU KNOW? MY MOTHER always told me that if I kept pulling a face and the wind changed, my face would stay that way forever," Jeanine comments, but her attempt to cheer me up hasn't worked.

"Maybe that's what's already happened to me," I say and move the books from the shelf.

"You don't have to help me. This is what I get paid to do."

"I know. I'm nesting I think." I've always nested. Since I was little I've been a thorough cleaner. Not to mention the fact I'm bored out of my mind and in need of something to do.

"Well, thank you, it's nice to have the company." She slides the couch along the floor and starts sweeping the dust that has gathered beneath it. "Oh and those cakes you made the other day, I thought I'd died and gone to heaven."

I smile a little. "Thanks. I think Nathan liked them. I came down the next morning and there was only one left in the centre of the plate." He was considerate enough to save me a cake that I made. I don't mind; it was nice to see they hadn't gone unappreciated. Besides, I never would have been able to eat the eight I made for Nathan and me.

Jeanine laughs at this as I continue to pile books neatly on the chair. This shelf needs a good polish. "Have you spoken to him at all?"

"Nope." Not in the past two weeks since we had that massive argument. I've made him breakfast, lunch, dinner and dessert every day, but I haven't seen him. "He's probably busy."

"That man will always astound me. He's so..."

"He's just the way he is." I cut her off, not wanting to slag him off behind his back no matter how badly he's pissed me off. "Not worth getting upset over."

It's at this point I hear a door upstairs slam and I wince. He heard me. Now I feel bad but I'll be damned if I apologize. Maybe he didn't hear me; maybe he just likes slamming doors.

I almost laugh at this last thought because Nathan has to be the quietest man I know. He slammed the door because he wanted to be heard.

"I think that shelf is sparkling as much as it can," Jeanine says, breaking me from my thoughts. "The next one needs a good clean."

"Right." I blink myself back to reality and start piling the books back on the shelf. Something just tapped me on the foot. That better not be a spider. Or worse... a rat.

I squat and pick up the small square of paper. It's a note I think, maybe a book marker of some sort.

My thumb hooks under the folded edge and slowly begins to part it.

"Everything okay?" Jeanine asks, reminding me I'm not alone.

"Yeah." I stand and tuck the small square into my pocket. "Just dropped a receipt."

"You know, this house is hundreds of years old. Don't let its modern interior fool you. I bet there are lots of little things left behind from Nathan's family line," she says, her voice high and thoughtful. There's no pulling the wool over Jeanine's eyes, that's for sure. "In fact, during my times of cleaning I've found a few things myself. Love notes, letters, old pictures and drawings. It's amazing the places they've turned up."

This fuels my curiosity further. "Where are they all now?"

"I imagine Nathan put them away somewhere. I gave them all to him."

"Great. If you ever find anything else, please let me know." I'm relieved when she agrees and hastily get back to my dusting. I shake every book, old and new, but find nothing else. I'm not sure why I'm interested. I don't even know if the paper in my pocket is a note. I'm definitely going to find out later when I'm away from curious eyes.

Jeanine leaves at eleven and I quickly start on lunch, glad to be busy again. Every day I come up with something even messier to make. I swear I'm doing this just so I have something to do.

Nathan doesn't come down, even after I've finished and sit at the table picking at my food. I don't blame him. Things are weird between us right now.

The weather isn't too bad so I pull on my walking boots and jacket after lunch and head out into the cool air. It'll be autumn soon and I can't wait. I can only imagine what these beautiful trees will look like when their leaves die in the most colourful way. It's a sad notion, it's sad when anything dies, but at least new leaves will grow in their place. Unlike Caleb. I'll never be able to replace Caleb.

This baby will never be able to have that father slot filled. I hold true to my word, the word I gave Caleb when he made me promise to never leave him.

I'll never leave him, never.

No man will ever replace him.

With my chalk in hand, I go a different route this time, my feet steady and sure as I plod along, marking the tree trunks as I go. This time I'm heading behind the house and through the trees that way. I'm not sure why but I just feel like this is the place I want to go this time. The trees are a lot thinner here and there is a foot path covered in small twigs and rocks. I still don't risk not marking the trees, even though there's a path to follow. I'll probably get lost either way.

As I walk along the dirt trail I pull the folded square from my pocket and slowly start to peel it open. It's not a note. It's a picture.

I gasp when I see what it is and instantly close it out of shock. It's Caleb, stark naked, aged seven at least. Blinking through my shock I open it again and laugh at the scowl on his face. He doesn't look happy being photographed nude, not that I blame him.

He's stood in front of a window, the light making his hair shine. I smile. He was adorable. Tears fill my eyes.

This is the only photo I've seen of Caleb as a child and, naked or not, I'm keeping it. I refold it and tuck it back into my pocket, happy to have a piece of Caleb with me as I continue along the trail.

My side is aching. I shouldn't have started walking so soon after eating. Oh well. I'm nearly at a clearing of some sort. Can't go back now.

When I make it to the edge of the trees, I nearly stumble on a fallen branch but manage to right myself at the last second. The grass here is long, at least up to my thighs. What if there are rats?

Who am I kidding? There most definitely will be rats, or foxes, or some kind of nature that wants to kill me.

Ooh, what's that?

My eyes pick up a piece of charred wood in the distance, poking over the long grass. Now I'm focusing on it, I see more charred pieces. How odd.

I really want to explore but I daren't wade through this jungle. Huff.

After a moment's deliberation I step forward, my leg instantly swallowed by the grass. I can do this. I can. My other leg comes forward.

The wind picks up making the grass sweep to the side like a million tiny hands beckoning me further.

Fuck this.

My rapidly beating heart urges me away. I follow its warning and run back the way I came. I'm never doing that again. Never.

Shudder.

I make it back home in record time due to the fact I'm running from imaginary rats that are nipping at my heels. My already ragged breath leaves me in a long heave as I make it inside and slam the door behind me. I place my forehead against it, relieved to still be alive.

I'm never going that way again.

Once my trembling has subsided I turn, only to crash into a familiar chest. Why was he standing so close? "Sorry, didn't see you."

"I've been stood here for three minutes." He smirks as I lean back to look up at him. His hands are gripping my biceps tightly but not too tight. "Are you okay?"

"Yeah, just imaginary demon rats," I mumble, causing him to cock his head in question. "Nothing. I was walking... ooh." I click my fingers. "I came across a field back there."

His body tenses. "Where?"

"Behind the house. I could see a load of charred wood."

"Oh." He runs his tongue over his lower lip. "It's an old barn that burned down not long after my grandfather died."

I cringe and place my hand on his chest between us. "I'm sorry for your loss."

"Hmm," he says but he looks pained to say it. He must have loved his grandfather very much. "Stay away from there. There are probably rats and other vermin I daren't name."

"I knew it," I whisper, my eyes narrowed and my mind flicking through images of demon rats lying in wait to feast on my poor pregnant body. "Did you eat lunch?"

He nods. "I did."

"If there's anything you want in particular, just let me know."

"You don't have to cook for me all of the time," he says irritably. "That's not why you're here."

"I know." I give him a shrug and manoeuvre past him. "Cooking is my passion I guess, or it used to be before..." Caleb. "But now it's just a way to get through the day."

"We should start setting up the nursery. How long do you have left?"

My mind goes blank for a moment. I never expected him to bring it up but I'm glad he has. "Less than seventeen weeks."

"That soon?" He shudders a little. "I hope you know that I have no idea what I'm doing and no intention of stepping into Caleb's shoes. I've never even held a baby. To be honest, they freak me out and gross me out all at the same time."

Oh. "Oh. Is that..."

"I'll do my best to help you but I think if you need it, we'll hire a nanny or a professional of some sort."

"I'm sure I can manage," I lie because there's no way I'll be able to manage on my own. I have no idea what I'm doing either. I've never held a baby, never even been near a baby, and children freak me out too. This is why I can't blame him or hate him for his admission.

"Caleb was great with kids from what I can recall," he says and my heart plummets. "Always smiling, always happy and playful. The kids flocked to him." His hand comes up to cup my cheek and his thumb presses against the corner of my mouth. "So I'm guessing the key is to be happy and smiling whenever in the presence of a tiny person."

Gulp. "I don't think that applies to new-borns."

His thumb lingers for a moment before his hand falls away. "We'll figure it out." We? "There aren't many places nearby that sell furniture suitable for an infant. I'll take you into the city next week."

"Nursery equipment is really expensive, Nathan," I say quietly.

"I have money. Besides, when I get my hands on Caleb's trust fund you can pay me back." He winks and my heart flutters with glee.

"How are you going to do that?"

He smiles wickedly. "I'm taking my father to court."

My mouth drops open. "Just for Caleb's trust fund?"

"Yes and my own, they're what our grandfather left us, not what my father gave us. The only reason he could touch them is because we were stupid enough to keep them in their original accounts. My dad had been placed on both accounts to oversee them before we became of age. I never thought he'd do something so callous." He steps over to the small desk where he usually leaves his keys and opens a small drawer beneath it. I watch as he flicks through a bunch of envelopes before finding the right one and tucking it into his pocket. "It's not a large amount; it's more the principle than anything."

"Wow." I'm not sure what to say. "So, this house used to be your grandfather's?" He nods in response. "Why'd he leave it to you and not Caleb?"

"Guilt," he says, his tone deep and dangerous.

"Guilt?"

"Yes."

I wait for him to explain but he doesn't. "Okay. Do you... umm... want to do something?"

He looks regretful for a moment. "I actually have to go to the city to deal with a few things."

"Oh, okay." I take a step away from the door. "Well, drive safely."

"Aren't you going to ask me how long I'll be gone?" He looks surprised for a moment but his blank mask quickly falls into place.

"You told me to respect your privacy," I respond and twirl a lock of my hair around my finger. "Have a good trip."

He thanks me and reaches for the door but stops before his hand touches the handle. "I'll be back late this evening."

"I'll leave your dinner in the oven."

His eyes burn into mine with an emotion I can't read and don't care to explore further. "Thank you."

I start to make my way to the stairs when he calls out my name. I wince and glance back over my shoulder at him. What does he want now? Light brown eyes linger on me for what seems to be a long time. "You have twigs in your hair."

My mouth drops open as my hands frantically feel my head for said twigs. When I manage to find the last one and pull it loose, Nathan has already gone.

He couldn't have told me that when he was stood right in front of me? Or maybe that's why he was stood so close. Maybe he was going to pull them out himself.

Nah.

I race up to my room and immediately take the picture of Caleb from my pocket. Taking a sticker from an old label, I rip it in half and stick that part over his nude area. I want to see his face, the rest I don't mind missing out on.

He looks miserable and it hurts my heart. Parents can be bastards. My mum has naked pictures of me and I used to scream at her when she got them out to show my friends. He also looks adorable. His almost chocolate irises are shining so brightly considering this picture is most likely an old Polaroid.

"I miss you, baby," I say softly and touch his chubby cheek. "I wonder if Caleb junior will look like you. Is it wrong that I want him to, almost as much as I don't? I don't know what will hurt worse, if he does or he doesn't. If he does, I'll be constantly reminded of what we've both lost. If he doesn't, I won't get to gaze upon your face every single day for the rest of my life." I fold it up and put it back in my pocket.

Tears fill my eyes as I imagine my deceased fiancé standing directly behind me, moving the hair from my neck like he did so many times and placing his lips in the spot he cleared. Every time he did this I shivered and my skin broke out in goose bumps. My knickers would soak in seconds and usually his hand would snake around my waist and slide between my trousers and my underwear.

Just thinking about it makes me tingle in ways I shouldn't. My own hand follows the trail that Caleb's hand left so many times. It's harder with my stomach in the way, so I pop the button of my jeans and dip my fingers directly into the wetness that seeps from my core. A sharp breath leaves me as I imagine Caleb's hand working that sensitive nub. I do it exactly the same way he used to, circling slowly, picking up the pace as his other hand came up to tease my nipple. My hand follows this movement and I squeeze my full breast in one hand, still teasing my clit with the other.

Burning spreads through me and my mind conjures how it felt to have his lips and tongue tasting my neck, as my ears pick up on words once spoken but no longer there.

It starts in my clit before spreading up and around to every sensitive spot on my body. My nipples become erect; at this moment he'd press it with his thumb like a button before rolling it gently between his thumb and finger.

A strangled cry escapes me as I bring myself to the edge, my hand working quickly in my pants. I want to push my fingers inside but I can't reach, my stomach won't let me.

"Oh god," I breathe and continue my movements.

My eyes seem to darken as the burning and tingling focuses on one place in my lower stomach. I gasp and rub harder, willing it to burst forth.

It does and I almost fall to my knees but manage to free the hand teasing my breast and grip the desk with it. "Ah," I cry out as my breath comes out in pants and the explosive climax tears through me, ripping my body to shreds before finally piecing it back together with the lingering pleasure that lasts a few seconds after.

With one final shudder I collapse to the ground and cry. My body is exhausted and sated but my true desire is nowhere near fulfilled, nor will it ever be again.

It's been a while since I felt like screaming, but now the need to is almost unbearable.

Instead I stagger into the bathroom, turn on the shower and step under the cool spray without removing my clothes first. I should never have done that. I've never needed to do that before. Caleb was always the one to turn me on and finish me off. Every single time.

Not once during our entire relationship did I ever pleasure myself.

Now I just feel guilty and dirty. Why did I do that? I shouldn't even be feeling horny after everything that's happened. I'm weak.

Weak and stupid.

I'm lonely.

I'm lonely and tired, tired of being alone.

CHAPTER FIFTEEN

I REMEMBER WHEN SASHA told me not to lose myself to a darkness I'll never be able to climb out of. She was right, but she was also wrong. Caleb was my light. Sure there's darkness that I can't climb out of, but not because I lost myself, it's because I lost him.

The week drags on and nothing new or exciting happens. I continue cooking for an invisible man and cleaning with Jeanine. I search for photos, notes and other things that may prove to me that Caleb once existed and ran through this house.

Unfortunately I find nothing and I'm beginning to wish I hadn't started looking in the first place. The amount of disappointment I feel each time I don't find anything just pushes me further into that darkness.

On Tuesday I went into town and printed off a lot of pictures from my phone, wishing I'd done so sooner. This brings me a small amount of joy and an even bigger amount of frustration because I can't bring myself to look at them. They still sit on my dresser in a closed envelope, gathering dust that doesn't exist in this bleach scented house.

Part of me was hoping we'd go baby shopping this past week. Nope. Either Nathan forgot or he's changed his mind or maybe he's been busy. I don't know and I don't want to ask.

His moods are never certain and I can't deal with pushing him over the edge right now.

Why is he such a recluse? It can't be healthy.

It's none of my business.

Why do I pick at everything when Nathan pops into my head? I don't do it over anybody else. What is it about him that makes me want to protect him and slap him all at the same time?

He's a riddle.

I manage to roll out of bed just after nine and get ready by nine thirty. By ten I have breakfast made and served, but I hold no hopes that I'll be dining with anyone this morning. Jeanine doesn't work Saturdays and Nathan has been a no show for the past week.

The baby tumbles and twists in my stomach. It's extremely uncomfortable.

With a heavy sigh I sit back and pull up my shirt to reveal the stretched skin. Its surface is shiny and moving as hidden limbs press against it from underneath.

That is really weird.

I can see it. Only slightly, but I can definitely see it.

"CAL..." I start to shout and bite my tongue to stop myself. "NATHAN!" I shout instead. He doesn't respond so I shout louder.

"Yes?" He calls and I hear his footsteps along the first floor.

I wait for him at the bottom of the stairs. "You have to see this. It's like something out of Alien."

"What is?" He looks perplexed, not that I blame him.

After walking into the room, I sit on the couch and slowly lift my shirt once more.

"What are you doing?" Nathan looks panicked.

I smile and beckon him closer. "Look!" I prod my belly and watch as it jiggles and moves ever so slightly. "Isn't that weird?"

He kneels on one knee by my legs to get a closer look, his brow furrowed. "That's definitely weird."

I snort and place my hand on the top of it, smiling as I feel the kicks as well as see them.

"May I?" He asks, his brows still furrowed.

I shrug. "Sure."

Teasing his lower lip with his tongue, he reaches forward and places one gloved hand on my stomach. The baby wiggles again and his hand moves back in a flash. He flexes his fingers and this time moves both hands to my stomach. "That's amazing," he says and strokes his glove clad hands all over my bump. His eyes sparkle as they meet mine. "Does it hurt?"

"It's a new feeling, so it is slightly uncomfortable," I admit and watch as Nathan continues to feel the baby move. "Your hair needs cutting," I say, reaching forward with my hand to tuck the longish dark locks behind his ear. It almost immediately pings back forward but it's nearly at the length that Caleb used to have it. "You've been hiding in your room for too long."

His fingers slide up my sides. I inhale a sharp breath. What is he doing?

They hook around the edge of my shirt and slowly slide it over my belly. His eyes come to mine and stare intensely. "Let's go out."

"Where?"

"To the city. We'll stay the night."

"Okay," I breathe, wanting to turn my eyes away but not having the willpower to do so. "Why?"

"Baby equipment, you only have four months left."

"Four months and two weeks," I correct him.

He rolls his eyes. "Don't split hairs."

"Ugh, my mum used to say that to me," I mumble and let him pull me off the couch.

"Stay here, I'll gather our things."

"Our?"

He gives me a quick nod before leaving the room. How does he know what things I need? I'm a little uncomfortable with him going through my underwear drawer.

On that thought I dash up the stairs and into my bedroom where a bag is open on my bed and Nathan is walking back and forth, placing things in neatly. "This is weird."

"I told you to wait downstairs."

"I couldn't resist watching you pack my bag. It's a little odd."

He frowns at me, all the while folding a dress top. "Didn't Caleb ever pack a bag for you?"

"Yes but..."

"Then why shouldn't I?"

Is he serious? "Are you serious?"

"Yes."

"Because I was... you know... with Caleb."

His lips twitch. "You were *what* with Caleb?"

I watch him place a top of mine into the bag, my cheeks heating. "I think that's pretty obvious considering my predicament."

He lets out a light laugh, his almost chocolate eyes sparkling with humour. "If I didn't know you were pregnant, I'd think you were a virgin."

Splutter. "I... This is not a normal conversation. Besides, we were all virgins once, it's nothing to be ashamed of."

His hand stops on the zipper midway across the bag and a dark look comes over his features. "Yes. Once."

"Shall we go? Or would you like me to pack your bag for you?" I'm joking obviously, but I don't think he knows that because his brow quirks. "I desire nothing more than to randomly start going through your underwear drawers."

"I was just trying to be nice. Besides, I didn't actually look. I only glanced." He sighs and places my bag on his shoulder.

"That's what they all say."

"Who?" He doesn't actually sound interested, more irritated and bored of my teasing.

"Men who're caught going through your underwear drawer," I joke and elbow him in the arm.

He sighs again and gives me a gentle nudge towards the stairs. "Quickly before I change my mind and give you a cardboard box and a single nappy to live on."

"Ouch." I grin and make my way towards the stairs. "I'll wait in the car." He nods and throws me his keys, sighing – yet again – when I don't catch them. They bounce down the stairs before sliding along the floor a few inches.

"Bad throw," I comment before he can tell me I'm a bad catcher.

I am, but he doesn't need to rub it in my face.

He responds with a scoff of disbelief as I scoop them up from the ground and rush out of the house. The air is chilly today, a tell-tale sign that autumn will soon be upon us. I don't mind autumn so much, it's winter that I can't stand. I'm more of a warm day on the beach kind of girl. Or I used to be at least. Not anymore. Now none of it matters because I don't have my favourite person in the world to spend it with.

Soon I'll have another person. I climb into the car stroking my belly. I wonder if giving birth to the baby will take away the pain. Maybe it will fill the gaping hole in my heart.

Nathan climbs into the car ten minutes later and we set off for the city. This time it only takes us an hour and a half; the traffic wasn't too bad on the way.

I'm so excited by the time we get there that I barely let him stop the car before I'm out and around to his side. This will be a great thing to focus on. Plus, what woman doesn't want to decorate a nursery?

"Which room will be the nursery? We haven't discussed it," I ask as I place my hand on his arm and allow him to guide me along the busy street.

"There are two more rooms on your floor. Take your pick."

"Which room was Caleb's?"

He looks down at me, his face a blank mask. "He didn't have a room."

"He didn't?" That seems a bit odd. "What about you?"

"Me neither. I'm staying in my grandfather's room, although I had it remodelled when I first moved in."

I chew on the inside of my cheek for a moment, wondering whether or not I should push further. Of course I should. It's in my nature to push. "You two must have been close?"

"That's one way to put it," he mutters conspiratorially. "Here."

"This is a brand store." I gawp at 'Baby Dreams', a pregnant woman's dream and the expectant father's nightmare. "This is too much."

"I can afford it," he states and pulls me through the automatic doors.

I'm immediately assaulted by a welcome blast of cool air from the fans in the ceiling, but it's not this that makes me shiver, it's the store itself. I'm in baby heaven.

"I should have written a list," I mumble as I take a few cautious steps forward.

"We'll start with the big things and work our way down." Releasing his arm, I head into the section where nurseries have been set up with a single wall behind each.

They're all so cute and homely. I can't wait to start papering and painting the walls.

"I love this," I say as my eyes immediately zoom in on a strange green colour wall with white tree patterns reaching to the top. The furniture is dark brown and glossy and I'm in love. "I really love this. It's neutral and it's... holy... mother of..." I start to choke when I see the price tag. It's not extremely expensive but it's a lot more money than I considered spending on just the heavy furniture.

"You're sure?" He smiles at my look of shock. "You're sure."

Three hours later my ankles have swollen so we make our way to a nearby restaurant to stop for lunch. Nathan hasn't said much although he insisted on glass bottles for the baby and everything that isn't made of harmful plastic. I'm not even allowed disposable nappies but I don't mind the washable ones; they're pretty easy and last years. They have little poppers instead of Velcro and can be adjusted as the baby sizes up.

He even made me order the wool and water wet wipes, completely toxin and fragrance free.

After a while I let him take over. I wasn't in any position to argue seeing as he'd done research and I clearly hadn't. I was happy that at least one of us knew what we were talking about. He won't even consider me using powdered milk and insists breast is best, which is right but also annoying. I was going to breastfeed anyway but I don't like being told I have to.

I'm happy with the amount we got and I can't think of anything else we need right now. Secondly I can't wait until it's all delivered and I get to see it set up.

Something else to look forward to.

We're seated at a table right at the back of the restaurant, out of the view of others. It's a booth so I have to push the table out to fit inside which is annoying, but I soon cheer up when I see the menu. It's very diverse and I am starving.

"Ordered enough food?" He jokes, sliding closer to me.

I shake my head. "I want dessert too."

"Have whatever you want." He smiles and glances at my stomach. "It's the only time of your life you have an excuse to eat like a very large man."

I laugh at this and rest my temple on his shoulder. "You know? I can't even remember why I was mad at you before."

His cheek rubs against my hair and I'm instantly reminded of our time on the Ferris wheel. "Good, I don't like it when you're mad."

"Then stop peeing me off." I tilt my head back and look at him through my lashes. "Reckon you can handle that for more than a few hours?"

"I'll try," he responds quietly and presses his lips to my forehead. "You always smell like vanilla."

Umm... "That'll be the shampoo I use, and the body lotion."

"It's good," he murmurs. I feel his hand slide onto the cushioned bench between us, his gloved pinkie finger so close to mine I can feel the leather tickling the tiny hairs. My hand moves closer, only slightly,

The waitress comes and for some reason I move away after feeling a pang of guilt for being so close to another man. What is wrong with me?

We fall silent after ordering. Nathan taps away at his phone as I twiddle my thumbs and wait for the food to arrive.

"Oh my god, Nathan?" A high pitched squeal comes from an unknown female with dark wavy hair and a smile wider than the world itself. "When Tracy called..."

Nathan stares at the female for a moment. "Diane?"

"Umm... yes." She puts her hands on her hips and pouts like an infant. "You do remember me, don't you?"

"Do you?" I tease him, which earns me a glare.

Her eyes immediately come to me and her smile drops. I'm hardly invisible. "Who's your friend?"

"None of your concern," he bites out and leans forward. "Can I help you with anything, Diane?"

I shrink in my seat. This is awkward.

She hesitates for a moment. "No, I just wanted to say hi."

"And who was it that told you I was here?" He's definitely irritated.

The waitress chooses this moment to bring out our food. I sit up and thank her in a whisper. She senses the tense atmosphere and quietly slinks away. I don't blame her. I feel like hiding under the table right now.

"Tracy called; she saw you come in. Though she didn't mention her." She nods to me and frowns. I give her a little finger wag and stare at my food. Should I start eating without him? Yes I should.

"Okay, well hello, Diane." He gives her a pointed look. She just doesn't get it. "Goodbye, Diane."

Finally she blinks herself out of her stupor. "Call me."

"Honestly?" I can feel his anger. Ooh, the waitress brought me sauces in cute little pots. "I could be sat here with my wife."

She looks at me. "You his wife?"

I open my mouth to respond but think better of it and continue testing the dips with spiced potato wedges.

"You need to leave," Nathan warns, his eyes narrowed. "And next time you see me, don't acknowledge me." Ouch, that one has to hurt.

Her mouth falls open and pain flashes across her eyes. "Wow. What an arsehole. I was just saying hello."

"And then you told me to call you in front of my pregnant wife." Wait... what?

She looks at me, her brows raised. "You his pregnant wife?"

I open my mouth to respond but Nathan cuts me off. "Stop talking to her."

"I'll talk to whoever I choose. Just because we fucked doesn't mean you hold any kind of authority over me."

Nathan closes his eyes briefly and lets out a breath.

I hold up a chicken wing in front of Nathan. "Want some?"

"In a second." His hand goes to my wrist and slowly lowers it back to the table. "Are you finished?"

"Definitely," Diane spits and turns on her heel. "You weren't that good anyway." Then she looks at me. "Good luck having a life without oral."

Then she leaves and I can't hold it back. I laugh and laugh and laugh. I laugh harder than I have in ages and, for once, I don't feel guilty about it. "A life without oral, huh?"

"Shut up," he bites out.

"I'm going to have to divorce you for that reason alone," I choke through my laughter and slide down my seat a little.

He shakes his head but I see his lips stretch into a smile. "It isn't amusing in the slightest."

"Oh, it totally is," I gasp and continue laughing. "Best lunch date ever."

"I'm almost certain I don't like you anymore," he adds but his body starts to shake beside mine. "Stop laughing, it's contagious."

I finally calm, a smile still on my face. "You're adorable, Nathan."

He rolls his eyes. "Just what every man wants to hear. Eat your wings."

"Want one?"

"No thank you," he says after a moment's deliberation. We eat silently. I occasionally tempt him with the wings that I've been craving lately as I eat my own food. I'm shocked when he suddenly blurts, "If she hated it that much, why would she tell me to call her?"

"In front of your pregnant wife," I add and start laughing again.

He chuckles for a while before sobering. "Well you could have been. That female has no manners."

"Who was she?"

He shrugs and turns towards me. "Just some girl I dated half a year ago."

"How many dates?"

"One," he admits. "I think."

"You're disgusting," I giggle and finish off my last bite of food.

"No worse than Caleb." He immediately regrets his words. I see this but it does nothing to ease the sharp pain that slices into my heart. His face drops and his hands come to my face. "I'm sorry, I was just kidding. I didn't..."

"It's fine," I cut him off and lower my face so he doesn't see the tears there. "We should be able to talk about him. We can't keep pretending like he never existed."

His eyes scan my face and his tongue trails across his lower lip. "Dessert?"

"I'll pass," I respond and push my almost empty plate away. "I'm stuffed."

"Me too. Let's go."

I wait for him to slide out before I join him. He holds out his hand and I immediately give him my wrist.

Wait... "Who's Tracy?"

"Sorry?" He looks at me, a confused expression on his face.

"The Diane person, she said Tracy told her you were here. Who's Tracy?"

He thinks on it for a moment, his gloved fingers scratching at his neck.

I laugh a little again. "You don't know, do you?"

"Nope."

"Your memory is worse than mine."

"I only remember people and things that I care to remember." His eyes land on me and I can't help but feel like he's trying to tell me something with them. They glaze over as a memory comes to his mind. I wonder what it is but I don't ask. That's something I won't prod for. His thoughts are his own. "Let's go have that wander around the city I promised you but never came through on."

"I'd like that." I smile softly at him.

Chapter Sixteen

"I THINK MY FRIENDS Tommy and Sasha want to come and visit soon. During the holidays, maybe." I run my fingers over the teddy bears in Toy World. "Would that be a problem?"

"For the day?"

"For the day and night." I pick up a giraffe teddy and place it in the basket that Nathan is carrying.

"I don't see why it should be a problem; we have the space. As long as it's for just one night. I'm still getting used to having you around."

I pick up a strange rattle with a plastic pocket full of water. Nathan takes it from me and puts it back on the shelf. It's then I notice that the giraffe has gone as well. "Seriously?"

"They're choking hazards."

"They're teethers and teddies, you control freak." Eye roll. "And thank you, I'll let them know. It'll be nice to see them. I owe them after all they did after Caleb died."

He places his arm around my shoulders. "I can't imagine what you went through, being the one to find him."

"I didn't find him," I bite out, willing myself to say the words. "He died in my arms. I was sprawled across his chest like I usually was when I woke up. That's not finding him. If I'd found him it would have been a lot harder."

"What do you mean?"

"His last moments were with me and our baby, comfortable in bed. If I was to die, I'd want it to be just like that, holding the man I love whilst peacefully sleeping."

He picks up the giraffe and places it in the basket. I almost smile at his attempt to cheer me up. It was subtle but it was still an attempt and I'm grateful for that. "Do you ever think you'll fall in love again?"

Wow. "No. I can't give away a part of me that he took with him."

"Maybe one day." His head is ducked down, looking at some kind of kids' bath toy, so I can't see his face to get a grasp on why he's asking me these questions. Maybe he's worried I'll betray his brother before his ashes have a chance to cool.

"I promised him I'd never leave him..."

This time his head whips up. "You promised him that?"

"Yes."

"I'm pretty sure that promise became invalid when he passed, Gwen."

I shrug. "It's still valid to me."

He blinks, his face set with a frown. "Let's go, this place smells of sweat and children."

"I know, right? It's a relief from the usual scent of bleach at home," I joke.

"You'll get used to it."

"Funnily enough, Jeanine said that when I first arrived."

***

We stay in the same hotel as the last time we visited the city. He must have made reservations before we came because they handed him two keys and we came straight to it. We eat and shower, the latter being at separate times obviously. I make his bed on the couch as he showers and climb into the super soft king size. I feel only slightly guilty for taking his bed, but then I get over it as I sink into the mattress and groan with delight.

My eyes close and this time I fall asleep before he exits the bathroom.

"Guinevere?"

He calls quietly as I drift into the realm between sleep and waking. His footsteps get closer. "Gwen?"

I'm shocked when the bed dips right beside me but I manage to keep my face relaxed. I'm not sure why I don't look at him; my curiosity has always been a flaw. Right now I'm curious as to what he wants, but for some reason I know I won't get the true answer if I'm awake.

"Gwen?" His voice is hushed and a lot closer than a moment ago. His heat sinks through the thick quilt and into me, making my stomach flutter. I feel the smooth leather that covers his fingertips trail up my arm from the dip of my elbow to my inner wrist. My arm tingles and tiny bumps break out over the skin he touches.

He leans forward and this time my breath does hitch. His face gets closer to mine. I can feel his mint scented breath fan across my cheek. My heart races faster than it was and I wonder if he can hear it.

My thoughts are a jumbled mess.

My entire world stops when I feel his nose on mine. It trails gently up to the bridge before slowly moving back down. A barely there touch but I feel it. I feel it everywhere.

I can't handle it. This shouldn't be happening and I don't know why it is. His hand comes up and slides between my cheek and the pillow. He lifts my face ever so slightly, his nose now against the side of mine.

"Gwen?" He whispers, his voice sounding pained.

What's he doing?

Panic overcomes me when I feel his top lip breeze across mine.

His own breath speeds up as I feel his bottom lip touch mine.

"Don't," I beg, my eyes burning and now open.

His eyes widen a fraction as they stare intently into mine. My hand comes up and takes a hold of his wrist and, as I slowly push myself into sitting position, I move his wrist away.

"What are you doing?" I hiss, keeping my voice low.

After tugging his wrist free he stands and turns around. "Go back to sleep."

"Nathan..."

"Don't," he begs and walks to the bag by the couch.

Now I feel like shit. "Nathan. Please..."

"I said don't," he bites out and I watch him pull on his jeans under his robe. The sound of metal clanging against metal lets me know he's doing up his belt.

With cautious movements I make my way out of bed and softly pad over to him. I'm not sure what I'm going to do, all I know is I don't want him to feel like this. I'm not sure what I did to make him feel like this in the first place.

What was he thinking? Christ I'm so angry right now, but he doesn't need me shouting at him. Our wires must have gotten crossed somewhere along the way. The best thing I can do right now is to just try and understand him.

"Nathan," I try again and place my hand on his shoulder. The soft gown stops me from feeling his skin but I can still feel the heat seep through. "I don't understand."

"You wouldn't," he grits out, his tone clearly saying this is my fault and he's going to hold it against me.

I step forward and slide my arms around his waist, pressing my forehead between his shoulder blades. "I'm sorry. Please don't fall out with me again."

He lets out a long breath and grips my wrists tightly with both hands. Turning slowly in my arms, he brings his arms around me and rests his chin on top of my head while squeezing tight.

Suddenly I'm airborne and letting out a choked cry as he bends and lifts me into his arms. He carries me to the bed and slowly lowers me onto it. "Go to sleep," he whispers and presses his lips to my forehead.

"Are we okay?"

He doesn't respond, he only moves away from the bed. Five minutes later I hear the door close.

Someone shakes my arm. No. I want to sleep. "Up, breakfast is ready."

"I don't care," I grumble and pull the blanket over my head, smiling to myself.

"Come on." He says and tries to pull the blanket away.

"No. You eat it."

He chuckles. How I've missed that throaty laugh. "I'll just come in there with you and then neither of us will eat the breakfast I made. Just for you."

"Go away, Caleb." I whine and feel him slip into the bed behind me. "You probably only made cereal anyway."

He scoffs, feigning offence. "I did not."

"Toast then."

"Damn it, you know me too well." He runs his lips over the curve of my neck, his hand resting against my moving stomach. "I miss this."

"Me too," I say quietly and turn to face him. His light brown eyes shine in the dark, bringing tears to mine. "I love you."

"I love you too, Gwenny." He wraps his arms tight around me, his cheek pressing against mine. I love the feel of his breath against my ear; it makes my body tingle in the most delicious way. "You're perfect the way you are. Don't ever change. Never leave me. Never. I know it's selfish but I..."

My heart starts hammering as Caleb's healthy face distorts for a moment and suddenly I'm staring into the eyes of a sick man.

"I'll never leave you," I promise. "Just do me the same. Don't leave me."

"I love you," he says, his eyes filling with tears. They fall as he presses his mouth to mine. "So much."

"Then why'd you leave me?"

"I almost forgot." He smiles and slides down my body. I feel his lips press against my protruding stomach. "Love you, baby Weston."

"Caleb." I reach down to haul him back up to me. My hands find nothing but air. "Caleb!" I try to sit up but something's weighing me down. No, I want to go with him. Let me go with him!

My body jolts, zapping an electric current all through my legs and heart. I sit bolt upright, facing a dark room with sweat beading on my forehead. The space in bed beside me is empty and my grief returns tenfold. I feel like I've just lost him all over again.

Nathan sleeps peacefully on the couch as it's still dark out. I don't want to wake him but I can't stay in this bed, so I climb out and pad over to the bathroom to splash some water on my face. It does little to refresh me.

I sit on the closed toilet and rest my head in my hands, my hair falling around me in black curtains, shutting the world out and locking the pain in. Tears pool in my eyes and when I blink the first tear falls and then another. They sting my cool face. Another reminder that I'm a lonely mess with serious issues. My grief outweighs any of the good I've felt over the past couple of months, although that's not saying much seeing as I've hardly felt any good.

The door handle is pulled down and the door clicks open. "Gwen?" Nathan says and I feel him squat before me. His hands go to my wrists and I'm blinded by light as he pulls my hands away from my face. "What's wrong?"

"Nothing." I inhale a deep breath, willing my emotions to settle. "I just need a minute."

"Is this because of earlier?" He looks pained. "Because I am very sorry for..."

I don't even want to think about that right now. "No. It's... that's not why I'm crying."

"Then why are you crying?"

"I'm always crying, Nathan," I admit and wipe my eyes with a piece of tissue.

Standing, I move away from him and stop in front of the sink, resting my weight on my hands which grip the edge of the basin.

"Talk to me," he pleads and stands behind me. I look at him in the mirror through swollen eyes.

"I miss him."

He takes a step closer and runs his fingers through my hair. It's relaxing, soothing, but it's not his hands I want. "Me too."

"Why'd he die?" I whisper, my eyes still on his. "Do you think he fought to stay alive?"

"I know for a fact he did. Caleb wouldn't want to leave you."

"But he did."

Nathan shrugs. "I know, and one day you'll leave. So will I. It happens every day."

"I know that, I know it happens. I've just... it's just never happened to me before. I've never lost anybody that I love." Touch wood. "And then I lost him, I lost the one person who made me feel like... he just made me feel. He was perfect."

"He wasn't perfect, Guinevere."

I scowl at him. "To me he was and always will be. That's what love is."

"Blind?"

He just doesn't get it. "When you're in love, you learn to accept everything about that person and you love them for it, so even though little things annoy you, you know that it's one of the many things that make them who they are. When you love them so deeply you can feel it in your bones, that's what makes them perfect because you appreciate everything they are and everything they do."

"I think you're a tad naïve. If that were true then there wouldn't be so many people out there battling alcoholism and gambling addictions and what not."

I blink at his blindness. "That's different."

"But you just said..."

"I know what I said but that's not what I meant. Those are conditions, illnesses. Those may shape a person but they aren't who you are."

"So, for example," he clears his throat. "If I were to leave the toilet seat up and, hypothetically, you were in love with me, you wouldn't care?"

"No."

"But if I were to gamble or take narcotics you would?"

"Yes."

"Why?"

"Because the little things can't harm you. The little annoyances can't hurt you or hinder your ability to live a normal and hopefully peaceful life."

He licks his lower lip. "And what about my condition?"

"That's part of who you are. If you decide to speak to somebody about it that's your choice and I'd support you, but I'd never force you to do that. It's a part of you and if I were to be madly in love with you, I'd be in love with your quirkiness too."

He frowns, his eyes narrowing. "I am certainly not quirky."

"Whatever." I wave him off, wiping the last few tears from my eyes. "Now do you understand what I mean?"

"Yes, if I ever fall in love I hope I'll feel it, rather than just have a basic understanding of it."

This makes my heart ache. "You've never been in love?"

"Not reciprocated love, not a lot of people enjoy my 'quirkiness'." His lips twitch at the last word.

Eye roll. "I find that hard to believe."

"You heard what that wretched girl said earlier." He smiles brightly and my eyes go straight to his mouth where perfect white teeth shine at me. "I don't do oral."

At this I blush. I slap his arm and step back into him so my back rests against his chest. "Why'd you try to kiss me, Nathan?"

In a second his body goes from relaxed to tense and his eyes widen briefly. "I shouldn't have. I apologize."

"That's not what I asked."

"It's the only answer I'm willing to give," he retorts, his tone clipped. He steps away from me. "You should go to sleep."

I'm not tired but I agree after apologising for waking him up. He promises me it doesn't matter and retires to the couch after making sure I get to bed safely.

My mind is a jumble of thoughts. I want nothing more than to shut off my brain and its stupid obsession with overanalysing everything, but I can't.

Am I truly naïve?

***

I decided on the room across from mine as the nursery. It's the same size as my room but longer and narrower. It also has an indent in the wall where the cot should fit perfectly.

Right now the room is in tatters. Nathan hired some guys to come and strip the walls and decorate it the exact way it's decorated in store. I'm humming with excitement. Once I see the room, everything will be real. This is as real as it has all gotten so far and I can't deny that it is scaring me despite the excitement. I can't wait to go for long walks with the baby in the stroller. I can't wait to change his nappy and feed him. Mostly I can't wait to get back a piece of Caleb because I hope that it'll stop my grief.

"What if the doctor's right?" I say to Jeanine as we open the windows in an attempt to get rid of the stench of paint.

"About?" She asks, giving me an inquisitive look.

"What if I hate the baby?"

She lets out a startled laugh. "I'm sure he didn't say that."

"Not in those exact words."

She lets out a long sigh and turns me to face her. "My sweet girl, you don't have it in you to hate anyone. You're too kind. It's a flaw, as well as a very sweet blessing." Her smile is warm and understanding. "I had postpartum depression with Julie, my first. It was tough but I got through it. If it happens, it happens. It won't last forever. Just don't expect miracles."

"What do you mean?"

"This baby won't bring back Caleb." I hate that she's right. "This baby won't *be* Caleb either. If you remember that then you should be okay."

Now this is something I'm not sure of. "Fancy going into town to get a coffee? This smell is making me want to vomit."

"Definitely," she chuckles and we go to grab our coats. "Your friends are coming down next month aren't they?"

I nod. "I can't wait. I miss them."

"I bet." She looks at me sideways. "How are you doing? You seem to have perked up a little more than usual this week, although Nathan seems to be in his usual foul mood."

We came back from the city just over a week ago and she's right, Nathan's mood has been foul. Although he hasn't aimed it at me, I've still felt the bite of his fury just by sitting close to him. I'm not sure what's bothering him; all I know is that he's taken a few calls that haven't ended well. His phone screen has a large crack down it, from throwing it I assume.

His voice has been travelling from his study all day. I couldn't make out what he was saying as it was too muffled, but I could tell he wasn't a happy bunny. Part of me wanted to go upstairs and console him but I knew by his silence at the dining table that he just wanted to wallow.

Nathan parked further down the driveway yesterday, paranoid that the decorators would scratch his car. I wish he'd parked a little closer. I can see the car about thirty feet away but that's a good thirty feet I could've avoided walking down.

"I'll meet you there," Jeanine says and climbs into her own vehicle.

While we're in the village we stop by a bookstore. There's a lot to choose from but nothing that interests me. Jeanine goes book mad, piling them in her basket before spending twenty minutes chatting to the girl behind the counter. Something glints out of the corner of my eye. I immediately head for the shelf and pick up the gorgeous leather journal with a brass buckle keeping it closed.

"What is this?" I ask, effectively cutting off their conversation.

"One of the leather journals I got in stock a while back. Only sold a few. I think that's the last one," she says from across the store.

My hand runs across the A4 sized book; the leather is patterned beautifully. "How much is it?"

"Fifty," she responds and I almost choke.

"Fifty?"

"Yes, it should be sixty."

Well I do enjoy a bargain. With a heavy sigh, I take the journal to the counter and hand over my card. Inputting my pin into the machine after a long moment's deliberation, I finally relax. Fifty pounds is a lot of money. There are a lot of things I could buy with that.

Nathan deserves this more. He's done a lot for me and something tells me he'll love this.

She wraps the book in parcel paper and places it in a bag for me. I take it with a thank you and follow Jeanine out of the store.

We part ways and I go home feeling a little better.

Tucking the leather journal away somewhere safe in my closet, I lie on my bed and stare at the ceiling, my heavy stomach bouncing around. Caleb was always moving, always. Maybe the baby gets it from him.

Knock, knock, knock.

"Come in," I call, still sprawled on my back with my legs over the side of the bed.

"Where've you been?" Nathan asks and closes the door. The paint smell seems to be bothering him too.

"I just went into town for an hour," I say, yawning as I raise myself onto my elbows. "You didn't need the car, did you?"

He shakes his head. I pat the bed beside me and flop back down. I'm shocked when he joins me. His head turns towards me, only a foot away from mine. We share a smile but his fades when I wince a little at the dull ache throbbing in my lower back. "What's wrong?"

"Back ache," I admit and wriggle a little. "It's okay, it'll pass soon."

I hear a thud when Nathan slides to his knees by the bed. A squeal escapes me as his hands grip the place behind my knees and pull me off the bed. My body spins until only my chest is resting on the bed and my knees rest on the floor.

What's he doing? "Nath..."

"Relax," he commands as his covered fingers lift my top up my back.

I try to look back at him but his hand presses my face back into the bed. Soon his fingers start stroking against my skin. I tense momentarily until they dig deep at the base of my spine and slowly work that area. Oh god, that feels great.

I barely register it when he slides a cushion under my knees, because one hand never stops massaging the aches out of my back.

"Don't stop doing whatever it is you're doing," I groan.

Am I drooling? I think I'm drooling.

He kneels directly behind me to get to all of the right spots more effectively.

My legs slip a little on the floor as I relax deeper into the mattress, the top curve of my stomach touching the side of it. Unfortunately Nathan's closer than anticipated and as if this position isn't already awkward enough, my arse connects with his groin.

He tenses and clears his throat, his fingers still on my back.

"Sorry," I whisper into the quilt and slide forward a little.

"No problem," he seems to choke out. Then, to make matters worse, he adds, "Your skin is flawless."

I blink in shock. "What?"

"Your skin," he repeats and brushes his fingers lightly over the curve of my hips, making me shiver. "It's flawless."

"It's pregnancy, it has many benefits," I mumble and move my hips a little. "Keep going."

His thumbs begin to circle once more. Oh god. That's so good.

"No," he murmurs, pushing deeper into my flesh. "It's just you."

Okay, I'm all for compliments but this is making me feel weird. The position, the touching, and the way he's speaking... "I feel better now."

"Relax." He presses into my back again and I half relent. "What did you do in town?"

"Went for coffee and for a walk." I groan; that feels amazing. It takes me a moment to collect myself and continue. "Then we went into the book store."

"It didn't have anything you like?"

"It did."

He waits for me to continue but I don't, I'm too drugged on this wave of relaxation that's sinking into me; making my skin burn and my blood warm. "Continue."

"If I do that I'd have to move," I grumble and feel him laugh silently.

"Just tell me the name of the book."

I don't even know my own name right now. "It doesn't have a name; it's unwritten."

"Now I'm intrigued."

I smile into the blanket, savouring the feel of his leather clad fingers circling and dragging across the skin of my back. Goose pimples swell over every inch of my skin. I feel his thighs brush mine, unintentionally I think; either way it makes me whisper a moan into the peach coloured fabric. My nipples pebble as his hands cup my hips and his groin brushes against me once more.

"I got something for you," I manage to say, willing myself to pull away but failing. Screams echo through my mind as I chastise my traitorous body mentally.

This time he deliberately presses himself into me. I feel the swelling in his pants and inhale a sharp breath.

This is wrong.

He acts normal even though his own body is betraying him. I feel the trembling in his hands as they explore my skin. "Why for me?"

"I just saw it and thought you'd like it. You probably won't."

"I will," he breathes and his thumbs dip under the seam of my trousers, gently caressing the curves of my behind.

"Nathan," I warn as his breathing deepens and he presses himself into me once more.

He lets out a quiet moan, almost like a whimper, and grinds into me. Heat pools in my belly, I can't help it. I'm twenty five weeks pregnant, my hormones are raging. I know this is wrong, so damn wrong.

So why does it feel so good?

"Nathan." This time my voice isn't a warning, it's pleading.

His hands trail down the outside of my thighs, dragging across the fabric as they go. I clench and ache with need. Tingles and fire burn through me when I feel one hand move to the button of my jeans. It slowly begins to peel them open, causing my breath to hitch and my heart to accelerate.

CHAPTER SEVENTEEN

A VOICE SHOOTS THROUGH my mind, one I know so well. One that doesn't exist anymore.

"My brother isn't normal. Stay away from him, Gwen. Okay?"

As if a bucket of ice is dropped on me, I cry out and scramble away, the tingles and fire now doused. Nathan instantly releases me; not that he had a chance to grip me as my action was rather sudden. I sit on the floor looking at his flushed face and wild brown eyes. They come to me and his hand reaches out, beckoning me to come back and finish what we just started.

"No," I say, my head shaking back and forth frantically.

He sits back, his legs bent in front of him, his hands resting on the curves of his knees. We both stare at each other for a long while, the heavy rise and fall of our chests synchronised.

What just happened?

I daren't ask him why he's doing this, mostly because I'm afraid of the answer.

"Gwen," he says calmly and stands slowly, his eyes never leaving mine. Placing his hand in the air, he waits for me to take it. I don't, I daren't risk it right now. I'm aching in places I shouldn't. I don't trust my body. I don't trust him to not continue whatever it was that made my body so delirious with need.

"Here." I lower my eyes and rush into my closet. Hiding under a few folded bed sheets is the journal I bought for him. My hands smooth the parcel paper as I walk back towards him, chewing on my lip nervously. "It's not much, nothing in comparison to what you've done for me." I wasn't going to give it to him yet but it seems like an okay distraction for now.

He stares at me with a frown. "You don't have to give me anything."

"I want to, it's what *friends* do." I add this last bit giving him an imploring look. See reason, please see reason.

Dilated pupils stare intently at my face as I look away. His hands take the gift from mine and slowly peel away the paper. I hope he likes it, truly I do.

The silence stretches between us as the journal finally comes into view. He looks from the leather bound book to me and then back again. His hands turn it over before stroking it to feel the patterned grooves that make the cover.

"This is wonderful," he says sincerely. "You said you got this from the book store in town?"

"Yes, it caught my eye and I immediately thought of you."

He smiles at me, his cheekbones turning slightly pink. "Thank you."

I wave him off. "Don't thank me."

His teeth sink into his lip as he looks at me. "Gwen."

We're both startled by a loud bang from across the hall. He sighs deeply and I watch as his lips pinch together with frustration.

"I should go and check on the decorators." His tongue teases his lower lip. "We'll go out to eat. The stench of paint is irritating me."

I smile fondly. "Everything irritates you."

"Of course." He grins and touches my cheek with his thumb. I shy away instantly but he doesn't seem offended. "Get ready."

"Okay." I scuff my sock on the ground, praying that his intense gaze lingers on me no longer.

"Fifteen minutes, Guinevere." He says my name quietly, like a gentle caress on my skin, before leaving the room completely.

Caleb's eyes catch me from my bedside table. I stare at him for a long time, imagining his eyes glaring at me with accusation.

"I'm sorry," I whisper, desperate for him to believe that it was nothing more than a moment of weakness and Nathan is nothing more than a friend. He doesn't believe me, I can feel it.

But it's true.

Whoa, dizzy. Strange.

Must be my low blood pressure. My eyes just turned black for a moment there. I need to stop stressing myself out over little things, it isn't healthy. Caleb isn't here and he's not coming back.

Even though I know I'll never let him go, I need to stop trying to run all of my decisions past him first. He's not here to answer me and I'm twisting what his answers would be in my mind to make myself feel worse.

I deserve it, I deserve to feel worse.

We enjoy a quiet dinner at a restaurant out of town. Nathan doesn't say much and neither do I. There's not much to say.

I spend the entire time looking at everything but him. It's really awkward so I'm relieved when my phone rings.

"Hello?" I answer, turning away from Nathan to give myself some semblance of privacy.

"I messed up." It's my mum. What? "I should never have sent you away. I was just so angry and disappointed."

"Okay." I move away from Nathan and his hand comes out and snags my wrist. Placing my hand over the speaker I turn to him. "I'll be one minute."

"Who is it?" He asks, making me quirk a brow.

I walk away without responding and step into the cold air.

"Where are you?" She asks on a sniff.

"I've travelled south for the winter," I respond and clear my throat. "I'm staying with a friend."

She lets out a long breath. "I want you to come home."

"Home?"

"Yeah, I want to be there for my grandbaby and my first baby. I know... I screwed up, but I want to make it up to you."

I shift nervously on the spot, placing my finger in my other ear to stop the wind from distorting my ability to hear her. "Why the change of heart?"

"I've had some time to calm down and think about it."

"You've had some time to calm down and think about it?" I scoff.

"I know what I did was wrong..."

A harsh laugh escapes me. "You're my mother. You abandoned me when I needed you more than ever."

"I..."

"And suddenly you want back in? Two months later? When you've had no contact?"

She remains silent for a long moment. I watch the occasional car blur by and move out of the way of people walking past. "I'm sorry. I know how awful I've been. I just never wanted this life for you."

"Hmm, I didn't notice," I remark sarcastically.

"Yet I've given you the same life that my parents gave me when I was faced with this. I don't want you to be alone."

"I'm not..." I look through the window and catch a glimpse of Nathan. He's cleaning his phone with hand sanitiser and a pocket tissue. I smile warmly at the display. "Alone."

"Good," she sniffs. "I'll work for it, for you. I miss you. I'm sorry."

"I have to go."

"Please consider coming home. I miss you. I want to be there for you. I'll be better."

"Well, I'm glad you've come around," I say and look through the window again, noticing Nathan's curious eyes on me. "I'll have to let you know if I'm coming home. I'm... it's complicated."

"Can I at least come and see you?"

Can she? Do I want her to?

She is my mum. Gah, this is so frustrating. I want to hate her for what she's done but the thought of my baby having a stable, loving grandmother in their life overrides my need to hate her. I just don't have the emotional capacity to hate her right now. "Sure. Just let me sort a few things first."

"You're, umm... not staying in a hostel or something are you?"

I smile a little. "No, Mum, I swear. I'm in a very good and safe place with a friend."

She sighs with relief. "I'm sorry for what I said. I should have been there for you."

"Yeah," I say, my eyes burning. "You should have."

I hear her sniff and my heart pounds a heavy rhythm in my chest. "I'll be there, I swear. Call me. I miss you."

"You too." I hang up and chew on my lip for a moment, my phone clutched tightly in my hand.

After taking a steady breath I walk back into the restaurant and make my way over to Nathan.

As soon as I get close enough he asks, "Problem?"

"No," I lie. It is a problem in a sense, something I need to talk about, but I don't want to bother him with my issues. How exactly do I deal with this? "It was my mum."

"The one who disowned you?"

"The one and only." I slide into my seat and rest my chin on my hand. "She said she's sorry, she was angry and disappointed and never should have reacted that way."

He scoffs and runs his fingers through his hair. "I don't care much for your mother."

"She wants me to go home." My voice is a low whisper, but he hears me. I know this because his body shifts and his tongue swipes his lower lip.

He clears his throat and casually moves his straw around his glass. "Are you going?"

"Not without speaking to you first." I watch his straw swirl through the clear liquid.

His face drops. "Would you like to go?"

Would I? "It'd get me out of your way. You could go back to your life without having to worry about me."

He softens and smiles a sad smile. "I'll always worry about you."

I look him directly in the eyes. "Do you want me to go?"

Blowing out a breath, he runs his fingers through his hair again. "No. Honestly I don't."

"I thought you liked your privacy? Your space?"

"And so far you've respected both. I enjoy your company. It is your choice, but think about it long and hard before you make any decisions." He waves his hand to signal for the waitress. She comes over and clears our plates, asking if everything was okay with our meal. We both nod and climb from the table. Nathan takes my wrist in his hand and guides me outside. I'm not sure exactly where we are, I just know that it looks like we're in the middle of nowhere.

"She wants to visit," I blurt as we walk towards the car.

His brow rises. "Does she know who you're staying with?"

"No, I didn't tell her." I chew on my lip for a moment, looking out at the curving green and yellow hills that touch the horizon. "Can I ask you something?" He helps me into the car and rushes around to his side.

"Sure."

Should I?

Yes. "Why did you hit Caleb?"

"What?"

Oh, like he doesn't know what I'm talking about.

He looks around for a moment, clearly uncomfortable.

I repeat my question. "Why did you hit Caleb that night? And then tell me to get rid of the baby?"

"It's a long story."

"It's a long drive." Why's he avoiding this?

He lets out a long breath of frustration. "It's not important. It happened and I'm ashamed of myself for acting so barbarically."

"It is important," I respond, feeling defensive. "You just walked in, cracked him one and left."

"You've never mentioned it before," he grits out and starts the car. "Why now?"

"Because I've been too busy dealing with my grief to think about anything else. I'd like to know."

"My brother betrayed my trust. I asked him to do something for me and instead he chose to let me down after swearing to me it would be done," he responds cryptically and now I want to know even more. "That's it."

"What did he swear to you he'd do?"

"Honestly, Guinevere, I really don't want to talk about this." He looks as agitated as I feel.

"You don't trust me?"

His face hardens. "I don't trust anyone."

Ouch. "'Kay."

"Don't take it personally." He sighs like I'm being ridiculous for feeling a little bit sad over this. "Trust is earned over time, not given freely on request."

My mouth drops open. "And I haven't earned your trust yet?" What an arsehole.

"Just drop it, would you?" He looks at me briefly. "Whatever happened between Caleb and I is my business. It's not for you to worry about."

I glare at his profile when he faces the road once more, my arms folded across the top of my belly. "What about what you said to me?"

"What are you talking about now?"

"You told me to get rid of the baby while I still had the chance. Why would you say that?"

He doesn't respond, staring blankly ahead, his hands gripping the wheel tightly.

"Nathan." I persist, wanting him to explain.

"I apologize for saying that."

"Clearly I've forgiven you already, but I'd like to know why you said it."

Like before, he doesn't respond. I rest my forehead on the glass. Out of the corner of my eye I see him look at me as if wanting to say something, but then he shakes his head and looks back at the road, his lips a thin white line and his jaw tense. "I have a meeting with my solicitor tomorrow in the city. I'll be away until the weekend."

"Don't do that," I snap, feeling my anger rise. "Every single time we have a heated discussion, you take off. Maybe I should just leave, then you won't have to keep doing that every few days."

"That's not why I'm leaving."

"I'm calling bullshit."

"Don't swear; it's not attractive."

I laugh humourlessly. "Seriously? I'm not trying to be attractive."

"Just don't swear and don't leave. It's not why I'm leaving."

Eye roll. "I'm always the reason you leave. It makes me feel guilty, knowing I'm in your house and you feel forced to stay elsewhere."

"You're being ridiculous."

Am I? It doesn't feel like it. "Whatever."

"I'm serious," he remarks, stopping the car so he can look at me. "That house... it holds some painful memories for me. That's why I leave on occasion."

I'm sceptical. "Why do these memories only resurface when you seem to be pissed at me?"

"Stop swearing."

"Sorry." I say this flippantly and continue on as before. "I don't get it, Nathan. Do you want me to leave? Tell me honestly. I don't want..."

"Stop reading into things that aren't there." He cuts me off; his tone is louder than it was a moment ago and it startles me.

"Like you can talk," I mumble and instantly regret it.

Pain flashes through his features before vanishing behind a hardened mask. "Is there something you'd like to say to me?"

My chest tingles and my eyes widen slightly. I look away and shake my head.

"Really? It sure seems like there is."

I shake my head again.

"Go on, I'm waiting."

I chew on the inside of my cheek. Should I say something? After what happened when he rubbed my lower back, things have been good between us but also awkward.

Should I?

"You tried to kiss me." My heart starts pounding against my chest. I regret the words the second I speak them.

"It won't happen again."

"I know that." This is so awkward. "Why did it happen in the first place?"

He shrugs. "I felt like it."

"That's the most ridiculous thing I've ever heard," I scoff, almost slamming back into my seat as he starts up the car once more.

We drive in silence for a while. He has to give me more than that. He can't just not explain this to me.

When we pull into the driveway I ask again; I can't help myself. He climbs out of the car, slamming the door with a bang, not even bothering to look at me or even help me out like he usually does.

"Nathan." I say sharply and grab his arm. "Don't walk away from me."

"What do you want me to say?" His brown eyes narrow on my face. "You're like a dog with a bone, just drop it. I've apologised. Let it go."

"I'd like to understand."

"Fine," he laughs once. "You honestly want to know?" I nod slowly. "I was aroused, you were available. Nothing more and nothing less."

A loud breath leaves me and I release his arm. "Seriously?"

"Yes." He starts to turn. "I won't do it again, you can be sure of that."

"I would never do it with you anyway," I clip and stroll past him. "Do you have any idea how wrong that is? I'm pregnant with your brother's child. Yet you'd try and use me because you're horny? That's unforgivable."

His eyes darken and he lowers his face to my ear, his presence dominating and a little frightening. "I don't want your forgiveness." He moves back slightly so he can see me. "You are mistaken if you think I look at you as anything more than my brother's whore."

My anger gets the better of me, fuelled by hurt at his words. My hand connects with his cheek, stinging my palm and instantly turning one side of his face a deep shade of pink.

"You struck me," he whispers, his face a mask of shock.

A tear falls from my eye. "You struck me first."

Pushing the door open I head inside and race up the stairs, wanting to put as much distance between Nathan and I as possible.

I hate him.

He doesn't follow me which I'm grateful for. I get to cry in peace. How did this day turn out to be so bad?

His brother's whore.

I was his brother's fiancée. Caleb loved me and this baby.

I've never been called a whore in my life! I was a virgin until Caleb and even then I made him wait for it. Not that sleeping with multiple people would make somebody a whore either. I despise that word. It's a vile, lowly, desperate attempt to insult a person.

After wallowing for a long while, I have a shower and freshen up. Powering on my laptop, I flick mindlessly through websites about babies. I should really research the whole baby thing. There's no use putting it off and it'll help to take my mind of the drama that is Nathan.

The doorbell rings and I hurry back down the stairs as is habit. Nathan never usually answers the door as he knows I'm closest when he's upstairs, so I'm shocked to see him pulling it open and greeting a very attractive Lorna.

She gives me a little wave and a smile as Nathan takes her coat. Nathan looks up at me, his expression emotionless and his eyes dull. The brown in them has lost their usual sparkle.

"Hey," Lorna grins and stops in front of me. "How are you and the bump?"

"Good." Lies. All lies. "Yourself?"

"I'm great. We should totally go for coffee or something tomorrow. I have the day off and there aren't many people around here that are our age."

I'm about to say sure but Nathan cuts me off. "She can't, she's leaving in the morning."

"Oh no," Lorna says, looking as shocked as I feel. "Where are you going?"

"She's decided her mum's is a better option for the duration of her pregnancy." And there is strike two. He's just gutted me with a blunt knife. "Come on." Nathan grips Lorna's arm and tugs her towards the stairs.

I see he's found his next object to relieve his arousal. Well at least he won't be kissing me any time soon.

"That's okay, Nathan, it won't take me long to pack my things." My fists clench by my sides. How can he be so heartless and mean? What did I do exactly, other than question him over his own actions? "I'll leave now."

"I'll take you in the morning," he orders, his tone clearly stating I'm not allowed to argue.

"No thanks, I'll call my mum. I wouldn't want you to have to suffer a three hour journey in a car with your brother's whore." I stomp past him. "Nice to see you again, Lorna."

She doesn't respond to me but I hear her whisper, "What just happened?"

"Go up to the room; I'll be with you in a moment," he orders and I hear his footsteps close behind me.

I push open my bedroom door and pad into the closet, my eyes tingling with the preparation of releasing tears. "You know?" I begin and pull my suitcase out, still not looking at his frame lingering in the doorway. "If you wanted me to leave, you didn't need to be such a dick about it. I would have left if you'd asked."

I get no response, though I feel his intense presence still lingering in the doorway despite the fact that my back is to him.

"What do you want?" Grabbing a few items, I fold them neatly and place them in the open case.

He takes a step inside and shuts the door. "Nothing."

"Then why are you watching me?"

He sighs and pulls the door back open. "When you're ready to apologise, I'll be waiting."

Me? Apologise? I'm about to shout at him when I notice that he's left the room. Grrr. I want to slap him again.

I fill my case with the essentials and wheel it into the hall. Getting it downstairs proves to be difficult, but I manage it. My anger rises with every step.

I notice his keys on the desk near the door and snatch them without an ounce of guilt. Call me immature but I'm taking his fucking car.

I feel naughty, my heart is racing and my adrenaline is pumping. I've not been able to enter a car so quickly for weeks.

Spinning the car around I take off, putting my phone on charge via the console in the middle and putting as much distance between me and the house as possible. This is so bad. What am I doing?

My phone rings; it's Nathan. I ignore it and head towards the village. I'm going to need a map if I want to make it out of here, let alone all the way home. The baby lies still which I'm grateful for. It's irritating when he moves while I'm trying to drive.

I know there's a post office around here somewhere; they'll do maps surely.

I only make it twenty miles out of town when I'm being pulled over by a god damn Police car. No! He wouldn't.

He would.

I have to sit and listen to the officer talk about how taking other people's cars without permission is stealing, but fortunately Nathan isn't pressing charges.

Fortunately... scoff.

A red car pulls up ahead of us and Nathan climbs out. He strolls over to the officer but makes no move to shake hands. It's a conspiracy; they obviously know each other. They talk quietly for a few minutes. The officer even invites Nathan for dinner. I hate villages!

"Move," Nathan demands when he makes it around to the driver's side.

I clamber out and pull open the back door.

"Get in the front," Nathan orders.

I ignore him and slide onto the backseat.

A muscle jumps in his jaw but he doesn't say anything, he just waits until I'm buckled in before climbing into his seat directly in front of me. I chose this seat so I wouldn't have to see him.

I've never been so humiliated in my life.

"I'm sorry," Nathan says as we start to drive.

"I'm not," I whisper and wipe my hand under my eyes. "I hate you."

His breath catches. "You'll get over it."

I laugh once, although I don't find anything funny. "You've completely humiliated me."

"You did that yourself. I told you to wait until morning."

He is so infuriating. "I'll wait until morning then."

"You aren't leaving," he states firmly and now I'm just frustrated and confused. Leave, don't leave. What the hell is wrong with him? "And don't bother trying. I won't let you."

"Are you suddenly collecting whores?"

The car lurches to the side as he pulls over. He waves at Lorna, who was behind us, to motion that she keep going. She does. I'm not relieved. In fact, I'm the opposite. Now I have no female support.

The car door opens and Nathan is half dragging, half carrying my squealing form out. He lifts me, much to my annoyance, and carries me around the car. Placing me on the bonnet, he stands in between my knees and wraps my long, black hair around his hand, tugging it slightly so my head tilts back.

"You're not a whore," he says, his eyes dark and furious. "Nor will you ever be a whore. I said a bad thing when I was angry. Nothing more and nothing less. As for leaving, I don't want you to go. I said yet another moronic thing out of anger."

"Get off me," I beg, but he only moves closer, his face inches from mine.

"As for why I kissed you, I couldn't resist. I'm a man and you're beautiful." My breath hitches at his words.

"That's a crap excuse, now let me go."

His eyes smoulder, their intensity startling me. "I wasn't lying when I said to you that I enjoy your company. I enjoy it very much. Too much." His body sags a little. "More than I should."

"Nath..."

"I promise I won't threaten to make you leave again." His free hand rests on the curve of my neck, his eyes now kind and full of... something I'm clearly imagining. "You have my word. Please, accept my apology for upsetting you."

"No." I shake my head and look at my parted knees pressed lightly against his hips. "I don't want to."

"I've earned it, don't you think? I deserve forgiveness." His eyes now glitter with regret, his hand tightening in my hair. "Please."

My lips pinch together. I swallow the lump in my throat and try to push him away with a hand on his chest between us. He moves even closer so I can feel his heat all over. It makes me hum in places I shouldn't be humming. "Stop."

"I don't want to. Not until you say you forgive me and startle me with that beautiful smile," he whispers, his breath fanning against my lips.

"Step back, Nathan," I warn as his hands hook under my knees and pull me to the edge, my body almost pressed against his.

It's useless. I try pushing at his chest but he won't move. His hands grip my wrists and he clasps them behind my back with one hand whilst grabbing my hair again with the other. "Forgive me." He presses his lips to my jaw. I gasp and a shiver runs through me. "Forgive me," he repeats and places another gentle kiss further along my jaw.

"Don't," I beg, but it comes out breathy and does little to convince either of us.

His lips hover over mine, his eyes flicking back and forth, scanning my face to see my reaction. "Forgive me."

He's going to kiss me. If I don't say yes, he'll kiss me. Why am I not saying yes?

His face gets closer. My eyes get wider. My lips twitch in preparation when he moistens his.

"Okay," I blurt, my body tensing. "I forgive you."

"You have my word," he whispers and I feel his top lip brush against my own. "I won't touch you again, not unless you want me to."

His hands release mine and I'm being tugged into his body. My belly gets in the way but I still feel his groin against mine briefly as he lowers me to the ground. My entire body spasms with it, heats with it, aches for it. I pull away abruptly and keep my head down.

What the fuck just happened?

CHAPTER EIGHTEEN

L IFE HAS BEEN SETTLED for a while now, which is a relief. I got tired of constantly walking on eggshells. Nathan has cheered up a lot it seems, although I'm quick to touch wood whenever I think this, because I'm scared my words will jinx it.

The nursery looks amazing. I spent an entire day washing, drying and ironing baby clothes before putting them away. Everything has a place. It looks like something out of a catalogue. Perfect.

My mum has been calling me every couple of days for updates. I still have yet to tell her who I'm staying with and I'm not sure why I'm postponing the inevitable. It's not like I'm doing anything wrong. Am I?

Nathan is spending more and more time downstairs with me, be it working on his laptop or reading a book. I'm enjoying it a lot. He's even helped me cook a few times. I'm not sure why there's a sudden change in him but I can't say I don't like it.

I can't seem to shake the memory of the other morning when he exited the basement after an hour of working out. I collided with him in the hall, making him trip backwards on my slipper and slam into the wall. His arms came around me protectively and I leaned on him for a moment, embarrassed at my clumsiness.

"Sorry," I murmured, pulling back to smile sheepishly.

He righted us both but kept his hands on my elbows. I immediately took note of the patches of perspiration on his chest and sides. My mouth became dry and my lips parted as I took every inch of him in.

"Are you okay?" He asked, turning me slightly as he checked me over.

"I'm making muffins," I blurted, nodding towards the kitchen. "Banana and oat muffins."

"I can't wait to try them." He tucked my hair behind my ears with the tips of his leather clad fingers and pressed his soft lips to my forehead. "I'll be down soon, Gwen." And then he jogged up the stairs and out of sight, leaving me feeling flustered and moronic.

My lips twitch as I recall the memory for the thousandth time since it happened. The way he sweetly kissed my forehead and said that he'd be down with such a soft tone...It melted me.

Sasha and Tommy are due any minute now and I'm nervous. I'm scared they'll see how much I've changed. But as promised, I have made Tommy a meal fit for a king. Sasha too, but it was Tommy's idea.

The dining table is full and the wine is poured, although I'm having juice. I hope they don't have trouble finding the house. That would suck.

"Something smells good," Nathan comments as he walks into the dining room. He reaches for a muffin but I slap at his wrist. The smile he gives me is cheeky and it's one I haven't seen before. He starts backing out of the room, his hand that I didn't slap behind his back.

"Nathan," I warn, my brow quirked. "Care to tell me what you're hiding?"

"Nothing." He shakes his head, his lips still twitching.

"Food thief," I joke.

His mouth drops open. "I paid for it."

"Details." I try to grab it again but he swiftly twists out of my way. I relent, my energy gone after cooking for so long. "Just let me know how they are."

He brings his gloved hand around and takes a large bite out of the blueberry and white chocolate muffin. The groan that comes from him does things to me. I instantly feel guilt and look away, hoping he didn't see the sudden flash in my eyes that would have surely told him of my brief, impure thoughts. "Amazing."

"Really?" I was a bit worried about the new recipe that I had fooled around with.

"Better than those chocolate ones you made two weeks ago."

"You mean the ones that were there when I went to bed but gone when I woke up the next morning, like all of the others before them?"

He shrugs. "Far too moreish."

There's a knock at the door. I smile and race towards it, almost bowling Nathan over on my way past.

I pull it open, still bouncing on the spot. Sasha and I both cling to each other like monkeys to their mother the second we spot one another.

"Oh my god, you are huge!" Sasha pulls away and looks at the boulder between us. "How long now?"

"Ten weeks," I reply and move her out of the way of the door so Tommy can step through. He smiles a kind smile, all the way to his eyes. "Hey you."

Strong arms wrap around me and squeeze me tight. "You look great, Gwen."

"So do you." I step away and look at them both. They both look so different yet the same, older and more attractive. Tommy's hair is longer than it was and Sasha's is a few inches shorter. They look great, they look happy. I wonder what they see when they look at me. "Come on, dinner is served."

"Where's Nathan?" Sasha whispers as she glances around nosily.

"Here." Nathan announces his presence from the doorway of the kitchen and both Sasha and Tommy turn statue as their eyes scan him. I'm guessing they're shocked to see how much he looks like Caleb.

They'll get used to it.

"It's great to meet you." Sasha breaks the silence and gives him a little wave. I warned them about his condition before they came so they know not to touch his hands. I'm grateful that they've remembered and haven't taken offence to it like some people do. "Thanks for having us."

"Yeah." Tommy dips his head. "Nice place."

"Thank you," Nathan says and leads us into the dining room.

Sasha lets out a long groan and grips my arm, her eyes round and dramatic. "I've missed your food. Consider me your new lodger."

"Fit for a king, just the way I like it," Tommy jokes and pulls out a chair for Sasha.

Nathan does the same for me, standing behind me as he pulls out my chair and pushes me in, much like Tommy just did with Sasha. I give him a questioning look but his eyes are on my friends, more specifically on Tommy.

Everybody helps themselves from the plates in the centre, moaning and groaning with every bite. This makes me happy.

Really happy.

"So, how is University?" I ask them both. They begin talking over each other, blaming each other for things I wish I'd seen. I love listening to them talk, telling me stories that once upon a time I would have been a part of.

After dinner we move into the living room and sit on the comfortable couches with music playing softly in the background.

"Tommy broke up with his newest girlfriend because of me." Sasha seems to think this is hilarious.

Tommy shrugs. "Tanya was jealous. She kept giving me ultimatums. It wasn't because of Sasha, it's because of her own insecurities." Tanya? What happened to Zoe?

"Bros before hoes," Sasha giggles and gives me a nudge with her elbow.

"Too right," I jest and rub my stomach, a habit whenever the baby starts to move. Nathan sometimes joins in as well. I've kind of gotten over the weirdness of it now.

Nathan, knowing without me asking, throws me a pack of Gaviscon tablets. I chew two and wait for them to kick in.

"Heartburn?" Tommy asks as Sasha places both of her hands on my moving belly.

I nod. "Apparently it means the baby is going to have a lot of hair. I hope his hair is worth it."

"You're having a boy?" Sasha squeals and lifts up my top without permission so she can see the baby move through my skin. My friend is weird.

"I don't know, I think so." I glance at Nathan. "I kind of hope so."

"We should put bets on it," Tommy suggests and I scowl good naturedly at him. "Unless you're afraid to lose."

"Stop it." Sasha slaps his arm and snuggles into my side, her eyes on my rolling bump. After a few more moments she groans and pats her flat stomach. I'm so jealous of her figure right now. "I'm bloated."

"I got bloated seven months ago and it's only gotten worse since," I say, making the others laugh. Even Nathan smiles a little. "Why don't we go for a walk?"

"Sounds good." Tommy smiles as Sasha groans. "Seriously?"

"Come on, Sash, you should see the outdoors before it gets too dark," I push but it doesn't work.

She shrugs. "You two go; I'm going to clean the dishes."

"Leave them." I glance at Nathan, whose eyes are on me. "Come on."

"No, I'll make you milk and honey too, it's Friday." She gives me a wink and sashays into the kitchen the only way Sasha can.

I smirk and look to Tommy for help. He stands and holds out his hand. Taking it, I let him pull me off the couch gently.

"Don't go too far, it's dark," Nathan tells me as he stands.

I give him a small frown. "You're not coming with?"

"I'll help your friend in the kitchen." He exits through the archway without saying anything else.

"I guess it's just me and you, pregger-belly." Tommy grins and throws his arm around my shoulder.

My frown turns into a scowl. "I'm not that fat."

"Sure you're not."

I elbow him in the side, making him stagger in jest. "I'm kidding, you're glowing actually."

"Yay."

"You still say that?" He chuckles, coming back to my side.

I blow out a breath. "Not much."

"So, spill all." Ah great, the serious tone.

"All of what?"

"Everything, don't hold back, I can take it."

But can I? "I'm doing better."

"No you're not." The look he gives me is one I've seen on Tommy before. It shows disbelief, sorrow and pity. I hate pity but I don't hate him, I never could, so I let it slide. "I mean, you are, but I can see that you still struggle."

"It's been a four months," I respond quietly, tucking my hair behind my ear. "It hurts every day."

"And Nathan?"

"Seeing him at first made it hurt more, but now it's gradually becoming a comfort. He's nothing like Caleb." I smile softly at how close we've become over the past month. "He doesn't have Caleb's easy smile, or constant hyper activeness and excitement for life. He's secluded, withdrawn but when he smiles, it makes all the bad stuff disappear for a while."

"What?" Tommy seems as startled by my words as I am.

I rush to defend myself. "I mean, at first I thought he hated me. I hated him a little bit, but now I'm happy to say we're friends. He's grumpy, completely intolerable but one of the nicest people I know."

"Huh." He looks up at the sky.

"How is university?"

"It's good, but you already know that. It's getting dark, we should head back."

"We've only been walking for five minutes." I laugh and tilt my head towards the greying sky.

"Yeah, well, Sasha's on her own," he lies because obviously she's not.

"Whatever." He's probably tired and doesn't want to admit it. "Thanks for coming, Tommy."

He smiles down at me, his arm still around my shoulder. "I've missed you." A shadow flits across his eyes. "I miss how things used to be."

That hits me hard, too hard. It's remarkable how things can change in just a few short months. "Me too."

The house comes back into view. I look up at its glowing windows and think about my future. A few months ago my future was with Caleb, in our little house, finishing school, getting a job and a decent placement.

Now my future is here.

As bright as that may seem, which it should be because I've been a lot more fortunate than most, it still fills me with a dread I can't explain, like an impending darkness is closing in on me. This isn't the life that I want, but it's the life that I have. I have other options but none of them seem better than the option I've taken.

Am I being selfish?

After all of this time am I now just realising that I'm using Nathan?

Am I using Nathan?

I don't think I am. I genuinely like him and I'm certain he likes me. It's all so weird. After seeing my friends in this atmosphere with Nathan instead of Caleb, none of it is clicking right and I feel like I need to explain the situation to them. I feel like I should defend myself and my choices, even though I know they're not judging me.

I feel guilt.

Well-deserved guilt that I should feel each and every day for still breathing when he's not.

Now that I can see my friends in front of me, I see my old life. I see my old life clashing with my new one. I'm assuming this is the reason I'm feeling so off about everything. Maybe it'll pass.

Hopefully it'll pass.

"Where's Nathan's car gone?" I ask aloud as we walk past his empty parking space.

"How should I know? Maybe he went to get milk or something." Tommy suggests and I snort. Like Nathan would go out at night to get milk. Not unless I asked. Plus we have milk, we have plenty.

I open the door and step inside before Tommy. Sasha peeks around the kitchen door. "Hey, the drinks are ready."

"Where's Nathan?" I ask, glancing around to confirm what I already know; he's not here.

"He left a minute or so after you guys, said to tell you he had some things to take care of."

"Did he mention what things?" I ask, knowing full well he wouldn't have said anything to Sasha.

She gives a shrug. "I don't know. He had a large brown envelope in his hands though."

A large envelope? "Probably something for work."

"Yeah."

How did I not hear his car? Or see it? We weren't that far from the house. He's like a ninja, even in a car.

"Okay," I say with a smile but inside I'm nervous. Nathan usually only leaves unexpectedly when he's pissed off about something. Also, he always tells me that he's leaving. "Where's my milk?"

"Do you still do that?" Sasha asks, handing me the warm cup of golden tinted milk.

What?

She notices my look of confusion and continues, "The milk and honey on a Friday."

"Oh." That. "Not often. Nathan did it with me once, not long after I came here. It's a family tradition apparently, one he doesn't stick to." I look at my friends and force a smile. "Come on, I want to know about you guys. Tell me what I've missed."

Sasha brightens a little. Tommy places his chin on his hands, his elbows resting on the table. "I'm dating someone," Sasha begins, her face animated with joy. "He's so sweet."

Tommy rolls his eyes when she's not looking, making me thin my lips in an attempt to stifle the giggle that's rising up my throat.

"He bought me flowers on the first date," she swoons. "And he opened the car door for me. It was so..."

"Sweet?" Tommy interjects and her face brightens further. "Exactly!"

"That's great." I smile at my friend. "It's about time you met somebody decent."

Tommy snorts and lowers his head. Sasha's smile soon turns into a frown. "What is your problem?"

"Nothing." He waves her off and looks at me. "If I have to hear one more freaking time about how freaking sweet this guy is, I'm going to gradually turn into sugar."

I snigger and Sasha shoots her frown my way. My hands go up in surrender but my smile is still there. "I think it's sweet. Tell me more."

"His dad is the manager of a restaurant in town and he wants to take it to new heights. He started late but his skills are impressive. He cooked for me and oh man, it was like an orgasm in my mouth." She groans with delight at the memory. It's almost disturbing to see. And this is just over his food. I can only imagine what she'll be like when they do the deed.

Wait. "Have you done the deed?" My presumptuous tone makes her cheeks turn pink, just around her nose. "Oh my god, you have."

"No!" She practically squawks. It's that 'bird like' of a noise, I'm surprised feathers haven't burst from her arms.

Tommy rubs his ears as his face scrunches in pain. "Ouch."

"Okay, so if you haven't done it, then what have you done?"

"I am totally going to bed right now," Tommy says and stands.

Sasha laughs with me as we order him to sit down with promises that the conversation will change.

It's just turned eleven and my mood has soared. The conversation has flowed so easily between the three of us and I've found myself willing to talk about Caleb and his goofy ways. Found myself smiling over it too. Almost been in tears because of it and so has Sasha. Tommy is better at handling his grief but I see it in his eyes. They were good friends, despite their rocky start because Caleb was jealous of our relationship.

Well, not jealous. More like he felt threatened. I loved it though, the sex was amazing when he was riled up. Telling me I belonged to him, promising me he'd screw every other guy right out of my head. Not that I had any other guy in my head, still, I appreciated the effort he put into it.

"What's going on with Nathan?" Sasha asks, making me choke on the water I'm sipping. Her eyes widen. "Babe..."

I shake my head, that guilt from earlier surging back. My heart hammers with it, every thump seeming to ricochet through my chest with a burning ache that lasts until the next thump, only to start up again even stronger.

"No, don't even go there. We're friends."

She lowers her voice until it's barely a whisper. "He looks just like Caleb, I'd understand..."

"Sasha," Tommy warns but I cut him off.

"No he doesn't," I blurt, my words rushed. "At first, yeah he did, but not now. I've seen him too much. I barely recognize the similarities." She opens her mouth to say something else and I'm shocked when Tommy's clipped tone interrupts, "Leave it, Sasha. You're pushing where you shouldn't."

Sasha's mouth hangs open. "I was just going to say that nobody..."

"How do you think you're making her feel, huh? Honestly? There's nothing going on between her and Nathan, yet you're spreading shit that's going to stick in her mind. That's Caleb's brother. She already feels fucked up enough about staying here with him. You putting extra on that isn't going to help her." He doesn't sound angry but he does sound something close to it. I'm grateful for him having my back but I wish he hadn't said anything. It's made this a little bit awkward.

"Christ," Sasha squeaks, her hand going to her mouth. "You're right, I'm so sorry, Gwenny." Gwenny... ouch.

She hugs me and I hug her back as best I can. "It's okay. Forget it."

"So, where's my room? I haven't seen it yet."

I gasp and my smile returns, my thoughts now distracted. "I haven't shown you the nursery yet."

We manage to finally get to bed after midnight. I send Nathan a text, asking him if he got to wherever he was going safe and sound. I don't expect him to reply. He usually doesn't and this time is no exception. I bury my head in the pillow and sigh before shutting my eyes and letting sleep claim me.

I awake with the sun streaming through the windows. Gah, who opened them? "Morning!" Of course, Sasha.

"Sleeping," I grumble and bury my face under the covers. My morning ritual.

"Up. I want to explore."

"Fine," I relent and slide out of bed. "Get me ready. I'll just sleep while I sit." My eyes won't open, they refuse to.

"Your phone went off about twenty minutes ago, one missed call and a text message from Nathan."

To read them would be to move. To move would be to wake up. To wake up would be to... ugh.

"'Kay." I yawn and reach at the table blindly. My phone falls to the floor. Darn. "I'll get it."

Sasha giggles and places it in my hand. "Maybe you should go and wash your face first. It might stop your eyes from sticking together."

"Good point," I say around a yawn and waddle into the bathroom. After splashing water on my face, I pull my hair up into a loose bun and apply a little mascara. Sasha watches me like a hawk, already dressed and ready for the day in dark blue skinny jeans and a thick, silver jumper that reaches to mid-thigh jumper. "Where's Tommy?"

Sasha nods towards the hall. "Getting ready." Which translates to, 'getting five minutes more sleep before throwing on whatever he can in two seconds and making it look like he's been getting ready.'

"I'll start on breakfast." I stretch, laughing when the bottom of my belly peeks out from below my top. "I think I need bigger clothes again."

"That's what we'll do this morning!" Sasha bounces on the spot, looking far too giddy, far too early.

"I don't think Tommy will appreciate that," I murmur and slide my thumb over my phone.

<u>Nathan</u>: I apologize for leaving so suddenly. Have fun with your friends. There's some money in the top drawer of your dresser. I placed it there before leaving. Spend it as you wish. Not including the obvious things I have a clear distaste for.

<u>Me</u>: Thank you, that's very kind. Is everything okay? I was worried.

<u>Nathan</u>: Everything is fine, Gwen. I'll bring you back something nice.

<u>Me</u>: Just bring yourself back, unless you want to come back with chocolate too, then I won't complain. When can I expect you home?

<u>Nathan</u>: Tonight, at about six. I wouldn't say no to those pasta parcels you make.

<u>Me</u>: Duly noted.

After tucking my phone into my pocket I head down the stairs and Sasha goes to get Tommy up.

I make a quick and easy breakfast, omelettes with mushrooms and cheese. I have to keep my stash of eggs hidden. Nathan has a really weird thing about eggs. If he can't see them, like in cake or pastry, then he's fine, but if I have any form of eggs, scrambled, fried, poached, etc., he freaks out and puts them in the bin immediately. I'm going to use his absence to enjoy a well-deserved omelette with my friends.

"I'm so glad you guys are here, I just wish you could stay longer." I pout slightly and place their plates in front of them.

Tommy wags his eyebrows. "And have me miss Halloween, the one night of the year where women dress like..."

"Sexy creatures of the night." Sasha finishes his sentence.

I look down at my belly. "I should just paint a bullseye or something on my belly."

"Or paint it so it looks like the skin's torn and make tentacles look like they're coming out of it." Tommy seems way too excited by this idea. "You know? Like off Alien vs Predator?"

We both look at him incredulously. Sasha speaks first. "You are not only weird but you're also disgusting."

"I second that vote." I raise my hand, wincing when Tommy slaps it down and throws a piece of cucumber at Sasha. "Violence solves nothing."

He shrugs. "I thought it felt pretty good."

"Slapping a pregnant woman felt good?" Sasha feigns horror.

He only sighs. "I'm leaving you behind if you don't stop bullying me."

"Like that'll ever happen," Sasha snorts quietly, knowing full well he can hear her.

"Me leaving you behind?" His face takes on a daring expression, willing her to say yes.

"Guys," I laugh and finish my breakfast. "Come on."

"Yeah, we're going to buy big belly some new clothing."

"You're such a bitch, Sasha." Even if her words are true.

She only smiles in return. "You'll be skinny again soon."

Shudder. "And mature."

"And a milf," Tommy adds, which makes Sasha throw the same piece of cucumber back at him.

I stand before they involve me in the food fight. "I'll just be a minute."

"Okay." Another piece of cucumber goes flying.

"And clean up that mess," I order and strut out of the room, ignoring the small hard lump of food unknown that hits the back of my head. I don't look either. I won't give their quiet laughter the satisfaction of seeing me react.

Back in my bedroom, I grab my bag and open the top drawer of the dressing table. Sure enough there is a small roll of notes. It's way more money than I need. Sigh. He needs to stop doing this.

I unroll the notes and stuff a few of them in my back pocket. It's then I notice a folded envelope with my name written neatly in script on the front.

I take it out and turn it over. The corner has something heavy weighing it down, making the paper bend when I hold it at an angle.

After tearing it open I dig for the source of the weight with my fingers and blink in astonishment when I see the ring. It has a gorgeous gold back with a cluster of diamonds spiralling around a larger one in the centre. My hands tremble as I take out the note. What is this? Why is there a ring in here?

My heart clenches as I unfold the note, the ring still in my hand.

My eyes scan over the short yet neat paragraph.

I've been doing some thinking and I believe that at this point it would be in our best interests to get married. I don't expect an answer right away. Think about it. I want my nephew to have a stable home and my last name and to be taken care of if anything should happen to me. I also don't want people thinking badly of you because of the circumstances. There's a lot I can offer you. There's also not much in the way of my being a husband but I'll try. I promise to keep you happy and you have my word that I'll respect, care for and protect you and my nephew until the day that I die.

Nathan.

I drop the ring like it's burning hot, the note too. My brain forces my body to propel me backwards, my eyes wide as fear and panic race through me.

Why would he ask me this?

I glance down at the ring already on my finger and notice how simple it is in comparison to the ring Nathan has gifted me with. His brother's ring. The one Caleb put on my finger.

How can he even... why would he... what is wrong with him? He can't honestly think I'd go for this?

Marriage means a lot of things, sex being one of them. I could never do that. Never.

He can't honestly want this... can he?

I feel sick.

"Are you ready?" Sasha shouts.

"C... coming!" I call and tuck the note and ring back into the envelope before thrusting it back into the drawer.

This won't ruin today, I won't let it. Nathan is just being noble, even though he has a weird way of showing it. It's not the eighteenth century, or whatever century that shit like this went down. It's not even necessary in any way shape or form. I don't care what people think of me. Caleb was the love of my life and they can go fuck themselves if they think I wasn't his.

He chose me. He died beside me. In my stomach is half of him.

Damn it, Nathan! What are you doing?

Why would he ask me this today of all days? Maybe so I could talk it over with my friends. Screw that. I'm not looking to see their reactions, that's something I'd rather miss.

I head down the stairs, fanning my face to rid it of the nervous perspiration that seems to be beading on my skin. "Let's go." I push open the door, my bag tucked close to my side. "There isn't much to see in the village but there is a nice clothing store. The women there are amazing at making clothes to fit you perfectly."

"Wow." Sasha remarks dryly. "How lucky for you."

I shrug. "I like it. I like the people and the coffee shop and what few restaurants they have, which yes, are all pub restaurants. They're cosy. Like something out of a movie."

"I envy your quiet life." Sasha again says this dryly.

Tommy opens the car door for me, forcing Sasha to get into the back. I'm grateful because once I got in the back I doubt I'd be able to climb out again. It's only a three door car. The front seats slide forward for access to the back.

Definitely not going to happen.

Sasha doesn't seem to mind, though. She leans forward between our seats and messes with the radio. Good luck getting that out here.

She gives up after ten minutes and turns on a CD as I direct Tommy to the village.

We stop at the clothing store first and Sasha cringes at almost everything. It is very... formal I suppose, but it's warm and comfy.

"EBay, Christ. Ever heard of it? Just because you're pregnant and living with a bunch of fogies doesn't mean you have to dress like one," Sasha whispers. I stifle my laughter and allow the lady to guide me into the back for measurements. She takes them in seconds, her memory clearly better than mine. After pointing at a few different things, I pay at the counter and meet Tommy on the sidewalk outside.

"That was fast," he comments, ignoring a still grumbling Sasha. "Now what?"

"Welcome to hell." Sasha looks up at the sky. "How do you not get bored here?"

"Nathan takes me to the city with him sometimes. That's fun. Jeanine the housekeeper is there every morning, so I get to chat with her for a while. Nathan also got me a laptop and there are loads of books to read and places to explore." Not including the rat infested grass that I tend to avoid. "He's suing his parents." I say this in a hushed tone, mindful of ears listening in on the empty streets. I'm probably being paranoid but I don't want to take any chances.

"He's what?" Tommy blinks and looks directly at me, his eyes full of curiosity.

I nod and chew on the inside of my cheek for a moment. "Yep. Don't say anything to him though. He won't like that I've told you. They went crazy when they realised I was staying with him and cut off his trust fund which wasn't theirs to take, just like they did with Caleb."

"Ouch, bastards." Sasha blows her fringe from her eyes and looks through a store window at the trinkets lined up perfectly behind the glass. "What is their problem?"

"I have no idea." But I really want to find out. "I don't get it; it makes no sense. This can't just be about the fact I'm not from a family of their choosing. I think this is something a little closer to home."

Tommy cocks his head. "What do you mean?"

"Maybe it's the whole rebellion thing. Or maybe they had women in mind for their sons. Who knows how they work?"

"Hmm." Sasha starts walking again and we start following. "It is all a bit strange but it does happen. Remember that guy I dated?" She looks up in thought. "What was his name?"

"Who?"

"The one with the strange flick at the front of his hair."

Tommy chuckles. "Reece?"

"That's the one." She clicks her fingers and smiles. "His parents were really strict. They hated it when they found out he was dating me. They wanted him to marry a girl from his neck of the woods."

Ah, I remember that. "That guy was an idiot."

"Yep," Tommy chips in and places his arm around her shoulders. "Not that it matters much seeing as you forgot his name after only two years."

Her hand whips around to smack his chest, her smile never faltering. "I was just using him for his car. When summer was over we dropped each other. He was sad about it, I just pretended to be."

"Bitch," I laugh in shock and kick a small pebble across the ground. "I thought me and Caleb would end the summer before I started University. I was so sure he was lying and saying pretty things to take my virtue."

"Nice."

I elbow her to shut her up and continue. "He kept telling me he was staying but I couldn't even comprehend the reality of a man as amazing as Caleb, after only a few days, promising me the world."

"He always did promise you the world," Sasha sighs wistfully, her hand clinging to mine.

"I don't think he ever realised he'd already given me it," I mumble, feeling that familiar ache of grief in my chest. "He was my world."

"Soppy." Tommy pretends to hurl on the sidewalk. Immature much?

"Do you think he'd be angry with me? I promised him I'd stay away from Nathan."

Tommy shrugs. "Probably not. I mean, the circumstances haven't been ideal. I'm sure he's grateful to his brother." Why don't I feel like this is true?

Sasha shakes her head. "Nah, he's definitely pissed. Caleb was the jealous type, but he'll understand too. I don't think you need to be worried about what he'll be thinking. He knows you're doing the best you can to get your life how you want it."

"I hope you're right."

"We are."

Chapter Nineteen

I CRY WHEN MY friends leave at five. They promise to visit again in a couple of weeks, so our parting wasn't too difficult. It was difficult hugging them and thanking them for all they did for me. It brought back painful memories but it needed to be
said.

When they left, I instantly raced up the stairs and pulled the envelope back out of the drawer.

It's been half an hour and I'm still stood slapping it against my other hand, wondering how I'm going to deal with this.

"Gwen?" Nathan shouts as the front door closes.

Oh bugger, I was supposed to make dinner. I hastily throw the envelope back in the drawer and jog to the stairs. "Sorry, I fell asleep." I'm lying. What I want to say is, 'You mind fucked me with your note and ring and I stared into space for god knows how long.'

He smiles, his eyes softening. "No problem. Go and rest, I'll make dinner."

"Umm, no, that's okay. You've been driving and I just... I'll go and..." I point to the kitchen. "That way."

His lips twitch. "Everything okay?"

"Yeah." I turn and walk straight into the small desk that holds a vase of fresh flowers that I stocked only two days ago. I grab it before it can roll, inwardly cursing at my clumsiness.

Nathan takes a few steps over to me. "Are you okay?"

"Yeah, just..." He asked me to marry him, in a note, which I guess is better than him asking me to my face. I don't think I could handle that. "I'm a little out of sorts. Is that the kettle? Did you press the kettle?" I begin my journey to the kitchen but Nathan's hand wrapping around the back of my shirt stops me. "Problem?"

"I was about to ask you the same thing." He's standing right behind me, like directly behind me. "Is there something you want to talk about?"

My mouth opens and closes. Do I? "I should start dinner if we want to eat before midnight."

Even though his chest is to my back and I can't see him, I know he's licking his lip. "I'll help."

"You don't have to." I tug forward but he pulls me back and my heart hits my throat, I can hear it in my ears.

"I want to."

"'Kay." Gulp.

He finally releases me and follows me into the kitchen. I collect the ingredients needed and start preparing. Nathan stands to the side waiting for orders.

"Could you pass me the milk?" I ask as I cut the pasta sheet into smaller squares and start filling each one. He looks over my shoulder as I dip the sealed parcels in the milk and place them in the boiling water. "Why did you leave last night?"

"I wanted to give you and your friends some privacy," he responds and I'm shocked by his honesty, although now I feel guilty. "Don't look like that, I didn't mind. I had work to do anyway."

"Well... thank you." I look at him with a grateful smile and grab the salad bowl. "How are things with your parents?"

"My father is furious but he's also scared. My mum isn't speaking to me and the business is suffering because my father refuses to change his stock and prices."

"That's not good." I shake my head a little as my hand wields the salad knife on rolled up lettuce. "What are you going to do?"

"Actually..." His lips purse as if thinking about whether or not he should tell me. "I was thinking of starting my own."

I stop chopping and tilt my head. "Your own jewellery business?"

"Yes."

My curious expression slowly melts into a smile. "Nathan, that's a brilliant idea."

He blinks as if shocked. "You think so?"

"I know so. You'll do great! The jewellery you showed me is fantastic. Better than anything I've seen of your dad's." It's true, his jewellery is really good, although I don't speak for everyone. We all have different tastes. But if his dad's business is failing then maybe that's the direction he should go. I tell him my thoughts and his face stretches into a smile I've not seen on him before. It makes him look very handsome. Too handsome.

"You have no idea how..." He clears his throat and chews on his lip for a moment. "You're amazing. Thank you."

"I didn't do anything," I laugh, enjoying his giddiness that makes him look his age rather than the age he pretends to be.

"Excuse me for a moment." He leaves the room and races up the stairs like a kid going for his favourite toy.

Still smiling, I look back at the meal I'm preparing and continue with it. This has been a very, *very* good day.

At dinner Nathan pulls out a large folder full of laminated sheets of paper. I glance at it as he flicks through each page. He uses a marker to write notes on certain items of jewellery and occasionally asks me what I think of the ones I see. Mostly I like them. A couple of them I don't, but not because they aren't good, only because they aren't my style. My opinion doesn't really matter, though, because he needs a diverse range.

Fortunately, having already been in the business, he knows how to kick start this kind of thing. I don't have a clue so I just promise that I'll keep him well fed and thoroughly entertained throughout the experience. His smile tells me he appreciates it.

After dinner he takes the folder, plus two more, into the living area and spreads them out on the table and ground. I watch as he brings down an easel of sorts and starts cutting out smaller images of his designs and placing them in groups on single sheets of A2 sized paper.

His concentration is mesmerising. I'm not sure why, but watching him in his element, murmuring to himself and darting back and forth, makes it impossible for me to keep my eyes off him.

Eventually he removes his jacket and rolls the sleeves of his shirt up.

I keep his coffee filled and nurse a Horlicks by the open fire.

"Just a second." His voice disturbs the silence, followed by him leaving the room.

I wait, although it's not like I'm doing much else.

"Here." And he's back. Damn, his footsteps are almost silent. I didn't hear him until he was walking into the room. "Lift your hair."

"Why?" I eye the arm that is hiding behind his back.

"Please?" He places his free hand on my shoulder and gives it a reassuring squeeze.

I relent and lift my hair.

"Close your eyes," he whispers, so I do.

Something flat and cool taps against the swells of my breasts, a thin chain following as his fingers trail around my neck and clasp it at the back. He pulls my wrists away, allowing me to release my hair.

I daren't open my eyes. Obviously I do eventually and my hand and eyes immediately go to the unique, flat pendant hanging from my neck. My breath rushes into my lungs and stays there. "Nathan..."

"I know you said you couldn't accept it before, but I need to see it on somebody. I want you to have it." He kneels in front of me. Is that a camera in his hand? "It fits you. Perfectly in fact."

Shit. What do I say? He's already given me so much. This is... it's beautiful and I adore it, but how can I accept it?

"I'd like to take a picture." His gloved hands rest on my knees. "If you don't mind."

"I look like a frizzy freak."

"Quiet, you look beautiful," He moves back and sits on the table. "It's just to capture the necklace against your skin."

Nothing to do with my boobs then? "Sure. How do you want me?"

Did he just squirm? Nah. I'm imagining things, although his cheeks are slightly flushed. It's probably because he just ran upstairs and back down again. "Okay." He raises the camera to his face and looks at me through the lens. "Relax."

That's hard to do when you're suddenly under a spotlight you never wanted to be under. I duck my head and tuck my hair behind my ear, waiting for him to finish.

"Hold it, with just your thumb and finger," he says and helps me move my hand into place. "Excellent." A few more clicks sound before he finally finishes and I release the breath from my lungs. "Thank you."

"Want a cookie?"

"You made cookies?"

I nod and climb to my feet. "I'll fetch them."

As soon as I enter the kitchen, I splash water on my face and pour myself a drink, trying to get rid of the heated feeling in my stomach, trying to get rid of his almost chocolate eyes dilating in between each shot. There is something horribly wrong with me.

Caleb. Forgive me.

I'm lost without you, mind included. I think you took it with you.

Could you please send it back at some point? If I'm to live without you, I'm going to need it.

"Gwen?"

"Jesus!" I squeal and drop the glass in the sink. It doesn't break but it does splash water onto my front.

He chuckles and hands me a few pieces of kitchen roll. "You're acting odd tonight."

My mouth drops open. Is he serious? "Yes... well..." I look at his sparkling eyes and relaxed stance and sigh. I'm not going to drag it up tonight. The proposal can be addressed another night, though I hope he doesn't think my avoidance of it is because I'm thinking about it. I'm not even going to consider it. I should just say no.

"I'm just tired."

"It has been a long night. Go to bed." He tilts his head to the side and assesses me for a moment. "Is there something you want to talk about?"

"No, not at all." I'm such a terrible liar. "I think I'll just go to sleep. You should too."

He smirks, his lips parting slightly in the middle. "Is that an invitation?" I gasp in horror as his hands fly up in surrender. "Kidding. I'm just kidding around."

"I know," I lie and push Caleb from my mind. His face keeps flashing before my eyes and, as much as I love seeing him, he shouldn't be witnessing this conversation.

I'm going nuts. It's official.

"Go to bed." He steps to the side, giving me space to pass. "Goodnight, Gwen."

"Night," I murmur in response and waddle as quickly as possible to the stairs and then to my room.

In bed I touch the necklace resting on my chest and admire the small red jewel at the top left of it. I wrap my hand around it, the one with my engagement ring. It's one of the only reminders I have that Caleb existed. The gold band lightly touches the flat gold disk and my tears of frustration fall.

I need to distance myself from Nathan. He needs to know that I can't ever be that to him. I know he thinks he's being noble or something along those lines, but he doesn't have to be. Why would he give up a lifetime of happiness to be with someone who will never love him that way?

Starting tomorrow I'll make it clearer. It'll be as clear as crystal.

We're friends and friends only.

Maybe I should leave but I can barely even comprehend the thought of going back to my mum's. I don't trust her. It sounds horrible but I genuinely don't trust her to keep her word and I doubt I'll be as happy with her as I am here with Nathan.

Plus... I think he needs me.

I think he needs me almost as much as I need him.

***

The next day I don't get a chance to hint to Nathan about our current relationship status as he left immediately after breakfast. He looked exhausted but determined so I packed him a lunch, straightened his tie and sent him on his way. Then I kicked myself for not keeping myself at a distance.

When he got home he had a quick dinner, almost sleeping at the table. I sent him up to bed immediately, a little worried about him.

It's now dinner time the next night and he's still up there. He hasn't left his room once. I want to go up to see if he's okay, but I daren't invade his space.

He's avoided me before but he's always come down at some point to eat something. Plus he has no reason to avoid me right now.

Maybe he's just tired. Or maybe he has company.

I'm not sure why but the latter annoys me and sends a spasm of pain through my chest.

Another hour passes and now I'm really worried. I've checked the fridge and nothing is missing. His breakfast went untouched, along with his lunch and his dinner.

Decision made.

I'm going up there.

Why am I so scared? It's like that point in a scary movie when they're facing the attic, knowing they have to go up there but really not wanting to. If that was me I'd probably poop a little.

I stand at the door at the far end of the long hall that leads to Nathan's space. My hand trembles as I grip the handle, my body tensing as if ready for an alarm to start blaring. It opens without issue or dramatics.

Phew. No ninjas then.

"Nathan?" I call out and flick on the light, showing a steep and narrow staircase, carpeted in soft deep blue. The walls match. "Nathan?" I call louder and, with one hand on the railing, I ascend. "Hello?"

Nothing.

Shit.

When I reach the top I see three doors. One of them is open, showing the inside of a closet, full of old boxes. I'm assuming they're files so I leave that and play eeny-meeny between the other two.

"Nathan?" I knock on door number one and then door number two. No response. Darn.

Door number one opens without sound. I push it only six inches or so and peek into the room. It's dark and large but I can make out a huge four poster bed. There's also a large lump in the middle.

I open the door further and almost gag at the scent of bleach. You never get used to it. No matter who says you do, they're lying.

Wow, it's freakishly tidy in here.

"Nathan?" I say, staring at the unmoving body shape on the bed hidden under deep blue blankets. My heart starts hammering. This isn't happening again.

Caleb was a one off. Nobody would be this unlucky.

But what if it's hereditary?

My nose starts to tingle as tears pool in my eyes, feelings so fresh come back to memory. I almost don't go to Nathan out of fear but I can't leave him.

I silently pad towards him, sniffing the air for any sign of that sickly sweet smell that seemed to suffocate me when I woke up next to Caleb. The bleach is too prominent; there's no room for another scent.

"Nathan?" I almost sob, but I hold it back and reach for the top of the blanket with a shaking hand. Imagining myself pulling it back, all I can see is a lifeless form. I'm so scared. I don't want to do this. "Nathan!"

I wrap my fingers around the edge of the blanket and, like a plaster, I rip it back over his head and to his naked shoulders.

Oh thank god. I've never felt such relief before.

He's lying on his stomach, the side of his face squashed into the mattress, his lips partly open but glistening with recent moisture from his tongue and quivering with each breath. One of his hands grips the mattress above his tousled locks that seem to have no clear direction in mind.

"Nathan," I repeat and gently place my hand on the back of his shoulder. He lets out a low moan and burrows into the bed further, sniffing a not too pleasant sniff through his nose. My hand jolts back from his hot and clammy skin and my body does the same.

The last time this happened... no I can't go back there. I just need to... shit.

"Nathan?" I roll the blanket further down his back and sit on the side of the bed.

He opens the only eye available and tries to lift his head. "Gwen?"

"I've been worried. You're burning up." I say this quietly and cautiously, hoping he doesn't get angry for my being here. "What's wrong?"

He coughs and it sounds like it rattles in his chest on its way up. "Flu."

"You promise?" I brush the hair away from his sweaty forehead. "Swear it."

He rolls onto his side, moaning pitifully. "I swear."

"Okay, I'm going to get medicine."

"Okay," he mumbles and closes his eyes once more.

I don't waste time. I reach the kitchen as fast as my legs can carry me and start rummaging through the medicine box. I find the usual pain killers and nasal sprays, so I round those up with a bottle of lukewarm water. My hands tremble the entire time I'm rushing around.

Honestly... I'm terrified.

Who can blame me?

He's still in the same position when I get back upstairs, curled up on his side, snivelling through his blocked nose.

"Hey," I say softly and switch on the lamp by his bed. He moans loudly and buries his head under his quilt. "Baby."

"What do you want?"

"I've got you medicine and water and some of those weird cracker things that you like."

"Not hungry," he grumbles, sounding childlike and actually kind of cute.

"You can't take painkillers on an empty stomach," I say firmly, letting him know there's no room for argument. I'm not taking any chances. "Please."

"Ugh," he says and sits up slowly. I fluff his pillows behind him and hand him a packet of tissues.

"You shouldn't be near me; you'll get ill," he says, his eyes heavy and hooded. Dark rings beneath them make him look as ill as he probably feels. "The baby."

I shake my head. "I had a flu shot a few weeks ago. They give them out like leaflets when you're pregnant." I hand him the packet of crackers and hold a napkin under his chin while he eats to catch the crumbs.

"I don't want to eat anymore," he states after having only two bites. "My throat hurts."

"Stop being such a guy." I smile softly and move the crackers back to the tray. "Here." I pop two pills into his hand, almost sighing when I see the gloves. He doesn't even take them off to sleep. That's just weird.

After watching him swallow them, he lies back down and tries to pull the blanket over his head. "Go back downstairs."

"One more thing." I wave the long and thin digital thermometer at him with a smirk.

He blanches. "Not a fucking chance."

Snort. "Relax, it's for under your arm."

"That's the baby thermometer."

"I'm sure he won't mind." I go to touch his arm and he flinches away. Right, the hand thing, but he didn't flinch away when I brushed his hair from his forehead. How strange. I somehow manage to wriggle it into the crease where his arm is pressed to his chest. After a few moments it beeps frequently.

Forty one.... FORTY ONE!

"Where are you going?" Nathan calls as I grab the tray and rush from the room.

I have to bring his fever down. This is all too familiar, all too close to home.

"What now?" Nathan sighs, his N sounding more like a D. "Can't you just leave me alone?"

"Are you naked?" I ask and pull the blanket down his back.

"Why? Do you want me to be?" He attempts to smile but it looks more like a grimace.

"Shut up." I place two thick and clean towels onto the bed beside him and he watches me through a small gap between his lids. He doesn't look impressed, only irritated. I really don't care. "Lie on here, on your back."

"Why?"

"Now, or I'll move you and you look heavy. Not a good idea for me."

His sluggish limbs shuffle him onto the towel and I'm glad to see he's doing as he's told. His eyes hold mine as I grab a folded damp flannel and place it on his forehead, being careful to not touch his skin with my hands. "How are you feeling?"

"Worse than I look." He cringes as I lay another damp flannel over his neck. "Why are you doing this?"

"You don't look that bad." I ignore his question and stare at his skin as it instantly tightens, tiny goose bumps forming along the surface.

"Are you done yet?"

My head swings back and forth. Nope. I'll never be done. Not until his fever has gone and I'm satisfied that his heart is going to continue beating. "Go to sleep."

"Leave my room and I will."

Ignorance is bliss. Well... it is at this point.

"I told you to leave."

"No."

His brow quirks, making it vanish under the flannel. "No? This is my room."

"Go to sleep, Nathan," I whisper and remove the flannels from him after ten more minutes.

He rolls off the towels and pulls the blanket back up and over his head. My entire body is shaking. My gut is screaming at me. Maybe I should take him to the hospital, just in case.

"You're staring." He lies flat on his back. "It's distracting."

Eye roll. "You're poorly; just shut your eyes." Maybe I should keep him awake. That would be selfish though.

"Stop staring."

I refuse, because I'm making sure he's still breathing.

"Sorry," I mutter and fluff up the pillows where the towels were moments before. I lean back against them, cringing at the heat coming from him. He's ill, that's for sure. "Maybe I should call a doctor?"

He doesn't respond. Why isn't he responding?

Okay, I can hear him breathing. He's sleeping, that's all.

My twisted mind is relieved when he starts shivering after twenty minutes or so. It's a sign he's okay. Sick as a dog but still alive. That's good.

I should leave. Why am I sat here? I just can't bring myself to leave.

Just another half an hour. I'm overreacting, he'll be fine.

His short breath becomes slow and steady after forty minutes. I relax minutely until I hear him take a shuddering one and suddenly I'm tense again. What is wrong with me? He's fine!

But just in case he isn't, I should check his pulse.

My two fingers almost sizzle against his skin, that's how warm he is. The feel of his artery pumping against my fingers does little to soothe my inner turmoil.

I should call a doctor.

I'll do it in the morning.

But what if he's not here in the morning? I'll regret it for the rest of my life.

I stare at his peaceful face in the dark and gently move his hair from his brow. His hair is amazingly soft, not like Caleb's. His was great but it resembled the feel of knotted silk. With Nathan's my fingers just slide straight through. He conditions.

I move my hand down to his chest and savour the feel of his heartbeat. I want to hear it. Is that weird? Probably.

He's too out of it to care.

Shuffling down the bed, I move my hair to my opposite shoulder and place my cheek on his chest. His chest is solid yet soft, with only a light dusting of hair. It's a nice chest. He doesn't move and his breathing remains steady so I know I haven't disturbed him.

Thump, thump, thump, thump.

Blowing out a soft sigh of grief and relief, I curl my legs and rest my arm across his abdomen, my hand fisting near my mouth.

I don't want to move from this spot. I will in a second.

Just a minute or two.

CHAPTER TWENTY

S O WARM. TOO WARM.

Why's my back damp?

Hot breath tickles my neck as I blink the sleep from my eyes and scan my surroundings. This isn't my room.

An arm tightens around my waist and a soft male groan accompanies the movement. The air rushes from my lungs as I realise where I am and what I'm doing. I'm spooning with Nathan.

I'm spooning with Nathan, who is roasting hot and covered in a thin layer of sweat. Why doesn't this gross me out? Maybe because I'm relieved to see that he's alive.

"Nathan?" I say and try to roll onto my back, but his arm holds me even tighter. I feel his nose against my neck and his forehead against my ear. His leg locks between mine, his thigh sliding so high I can feel the heat against a place I shouldn't. "Nathan?"

"Umm," he hums against my neck, sending a tremble through my entire body.

"Are you okay?"

His only answer is to run his nose up and down the back of my neck. Fingers that were wrapped around my ribs trail over the swell of my stomach before flattening directly below it. Gasp. His hand is far too close to my... oh god.

"Gwen," he mumbles and I feel him grind himself against my arse. My mouth drops open. I'm frozen on the spot. What's happening? Well, whatever is happening, there's now solid evidence of it pressed against my arse.

"Oh my god," I mime, not making noise when in reality I should be running and screaming.

I feel him tense behind me and squeeze my eyes shut. It takes everything in me to relax my breathing and my face.

"Gwen?" I'm shocked when he doesn't instantly move his clearly throbbing, well-endowed length from my backside. Instead he moves his arm back to its original spot above my stomach and collapses back onto the pillow with a groan. "I know you're awake."

Oh shit. I still feign sleep.

"I should move away but..." he snuggles in tighter. Gulp. "Your warmth is comforting."

And your warmth is disorienting and scalding.

He lifts up again and leans over me, pressing me deeper into the mattress. His groin still hasn't left my arse. If anything it's pressing harder as he reaches for the water bottle on the bedside table.

I gasp when he grinds once, then twice and quickly shift away from him, only to meet a boyish smile I've never seen on his face before. "What's wrong, Gwen?"

"You're a pig," I comment and kick the blanket off me.

"No morning kiss?" He taps his chin with his finger.

My mouth falls open. "You're clearly still delirious. Take your medicine." I throw the boxes at him and gather up the damp and dry towels that I folded and placed on the floor last night.

"I'm only playing." He starts to cough and falls back onto the bed.

"Where do you keep the bed sheets for this room?"

"In there." He points to the door behind me, his eyes narrowing. "Why?"

"So I can change these and wash them. They're damp, and soaking in your own illness won't help you get any better."

"Thank you." He rolls onto his front and pulls the blanket over his head.

"Aren't you going to have a warm bath or something?" I tap my foot impatiently and place the towels by the door.

"No."

"Why?"

"It hasn't gone to sleep yet," he mutters so I can barely hear him.

My lips pinch together but it's not enough; a giggle bubbles up from my chest and spills forth. I rip the blanket from his body, revealing his tight black boxers that fit his frame oh so well.

"It's cold."

Ignoring him, I set to work stripping the sheet from the blanket. He grumbles to himself and pulls his body into a sitting position on the side of the bed. "I'm going to have a shower." On shaking legs he stands, his back to me. I take this moment to strip the sheet from the bed, rather than stare at his back.

Stop it, Gwen. Stop it!

Then he turns. "Holy…" I cover my eyes and turn, ignoring his laugh as he walks towards the door which I now know is the bathroom.

"I did warn you."

I peek between my eyes when I hear the door close, but he's still there. Tented boxers and all. Christ he's big… I mean… look away damn it!

"Get out," I squeal and turn around.

I can't see it but I know it's there, a smug smile is definitely on his face. Arsehole. What's he playing at?

I quickly remake his bed and grab the towels and sheets before exiting his room.

As soon as I have them in the washing machine, I make soup. He needs it and I enjoy soup so it's all good, although it'll probably take a while. I'm sure he'll be okay for the next hour or so.

Should I check on him? What if he fell in the shower?

No. I'll leave him to rest before bothering him again.

The chicken simmers in the pot of water, almost ready to eat, as the bread warms and rises in the oven, filling the house with a delicious scent that makes your mouth water. Jeanine arrived not long after I began cooking. I didn't realise how early it was. She took over the soup for a moment while I had a shower and got dressed. No need to walk around in my pyjamas all day, smelling of Nathan's sweat.

Not that his sweat stinks or anything, just that… well… it's Nathan.

I serve the soup into two bowls as the bread cools and place them both on a tray with two glasses of water and a bottle of cough medicine for the man upstairs. Jeanine cleans around me as I cut the bread and place the slices on the tray. I also grab a table cloth and go on my merry way.

My cheeks heat as soon as I step into the room. He's half asleep on his front, looking pale and weak. "Nathan?" I whisper into the silence and place the tray on the small table beside him.

"Yeah?" He sits up and glances at the silver tray. "Soup? What am I, a child?"

"I'm still debating," I mutter and fluff the pillows behind his back, which he frowns at.

"I can do that myself."

Sigh. "You shouldn't be doing much of anything."

"Which I wouldn't be if you'd leave me alone."

Touché. "Okay, grumpy, just eat and I'll leave you alone."

I open the table cloth and fan it out over the bedding. Nathan smoothes it down with his hands. Climbing in beside him, I reach over and carefully pick up the tray before placing it on his lap. I take my own bowl and immediately soak a corner of the bread in it.

Nathan grimaces as he swallows the first bite. "I wish I could taste it."

"It's fabulous," I brag with a smile. "And full of protein and vitamins."

"Is there any left?"

"Yes, plenty."

He nods. "Freeze some, so I can try it when my tongue isn't as thick as a foot and as dry as sand."

"Sure." It really does taste good. "Is there anything you need me to do while you're out of commission?"

He thinks on it for a moment, swallowing the food in his mouth so his long, corded neck bobs, causing my eyes to zoom in on that area. My mouth has just gone dry. "No, but thank you for offering, Guinevere."

"I'm sorry for coming into your room without your permission," I blurt, cursing my conscience. "I got really worried when I hadn't seen you all day."

He shakes his head and waves me off, before sliding the tray onto my lap. "Thank you for the food, but I'm full."

"Okay." I stare down at his almost full bowl and frown. Nathan can eat like a starving horse. He'll lose weight if he goes through another day like this. He's already lean and obviously toned, but any more off him and you'll be able to see his ribs. "I'll just take these away and leave you to rest."

He nods, his eyes watching me as I gather up the tablecloth, careful to keep the crumbs inside, and pick up the tray. I switch out the light with my elbow and use my belly to balance the tray with one hand as I shut the door behind me.

Now what can I do?

I don't want to leave the house just in case. Oh shit, I should have made sure he had his phone and that it was fully charged. I doubt I'll be able to hear him yelling from all the way up there. Although I'd probably hear something if I were in my room.

That's what I'll do. I'll do another jigsaw puzzle on my bedroom floor. There are a few in the closet in the room next to mine. I grab one at random and waddle back into my room. I tip the pieces on the floor after sitting on a pillow.

This is going to be a dull few hours until dinner time.

"More soup?" Nathan sounds awful. We situate ourselves on the bed like we did earlier at lunch. "Vegetable?"

"Leek and potato."

We eat in amiable silence for a while. I'm pleased when he finishes the last of it with his bread. I remove the tray and table cloth and leave the room silently.

Nathan texts for me to go upstairs not long after I retire to my room and get ready for bed. I don't hesitate to race to him like a lioness to her cub. Probably a weird comparison.

"What's wrong?" I'm a little out of breath and the baby doesn't appreciate the jostling around. If its insistent kicking of my internal organs are anything to go by, I'd say he's pretty darn pissed at being disturbed.

I see Nathan's hand in the dark, covered in black leather, and it pats the bed beside him where the blanket is pulled back, almost doubled over on his side.

My mind tells me not to sit so I don't. I look down at him, only a few inches from the bed. "What?"

"Sit," he mumbles, his eyes closed.

"Why?"

His eyes open, the light brown almost glowing in the dark. "Sit."

"'Kay." I sit. I don't feel comfortable because for some reason I feel way too comfortable. Part of me is clenching inside, whispering things to my brain, telling me to fill it with a forbidden tool.

I'm a slut.

His arm snags me around the waist, forcing me back into the pillow. My body tenses. "What are you doing, Nathan?"

"Using you as my radiator," he lies and I know he's lying because he's making no attempt to hide the fact that he's hard.

"We shouldn't be doing this." It's wrong, so wrong.

"I know." He doesn't sound like he cares though. "I like having you with me like this."

"Nathan..." I warn.

He continues, ignorant of my tone. "Just while I'm ill. Just tonight. I won't have the courage to ask you again."

"This is a bad idea." I sigh but find myself relaxing into him. "But it's nice too."

"Yeah." He nuzzles the back of my neck, causing me to tense. "Relax."

"Your thing is between my legs, Nathan." I try to frown but it doesn't come, especially when I feel him twitch. A fit of nervous giggles bubbles up from within. Nathan's body starts shaking with mine, his laughter silent. "Stop it, it's not funny."

"My head hurts," he moans and seems to bury his face in my hair.

"Have you had any painkillers yet?"

"Yes, Mum."

I shudder., "Calling me that, right at this point in time, makes this even seedier."

"Yes, ma'am."

"Go to sleep, Nathan." I place my hand on the pillow by my head and let out a long breath. "Nathan?" I call quietly into the darkness, my head swimming with thoughts.

He doesn't respond. The only sound that can be heard from him is his soft breathing.

A line has been crossed. A line that should never have been crossed.

I sit at my vanity table freshly showered and preparing for the day. The mascara brush is held tightly between my fingers as I pull it along my long lashes. Green eyes stare back at me in the mirror. Troubled eyes with a million secrets and emotions hiding behind the clear irises.

I place the wand down on the desk and chew on my lip as I gather my thoughts.

This morning I snuck out of bed before Nathan awoke. It's now only seven fifteen and I doubt he'll be up any time soon. I feel the need to flee before he wakes. At least I have a plan for how to handle this situation, albeit not a very good one.

My hopes are dashed when my bedroom door swings open and he strolls in, looking freshly showered and ready for the day. I'm annoyed that he didn't knock first. "We need to talk."

"Yeah," I agree because we really do need to talk, even though I don't want to address anything that has happened between us lately.

His long legs carry him to me in three quick strides, his hand reaching for the desk drawer. I watch him pull out the envelope that has been the cause of my nightmares as of late. "You haven't brought this up, but I can see you've read it."

My eyes meet his in the mirror, my mouth falling open. I have no words to explain why I've not said anything, other than the fact I just don't want to. That and he's been poorly.

"I can only assume this means you're thinking about it?" His sentence is a question and I notice his nerves. Nathan is nervous. I'm suddenly realising a side to him that I didn't know existed. Never has he looked more vulnerable than he does now, despite the hardening features. He lets out a laugh. "Or, by the looks of your panicked eyes and trembling hands, I'd say you already have an answer and I'm guessing it's not the answer I want to hear."

My mouth closes, then opens and then closes again. I let out a sigh and let my head fall forward, my hair creating a curtain between me and the room.

"You won't even consider it?" My eyes are once again drawn to him when I hear the sadness to his tone.

Honestly? "I can't."

He stands silent, his stare unwavering. "Very well."

"Nathan." I reach out, twisting on the bench so I can grab his wrist. "It's not you."

"No," he snarls and tugs his wrist free. "It's Caleb."

What the hell is that supposed to mean? "I love Caleb. I'm his fiancée, Nathan." I follow him out of my room and practically chase him down the stairs and into the living room. He stops at the window, his hands gripping the frame as he stares through the rain splattered glass.

"It's time for you to move on, Guinevere." I daren't open my mouth for fear of crying or verbally attacking him. "I'm sorry he's gone, truly I am, but you need to let go."

"I don't want to talk about this," I say to the floor, wishing I could curl my legs to my chest. Stupid fat belly.

"You need to talk about it sooner or later."

I shake my head slowly, closing my eyes for a moment. "Yes and when I do, it won't be with you."

"What's that supposed to mean?" He sounds genuinely affronted. "He was my brother. If you talk to anyone it should be me."

"You have no tact." I look him dead in the eye. "You have no tact and no compassion. I'm his fiancée and this is my decision. When I'm ready to let go, I'll let go."

"Therein lies your problem." Why is he speaking to me like this? "You said '*I'm* his fiancée'. You *were* his fiancée. Past tense."

"Christ, you're a dick," I snarl and instantly realise my mistake.

He's away from the window and in seconds he's in front of me. I cower under his harsh glare and scramble away from him. Darting for the hall, I don't even make it through the archway as an arm wraps around my waist directly above my stomach. It doesn't hurt and he's not rough but it's strong enough to stop me in my tracks.

I feel the cool leather of his gloved hand as it moves my hair from my shoulder. His chest is pressed against my back and his lips slightly touch the shell of my ear.

"Let this be your last warning," he whispers dangerously into my ear. "If you disobey me again, I will put you over my knee, pregnant or not."

"That's not even possible. Have you seen the size of my belly?"

I feel him tense.

"I'm not a child. If you hit me, I will report you."

He tenses further.

My body is trembling and I can't stop it. I've never been so scared in my life.

I feel his chest shaking and for a moment I think he's crying. I'm wrong, he's laughing. What the hell is wrong with this guy? "If you say so, Gwen."

"This isn't funny."

He stops laughing and his body stills. "No, it's not funny, you're right."

"We need to get past this and we needed to do it yesterday." Pulling away from him, I walk a few steps before turning, my body tense in preparation for the argument that we're no doubt going to have. "I don't know what's going through your mind and I don't know how you've rationalised this, but it doesn't make sense."

"It makes perfect sense," he responds, his tone loud and a little smug.

Okay, let's try this another way. "You're his brother. This is the twenty first century. Things like this don't happen any longer and if they do, they're frowned upon."

"You genuinely care what people think?"

I scowl, my annoyance turning into anger. "I care what Caleb thinks."

"Caleb is dead." Why does he have to be so cold? "Don't give me that look, it's the truth."

"And one day I'll be dead and I'll have to go up there and deal with the pain he feels knowing that I was sharing a bed with his brother just a few short months after his life ended so quickly."

He rolls his eyes. "You're romanticising reality. He's gone, I'm here. It's that simple."

"You're tarnishing your brother's memory by even suggesting I marry you," I shout, my hands in fists by my sides. My face feels warm. "I won't."

His eyes darken. "And why not? Just because of my brother?"

"Because I don't think of you in that way!"

He laughs cruelly. "I'd believe you if your eyes weren't flickering all over the place, Guinevere. You don't lie very well. You're too honest to lie."

A growl-like noise escapes me. "You are unbelievable! And deluded."

"I'm realistic. An attractive woman and an attractive man spend their time at home alone, sharing meal times and conversation. I don't have female friends. I have female acquaintances." He steps into me, his eyes boring down into mine. "And I have females that I fuck."

"Oh, so you're allowed to swear? I'm done with this conversation." I try to step around him but he dominates my space, his arms coming up to cage me in. I feel the hard muscles of his stomach press against my belly. "Christ, you are really driving me crazy. Seriously, I'm ready to... to... Gah."

My hands press against his chest but he doesn't budge. "I'm going back to live with my mum."

His smile becomes cocky. "No you're not."

"Yes I am."

He leans in close and I can smell the cleanliness of his skin. Soap and Nathan. "You're not."

"Please move." I look over his shoulder, refusing to make eye contact. "I don't know why you're doing this to me but it's not fair. I've done nothing to you." Now I do look him in the eye, in an attempt to make him understand me. "I just want to be friends, but now I'm not even sure if I want that."

"I'll let us remain friends for now, but things will change." My lip vanishes behind my teeth and his heated eyes darken and stare at that area. "Maybe I should just kiss you now. We both know you won't resist."

I want to argue with this but I can't. I'm like a rabbit in headlights.

"But I won't. I won't kiss you until you're ready." His fingers tuck my hair behind my ear and his thumb swipes across my cheekbone. "But make no mistake, I don't want to be your friend, Gwen. You know this now, you know my intentions. One day I will kiss you and one day you will be mine." His smile softens. "Until then I'll play along."

"I hate you right now." I whisper, tired of this game and this conversation.

"Hate is an emotion I can live with." He smiles wickedly and straightens, his arms by his sides. "There's a very thin line between love and hate and the opposite to love is indifference. So..." Soft lips touch my forehead for an endless moment. "You can still love me and hate me at the same time."

"Deluded." My legs finally do their job and march me past him. "I'm leaving."

"You're not." Grr. He is really pissing me off now. "If you try, I will drag you back kicking and screaming if I have to."

"You need help. Mental help."

His smug grin flickers. "Perhaps."

I leave the room and lock my arms together across my belly. It doesn't stop them from trembling but it helps me feel a little bit safer.

I'm about to grab the keys from their usual spot when memories of the last time I did this crash through my brain like endless angry waves against a cliff. There's no way I'm going through that again.

As I ponder what I'm going to do, coming up with zero answers, there's a knock at the door. Maybe Jeanine forgot to bring her keys.

Before I get a chance to open it more than an inch, it's being pushed with a force that sends it flying into the wall. If there weren't a doorstopper at the base the handle would have left a nasty indent in the plaster. "NATHAN!" I shout when his father storms past me and up the stairs. "NATHAN!"

His father isn't interested in me, he completely ignores me. Should I call the Police? I don't know what to do.

Mr Weston reaches the top of the stairs but Nathan is stood there already. "You absolute cunt."

His father's words shock me but Nathan doesn't seem affected. "Leave."

"You absolute cunt, it's not enough that you're suing me but now you're trying to take my business as well?"

Nathan's body goes tight. "I assure you I'm not touching the family business. I'm starting my own."

"Same fucking thing!" His father rages, his face purpling with anger and spit flying from his mouth.

Nathan stands his ground. I wish they'd move away from the stairs; it's making me nervous. All I can picture is one of them falling. "Nathan," I say quietly, but his eyes don't come to me.

"You're drunk," he states to his father.

"The Petersons have been a part of my company for years... so imagine my shock when they told me they were terminating our contract."

Nathan shrugs. "They came to me after I spoke to Harrison." I have no idea who any of these people are. "He's selling me one of his smaller stores."

Well that's good.

"It won't work." His father sways slightly as his arm lifts to point a finger at Nathan. "Your jewellery is amateur."

"Better than old fashioned," I mutter and the angry drunk sneers at me.

"Nobody respects the opinion of a whore," Mr Weston growls at me, his tone full of malice and hate. Totally undeserved.

Nathan's body tightens and I feel the space around us fill with his anger, his fury. It's so potent I can almost see it. I really wouldn't like to be his father right now, who is oblivious and staring at me.

"She's still here." His eyes are on me but his words are aimed at Nathan. "We had a deal."

"And when you received the papers from my solicitor, that should have told you I had no interest in making a deal with you. I have no interest in you at all actually."

Go Nathan!

His father begins to descend the stairs. Nathan cuts ahead of him and puts himself between us. "You always were a failure, Nathan. Failed as a son, failed college, failed university, you'll fail this too." What?

"I don't care. I'm bored of hearing you say it." Nathan sighs and pinches the bridge of his nose. "You need to leave before you make a bigger fool of yourself."

Mr Weston leans around his son. "He'll fail you too." His cold eyes go to his son, his body still swaying from the effects of whatever alcohol it is he's consumed. "Like he failed me and his brother."

Gasp.

Nathan takes a step towards him but my hand shoots out and grabs his arm. "Nathan."

He looks back at me, his eyes sad and showing his wavering control. His father doesn't stop. "This business will fail. You don't have what it takes. You're lazy, incompetent and stupid."

"I wonder who he gets that from," I remark dryly.

"Stay out of this, Gwen," Nathan warns and runs a hand through his hair. "Leave us."

He's asking me to leave? No, not asking, telling. "What?"

"Take the car keys and go out for an hour. There are things I need to speak to my father about."

"I'm not leaving you. Not with him." My face contorts in disgust.

Nathan flies around and tilts his head to catch my eyes. "I said leave. You're my guest, you'll do as you're told. My father and I have things we need to talk about, without you present. Contact Jeanine, tell her not to come."

I want to be angry but the pain in his eyes wipes that away in an instant. I speak in a hushed tone. "Are you going to be okay?"

His eyes soften and his body drops an inch. "Yes. Please. I don't want you to be here while he is. Let me speak with him and then he'll never have a reason to return."

"I don't like it," I admit, but feel my previous decision begin to waver. "Call me if you need me."

Nathan reaches into his pocket and pulls out a bunch of notes. I go to back away but he shoves them into my back pocket and nudges my forehead with his nose. I find the strange display of affection comforting, even though I shouldn't.

"Paying for her services already?" His father bates but I ignore him. Nathan doesn't though, he twists and grabs his father by the throat. I squeal and press my back against the wall as Nathan whispers into his father's ear. I can't hear what he's saying and I'm not sure Mr Weston can either. His face is almost purple.

"Go. I'm not giving him the ability to speak until you're gone." Meaning if I don't leave right now, his father will suffocate in about twenty seconds. I duck my head and flee the house, grabbing the car keys on the way.

Jeanine is pulling into the drive as I exit the house so I immediately rush to her and lie the first lie that comes to mind. "Nathan wants to be alone right now. He's just had some... umm... bad family news that he needs to deal with."

She doesn't believe me, not in the slightest. She does promise to follow me back into the village for a drink, though. I need a coffee. Decaf or not, I still need it.

Mr Weston is vile. VILE! Grr, I just want to poke him in the eye.

Who would say that to their son? It's disgusting. Nathan isn't a failure. He's talented and smart and he can actually be quite funny at times.

***

"Whatever it is, it's none of your business," Jeanine says softly, her hand cupping mine over the table. My free hand nurses my coffee close to my chest. "You've been mulling over whatever is on your mind for far too long. It isn't your business and it isn't mine."

"I know."

"Do you? Nathan is a complex man. There are secrets in the Weston house that even I dread to think about. If you want to help him, just be there for him."

I nod quickly and chew on my lip. "I don't think I like it here anymore."

"Did you ever?" She seems to be joking but I can tell it's to soften the tone of her sincerity.

I nod again. "Yes. Nathan is actually a joy to be around sometimes."

"He's no Caleb," she comments, causing me to wince. "He'll never be Caleb."

"I know." Why do people assume I don't know this? "I don't want him to be Caleb. Caleb doesn't even enter my mind when I'm with Nathan." Oh shit. Wrong choice of words. "I mean... he does but not in a comparison type of way... you know what I mean, Jeanine."

She smiles, showing sparkly white dentures. "Yes. I do." Her body tilts closer as her eyes scan the people around us. "Don't try and figure it out."

"Figure what out?"

"Why Caleb was loved and Nathan wasn't. It..." She sighs heavily and leans back. "Forget I said anything."

Oh no, she can't leave it like that. "What do you mean Caleb was loved?"

"I've said too much."

"Then say something more, what's the difference?"

Jeanine frowns, her eyes shadowing over with past memories I'm eager to know. "I signed something. If I say anything to anyone, Nathan will take pleasure in destroying me."

"Can't you give me even the slightest hint?"

She looks out of the window and shifts in her seat. I want to shake her, scream at her, make her tell me what I want to know. "My daughter is only a year older than Nathan, as you know. She was playing out by the old barn," the barn that is no more than charred wood I'm assuming, "when she saw some things that... well let's just say it took quite a bit of therapy to help her get past it."

"What things?"

"I'm not telling you to fuel your curiosity, I'm telling you because whatever secrets Nathan has, he likes to keep them that way. The entire family is one huge riddle and trust me when I say they're a riddle you don't want to solve. Nathan and Caleb are and were good men. He'll look after you. That's all you need to know. Other than that... don't get involved." Her stern tone is quiet, only loud enough for me to hear. What is she talking about? I need to know. "Don't try to dig anything up, and keep out of Nathan's way."

"I don't understand."

She rubs her tired eyes and shifts again, her discomfort obvious. "You don't need to. Just don't get attached."

"Why?" Not that I'm planning on it, for obvious reasons. "He won't hurt me." Why am I arguing this point? I don't want to get attached in the way she's assuming anyway.

She chuckles sadly, her eyes still gazing out of the window. "That's not what I'm worried about, sweetie. I'm worried you'll hurt him."

My breath leaves me. Jeanine stands, thanks me for the coffee and exits the café with her head bowed. I mull over her words again and again until I no longer remember the exact conversation. Only her parting words stick in my mind.

How could I hurt him? Nathan is... he seems impenetrable. He's his own fortress and nothing seems to affect him. I'd never hurt him intentionally. I've been clear about my feelings from the start. I think.

Although he is insistent that we'll be more than friends.

Maybe he's just toying with me, testing my loyalty to his brother. Do I even have any loyalty to Caleb anymore? It sure doesn't feel like it. I've betrayed him numerous times since he died.

CHAPTER TWENTY-ONE

I T'S BEEN THREE HOURS and I've heard nothing from Nathan. I decided twenty minutes ago that I wasn't staying away any longer. Now I'm sitting in the car outside Nathan's house, twisting my hands on the steering wheel and staring at the front door through the windshield.

The front door opens and Nathan stands there, motioning for me to come in. I climb out of the car and walk towards him, noticing two bags on the floor behind him.

"What's this?" I enquire, my brows furrowed and my worries heightened. Is he kicking me out?

"We're going to the city," he responds. "Check your bag, make sure I've packed everything."

I do as I'm told, hiding my annoyance that yet again he went through my things. "Everything is here. Why are we going to the city?"

"You'll see." Gah, a surprise. I hate surprises.

Well, actually I love them, I'm just impatient for them. "No clues?"

"I need..." He makes a squelching noise with his mouth. "I need your help with something."

"As long as it doesn't involve belly dancing or sky diving, I guess I can do my best." He helps me into the car, his eyes distant. His mind is clearly troubled with things unknown. Not even a smirk? "Tough crowd."

"Sorry," he mumbles and closes the passenger side door.

"Let's play a game," I suggest after he's seated.

He looks at me with a quirked brow and I slap his arm. "Fine, fine. What game?"

"Well, it's not really a game." I twist my fingers on my lap and look out of the window to the passing countryside.

"Then what is it?"

"I ask a question, you ask a question."

I don't need to look at him to know he's frowning. "That doesn't sound like fun."

"What's your favourite colour?"

He chuckles. "Fair enough. It's dark blue. Yours?"

"That counts as your question. Mine's dark pink." I sort through my compiled questions. "What's the happiest memory you have?"

He blanches, his eyes widening before the shutters come down. "Pass."

"You can't pass."

"I can."

Oh... the reason dawns on me. OH. It's a sexual one then. Okay. Moving on. "What's the saddest memory you have?"

"Pass."

"You suck," I grunt and move onto another question. "You have to answer this one."

He smirks, his eyes lit with humour. "I do, do I?"

"Yes." Nod. "Have you ever been in love?"

His smile fades in an instant. "You're terrible. You know that, right?"

"Yep."

"Fine, yes I've been in love."

Score. "With who?"

His brows hit his hair, which isn't difficult considering the length of it at the moment. The bottom brushes the base of his neck. I like it, it suits him. "It's my question now." Oh, right. "What's the happiest memory you have?"

The cheek! "You can't expect me to answer that!" So not fair.

"I can."

Growl. "Meeting Caleb, best day of my life."

His face is blank so I can't see what he's feeling and I'm not sure why I want to. "So not when he proposed?"

Hmm... "No, that's number two on my list of favourite memories." I turn my body towards him. "My turn. Who have you been in love with?"

"It was a while ago," he says with a shrug. "I didn't know her name."

How's that even possible?

"I used to see her walking a lot, around town. I never did pluck up the courage to talk to her." His eyes glaze over for a moment and I wonder if he's still in love with the memory of this girl. "It's stupid, I should have done. I've regretted it ever since."

"Why?" I know it's not my turn but I need to know more.

His tongue dampens his lower lip. "Because I could have had what you and Caleb had. I missed out on that."

"You're still young; you could have that."

His lips twitch. "Possibly. My turn and I get two questions."

"Go for it," I spur him on whilst staring at his profile.

"Okay." His gloved fingers run through his longish locks. "Tell me about your parents."

Hmm, where to begin. "I have no clue who my dad is. My mum says he knows I exist, saw me once and never came back." He's about to apologize and I cut him off because it's really not a big deal. "My mum, she loves me in her own way and she's always supported me with everything but this and the engagement. She wanted me to have the life she didn't."

"That I can relate to."

"Hmm." I bet he can. Poor Nathan. "I was always an inconvenience more than anything. She was never mean and I was always well dressed and never hungry, it was more duty than love though." We share a moment's silence and I wonder if he can relate to this too. "Caleb said his parents were great to him as he grew up, but his dad expected things of him that he didn't want."

"Yes, he was the apple of their eyes."

Dare I tread? "Why weren't they like that with you?" Yep, clearly I dare.

"Honestly?" He blows out a breath, his left arm flicking the indicator down. "I have no idea."

"You're not a failure, Nathan," I tell him but I can see he doesn't believe me. I don't expect him to. He's been treated badly all of his life by the sounds of it. Why would he believe my word over something that's been drilled into him for god knows how long?

"Was Caleb your first?"

My mind is still spinning with thoughts when he asks this so I don't click on immediately. When I do I choke on air. "That's a personal question."

"It's the question I'm choosing."

"Your questions are not nice questions." I shrug a little. Whatever, I'm not ashamed. "Yes he was my first." And I wish he could be my last, but I'm not stupid enough to make that promise. Time goes by and as much as the thought of sleeping with someone else repulses me, it'll probably happen eventually.

Pulling myself from my thoughts I look at Nathan, mainly because his leather gloves are squeaking on the rubber wheel. He does this when he's frustrated. Why's he frustrated? "Your question."

"Okay, how old were you when you lost your virginity?" My smile is cocky, two can play at this game.

"Young, I don't remember." Oh he's lying.

"You're a terrible liar too."

"I don't want to play this game anymore."

"Boring."

"Bored," he retorts and raises his chin defiantly. "Let's just listen to the radio."

He's so secretive, it drives me crazy. Maybe that's because I grew up with just me and my mum. It has made me eager to see how much greener the grass is on the other side. Or the opposite.

It doesn't take long to get to the city, even though we stop for lunch on the way. When we arrive we pull up outside an empty looking store on a busy street. Nathan helps me out of the car and pulls a ring of keys from his inner jacket pocket.

He first opens the shutters via a keyhole in a small grey box beside the shutters. They slowly ascend, revealing two wide windows with a door in the middle. Next we step inside and I'm relieved to see it's not dusty. Dust bugs the hell out of me.

From what I can see there are glass cases on top of dark wooden settings spread out around the room. Glass encased shelves line the walls. Even the counter is one long display box.

"What do you think?" He asks, worrying his lip between his teeth. "Think this is a good place to start?"

I nod slowly, observing the room. "I think it's great. A little dull though."

"Agreed, we need to set it apart from the rest." We? "It opens in a few months hopefully, I'm just waiting on stock and staff and I need to expand my jewellery selection and find a supplier."

"You'll do great, Nathan," I say honestly because I know he will. "Your jewellery is amazing."

His cheeks pink slightly and for the second time since I've met him I get to see a sweet vulnerability shine through. "I'm nervous."

"You're human." I place my hand on his shoulder as he leans forward on the counter display case. "You'll be fine and, if you're not, you'll still have me as your number one fan."

He looks at me, a handsome smile on his face. "You're a lovely person, Guinevere."

"So are you, Nathan."

"You bring that out in me." His lips purse slightly. I can see he's battling with himself on whether or not to say anything. "A few months ago I wanted to do this to destroy my dad's business, a revenge mission so to speak. Because of my family name I know this will get attention, the son of a well-known business man branching out on his own. I wanted to bring him to his knees, make him regret the day he called me a failure." I listen intently, wondering where he's going with this. "And now..." He pauses and looks at me, his hands coming up to cup my neck. "Now I just want to succeed to prove that I'm worth it."

"You are worth it." I stop myself from rolling my eyes. "You're worth everything." I'm not sure if this makes sense but I know what I'm talking about.

"No." He steps closer. "I mean... with you."

"You're worth a lot to me."

"Not as much as my brother," he grits through his teeth.

My hand comes up and grips his wrist. I stare him in the eye. "The same. You're worth the same to me as he was. It's just a different kind of worth."

"Don't," he sighs and presses his forehead against mine. "Don't give me false hope."

Gulp. "False hope for what?"

"That maybe one day you'll look at me the way you looked at him."

My heart skips a beat. "How do you know the way I looked at him?"

His phone rings, disturbing our intimate moment. I want to smash it but instead I step away to give him some privacy. He looks at me apologetically and puts his phone to his ear.

"I'll wait in the car." I have words to erase from my mind.

"We'll talk later."

Or never. Never is good too.

Nathan doesn't take me back to the hotel. He takes me for a long walk around Piccadilly Circus. He even takes a few pictures when I request them and a few when I don't. It's great, I love the city. I wish I could spend more time here before the baby arrives. I don't think pushing a pram around here is such a good idea.

I even manage to get a few pictures of him, which is great because I don't have any. Even though he doesn't smile, I still appreciate them.

I don't want this to end, what we have now. Maybe it's selfish of me. No maybe about it. It is selfish of me. Nathan's right, I'll never look at him the way I looked at Caleb. I'll never love him the way I loved Caleb, but I've come to love him in my own way. He's my best friend, possibly my only friend right now.

Well, the only friend I have within walking distance.

I care about him a lot, more than I should, and I'm not ready to give him up yet.

I am selfish. I can't argue with this. Of course I'm not using him but I need him and the thought of his attention being on somebody else makes me feel sick. Maybe it's the pregnancy hormones.

So I walk through the street with my arm around Nathan's, a smile on my face and a decision made in my mind. Right now I'm not letting him go. Right now he's mine and I'm going to enjoy that for as long as it lasts.

We arrive home when the sky gets dark. We go to our own rooms and I toss and turn as I try to sleep, missing his heat against my back and hating myself for it.

There's only one thought that enters my mind before I drift into the land of slumber. We didn't finish our talk and, for some reason, that makes me sad.

***

The weeks go by, my due date gets closer and my stomach gets bigger. All is healthy and well in my womb and my body is okay... to the extent that it's not under any stress. I feel like a whale though.

I knock on Nathan's bedroom door. It's eleven and he's still not down yet. I hope he's not ill again.

"Come in," he calls, so I do.

I place his coffee on the trunk at the end of the bed and then sit on the bed. He stands in front of the full length mirror buttoning the sleeves of his white and blue striped shirt.

"You look handsome," I comment, nursing my cup between my hands, the bottom of it balanced on my stomach. Nathan hates it when I balance things on my stomach, especially hot things. He's a little bit stressed when it comes to my pregnancy at the moment. If I didn't know any better, I'd say he was nervous. "It's snowing by the way."

"Seriously?" He doesn't look happy about this and immediately strolls to the window. I can see the large white flakes from where I'm sitting. "Great. It wasn't forecast until next week."

"Yep, they reckon twelve inches minimum in this area." I smile at the thought. I love the snow. "We can build a snowman."

"No we can't."

I glance at my planet and sigh. "Yeah, you're right. You can build a snowman and I'll watch and help you decorate it at the end."

"No." He raises his chin, his throat stretching as he buttons his collar. I stand and waddle towards him. "You look adorable when you walk."

I scowl playfully. "I look like a whale balancing on two toothpicks."

His smile widens. "At least you're a pretty whale."

"You're not funny. Not in the slightest."

"And an angry whale," he jests, his eyes glittering with amusement.

"I will sit on you," I threaten and pull his tie around his neck. "So, the dear old doctor called this morning. He wants to come out on Wednesday to check my lady parts." I loop the thick end around the thinner end. "He said he's going to come here. He wants to check our nursery I assume."

"What do you mean check your lady parts?"

I shrug; hell if I know. "Maybe to see if I'm dilated or something."

"That sounds uncomfortable." We both make a face. It does sound uncomfortable. Very much so. "Are you nervous?" I chew on the inside of my cheek and nod. He exhales a long breath after I repeat his question back to him. "Petrified."

"Why? You said you didn't want anything to do with the baby." I'm kidding. I mean, he did say it but I don't think it's true anymore.

He confirms my thoughts. "Things change. I don't want you doing this alone."

Aww, my heart just melted. "Thanks, Nathan."

"I also don't want your mum staying here for more than a few nights. I'm not fond of her." Well this is no secret. They met a month ago when my mum came to visit. She was shocked about the entire situation, not that I blame her. Although he took it all in his stride, she was rude to Nathan on more than one occasion, asking him about other girls and his private life, trying to convince me that he would throw the baby and me out when he gets a new girlfriend. I can see her logic and I understand her way of thinking. These same suspicions have plagued my mind for a while now.

If Nathan does happen to move on with his life, I'm certain his girlfriend won't be happy about the situation we're in.

"I'm aware of your opinion of my mum. If your two days of moaning and bitching after she left were anything to go by, I'd say you hate her."

"Hate is a strong emotion your mother isn't worthy of," he responds smugly and feels his now completed tie with one hand. "Thank you."

"Just making myself useful." I go back to the bed and lower myself onto it. "I look like I'm carrying twins."

"You look like you're glowing. Stop moaning about your appearance."

Resting back on my elbows I watch him pull his jacket on and smooth down the lapels with his hands. "Stay inside. No wandering around in this weather. I'll be back by dark."

"Can't I come?" I pout, tilting my head back to plead with him, eye to eye.

"No."

"Why?"

He smiles wickedly. "It's a surprise."

"I hate surprises," I grumble, swinging my legs side to side.

Nathan drops to his knees in front of me, pushing my legs out of the way so the top of his thigh connects with the side of my left hip. "You love surprises, you just hate waiting for them." His finger flicks at my lower lip. "And stop pouting."

"No." I pout even more and it soon turns to a squeal when he lunges forward and I feel his teeth latch onto my lower lip. He releases me after a few torturous seconds and kisses my forehead. "You just bit my lip."

"Don't pout." I want to pout for not being allowed to pout. Instead I flop back onto the bed, cringing as the baby swims around in my stomach. Nathan lifts my shirt and watches with his head slightly tilted. "He's running out of room."

"Yep." I close my eyes and remain relaxed when Nathan prods at the flailing limbs poking under the surface of my skin. He chuckles to himself, his fingers grabbing at feet and knees. "You're making him do it more."

"Your belly feels really tight," he remarks and I hum in response. It does, he's right, and I have no clue why it's doing that. I'll ask the good old doctor on Wednesday. Nathan goes back to playing limb grab with the baby. My eyes close. I'll just keep them closed for a moment. Only a moment.

My entire body tenses when I feel his soft, stubble free lips along the lower curve of my stomach. He doesn't stop there, he kisses further up sending tingles along my spine and continues going up. His kisses linger, each one a gentle caress. Leather clad fingers trail up my bare side, his thumb skimming over the swell of my breast. A shudder rips through me as a light moan leaves me.

My skin heats, my stomach tingles and I gasp when I feel the bed dip. His hand cups my chin, pulling it to the side. With my eyes closed I try to pretend this isn't happening. I try to pretend that after over two months of no contact from Nathan, he isn't doing this now. I can't push him away. I want to but my body is on fire. I'm surprised I'm not trembling with need.

He climbs up beside me.

A loud gasp rushes from my throat as he kisses the side of my neck. His tongue comes out to taste my skin as his hand holds my chin, stopping me from turning towards him and making the skin less tight and sensitive where he's kissing.

How can he want to do this with me? My body is hideous right now.

"Nathan," I manage to say through my panting. Am I telling him to stop? I don't know.

"Do you have any idea how beautiful you are?" He whispers in my ear and bites down on the lobe. "You're the only woman I've ever felt the need to touch, the need to taste." His tongue flicks at my neck, the spot below my ear that makes me purr.

"Stop," I say, my mind a war of emotions. "You... we... stop..."

Why's he shaking me? Why's my brain so foggy? I blink open my eyes, noticing the heavy feel of sleep pressing against my lids. "Huh?"

Nathan looks down at me, his lips twitching with a knowing smirk. "I lost you for a moment there." We weren't kissing? "Sounded like a fun dream."

"What?"

"Are you okay?" He's used to me falling asleep at random moments, but this is strange. It didn't feel like a dream. "You look a little disoriented."

"I... we..." I rub my eyes with the heels of my palms and slowly sit up. "When did I fall asleep?"

He shrugs. "I was trying to grab his feet. Two seconds later you were gone."

"Oh." So he didn't kiss me then. My guilt dissipates to a low murmur in my chest and mind. It lingers because I just had a dream about another man, but it's dull because I can't help who or what I dream about, especially right now. The past month or so has been hell. I've never been so horny and I can't reach down there to deal with it myself.

I had to get a bikini wax the other day. It fucking hurt! A lot!

No way in hell am I allowing my baby to pass through a jungle on his way out.

"Go to sleep, I'll be back in a few hours." Nathan pulls me up the bed and pulls the blanket over my body. He even shuts the curtains for me and pinches my nose. "I'll wake you when I get home."

"Uh-huh," I mumble and close my eyes. I love this mattress. I want this mattress. "Drive safe."

"Promise." He leaves the room after hovering in the doorway for a while. I imagine him looking longingly at the bed, wishing he could climb in and forget the world much like I'm doing. I'm being ridiculous though, I know this. Or maybe I'm the one who is wishful thinking. There's a heavy thought I don't want to address.

"Hey." It feels like I've only had my eyes shut for an hour when Nathan wakes me up again. I check the clock. It's been six. Christ, my nap turned into a coma.

Yes, bump, I blame you.

"What?" I rub my eyes and sway a little after sitting up. "What is it?"

Nathan takes my elbow and pulls me from the bed. I really don't want nor do I need to be awake right now. "I did something."

"Uh-oh," I feign horror. "Did you cook again?"

"It's almost six at night and you haven't fed me." We step into the dark hallway. Why aren't the lights on? I hate the dark.

"You're getting me out of bed so I can feed you?" I ask, my tone incredulous and impatient. I'm not the nicest person when I wake up. I try to turn around. "Order pizza."

His answer is to pull me down the stairs whilst chuckling.

Hey, the archway is glowing. Oh my god.

Christmas lights!

They hang loosely along the top and sides of the archway, twinkling purple and white in no particular pattern. The wooden floor holds the reflection of other dancing lights. I notice this as I make it to the last step. Nathan steps behind me and covers my eyes with one hand whilst guiding me by the elbow with the other.

"Okay, so, I've never actually done this myself before and it probably looks awful." He's nervous. I love it when he gets nervous. It reminds me that he's human and not a robot.

I know what he's done, he's decorated the room for me. But the anticipation and excitement to see it for real is strong.

"Ready?" He asks and I hear him gulp.

"As I'll ever be." His hand moves away and I gasp. "There's a tree!" I squeal and clap my hands before turning to look at the large room properly. My feet carry me to the fireplace where two stockings hang. I laugh and touch the red faux fur between my fingers and thumb.

There's not a surface without something Christmassy, it's amazing!

"Nathan," I sniff, my eyes tearing with emotion. "I can't believe you did this." He shrugs, his head lowered, seemingly shy all of a sudden. I step into him and wrap my arms around his waist. "This is amazing. You... are amazing." His arms come around me and we stand in the centre of the room, multi-coloured lights dancing across our bodies. The scent of pine wood and cinnamon fills the air.

It's almost Christmas.

***

We spend Christmas day just the two of us. I cook for obvious reasons and Nathan cleans. We didn't get each other much, mostly because we didn't know what to get. Nathan made me a bracelet to match my necklace and a new phone, which is way too fancy and complicated for me but I love it all the same. I got him ten new pairs of gloves, which he laughed his arse off at and a new jacket which cost half of my savings. He claims to love it and wears it proudly, but secretly I think he hates it and is just too kind to say anything.

Dinner is divine as I knew it would be and I made far too much. It doesn't matter though, I'll be having turkey and stuffing sandwiches for the rest of the week. I don't know a thing that's better.

Mostly we watch the Christmas movies on TV and play old board games that have more dust than pieces. We even try to play twister but I can't bend so that was a bust.

By the time midnight rolls around I've drunk my weight in alcohol free Baileys and I'm stuffed to the brim with food. Exhaustion seeps into me, making me feel heavy and lethargic. Nathan sees my eyes drooping and takes me to bed.

I should feel guilty that on Christmas night I fell asleep with a man other than the one I claim to love so profoundly, but I don't. If anything I'm just happy that even though Caleb's gone, there's a good man looking after me in his stead who wants to hold me tightly throughout the night.

I'm selfish, it's true, but I can't bring myself to end this... whatever this is... between Nathan and me.

New Year's Eve passes uneventfully. We didn't bother with fireworks because they scare the crap out of me. I told Nathan to go out and have fun but he insisted that he'd rather be at home reading. He stayed at home with me but he did no reading. There was a lot of eating and baking, though. He can now make scones successfully which is actually harder than it looks.

I'm now only two days from my due date and I'm scared out of my mind.

The snow is thick on the ground. When I go outside I have to wear wellies as it comes to my ankles in some places. I want to build a snowman but Nathan won't help me. He hates the snow and has avoided leaving the house while it lays on the ground in one huge, white blanket of doom, as he dramatically calls it.

Spoil sport.

Fingers crossed it melts by tomorrow. My stomach has been twinging slightly all day and I'm concerned I'll go into labour during this stupid weather. Although the weather forecast says it'll stop snowing by tonight, it's now one in the afternoon and although it has stopped I don't trust the forecast. They've lied to me too many times before.

As it is, I don't tell Nathan that I've been getting twinges. The last time I did that he took me to the hospital and it turned out to be gas. It was humiliating and he still laughs about it from time to time. Mostly because when the woman leaned over me, her fingers grasping at my cervix in an attempt to see if I'm dilated or not, she must have pushed the wrong button because I farted and it didn't stop for about seven seconds.

The room went silent and still, save for my loud and squeaky, endless fart. Then Nathan burst out with laughter so hard that tears streamed from his eyes and he turned red from not being able to breathe. What's worse is, it stank really, *really* bad. This only made him laugh harder. I thought I was going to die of embarrassment.

He laughed all the way home too and all day the next day. Even now sometimes he'll look at me and his body will start shaking as he tries to contain it.

My twinges seem to stop by the time I'm ready for bed which I'm severely grateful for. I climb under the covers without a care in the world. Nathan climbs in behind me and holds me tight like he does every night.

I don't feel lonely. I feel good, not great, but good.

My smile remains on my face as I fall asleep, eager to see what this year will bring.

I'm not sure what time it is when I wake up with an awful pain in my stomach that rivals that of a strong period pain. An arm around my waist stops me from sitting up with it. I rub my lower stomach. It's probably just gas like last time, which would be embarrassing due to Nathan sleeping next to me. What time is it?

It's only ten fifty at night. I've been asleep an hour or so.

I lie back, my neck on top of Nathan's outstretched arm, his breath fanning across my cheek. Another pain rumbles in my lower stomach, making all of my limbs want to curl. I bring my knees up as high as I can get them and roll onto my side. My breath leaves me as the pain leaves my body. Nothing but a dull ache remains.

What the hell's going on?

Oh... shit.

Nah, it's just false labour.

I need to pee.

"Nathan," I mumble and prod him in the chest.

He stirs and blinks his eyes open, looking tired. "What's wrong?"

"It hurts," I moan and roll onto my back.

Nathan looks panicked. "What does?"

"My back and my stomach." I sit up and he follows suit. "I need the toilet."

"Okay." He shakes himself out of his stupor and climbs from the bed. His hands grip me under the arms and help me up. "Are you okay?"

"Yeah," I lie because I'm not; I'm terrified.

Another pain grows within, starting in my lower stomach and radiating through my back. My body lurches forward and my hand grips Nathan's bicep. The skin all over my stomach tightens and I feel a horrible pressure down below.

"Oh god," Nathan mutters and rubs my back soothingly. "You're in labour. I need to call the doctor."

"I need to get to the hospital," I say calmly and stand once the pain fades. "I'm going to the toilet; you call what's his name."

"You shouldn't go alone," Nathan says softly and helps me to the bathroom. "I'll give you privacy but leave the door open."

Eye roll. "I'm not leaving the door open."

"What if you..."

"Nathan, it's labour. I'll be... bloody hell..." My body doubles over again and Nathan holds me up as an awful pain twists my insides. "Okay, I'll," pant, "Leave the," breathe, "Door open."

He waits for me to finish peeing and I take this moment to quickly wash my face and brush my teeth. "Lie down here. I'm going to put your overnight bag in the car and call the doctor," he says softly and guides me to the bed. Pulling back the blanket, he lowers me onto the mattress with one arm. "Don't move."

"Okay." Like I'm stupid enough to try moving right now. Holy shit that hurts.

"Will you be okay?" He rubs my lower back after I roll onto my side.

"Go." My hand waves at him a little frantically. "Can you get me a drink too, please?" My mouth is dryer than sand right now.

"Sure." He kisses my forehead and races from the room.

I time my contractions, using my phone to log them. This hurts so bad but I doubt I'm too far along in labour yet. They're every four minutes but they aren't so bad that I need to scream.

It's the discomfort that is crippling me.

I sit up after placing pillows behind my back, then bring my legs to my chest as best as I can. It aches, my back hurts and I feel a little bit sick. I'm also starving. It's an odd combination.

Where is Nathan? He's been gone twenty five minutes.

It's another five minutes before he returns, looking flushed and slightly panicked. "Are we going to the hospital now?" I ask, noticing that he's on the phone.

He shakes his head. "How far apart are your contractions?"

"Four minutes or so."

He repeats my answer to whoever is on the other side of his call.

"And on a scale of one to ten, how painful?"

Good question. "About a six."

He leaves the room again which irritates me. Can't he see I need him to stay with me right now? I pick up my phone ready to text my mum, Sasha and Tommy to let them know that it's time. Nathan chooses this moment to swoop in, take my phone and hand me a drink. "I'll deal with that, you rest. Try and get some sleep. The doctor said we should wait a while. He's on his way."

"Can I get a pain killer?" I rub my belly and roll onto my side again. "And my ball."

"Sure." He rubs my back absentmindedly with one hand, tapping away on my phone with the other. "Do you want me to turn on the TV?"

I shake my head and sip my water, breathing deeply to help with the pain. "No thank you. Be quick, I don't want to be on my own."

He is quick. I'm glad when he brings my laptop and plugs it into the TV on the wall so we can watch a movie, although my thoughts aren't on the movie, they're on the ever increasing pain in my stomach. Nathan is being great. His back rubs are helping and his calm façade is soothing. If he starts panicking I think I'll lose it and start blubbering.

I'm terrified. I just want this labour over with.

"Hurts," I moan and lay my head on Nathan's lap. I should be embarrassed that my arse is sticking in the air but this seems to be the only comfortable position right now.

"I bet it does." He rubs my back with one hand, still texting with his other.

"I think we need to go to the hospital now." A long moan rips from my throat as the clenching in my stomach persists with a vengeance. The pressure is getting worse and the contractions are closer together and killing me. Another one follows almost immediately after the last. I cry out loudly from the pain, I can't help it. It hurts so badly.

Nathan slides out from beneath me and stands behind me, his thumbs pressing into my back. Why aren't we going anywhere? I ask him this and hear him sigh. "We're sort of... damn it." Pause. "We're snowed in."

"That's really funny, but totally not appropriate to make jokes right now." I snap burying my face in the pillows. "Can we just go already?"

Nathan falls silent and his words sink into my pain fogged brain. Oh no. No, no, no, no, no. "I've called an ambulance but it's having trouble getting here. We're up a cliff; the snow around this area is about a foot deeper than everywhere else. Possibly two."

"Oh my god," I whine, my body now running on panic alone. "What about the doctor? Doesn't he have skis or something?"

"He's... stuck in the city." Where the closest hospital is.

"Then find me another one!" I shout and I don't feel guilty for it at all. Tensions are high and I need release.

I roll over and slide from the bed onto my exercise ball. "We'll figure this out," Nathan whispers softly after crouching beside me. His hand continues to rub circles on my back. "We have time."

There's an odd popping feeling inside as I roll my hips on the ball and bounce a little. My trousers feel wet. "No we don't."

"We do..."

"Nathan," I grab his shirt beneath his chin and pull him to me. "My water just broke. You *need* to get me a doctor."

His face pales and his thumb taps frantically at his phone screen. He calls numerous people, the hospital, nine, nine, nine. He tries everyone but nobody can get to us.

"Jeanine has had kids."

He nods and calls her. I don't listen to their conversation. I'm in too much pain and I'll never forgive the snow for this.

The reality of the situation sinks in. "Oh my god. I'm going to be..." Another pain rips through me. I cry and tense, my teeth gritting in an attempt to help it pass. "One of those women who has a baby on the living room floor!"

"We need to get you downstairs," he blurts. "If... I mean..."

I'm suddenly airborne, which is a good thing because there's no way I can walk right now. My trousers are soaked and I know Nathan must be freaking out about that. Fortunately he doesn't seem to notice and I don't point it out.

"I have no idea what to do." Nathan's panicking.

"Don't you dare," I shout at him as he places me on the couch. "Don't start freaking out now. I need you to stop me from freaking... fucking hell this hurts so badly." I drop to my knees and roll onto my back, placing my legs on the couch so they're elevated. It brings little to no relief. "Please get me some clean trousers."

Nathan does as he's told and I use this moment of privacy to cry. I could still be in labour for hours. My water breaking doesn't mean a thing. Something tells me I'm going to be unlucky and this baby is going to come soon whether I like it or not.

I turn the TV on and flick straight to the news. The weather forecast comes on after a few minutes. Worst snow they've seen in England in four years. Great. Fucking great.

I'm only slightly aware of Nathan kneeling beside me and peeling my trousers off. I'm in too much pain to care. I feel drunk.

"You don't need to push do you?" He asks me, after I stop screaming through another brutal contraction, whilst pulling a loose pair of shorts up my legs.

I shake my head. "I don't think so." But the pressure is there. "Is anybody coming?"

"They're all trying." His hand works at my back but it's just annoying me now. I bat it away and push him onto the couch.

With my arse on the exercise ball, I cross my arms on his knees and try to relax as his fingers rub the back of my neck and along my spine. "It hurts. I don't want to do this anymore."

"You're doing great," he reassures me and runs his fingers through my hair. "Honestly, you're being so brave right now. I'm sorry we're stuck here."

"Not your fault." My hands squeeze his thighs as it builds and builds before peaking and finally unleashing. "I'm scared. What if..."

Nathan places a hand over my mouth. "Don't. I'm barely holding it together here. Please don't put things in my mind that aren't there right now. We'll get through this."

"But I don't want you to deliver my baby." Tears flow from my eyes, my tired body sagging onto his lap.

"It's not on my bucket list either," he jokes and wipes at my tears with his thumbs. "It's going to be okay."

"AH!" I scream and clench my fingers around his thighs. "We should prepare, if it's..." Holy fuck.

"Good idea." Nathan nods and lifts me from him, replacing my head and arms on the couch moments later. "I'll be a second."

"I'm going to resurrect your brother," I pant through my ragged breathing. "And then I'm going to kill him again."

Nathan chuckles and drags my overnight bag towards me. "I'll help you."

"Great. We need towels or something."

"Hot water?"

I shake my head. "No. Just towels, old ones because they'll..." Ouch, ooowie, ouch. "Fuck." I wince at my own swear word and immediately apologize. "Load a video on YouTube or something! Don't just stand there."

"Right." And he's gone again.

This sucks. This really... oh thank god. Jeanine is here!

I hug her when she gets close and hold her tight for a while, almost breaking her neck as my belly contracts. "Nathan!" She shouts and Nathan looks as relieved to see her as I do. "I need to change and wash my hands. Stay with her. I'll deal with this."

Nathan does as he's told but not before asking, "How did you get here?"

"With difficulty, it's about two foot deep out there. I had to put bin bags over my trousers to keep the wet out."

"That's all well and good, but I've got a melon in me wanting to get out. Can we please share survival stories later?" I pant.

Jeanine vanishes for a few minutes. I vaguely hear the taps running and quick footsteps before she returns.

"Move her, I'm going to grab these pillows." I'm not sure what they do. All I know is one minute I'm on the ball and the next I'm leaning back against Nathan's open legs and my shorts are off.

The pain radiates throughout my body before focusing on one spot. The pressure is unbearable.

They keep talking to me, keep saying things, but I can't hear them. I can't focus on them. The pain is too much.

"Need to push," I grit out and I'm moved again. My back is against something soft and the couch cushions have been placed on the ground. It's comfier than I was.

I can hear screaming, I can hear growling and cursing. After a moment I realise it's coming from me. All sense of time has gone. I have no idea how long this pain has been going on, all I know is I want it to stop.

Fortunately my body seems to know what it's doing and pushing with it brings me a small amount of relief. The pressure is unbearable, it's burning so bad. I want to escape it, I can't keep my legs still.

Nathan is holding one up to my chest I think. I can see him but I can't focus on anything. Everything that's happening is going through my eyes and not registering as reality.

So much pain.

It's stretching, it's burning. "He's crowning," I hear Jeanine say excitedly. "Come on, Gwen, you're doing brilliant."

Nathan kisses my temple and holds my hand. His words are encouraging and the tone they're delivered with is full of fear and excitement.

He's crowning. It's almost over.

Another pop seems to happen and I feel more water flood from between my legs.

"Bloody hell," Nathan blurts in my ear. "The head's out."

Jeanine squeals with delight and orders me to push as soon as I feel the need to. Well... it's not like I had other plans.

It seems like forever before I hear it, that beautiful cry that could pierce a fragile ear drum. Something is dropped onto my chest and my attention focuses on him.

"Well, he's definitely a boy," Nathan laughs and rests his chin on my shoulder.

He's perfect, so damn perfect. His damp and gooey head holds a thick layer of dark hair. My hair.

His face is all Caleb, the shape of the eyes, the pouty lips and the nose. It breaks my heart and fixes it all at the same time.

"Well done," Jeanine sniffs and dabs at her eyes with a hankie. "You did so well."

"Why won't he stop crying?" I ask, my tiredness showing in the sluggishness of my voice.

"He's hungry," Jeanine chuckles and begins wiping him down with a towel. "Leave the cord attached until the ambulance gets here. It's better not to mess with that." I didn't even notice.

He's hungry? Oh god...

There's a loud knock at the door a few second later. Good timing. Jeanine stands. I don't think Nathan wants to move right now. I don't want him to move right now.

Two paramedics walk in a few moments later and I'm relieved to see my doctor with them.

"Doctor Meadow." Nathan gives him a polite nod.

The older man with slightly greying hair kneels down and holds out his hands. "May I?"

I nod and hand him the baby boy that I still can't believe is mine. He places him on a white blanket that covers some kind of device that looks like a large set of kitchen scales. "Eight thirteen," he says and one of the paramedics scribbles it down. He clears the baby's nose and mouth and pushes on certain parts of his body with his hands. I watch him take his temperature and check his vitals before cutting the cord and handing him to Nathan.

Nathan had no time to say no and now has my son in his arms. He stares down at him looking frightened and full of wonder, like a rabbit caught in headlights. I don't think he's noticed that the baby is gunky and naked and it's rubbing off on his bare arms.

"We need to deliver the placenta," Dr Meadows says softly, his smiling eyes on me. He gets a paper hat shaped thing under my chin in time to catch my vomit. Gross.

The next few minutes blur by. I'm only vaguely aware when Nathan, with Jeanine's help, gets the baby in a nappy and dressed. I'm being sewn up and cleaned up. I've unfortunately had to have stitches, which sucks because I'm going to be extra sore for a few days.

"We need to try feeding now," Dr Meadows announces and Nathan hands the baby to Jeanine before lifting me onto the couch. That's better, so much more comfortable.

Breastfeeding is an interesting experience. It's not pleasant but it's not unbearable either. Fortunately the little bundle gets the hang of it immediately. I love him. He's perfect.

I should be embarrassed that I'm sat almost naked in nothing but a gown in front of strangers with one of my breasts hanging out, but after that ordeal, I just don't care.

"We still don't have a name for him," I groan and rest my head back against Nathan's shoulder.

"We haven't really discussed it," Nathan says thoughtfully. "I thought you'd already chosen one." I shake my head in response. "Are you not naming him after his father?"

Good question. "I... I don't want to call him Caleb."

"We'll figure it out, there's no rush." Nathan kisses the curve of my neck. "You were amazing."

"You were loud," Jeanine jokes. I give her a playful scowl and look down at my son.

Caleb should be here for this. He'd love him. I can just imagine how excited he would have been, if he were here. But he's not here and this little boy will never get to experience his daddy.

My heart breaks as I grieve my son's loss for him. My fingertips move over his chubby, rosy cheek. I've never felt a love so intense before. I can feel it in the very centre of my soul.

"Let me take him for a while," Jeanine says when my son finishes feeding. "Nathan, go and run her a bath."

"Am I not going into the hospital?" I blink in shock and stare at my doctor.

"No," he responds with a smile. "You're both healthy and fine, it's not necessary. I'll be staying in the village anyway. I'm only a phone call away."

"You'll need to purchase a set of skis. I don't feel comfortable letting her stay home after that ordeal. What if she haemorrhages or collapses or something worse?"

Dr Meadows places his hand on Nathan's shoulder. "I assure you, she'll be fine. We're classing this as a home birth. I have no concerns."

"I'm fine, Nathan," I croak as I hand the baby to Jeanine. "I'm just tired."

He seems to relent but doesn't look happy about it. "Fine. Jeanine can you see them out?" I'm carefully lifted so I wrap my arms around Nathan's neck and hold on tight as he carries me up the stairs. "You feel so light now."

I smile and rest my head against his neck. "Sorry about the mess."

"Don't, it's not your fault."

A yawn tears its way up my throat. Nathan places me on the closed toilet, in the bathroom that I use, and crouches down beside the bath. The room fills with steam as the tap pours hot water into the large tub.

"Are you okay?" Nathan asks me for the twentieth time since I gave birth. "That looked like it hurt."

I give him a look, my eyes heavy with exhaustion. "It did."

"We'll be quick. I fear Jeanine may kidnap our son." He laughs.

Our? "Our?"

"What?" He looks at me over his shoulder, his eyes tired and full of emotion.

I blink and ask warily, "You said our."

"What are you talking about?" He looks completely oblivious. Maybe he didn't mean to say it.

"You said 'our son'."

"No I didn't" He frowns and shakes his head. "I said your son."

"I heard you..."

"You're tired," he points out. "Don't put words in my mouth. I know he's not mine and now isn't the time to argue about this."

Maybe he's right. I probably misheard him. Sigh. "Sorry."

"That's okay." He stands before me and slowly begins to slide the gown off my shoulders. "It's warm enough now."

I give him a pointed look and point to the door.

"I'm not leaving you right now. I've just seen you naked."

Scowl. "This is different."

"No it isn't. I'm not leaving this room. I refuse."

"Please?" The pleading in my tone causes him to relent.

He sighs, nods and takes a step back. "Fine, but I'll be sat out here. Okay?"

I thank him and carefully step into the bath once he's gone. The water stings my core but it also feels amazing.

I've just had a baby.

I've just had Caleb's baby.

Emotions overwhelm me, emotions I should have felt the moment my child was placed in my arms. Sorrow, loss, pain, frustration, anger. So many emotions. I'm too tired to sift through them properly.

I bring my knees to my chest, happy that I can finally do this for the first time in months, and cry into the top of them. Tears spill and mix with the dampness on my cheeks, sobs tearing through me, quiet ones. I want to scream, I want to shout, but I don't.

My body feels empty and I don't just mean the sudden lack of baby. I mean all over. There's love there, an instant bond I formed with my son on first glimpse, but that hole that Caleb left behind only seems to have stretched further.

There's a light tapping on the door. "Are you okay in there?"

"Yes," I lie. I'm not okay. I'll never be okay again.

Quickly and thoroughly I scrub myself down, hating the way the water turns pink. I climb out and dry my body carefully. I then wrap a towel around myself after placing a pad in a pair of my lady boxers and tugging them on.

Nathan, hearing me move around, opens the door and steps inside. "All set?"

I nod and stretch my body. "I feel so much lighter."

"He's a big baby, I'm not surprised." Nathan stares at me with a fondness in his eyes that I've never seen coming from him. "I know women give birth to babies every day, but I want you to know that right now, I'm in complete awe of you."

"I'm in complete awe of myself," I choke and rub a hand across my aching breasts. Ouch.

"Here." Nathan hands me a nursing bra with nipple pads already attached. I notice he hasn't got his gloves on. How odd. I don't bring attention to this fact though as I don't want to make him aware of it, just in case he's not already.

"I'm disturbed by how comfortable you feel handling my underwear." I take it from him and motion for him to turn around.

After a few moments I hear the sound of my son squawking and my boobs tingle. "Well that's new."

"What is?"

I shake my head, my cheeks flushing with colour. "Nothing." Just the fact my breasts seem to know that my child is hungry.

Jeanine is sat in the armchair by the window, my son in her arms clothed in a lemon coloured all in one and a little yellow hat with matching mittens. I pad over to the couch and carefully curl my legs to the side.

Shock overcomes me for a moment when Nathan, with a bright smile on his face, takes the whittling baby from Jeanine with his bare hands and holds him up before him, one hand behind his head and shoulders and the other under his round bottom.

I take a sneaky picture on my phone, I can't resist.

He brings him over to me and places him on my chest.

"I'll put the kettle on. I hope you don't mind if I stay the night, I doubt I'll be able to get back on my old legs," Jeanine says and smooths down her trousers.

"Not at all." Nathan doesn't take his eyes from us. "Thank you, Jeanine. I don't think I could have handled it without your help."

"Sweet boy," she chuckles and gives me a wink as she passes. "I think he's hungry again." She means the baby.

She'd be right. I look down at my son and smile at his attempt to find milk in my collarbone. "He's going to give me a love bite if he doesn't stop."

Nathan sits beside us, his arm resting along the back of the couch and his fingers teasing my hair. Tilting my head back slightly, I relish the feel of Nathan's gentle fingers soothing me as my son sucks the life out of my breast.

"He needs a name." I scrunch up my face as I think. "I'm drawing a blank."

"As long as it's not something hideous." He leans his head back and closes his eyes for a minute or so. "George?"

"No."

"Travis?"

"No."

"Dillan." He gives a small shrug when he sees my look of disbelief. "I like Dillan."

"Dillan." I test the name out a few times. "I love it." Yes. Dillan. It just sounds right. "Dillan is great."

Nathan's smile blinds me and if I weren't so tired I'd smile back. "Really?"

"Yeah, Dillan is perfect." I yawn, it's loud and unattractive. "Thank you. For keeping cool today and for being my rock."

He doesn't say anything but we share a look of mutual respect.

After burping my son I pass him back to Nathan, who seems eager to take him. As much as I want to hold my child, I daren't do it for a second longer as my eyes won't remain open.

CHAPTER TWENTY-TWO

THIS WHOLE PARENTING THING is hard. I don't remember much after falling asleep on the couch. All I know is I'm now in bed and this is the third time I've gotten up to tend to Dillan.

Dillan. The name suits him so well.

I look over at his Moses basket that rests on a stand about two feet from the bed. Nathan must have brought it in here, obviously not feeling comfortable being so far from his nephew.

Standing slowly, I bend over the basket and collect my son with both hands. He stretches in that cute way that only babies can stretch and lets out a little yelp. He's not happy being moved. Grumpy boy.

Carefully I climb back into bed and prop the pillows up behind me. Nathan, who is asleep to my right, instantly rolls back into me and wraps his arm around my middle.

His bare hand grabs at my flesh as if scared I'll move again.

As much as I want to be angry at his assumption that I want to share a bed with him, I can't because his assumption is true. I don't want to be alone right now.

Actually... he probably doesn't care if I want him here or not. This is him telling me he wants in my bed so he'll get in my bed.

Still, I can't force myself to be angry.

When Dillan has finished his feed, I lay him on the bed between myself and Nathan and roll onto my side. My face is level with Nathan's. He looks so peaceful while sleeping. He really has been my rock.

I'll never be able to repay him for all he's done for me.

Leaning forward slightly, I press my lips to the corner of his mouth. His eyes open immediately and his lips part. He looks at me curiously for a moment, as if trying to work out my intentions.

Then his hand comes up and rests on my cheek. I hear him inhale a shuddering breath as his thumb swipes over my lower lip. Something between us connects, clicks, falls into place. Without removing his gaze from my eyes, he leans forward and runs the tip of his nose along the bridge of mine.

His hand strokes my cheek and neck before his thumb rubs a circle on my pulse. He looks at me like he can't believe I'm real. I look at him and try to tell him how grateful I am with my eyes. How much he's worth and how much he deserves to be happy.

"Go to sleep, Gwen," he whispers, his breath minty and sweet.

My son is lifted to his chest. He cradles Dillan softly and presses his lips to his wrinkled forehead. Dillan lets out a squawk when Nathan places him in his bed, tucks him in tight and climbs over me to get back to his side.

I turn towards him, something I've never done before, and wrap my arm around his bare chest. He squeezes me tight and lets out a sigh of contentment.

I don't wake up again until eight the next morning and both my son and Nathan have vanished, only to be found wandering around on the ground floor having a one sided conversation that I can't hear.

Looking at them together, looking at Nathan with Dillan, I can't help but be relieved and admit that my fears are gone. Caleb might not be here, but right now, we're not alone.

***

"Can I ask you something?" I say quietly after walking into the nursery and watching Nathan with Dillan to his chest. His gloves are off and Dillan is drooling on Nathan's skin, yet I've never seen Nathan look so content. It's been eating at me for a couple of days now, since Dillan was born.

Nathan has an issue with germs but recently he's been wearing his gloves less and less.

Nathan blinks up at me, seeming to slowly come out of a daze. "What's wrong?" The chair on which he sits continues rocking slowly. His ankle is resting on the top of his other leg, which gently pushes the chair back and forth.

I walk over to him and sit on the padded arm, looking down at them both, my heart singing with happiness at the sight. As much as it hurts that Caleb can't be here for this, I'm glad to see that my grief hasn't fully gone to waste. Seeing Nathan look so peaceful and happy fills that hole in my chest a small amount. Enough to make the days go by easier.

"You rarely wear your gloves anymore," I whisper, my fingers stroking the back of his longish hair. He leans back and closes his eyes, as if seeking out my touch. "I've been wondering whether to mention it or not. I've been worried I'll trigger the need or something."

His irises peek from beneath hooded lids. "I don't know why." A small smile touches his lips and I want to trace it with my thumb but I don't. "When you had him, I got covered in more fluids than I care to admit." Snort. That's true. I cringe a little. "I think the panic overrode my fears at the time because I found it didn't bother me. I was too worried about you." His hand leaves Dillan's back and rests on my thigh. "Before he was born I was worried I'd run from the nappies, vomit and snotty events that will likely happen in the future. But seeing him born," his closed lip smile widens and his lips part, showing his shiny white teeth as his eyes gaze upon my son. "I've never witnessed anything so disgusting." My mouth drops open as I feign offence. He chuckles and continues, "Or amazing in my entire life. Nothing he can produce bothers me." His eyes come back to mine and my breath fails. "Or you. I don't know if it's because we've spent so much time together or because I've already been covered in your bodily fluids." Nice way of putting it. A soft look comes over his eyes and once again I'm shown a flash of vulnerability that makes Nathan seem so much younger than he is. "I don't mind touching you anymore. In fact... I've come to enjoy the contact."

My eyes burn, knowing that in some small way I've helped him along with the healing process. Even if it only applies to me and Dillan, I'm glad to have helped in some way. "You're an amazing person, Nathan."

His tongue comes out to tease his lower lip, his eyes going back to the window where they were looking when I first walked in. "I'll never intentionally hurt you. You know that right?"

Well that's a random conversation flip. "I know." And I do know. I trust him more than anyone else.

The mysteriousness of this new conversation doesn't end. "I make a lot of mistakes when I'm mad. I didn't..." He pauses, thinking on his words for a moment. "I didn't have the best upbringing. That's not to say I want you to feel obligated to me in any way. I just want you to know that I'm not used to being this close to somebody. Even Caleb. I've always been secluded." He laughs coolly, his lips a thin line. "I don't even have any friends."

"I'm your friend."

"Yes." His eyes become distant for a moment. "You are. But just know that whatever I do, if it hurts you, it's not intentional. I just don't know how to do this."

"What are you talking about?" Why do I get the feeling like he's warning me for something that has yet to come?

"Nothing, I'm just pointing out a major flaw in my personality." He sighs long and deeply, the lines around his eyes showing how many concerns he has on his mind.

I don't say anything. I'm not sure what to say. Instead I slide onto his lap, mindful of the baby on his chest, and rest my head against his neck. He presses his lips to my hair and strokes my arm with his free hand.

"Oh my god, look at him!" My mum sniffs and cradles Dillan to her bosom.

Nathan keeps his eyes on his newspaper but the way he spreads it out is slightly more aggressive than usual, his arms jerking to flick it in the air, stopping it from bending. He really doesn't like my mum and she's only been here an hour.

"And look at you, I wish my body got back to normal that fast." She gives me a pout whilst eyeing me up and down. Her gaze is nothing but friendly though so I don't mind it. "And I love the name. Dillan suits him."

"Nathan picked it," I blurt, feeling the need to give him the credit he deserves. "His middle name is Caleb." I picked that for obvious reasons.

"Beautiful." She beams and places her finger in Dillan's hand. He squeezes it, his eyes now open and unfocused. I'm eager to see whose colour eyes he gets. "I'm so proud of you." She looks at Nathan. "And you, for stepping up when it wasn't your job to. Your parents must be proud."

Nathan seems shocked by her words and his demeanour towards my mum softens after this.

I'm exhausted. I haven't slept for three weeks since Dillan was born. I find napping when the baby naps is the best way to stop myself from crashing during the day. My mum is also here for a few days, which is great. She's going to teach me how to express milk. I can't for the life of me figure out how to use the breast pump comfortably.

I had this image in my head of being milked like a cow and having it squirt out in one flow, enough to fill at least six bottles. That's not the case at all. Some days I produce more milk than others and mostly I can only produce and ounce or two.

At least I'm getting the hang of it now. I can freeze it too which is even better.

Nathan has to leave soon. His store should be opening in a couple of months. He has a lot to get through to finalise it but I think he's having trouble leaving us.

Things have been a little bit tense with him lately, not with us but with something he won't discuss with me. Almost every single morning for the past few weeks there has been a package on the doorstep. I'm not sure what it is but I know it's causing Nathan stress. I've asked him about it but he only tells me to mind my own business, not in the mean way he used to but the stern tone is still there so I daren't ask again.

I'm worried about him.

Part of me wonders if he's being blackmailed, what with everything going on with his father. I'm not sure what's going on with that either. All I know is that he has court soon. Nathan won't tell me anything about anything. In his mind he's protecting me from unnecessary stresses. He doesn't understand that if it's upsetting him, then to me it is a necessary stress.

I almost got my hands on a package five days ago but he took it and made a few calls. Since then there hasn't been another. I know that whatever it is, somebody wants me to see it. Or at least that's my theory. My curious nature drives me around the bend. I wish I could push it out of my mind but I can't. What is it that has Nathan so uptight at the moment and why won't he confide in me?

What does he have to hide?

My mum is here though so I have to get over it for now. It's been a while since I saw her and honestly... I've missed her. She's asked me how everything is and I've told her all is well with me and Nathan. I know she doesn't approve of our current situation but she can't say anything.

As long as I'm happy and Dillan is happy, that's all that matters.

Nathan won't even let me sleep alone. To say he's become clingy would be an understatement. The problem is, I don't want to sleep alone and I like having him hold me as I sleep every night.

I'm extremely pleased to see that Nathan still doesn't have any issues with Dillan and me where his bare hands are concerned. Dillan's potential germs don't seem to bother him at all. He's been amazing; if Dillan needs changing, he'll just get up and do it. Of course I do it as much as he, but I never even have to ask.

Not that I would, mind you. Dillan is my responsibility but it's nice having the help.

Things are changing around here and I'm not sure how or why. I'm not totally convinced that I don't like the changes either.

"Can I have a word?" Nathan asks me and nods towards the archway.

I agree and kiss my sweet baby boy's head, leaving him with my mum.

"What's wrong?" My hands rub up and down my arms as I lean against the kitchen wall.

He scrapes his teeth along his lower lip. "I really don't want to go but I have to. My court hearing is soon, then I've got the store and I really need this sponsor."

Why does he look like I'm going to get angry? "I know. I understand."

"I don't want to go," he sighs and leans against the wall beside me. Both of us stare at the far wall as if it holds all of the answers to our conflicted feelings. It doesn't; it tells me nothing.

"I don't want you to go either but you need to."

He lets out a long breath. "Can't you both come with me?"

Blink. "What?"

"I'm serious, just come with me. It's only three days in the city. Just me, you and Dillan. It'll be fun."

"My mum's here." Is that the best excuse I have?

"She leaves Tuesday. Join me then."

"I'll think about it," I respond and kiss his cheek. "Go and conquer the world, Nathan."

He gives me a smile that could stop a thousand women at a female rights protest. My heart just stuttered. "I'll miss you."

"We'll miss you more." I step away and watch him walk through the hall. His eyes catch me over his shoulder as he grips the handle and pulls. "Drive safe."

"Always do." With one last look, he finally leaves.

I let out the breath I've been holding and re-join my mum in the living room. She gives me a knowing look. I roll my eyes and sit on the armchair by the fireplace.

"Well, I didn't hear much but from the looks of things that boy is…"

"Don't," I beg with a shake of my head.

"He's Caleb's brother." The way she says it tells me she's disgusted. "Imagine if your roles were reversed and Caleb fell for your sister."

"I don't have a sister."

She rolls her eyes. "Hypothetically."

"I'm not falling for Nathan either."

"If you say so." She purses her lips. "It's your life. But be warned. I don't agree with this at all. There's something not right with him."

It's my turn to roll my eyes. "Don't insult him, mum, I'll never forgive you."

Her mouth drops open.

"I care about him. He's done a lot for me."

"I'm just saying I think maybe you should be careful. He's not normal. He has issues."

She can say that again. "He's working on them."

"I'll stay out of it, I swear. Just… be careful. I don't want to see you get hurt." She rolls her shoulders. Clearly her arms are aching from holding the baby for so long.

"Do you want me to take him?"

"No." She moves away a fraction. "I'll hold him until my arms drop off. Who knows when I'll get to see you next?"

"You can visit as often as you like." She's my mum. Even if she is a bit of a bitch at times, that doesn't mean I want to exclude her. "I want you in his life."

"Not as much as I want to be in it." She gives me a teary eyed smile. "I won't let you down again."

I give her an amused smile. "And I won't get pregnant again."

A pillow hits me in the face. I snort and place it behind my head. "Hungry?"

"Starving."

"I'll put dinner on. Tell me what's going on with you. How are things back home?" I stand and walk into the kitchen. Pulling things from the fridge, I smile when she puts Dillan in his swinging chair by the door. It's away from everything but I put him in there when I'm doing the cooking and what not.

Conversation flows easily over dinner. I find myself laughing more in one evening with my mum than I ever did in my entire life of living with her.

When the time comes for her to leave, I find myself feeling rather sad. Dillan, who is sweetly oblivious to everything but his feeding, pooping and sleeping times, even seems to cry when she leaves.

She hugs me and it's stiff but she's trying.

For the first time since Dillan was born I'm in the house alone. I miss Nathan.

I miss him a lot.

Sasha and Tommy came to visit a week before my mum and they both want to come again soon. I'm looking forward to it but for now I just want some quiet with my son and my... I mean Nathan.

Dillan is almost one month old already. He's lifting his head and his feeding has settled. I can't wait to see his first smile. So much so, that I'm constantly playing with him, trying to get more than gas from him and baby vomit.

Placing Dillan in his cot, I switch on the baby monitor and head downstairs, flicking on lights as I go. I wonder when Nathan will be back. It's getting late and I know he dislikes driving in the dark.

Hmm, I fancy a Horlicks.

As I'm boiling the milk in a saucepan, the front door opens and closes. I hear the tell-tale signs of Nathan taking his jacket off and hanging it up.

My face immediately lights up with a smile and my legs carry me into the hall at a record speed.

"Oomph," Nathan steps back as I collide with him, arms around his neck. "Miss me?"

"How did it go?" I tilt my head back and look at him. "I want to know everything!"

Uh-oh, his face drops and my heart drops with it. He was relying on this person. I'm not sure exactly how it works but I know Nathan won't be able to go forward until he finds someone to help him create his jewellery.

"Hey," I say softly. "It'll be okay."

"Yeah," he nods, his hands on my hips. "It will." I'm blinded by his sudden beaming smile full of joy and excitement. "I got it."

"No way," I choke. "You're kidding?"

"Nope, I got it. We start Monday."

"Oh my god," I squeal and hold him tighter, my face going to his neck. "I'm so happy for you."

"Where's Dillan?" He pulls back slightly, his eyes scanning the immediate area for the baby.

"Sleeping upstairs." I tap the baby monitor that's attached to the loop of my jeans. "We should celebrate... oh crap!" I pull away from him and race back into the kitchen.

Well... the milk is hot, that's for sure.

"Oops," I mumble and take the saucepan from the hob where the milk has bubbled over and spilled everywhere.

"I'll do that," Nathan says as I grab a cloth.

I wave him off. "You've been working hard, go and sit down. Are you hungry?"

"Not really, I ate before I left the city."

I give him a teasing smile. "Oh, well then I guess you don't want the cookies I made."

He instantly perks up. "Cookies?"

"Yep," I laugh when he darts for the oven and takes out the foil wrapped plate full of chocolate chip circular treats. "Share." I open my mouth and wait for him to pop in a small mouthful.

He grins, places it in front of my mouth and as soon as I go to close my mouth around it he puts it in his own mouth and swallows with a groan. "Too good to share."

"I made them," I argue, still cleaning down the hob.

"I purchased the ingredients." This time he does place a piece in my mouth.

He's so right. Way too good to share. I snatch the plate from his hand and run.

"Hey," I hear him whine before his footsteps follow mine right before he snags me around the waist and pulls me back into his chest. "They're my celebration cookies!"

"Actually, they're your welcome home cookies. Your celebration cake is in the fridge."

He immediately forgets the cookies and prowls back into the kitchen.

The large white chocolate cake covered in dark blue icing sits proudly on the shelf in the middle. Placing the cookies on the side, I pull the cake out and show him the silver icing that spells, "CONGRATULATIONS!"

"What if I didn't get it? This cake would be like a kick in the teeth," he says quietly and stares at the amazingly decorated cake, if I do say so myself.

I place the cake on the counter and wrap my arms around his waist. "I knew you would."

"Gwen, even I genuinely thought I wouldn't. How could you have such faith in me?"

"Because you're talented and amazing." I tip my head back and wink at him. "You should have faith in yourself."

"You spoil me." He grins, his fingers squeezing my back for a moment. "Give me it."

I serve two slices and hand him his, then we make our way to the dining room and sit at the table. "Tell me everything," I demand.

"Well, I do have some other news. Good and bad."

Hmm... I don't like bad news. "Bad first so the good can cheer me up afterwards."

"Okay." He swallows his mouthful of cake and laces his fingers beneath my chin. "You won't be getting Caleb's trust fund. Unfortunately due to you not being married at the time of his demise, his money went to his next of kin, which was my father and mother, although my solicitor informs me that we may be able to transfer the trust fund over to Dillan. We'll just need proof that he's Caleb's."

Well that just sucks. My face falls as I realise it doesn't look like I'll be leaving here any time soon. Not that I want to, but it'd be nice to stand on my own two feet. It's great that Dillan might get it though. I'll never have to worry about affording his school expenses.

"What's the good news?" Please be brilliant, life changing news.

"The store will be up and running in two weeks and I received my trust fund plus interest." He pauses for a moment and I bite back the urge to squeal with delight. "So... I got you a gift."

What? "That's great, but you've already given me enough."

"It's mostly because I'll be travelling a lot again. I want to open a second location if this store does well." He runs his tongue across his lower lip and pulls out a single black key from his pocket with a BMW key chain. "I got you a car. It's perfect for families and has a fix for the baby seat so you won't have to strap his car seat in every time. You'll need it if I'm away."

I stare at the keys on the table between us. "I don't think I can accept it."

"Don't over think it. Just say 'thank you, Nathan', kiss me and try it out tomorrow."

I giggle and stand. Taking a step towards him I lean down and press my lips to his ear. "Thank you, Nathan."

He grabs my arm before I can move away and pulls me onto his lap, making me squeal. "You didn't kiss me."

He's right, I didn't. I roll my eyes and move my mouth to his cheek, planting an extremely moist kiss below his cheekbone.

"You are disgusting." He cringes playfully and wipes his cheek on his sleeve.

Dillan's screeches sound through the baby monitor. I step back, ready to deal with him, but Nathan guides me back to the chair and tells me to sit and that he'll sort it. I thank him and clear the table as soon as he leaves the room.

When I've finished cleaning I take my usual spot on the couch in the room and listen to Nathan talk to Dillan through the baby monitor.

"You really need to start smiling soon. If I have to listen to your mummy play peekaboo one more time, I'm going to gag her." I snort at his sweet baby talk tone. His threatening words sounding so non-threatening and cheerful. "Although it'll probably only get worse if you do smile at that. So do us both a favour and smile at something I enjoy." I hear a gurgle come from Dillan and laugh with Nathan, even though he can't hear me. "Good boy." There's a pause. I hear Nathan sigh before his tone becomes quiet and sad. "You look so much like your daddy it's almost painful." Pause. My breath hitches. Nathan rarely talks about Caleb and when he does it's usually just a few words of agreement about something I've said. "Mummy loved your daddy very much. Uncle loved your daddy very much. I'm sorry you'll never get to meet him; he would have loved you more than anyone and anything."

I choke back a hiccup and turn the monitor off. This isn't my conversation to listen to. It's private and it's their moment.

Wiping my eyes, I quickly fire up my laptop and try to distract myself. Instead all I see is Caleb staring back at me from my desktop background. I touch his face with my fingertip and slam the screen down after a quiet moment. I can't break down right now, Dillan needs me to keep it together.

Why's it so damn hard?

Nathan joins me half an hour later. He's slightly distant and solemn looking but otherwise okay. We watch the television in a companionable silence, my head resting on his shoulder and my hand across his chest. He doesn't play with the ends of my hair like he usually does.

When I look up, I realise it's because he's fallen asleep with his head hanging over the back of the couch. I laugh quietly and run my fingertips over his brow, smoothing his hair from his face. He's had an eventful day by the sounds of it, no wonder he's exhausted.

"You're staring." Nathan's lips twitch and his closed eyes flutter open, only to confirm his suspicions.

"How do you know when I'm staring?" I mutter, feeling my cheeks heat. He shrugs. "I don't know. It's kind of strange actually."

"Yep," I completely agree with that comment. "Bed?"

"Yes." Staggering slightly as he stands, he holds out his hand. I give him my wrist, as is habit. I'm shocked when his fingers slide from my wrist and push between my fingers until they're laced together.

I get changed in the bathroom after brushing my teeth and washing my face. Nathan gets changed upstairs. By the time he's done I'm already in bed.

It's rare that we go to bed together. I know it's wrong but I can't help it. I like our night time cuddles far more than I should.

He slides in usually after I'm sleeping and doesn't wrap himself around me until he's in the land of slumber himself. This time he instantly presses his front to my back and curls his legs with mine.

"I never thought I'd enjoy sleeping with somebody," he admits quietly, his breath blowing the wispy hairs that lay over my ear and down my neck. "But now I can't imagine a night without your body heat."

That and my arse seems to be the perfect seat for his penis. Speak of the devil... ping.

This happens quite a lot. Normally I don't notice until the morning. I don't say anything though and neither does he, though I just felt him tense slightly as if waiting for my reaction. In the mornings if I wake up before him I stay perfectly still and wait for him to notice. He usually rolls away from me or climbs out of bed and gets ready for the day.

Now it's like there's an elephant in the room. I should say something but what is there to say? The last time this happened and we were both awake it was awkward and funny. This time it's not funny, it's just awkward and a little bit of something else. Arousing.

We both lie perfectly still, as if waiting for the other to say something or to move. I bite down hard on my lower lip, a bit unnerved about what to do.

My leg starts to cramp so I relax back, wincing when his plaid pyjama bottoms tighten on his erect member as it slides between my thighs. His answering gasp tells me he definitely felt that too.

Soft fingers trail along my forearm, causing me to shudder. They travel up my bicep before tightly squeezing my shoulder and moving down my ribs. A warm hand comes to rest on my hip and my heart beat skips a few before beating a heavy rhythm in my chest. Everything tingles and I feel goose pimples rise all over my heated flesh.

A flash of pleasure uncurls in my stomach as his hand pulls my hip back into him. My hand clenches tightly around the pillow case near my nose. A whimper escapes me and I hear him let out a breathy moan.

His hips pull back. I know he's not wearing underwear beneath his pyjamas because I can feel his warm skin move over his solid length beneath the thin cotton. For some reason this causes me to tremble and ache. My eyes squeeze shut as I let his slow movement torture and tease me with something I can never have.

He pushes back between my thighs slowly, exquisitely. A quiet groan escapes him. His chest vibrates against my back and his lips come into contact with the curve of my neck.

Blood boils beneath the surface of my skin. I become overwhelmed with a hot flash of heat that won't dissipate. Need unfurls in the pit of my stomach and travels the length of my spine as his teeth gently bite at the skin below my ear.

This is so wrong but I can't stop it. The head of him pushes between my lower lips, forcing the fabric of my pyjama shorts to ride up in the most delicious way. It bumps against my clit. A cry escapes me and Nathan takes this as permission to give me more.

His hand tightens its hold of my hip and his pelvis grinds into me again. We shouldn't be doing this. I shouldn't be enjoying this but I can't help it. I'm only human.

Ragged breathing is now against my ear, the sound mingling with my own. The burning follows my blood flow, reaching the end of every limb. I whimper, my hand wrapping around Nathan's, my hips pushing back to meet his. Oh god.

Can't breathe.

Lights pop behind my eyes when I hear a hoarse cry rip from his throat. I need more, I'm suffocating with want and pleasure.

Dillan cries and we both tense.

Reality seems to hit us both at the same time.

"I've got it," I blurt and in seconds I'm out of bed and across the hall, my hands trembling, my legs jelly. Scooping Dillan up with a strength I shouldn't have right now, I quickly change him and give him my breast. The discomfort of it helps me to gather my thoughts.

What the heck is wrong with me?

I'm cuddling Dillan and rocking him for only ten minutes before he's asleep again. I need to speak to Nathan. We need to stop this. We can't let this continue. It's wrong and... it's just wrong.

Caleb... I touch the picture of his gorgeous face that I hung from the cot mobile only a week ago. His smile makes me feel so damn guilty for whatever it is I'm doing.

The picture turns with the soft tinkling tune that plays as the mobile spins slowly. Tiny beige stuffed animals hang from its wooden points. Like being in a trance, I stare at the slowly moving mobile and lose myself for a moment, imagining what could have been.

Tears fall from my eyes as I think about what I've done. I wouldn't even consider doing this if Caleb were alive. It would be so morally wrong and taboo. Nathan is his brother! This is the kind of stuff you see on the TV happening to other people, reality shows where they have paternity tests to determine the father of the child.

Yet it's happening to me.

My heart is so confused. My head tells me this is wrong but whenever I'm with Nathan, my heart is conflicted. One part screams for Caleb and the piece he took with him, the other half tells me how much I love being around Nathan, how good he makes me feel. How cherished he makes me feel. How protected.

Sucking in my fear, I bury it deep down and slowly make my way to my room.

Where's Nathan?

I step back out and notice the door at the end of the hall is open, the one leading to his bedroom. I should leave him alone. Maybe he doesn't want to sleep with me now. That isn't a bad thing. We've taken this too far.

For some reason I can't leave him. I start forward, my pulse throbbing with every step, my nerves rising. The last thing I want is to hurt him or to push him away, but he needs to understand that this, whatever this is between us, can't happen.

I slowly and quietly ascend the stairs. There's no light coming from beneath his bedroom door.

It's shut. I should knock but for some strange reason I don't. Maybe I'm worried I'll wake him. At least... that's what I tell myself.

The door opens an inch at a time with the assistance of my hand.

I hear his breathing, his heavy laboured breath. Another noise accompanies it. My head screams at me to look away but I can't.

Instantly my mouth goes dry as I stare at Nathan's profile through the crack in the door. He's standing, one hand leaning on the chest of drawers by his bed, the other... the other is wrapped around his swollen and angry looking length. His blue and white pyjama trousers are still up so I'm assuming he's only pulled the front down.

Slowly his hand strokes back and forth, a leather glove on it. That's weird. Maybe he likes the feel of it.

His shoulders tense and his muscles bulge as he continues working himself. It's an amazing sight, one I shouldn't be appreciating.

"Damn it," he whispers, his eyes on something on the desk in front of him. I can't see what it is; the room is too dark and it's too far away.

The muscles in his arm tense and flex as he picks up the pace, his hand now working almost furiously on himself. My stomach clenches and I feel myself become slowly wet as I watch the scene before me.

Gulp. He pulls on himself faster and harder. It looks almost painful. So raw, so... desperate.

I lean closer to the door. Big mistake.

My jellified legs buckle slightly as I lean and I catch myself on the door handle, causing it to click.

My heart stops and I begin to shake. Oh crap.

He freezes, his eyes closed, the whites no longer shining in the dim light coming through the open curtains.

I contemplate running but I'd just look like a creeper. Hell, I am a creeper.

Shiny beads of sweat glisten on his forehead like tiny diamonds. I have the urge to wipe them from his brow but I don't. Instead I stand in the doorway, my mouth parted in silent shock.

He's going to get angry, I just know it.

"Are you going to just stand there?" His voice is deep and hoarse. I've never heard it sound this way before. It caresses me in places like a hand would. "Seeing as you've already invaded my privacy, a few more steps won't hurt."

Gulp.

He turns, tucking himself back into his pyjamas, forming a tent in the front with his straight and impressive erection.

"I... I'm sorry... I came to..." My thoughts won't gather, my mouth is too dry, my eyes won't leave his twitching length. "To talk."

"Talk?" He smirks in the dark. "What about?"

"About," something to do with something. "Something." Face palm. "Downstairs, in bed."

His smirk widens. "Care to elaborate?"

"I..." Oh crap. "I'm sorry, I shouldn't have... I just..." I'm an idiot. "I'm sorry."

In four long strides he's grabbing me and pressing me against the wall, his faces inches from mine. "Did you enjoy watching me?"

Oh my god. "I should go back to my room." Nodding frantically I try to squeeze from between him and the wall.

"There's nothing wrong with feeling aroused." He traps me by pressing his body against mine, his thickness pushing up between us, resting between our pelvic bones. "If I touch you down there, will you be wet?"

Yes. God yes. "Nathan," I don't know whether I'm pleading or warning.

"I'll take that as a yes," he chuckles and nips at my neck, making me want to arch my back and push my aching breasts against his chest.

No. I didn't come up here for this. "I should go."

"You don't want to."

I place my hands on his chest between us and push him back a step, slowly and gently. "I need to."

He looks at me for a long moment before speaking and what he says shocks me so badly, my mind goes blank. All previous thoughts flee. "I know you're not ready yet. I don't expect you to be. I also don't care how long it takes." He winds a lock of my hair around his gloved finger, reminding me of where that hand was not moments ago. Oh god. "I won't stop trying."

"T... trying what?" I stammer and lick my dry lips.

"To make you mine." Thud. My heart just hit my ribcage in an attempt to run screaming. I blink in shock. "This is more than just an obligation to you and Dillan. I can't hide it anymore and I can't keep pretending that we aren't perfect for each other when clearly... we are." The arrogance in his tone should make me angry, the things he's insinuating should make me really angry, but they don't. I only have one thing on my mind right now. It begins with S and ends in X. His words only fuel my desire and it takes everything I have to stop myself from wrapping around him like a koala and clinging on for dear life. "But I won't push you like I have. I want you to come to me when you're ready." His admission brings me back to earth for a flicker of a second and the guilt I feel pierces through my lusting state.

"And what if I don't?" I ask, because I doubt I will. No matter how badly he seems to be affecting me, I could never betray Caleb like that.

Pain flickers in his eyes for a moment. "Then I'll just have to enjoy you in any way I can get you."

"And if I do?" Why did I ask that? It just came out.

I open my mouth to tell him not to answer but I'm too late. His words are firm and sure, his smile gentle yet cocky. "Then I intend to marry you and keep you for a very long time."

My mouth forms the shape of an O, like Bridget Jones when she walks into the party wearing a bunny suit. "Oh."

CHAPTER TWENTY-THREE

I'M STOOD AT MY car outside of the supermarket, piling my groceries into the boot, when a tall and odd looking male approaches me. "Excuse me, sweetheart." He runs his fingers through his greying hair and blows out a long breath. "Sorry to bother you, I'm Carl."

I don't respond. I'm not a fan of being approached by strangers, no matter how friendly they seem. Where the hell is Nathan? He only went to change Dillan while I took the trolley to the car. He should be here by now.

He notices my lack of response but doesn't seem offended. "I'm sort of a messenger."

"Okay." Where is he going with this?

"I was told to deliver this directly to you." He holds out a large brown envelope that's bulging at the bottom.

I stare at the envelope, my eyes blinking stupidly. Should I take it? Maybe I can...

Dillan is thrust into my arms and I barely manage to catch him before Nathan is on Carl. I let out a scream when Nathan brings his fist back and swings it around. It connects with Carl's cheekbone but he quickly retaliates.

The hit didn't even daze Nathan and it was a hard hit.

"You stay the hell away from her!" Nathan shouts, blocking Carl's next swing and grabbing him by the throat. "Get Dillan in the car, Gwen."

I don't need telling twice. I quickly climb into the back and strap Dillan into his car seat. He lets out a baby cry but soon settles, which I'm grateful for.

During this time Nathan has Carl pressed up against the back of the car. I scramble out, convinced that Dillan will be okay for a moment. Nathan needs me.

Two men come over and separate the fight, not that it can be called that. Nathan was kicking arse until they showed up. I actually feel bad for Carl and his broken nose and his lip that's bleeding so profusely from the side, I have a terrible feeling it'll need stitches.

Nathan scoops the envelope up from the ground and tucks it inside his jacket. His hand trembles as he grips my arm, guides me to the passenger side and forces me in.

His angry brown eyes glare at Carl who is still being restrained and ordering that somebody call the Police. Everybody seems a little bit stunned by the events. This is a small town, this just doesn't happen here.

"Are you okay?" I ask softly, not knowing what else to say. His lips are a thin white line and a vein bulges on his forehead. He turns on the ignition and reverses out of his parking spot, causing two people to leap to the side out of the way. Christ. Is he crazy? "Calm down."

He ignores me and races out of the car park way over the speed limit. His anger is obvious, so much so, I'm surprised he's not glowing red. Actually, he looks like he kind of is.

"Do you want to tell me what's going on?" I snap and look over my shoulder at Dillan waving his chubby arms around. Nathan finally slows when we reach the end of the street and my body relaxes a fraction but not much. "Nathan. What's in the envelope?"

"Don't ask." He doesn't sound angry or even irritated, he sounds desperate. "Please. Just... don't ask."

"Why?"

"Because you'll hate me," he says this brokenly, as if this is worse than any other possibility.

"I doubt that." I place my hand on his arm. "Tell me."

"I refuse!"

Gah. "Fine. I won't ask." At least not while I can see how clearly upset he is.

We drive home in silence. It's tense and uncomfortable and brings back memories of our first couple of months together.

"Nathan?" I call as he makes his way into the house. He stops to unlock the door before coming back to help me unload the boot.

"Take Dillan inside," he demands. "Oh, and next time I leave you alone for five minutes, don't talk to anybody. Not even Paula or Jeanine."

My mouth drops open. "What?"

"You heard me."

"You expect me to ignore my friends because of something you won't tell me about? Something that will clearly affect me."

His broken and pleading gaze comes to me. His tone matches his eyes. "Yes."

"This is..." I pick up Dillan and hold him tight to me. His eyes peek up at me as I clutch him to my chest. "Ridiculous. Just tell me what it is, rip off the plaster. I'm not stupid. I know you're being blackmailed, that much is obvious, especially now."

"Take Dillan inside," he hisses, his tone telling me that he's not to be trifled with.

"I'm going to take him inside and then we're going to talk."

"No we're not."

I give him the same look he gave me only moments ago. "Oh, we are."

His face registers shock. I've never spoken to him this way before. If I didn't know any better I'd say he was amused for a moment before realizing that this time I'm not going to relent.

I'm confident that Nathan won't leave to avoid me, not when he's obviously trying to hide something and whoever is trying to deliver it is being relentless about it.

Dinner is as silent and as tense as the drive home. Whenever I try to speak to him he completely blanks me as if I'm not here. To say I'm frustrated would be an understatement.

"Still talking to myself I see," I mumble and follow Nathan up the stairs. He continues up to his room and even has the gall to slam the door in my face. "You can't keep hiding from me. You're going to have to talk to me eventually."

I try the handle but he's locked it from the inside.

"Nathan, please."

"Go away, Gwen." He pulls the door open, his face now inches from mine. "I'm serious. Go away."

"Arsehole," I swear, looking for a reaction. His jaw tenses. "Dick. Shit. Bitch. Bollocks." A hand slams over my mouth and a very tense looking Nathan glares at me. I continue with my cursing, even though it's muffled by his palm.

"You're going to keep pushing me aren't you?" He sighs, his hand still covering my now silent mouth. "I'm not going to tell you, so please, just drop it."

"It's clear to me," I begin when he removes his hand from my mouth. "That I'm going to find out eventually. Maybe you should just trust me with this, tell me before somebody else does."

His face pales and his eyes glitter with sorrow. "I can't."

My heart lurches and my hand immediately comes up and grips the back of his hair. "I can see that it's hurting you. Trust me with it."

He seems to think on it for a moment, then the shutters come down, hiding all emotion from me. "No."

Seconds later he's gone and the door has been slammed and locked again. I'm half tempted to go outside and wait for another messenger, but I don't.

Instead I retreat to the nursery and play with my baby boy. He still hasn't smiled yet and he's now officially five weeks old. Time flies. I can't believe how well he's holding his head up. It's madness.

"Peekaboo!" Nothing. Nothing but a blink. I guess he doesn't like peekaboo any more than his uncle likes it.

This entire situation is so frustrating. I hate being kept in the dark. I'm not used to secrets. I don't have many friends and the friends I do have tell me pretty much everything. My mum didn't have any friends or family as I grew up so there were no secrets there either. As for Caleb, he never kept anything from me. There wasn't a point in our relationship where I felt like he was hiding something. Not that I can recall anyway.

Caleb, if you're up there, please give me a clue. I have no idea what I'm doing and I'm scared. Fear is one of my quick to react emotions. It's usually the first thing I feel when faced by a difficult situation. Although I'm not a coward by any means, I tend to face my fears head on. I just hate feeling fear.

I need it to stop. I need to get Nathan back to his normal self.

Why do I have a terrible feeling that it'll never happen? Why do I have a terrible feeling that I'm about to lose another part of me?

A week goes by. Nathan left the first morning after the incident. I don't know where he is or why he's dared to leave me. All I know is that I've left the house with Dillan, expecting someone to come up to me with this bloody envelope that clearly hides something tremendous, yet nobody has.

Which means Nathan has dealt with it.

This thought brings me a small amount of relief. At least my world isn't about to turn upside down. I've come to rely on Nathan too much and this past week has been hard. Harder than it should have been.

I just wish he'd come home, or at least answer the phone when I call.

At least I have Dillan for company. That's a relief.

Of course I tried to search for the envelope too. I didn't just hang around and wait for one to be delivered. Unfortunately Nathan's office and bedroom were both locked and I couldn't find a trace of it anywhere else.

I'm woken by the sound of soft words being spoken through the baby monitor. I can't quite make out what's being said but I can tell it's Nathan. Checking the clock I see that it's just turned midnight. Relief fills me when I fully register the fact that I'm not dreaming and Nathan is in fact home. I scramble from my bed and quietly creep to the nursery.

The door is open and Nathan is sat in the rocking chair with his back to me. I can see the top of Dillan's head resting on the curve of Nathan's arm as he rocks backwards and forwards.

"Hey, I didn't hear him wake," I say softly, noticing Nathan's body tense as I move closer.

My gorgeous little boy is fast asleep, swaddled in a beige blanket. Nathan lifts him to his lips and kisses his chubby cheek before placing him in his cot and tucking him in. He stands with his back to me, his hands gripping the wooden railing.

"Are you okay?" I don't know what else to say and this seems the most diplomatic thing to say considering the circumstances.

Nathan shakes his head. "Just saying goodbye."

"You're leaving again?" My voice comes out breathy and full of panic and disbelief. "If this is…"

"Not here." Cold, calm and emotionless brown eyes come to me. A draft hits my body as he passes, causing me to shiver slightly. Or maybe that's his cold demeanour making me feel slightly chilled.

I follow him into his office and sit in the chair beside his desk. He stares down at a few sheets of paper in front of him, his tongue running across his lower lip. Please don't be leaving. Don't leave us.

I say this out loud, my tone pleading, almost begging. Hell, it is begging. I'll beg if I have to.

"I'm not leaving," he says calmly and looks at me, his inner businessman shining through. "You are."

Thud... my heart just hit my stomach. "What?"

"It's time for you to go back to your mum's."

I... I'm leaving? "What?"

"You heard me." He looks down at the papers again and spreads them out along the desk. "You may leave now."

I stare at him, my body frozen in place, my heart beat non-existent.

"I said you can go."

"I heard you, I just... I can't move," I mutter, my body still with shock. "You're throwing me out." This is a statement, not a question.

"We knew this time would come eventually."

"But... you promised you wouldn't, so no, in fact I didn't know it would come," I argue. "What about Dillan?"

His calm and uncaring expression doesn't change. "I'll see him when I can." And the promise? I get no apology for his breaking that?

"You're kidding," I breathe, grabbing at my stomach like I've just been punched. "Please tell me you're kidding."

"Do I look like I'm joking to you?" He hisses and holds his hand out, motioning for me to leave.

"Is this because of what happened?" It suddenly dawns on me. "You're doing this on purpose, pushing me away to stop me from finding out whatever it is you're keeping buried."

"No," he sighs and rubs his face with his hands. "This is because I'm bored of playing daddy and loving husband to a woman who..." His jaw clenches and his words stop.

"Look," I lean onto the desk. "If this is because I... it's just... gah. I mean..." I won't ask again. You're more important to me than whatever the hell it is that's ruining our bubble right now. "I won't bring up the envelope again, I swear. Just let me be here for you."

"It's not about that," he says, almost sounding bored. "I'm over that. I made a serious misjudgement and I won't be making it again. The envelope has been dealt with."

"I don't believe you," I state defiantly. This is rubbish, utter rubbish. I'm not falling for it and I'm not letting him push me away.

"Guinevere..."

"No." I walk around the desk and kneel on the ground before him. My body is aching with a pain I don't recognise. It hurts, a lot, and I need it to stop. I grip his knees and peer up at him through my lashes. "I promise I won't ask and if I do happen to find out, you have my word that..."

"Don't make promises you can't keep," he snarls, his gloved hands pulling at my wrists in an attempt to get me to release his legs. Why's he wearing his gloves again?

I stand immediately and take a large step backwards, seeing that he needs space. "Okay." My hand goes to my throbbing chest in an attempt to stop my heart from smashing through my ribcage and throwing itself out of the closest window. I try a new tactic. "I know what you're doing and you know that I know what you're doing. It won't work. Do your worst. If you think I'm leaving you when you're clearly going through something that's dragging you down, you're wrong." I give him the bravest face I can muster. "You're my best friend. Besides, what happened to never stopping until you had me? Does that no longer count?"

"No." He clears his throat and waves me away. "This was a misjudgement made by me. I thought we should have been more. In reality I'd just deprived myself of sex for too long."

Why does this hurt? Why do I want to smash something? "Oh."

"I'm seeing somebody."

Eye roll. "Oh yeah? Who?"

He continues like I haven't even spoken. "So I'll need you to leave. It was awkward enough when I had Lorna visiting while you remained here and she didn't mean anything to me." His eyes darken and his lips curve with a sneer as he looks me up and down like I'm a chip in comparison to a steak. "Aisha is a woman of... class." Ouch. I'm guessing she's the steak then. "It wouldn't suit us to have another woman around, especially my brother's fiancée and his..." He hesitates for a moment, his eyes straying from mine. "Bastard child." I heave at his words, a fierce pain tearing through me.

He's doing it on purpose but that doesn't make it sting any less.

But what if he's being serious? What if I'm wrong?

No. I'm not wrong. I can see it in his eyes, he's playing me. He's forcing me out.

Why though?

"It's not going to work," I whisper angrily, my fists clenching by my sides. "I get what you're doing and I'm telling you now. It's not going to work."

"I'm not playing a game, Guinevere!" Nathan shouts and carefully puts the papers in a folder. I see that they're just pictures of his jewellery, nothing important. I'm guessing he's using them as a diversion to limit eye contact with me, another reason I know he's lying. "Accept it and be on your way. Be grateful I'm not charging you for the amount of money you've spent since arriving."

My temper spikes, my chest tingling and my stomach twisting as I wrap my head around whatever the fuck this is.

"How dare you!" I spit. "I never asked for anything from you; you offered everything willingly. Stop doing this. I'm not leaving. You're just causing me unnecessary hurt!"

"As you wish," he laughs cockily. "But when you meet Aisha, don't say I didn't warn you."

My head shakes back and forth angrily. "If she even exists."

His eyes darken. "She does."

"Then I'll calmly explain to her that I don't believe a word you're saying!"

"Believe it."

"What the hell is wrong with you?" I cry, my eyes burning. "I'm going back to bed."

He shrugs and places the folder in the drawer. Now he has to look at me and I hate the cold stare aimed my way. "I'm not being cruel. I'm being honest."

"Yet another lie. I won't accept it. I don't accept any of the crap you've just said."

"Then don't accept it," he shouts, his face turning red with anger. "But if you know what's good for you and Dillan, you will."

"Fuck you, Nathan."

"Language."

"You can't tell me what to do anymore," I laugh incredulously. "You've just lost that right. And if you honestly think I'll be pushed out of my home because of some stupid secret, then you're wrong. Don't you think this is all a bit backwards? You're pushing me away when that's the thing you're trying to prevent?"

Nathan lets out an exasperated breath. "Now you're being ridiculous. Listen to what you just said. Why would I push you away to protect myself from your hate?" He has a point. Is he being serious about all of this? I can't tell anymore.

No. I won't talk myself into believing him.

Not unless he's being a martyr and forcing me to hate him so that I escape some other kind of hurt. What though? I need to know.

Just leave the room, Gwen, just leave it and speak to him tomorrow.

"I don't want to listen to this anymore." I wipe the tears from under my eyes with the back of my hand. "I'm going back to bed."

"I don't want you here anymore, Guinevere." His voice sounds hoarse, dare I say pained? "Take the car and I'll even pay for Dillan's private schooling when he's older."

I laugh humourlessly and walk to the door. "No thanks."

"Guinevere..."

"What?" I sigh, my exhaustion sinking into every cell of my body. I no longer have the strength for this. "What do you want now?"

"Don't fight me on this. Everything I'm saying is the truth."

"I won't argue with you on anything anymore." I look at him straight in the eye. "But I'm not leaving."

Nothing, not even a flash of emotion. The only thing he does is clench his jaw and his fists.

A sob tears through me as I push the door open and close it gently behind me. Sure, I'd love to slam it but that would be childish. Nathan didn't abandon me when I needed someone. He stuck by me. I can't leave him now, not when he clearly needs me.

This is stupid. What is he playing at? This makes no sense.

Nathan doesn't come after me and I won't lie, half of me expected him to. The other half wanted him to.

This is so messed up. Nathan's right.

Oh my god.

Is he really seeing someone else? Why is it that this thought hurts more than everything else? Maybe because I'm so used to Nathan circling around me and only me for such a long time. Have I somehow mentally made him my property?

No, I'm just pissed off. I don't care who he sleeps with.

I'll be even more pissed off if he chooses her over us, if he so willingly throws us out because of a new fling.

I'm not sure what to do. I'm not sure if I'm right or not. I have to stick this out. I can't leave him.

Dillan wakes three times in the night, although it doesn't bother me too much as I don't sleep a wink. Nathan leaves at seven, way earlier than usual. Is he avoiding me because he can't be bothered to argue? Or is he serious about it all and can't stand the sight of me?

I hate him so much for making me feel this way. My anger is trembling under the surface of my skin, causing my blood to boil. Lashing out seems like a great idea right now, but for some reason I just can't. As much as I want to throw things at him, deep down I know that he doesn't deserve it. He's been so good to me and Dillan. How can I hate him for wanting his life back?

If anything I should hate Caleb for leaving me in the first place.

But what's the truth? Somebody give me the answers before I drive myself crazy.

Chapter Twenty-Four

"You need a break," Jeanine tells me and she's right. "You've lost weight; you look exhausted."

I yawn loudly, pretty much proving her words. "Things aren't great right now."

"I can tell," she mumbles and lets out a long sigh. "Do you want to talk about it?"

I shake my head. "Not really. I've just got a lot on my mind." And Nathan still isn't speaking to me. After our argument last night I genuinely hoped it would have all blown over. Instead he walked downstairs, saw me sat in the dining room with Dillan and asked, "Still here?" He didn't wait for an answer, his tone clearly stating he didn't like the fact that I'm still here. After grabbing his food that I made, he vanished upstairs. I heard his office door slam shut and let out the breath I'd been holding.

I need to find a way to get through to him.

"Why don't you come over for dinner tonight? Bring Dillan obviously." That actually doesn't sound too bad.

"A word please, Jeanine," Nathan snaps. I wince, praying I haven't gotten her into trouble. She rolls her eyes and gives me a wink before following him out of the room and up the stairs.

Of course I follow, how can I not? They don't have to know that though.

"Yes, I'm serious." I hear Nathan say.

My ear is pressed up against the door. I feel like I'm in a movie.

Jeanine laughs as if he's said the funniest thing in the world. I don't have to wait long for an explanation. "Oh, Nathan. You know I don't have to work. The only reason I do work is because I'm the only person who keeps your house the way you like it." She laughs again. "But by all means fire me. It won't stop me from speaking to Gwen. She's become a friend and I don't treat my friends with such disrespect."

Nathan doesn't respond but I can feel his annoyance seeping through the wooden door.

"Will that be all?" Jeanine asks and I quickly run away. They probably know I was there, but to be honest I don't care.

I can't believe he threatened to fire her if she continued speaking to me. Or at least that's what I understood from their short conversation. What an arsehole.

Is he really that desperate for me to leave?

My answer is yes. I get this answer by suffering another two days with him.

"I didn't want lasagne. If you're going to stay in my home even though I've asked you to leave, you could at least prepare food that I actually want to eat." I watched him take his plate and scrape the untouched food into the bin. That was yesterday at dinner.

"This room is horrendous. It stinks of nappies." This was said this morning after I had just changed Dillan's nappy. He knew very well I'd just done this as well, as I was in the middle of wrapping it up in a nappy bag.

About half an hour later I was trying to connect to the internet. It didn't work. Nathan stood in the archway and explained harshly, "The internet isn't free, you know. Have some self-respect. Pay for your own things."

I didn't respond. I played minesweeper instead as Dillan had his nap. I can only pray that it gets better.

Which brings us to now.

Not even twenty minutes later Nathan returns, picks up my laptop and takes it away. He comes back with my old phone, takes my new one from my pocket, swaps the sim cards and places my old phone back into my pocket.

"You paid for the nursery. Are you going to take that away too?" I comment dryly, my eyes narrowed.

"No, I'll need that room empty and I doubt I'll get my money back on such poorly looked after furniture."

I let out a laugh. "Considering you've used the furniture as much as me, that's an insult to yourself."

He only leaves the room. I sit and twiddle my thumbs, my irritation at a new level. I'm finding it hard to keep it together and it's only been one day.

Oh god. What now? He's back. It hasn't been fifteen minutes since he left the room.

Oh wait, it's okay, he's going to the car with my... why the hell does he have my nappy bag? I watch him walk back to the house through the clear glass of the window. His face is a hard mask.

He steps into the room and throws Dillan's coat at me. I catch it before it hits me in the face. "Take Dillan and get out for a few hours. Your nappy bag is packed with the right amount of everything."

"What?" He's kicking us out for the day?

"You heard me, I have to concentrate. Get in your car and go."

Will he let me back in if I do?

He sighs at my lack of action and snatches the coat from me. "Honestly, you're his mother. The least you could do is get him ready to leave. That's all I'm asking." I'm going to punch him.

I watch him dress Dillan quickly and efficiently. God damn him. Now he's leaving the house.

I quickly chase after him and my son. He places Dillan gently in the car seat in the back of my car and tosses the keys at me. Catching them like I did the coat, only an inch from my face, I grit my teeth and climb into the driver's seat.

"You forgot your coat; it's cold," Nathan snaps, his hand on the doorframe.

A thought comes to mind. I climb back out of the car and stomp towards the house.

I grab my coat but as soon as I get near him, I click my fingers. "Oh, wait. I totally forgot." I lift my t-shirt over my head and throw it at him.

"What are you doing?" His eyes widen as he takes me in wearing nothing but a bra and trousers.

I kick off my shoes and tug my trousers down, ignoring the horrid feel of the wet dirt beneath my socks.

"What do you think you're doing?" Nathan hisses as I kick the jeans at him.

I slip my feet back into my shoes and snatch my coat from his hands. Shrugging it on I give him a friendly smile. "You bought those too."

"You can have the clothes." He gawps, disbelief plain on his face.

"No thanks. I don't want anything from you. Not unless it's for Dillan." I button my coat up at the front, ignoring the fact that it doesn't even cover my thighs, and lean into the back of the car to grab Dillan. I'm probably giving him a spectacular view of my lace knickers right now.

"Now what are you doing?" He snaps as I cradle my son to my chest and walk casually to the boot. With one hand I pull out his pram and unfold it with the aid of my foot. I place Dillan inside and wrap him tightly in his blanket. I use the rain cover to keep the cold air from attacking him. "Guinevere!"

"Yes?" I enquire sweetly, stopping a few feet from the car.

"You've made your point."

I pretend to be confused, almost laughing evilly at the look of defeat on his face. "Point? What point? I thought you wanted back everything you bought for me?"

"Gwen," he sighs, looking exhausted. "Stop this."

"Nope. If you want to be an idiot, then I'll just be an idiot right back." I click my fingers again. "Now that I think about it," I let out a little laugh and shake my head as if telling myself I'm stupid. "You bought me this underwear too."

His eyelids stretch as far as physically possible, his mouth dropping open. "You wouldn't. Anybody could see you. You'll get ill."

"I didn't realise you cared, Nathan." I bat my eyelashes and lift up the hem of the coat. My thumbs hook into the edges of my French knickers.

He gulps, his eyes almost daring me to do it. "That's it!"

I let out a scream which is half a reaction to being startled at the fact I'm now over his shoulder and half triumphant at the fact I cracked him.

His shoulder digs into my stomach as he carries me back to the house. He uses his other hand to push the pushchair. I smile. Score one to me.

"The only reason..." He begins but I scowl deeply at him and admonish, "Save whatever horse crap you're about to try and feed me. You care. You just proved that. I win this round."

His phone rings and he holds up his finger to tell me to be quiet. I'll give him this respect.

No words leave his mouth during the duration of the call. He only listens quietly, his body tensing. I can't hear what's being said but I can hear an angry male voice. Nathan hangs up the phone and pushes me towards the stairs. "Get dressed and pack. I'm serious."

"Nope." I return firmly, giving him a smile that I know is annoying the hell out of him. "But thanks. Are you hungry? What would you like to eat?"

He stalks towards me, his eyes a fiery blaze of fury and something else. I'm not sure what the something else is but I have a feeling I'm about to find out. "Pack your bags." His voice is menacing, almost vicious. His face only an inch from mine, I almost cower. Almost but not quite. Although I do gulp. "And leave."

"No."

"Fine," he says and moves his head side to side, causing his neck to crack. "Have it your way."

"Okay." I give him another smile and race up the stairs. "Be a sport and watch Dillan for me."

"I have things..." I don't hear the rest of what he's saying because I'm in my room and searching through my closet for something to wear that he didn't buy.

I can't believe I just got undressed in the driveway in front of Nathan. I've officially lost the plot.

The next few days are the same. Nathan either ignores me or insults me. If he insults me I ignore him. It's an endless cycle. It's also making me miserable.

Nothing I say or do gets through to him.

I need to find a way to bring the old Nathan back. I have to do something.

With this thought in mind, I drop Dillan off with Jeanine for a while and head to the supermarket as was her suggestion. She thinks I should try and remind him of the good times we've shared, so that's what I'm going to do. Nathan got rid of all of my eggs and I'm going to need some if I want to get on his good side with food. This is the only weapon in my arsenal, baked goods. I'm keeping my fingers crossed but I'm also not holding out hope.

If only he'd tell me. If he'd just tell me then we could move past this. What's so bad that he has to make out like he hates me?

I don't want him to know what I'm doing so I spend the morning baking cake after cake and cookies after cookies and treat after treat, using Jeanine's kitchen. By the time I'm done it's almost two.

Jeanine insists I leave Dillan with her while I do this. I thank her profusely and, after loading the baked goods into my car, I set off for home. The entire way I beg the skies for strength and help.

Now I just need to figure out what to say.

I gather as many cakes and things as possible and step into the house, relieved that the door isn't locked.

"Nathan?" I shout as I place the last of the boxes on the kitchen side.

My phone alerts me to a text and I open it.

<u>Nathan</u>: I'm in the nursery.

Well, that's an improvement already. Maybe he can smell my surprise treats and has decided to suddenly be civil.

The only thing I take up with me is the small bag of homemade donuts that taste way better than anything you'll find at a theme park. In my mind that was the night that Nathan and I connected, that was the night we became friends, and now I just have to remind him of that.

"Okay," I start shouting as I head upstairs. "So I went slightly overboard on the baking but I thought we could…"

Nathan's eyes meet mine and they wince at whatever he sees in them.

It's heartbreak he sees. My heart shatters into fragments so tiny they couldn't be seen under a microscope.

My phone beeps as I stare at the empty room. There's no nursery furniture in sight.

He's throwing me out.

<u>Mum</u>: Would you care to explain why a van full of yours and Dillan's things has just arrived on my doorstep? Are you coming home?

It would appear so.

"I told you I wanted you to leave," he says but there's no emotion to his tone. His hands tremble by his sides.

I don't know what to say. I'm dazed, totally and completely dazed. I think I just lost my mind.

"What about Dillan?" It's the only question I can manage to ask. I don't want an answer to any of the others.

He shrugs noncommittally. "I'll see him when I can. If you allow it."

I nod quickly and a little frantically, my body tense as it struggles to keep my emotions bottled. I won't give him the satisfaction. "Sure. You're his uncle."

"I appreciate that." He chews on his cheek. "I warned you..."

My hand shoots up, silencing him immediately. "I know. I should have listened. I didn't think you were serious. That's my mistake."

His eyes watch me warily for a moment. "Are you okay?"

A tingle erupts in my chest, forcing a lump up my throat. I swallow it down. "Fine. Are you sure they packed everything of ours?"

He looks me in the eye, his face now one of concern. "Are you sure you're okay?"

Am I? I feel okay. Shocked and maybe a little sad but I'm otherwise okay. "Yeah."

"I'm sor..."

My hand shoots up again. "You don't owe me an explanation, Nathan."

"I..."

"No." I throw the bag of donuts at him and he catches them with ease. I watch for his reaction as he peels the bag open. His eyes sparkle with the memory of that night.

"One of the best nights of my life," he says quietly and looks at me, his gaze unsure. "Thank you for these."

I ignore him and his strange look. "I have a bag of my things in your room, did you remember those?"

He cringes. "No. Sorry, I forgot about the time you stayed upstairs with me." Yeah right. More like he wanted an excuse for me to come back. What game is he playing? Do I even care?

How do I even feel?

"I'll just grab them now." My voice sounds weird. Why does it sound so... hollow?

He follows me up the stairs and into his room. Unfortunately he doesn't remain silent. "I expected you to be angry." Yeah, me too. "I don't like this."

"You don't like what?" I mutter and turn on the light. My bag is under the desk in the corner. I pull it out by the handle and sling it onto my back.

"This calm..." he waves a hand at me, as if referring to all of me rather than just my expression.

I give him a shrug. "Thanks for everything. Honestly. You've done so much for me. I guess I just can't seem to blame you for wanting your life back."

"That's not what this is." He takes a step towards me, almost as if he wants to touch me but thinks better of it and leans against the wall instead.

"Then what is it?"

He opens his mouth, closes it, opens it, lets out a frustrated growl and runs his hand through his hair.

A familiar cool disk taps the curves of my breasts. I'm so used to wearing it I forgot it was there. I wrap my hand around the circular pendent and pull it from my neck and the chain breaks. If this had happened yesterday, I would have been devastated. Now I don't care. "Here." I hold it out for him to take.

The pain in his eyes does nothing to me. He shakes his head, looking like I've just killed his puppy. "I don't want it back. I made it for you."

"Exactly." I toss it at him but he makes no move to grab it. We both watch as it flies past his arm and slides along the floor into the darkness of his closet. I feel nothing. I'd throw the matching bracelet too but I'm not wearing it. "There are twelve boxes downstairs in the kitchen, all of them full of your favourites. You can freeze them because I doubt even you will be able to eat them all in two days."

"Gwen," he whispers softly.

"Don't," I say and rub my eyes. "I'm going to call for a taxi."

"Take your car," he implores, following me down the stairs to the first floor where my room resides. "That's more for Dillan than it is for you. You said you'd keep stuff for Dillan, right?"

I blink at him like he's stupid. Hell, he is stupid. "Nathan, how the hell do you expect me to afford it? The insurance is ridiculous and it eats through fuel like we breathe air." He opens his mouth to speak but I don't let him. "I don't have a job, I have no money and my mum won't let me stay for longer than a month." He opens his mouth again but, like before, I cut him off. "And this isn't a guilt trip. It's the truth. I don't want anything from you."

"I'll provide for you both until you get back on your feet." His voice is barely there. I can see a flicker of emotion in his eyes. Is that remorse? "I'll rent an apartment for you. There's a really nice one in the..."

"Can you just call me a taxi? I need to go and pick up my son." I show him my phone which has just this second died due to me failing to charge it last night. "No power."

"Only if you promise to let me pay for it," he demands, hiding his phone behind his back. "Or better yet, let me drive you to your mum's."

"No," I refuse adamantly and check around my bedroom for anything that he may have left behind. "Thanks, but you've done enough for me already."

"Then let me do something more."

A tiny zap of anger pierces through my bubble of numbness. "No. I don't want anything from you anymore. You've made your feelings on us loud and clear."

"Us?" He blinks in astonishment. "What do you mean us?"

"I meant me," I correct myself, cursing for my idiotic slip up that he'll no doubt read into.

"You said us."

"Well excuse me if I'm a little out of sorts, Nathan," I hiss and prod him in the chest. "I don't know if you've noticed but I've just lost my entire life... yet again."

His skin turns an odd shade of yellow. "That's not what this is. You get to go back to your friends. You get to..."

"This is my home. No... sorry. This was my home." My heart plummets, its beat no longer existent. "You were my home."

He staggers back a step, his hand gripping hold of the desk. "Caleb was your home."

"Yeah," I laugh coldly. "He was. But he's dead and I lost that." I realise something and mentally kick myself for not realising it sooner. "You gave me that back. Just in a different way."

"I didn't know you felt that way. I thought..."

"Stop thinking. It doesn't suit you."

"Maybe we can talk about this. Maybe I've rushed my decision."

"Maybe you can call me a taxi so I can get my son and find a way to get to my mum's. A way that doesn't involve you. Besides, it's not going to change anything, is it?"

He lets out a growl of frustration, answering my question without words. Instead he says, "At least let me give you a ride to Jeanine's." I go to pass him but his hand wraps around my bicep. "Please."

Sigh. "Fine. Give me a minute, I need to call my mum."

He nods and ducks out of the room after I nod towards the door.

"Explain," my mum says, sounding curious rather than irritated or put upon.

"I'm coming home."

"Well, I guess it's a good thing I unpacked your things then." I can hear the smile in her voice. "I'm looking forward to seeing you. Text me when you're on your way."

"I will. Thanks mum." I hang up the phone and stare at my empty room. I failed.

Nathan doesn't say anything as he drives me to Jeanine's. I don't say anything either. I'm not entirely certain there is actually anything we can say. He's made his feelings clear and I'm not sure what my feelings actually are right now.

He pulls up outside of Jeanine's house, which isn't too far from Nathan's but is far enough for me to want to drive there.

Before I can reach for the handle, the doors lock. I give it a tug, sigh and sit back in my seat. "What's the problem, Nathan?"

He nods, his tongue creeping out to moisten his lower lip. "I promised you I'd never hurt you purposefully."

"That you did." Where's he going with this?

"I'm not doing this to purposefully hurt you either." He mutters conspiratorially. I really don't have the brainpower for this right now.

"Look…" I place my hand on his that rests on his thigh and give him a soft look. "I don't blame you. You don't need to feel guilty. Dillan and I aren't your problem, we never were. Thank you for the ride."

The look he gives me shows far too much regret than any person should have to deal with. "Everything I've done, I've done it for you."

"That's why I'm not blaming you now."

With one last lingering look at me, he finally flicks the locks on the doors. "I'll miss you, Gwen."

My heavy heart pounds. "Why are you saying that like we'll never see each other again?" Panic follows, I don't like this. "What about Dillan?"

He doesn't respond, he only twists his hands on the steering wheel and stares straight ahead.

"Nathan?" I prompt, my voice breaking. "What about Dillan?"

"I..." He looks away from me. "I don't know."

"Don't do this," I whisper, full of pain and desperation. "You promised me a home..."

"I gave you one."

"And now you're ripping it away." I sniff, trying so hard not to cry. "You're my best friend."

"Get out of the car, Guinevere," he says gruffly.

"No."

He leans over, keeping his face turned away from me and pushes the door open with his hand. The cool breeze dries the burning tears on my cheeks. "Get out of the car."

Shaking my head with disappointment, I lean over and press my lips to his cheek before climbing out of the car. He inhales a shuddering breath as I close the door and wave at him through the windscreen.

I'm grateful that he doesn't leave until I'm inside, hearing the engine slowly quieten as it leaves the driveway is hard enough. Watching it would probably break me.

"It didn't go well then?" Jeanine says as I step into her house. She's stood near the window by the door so I'm assuming she was watching. I take Dillan from her arms and hold him at arm's length.

"Did you miss me, baby? Did you miss me?" I coo in a baby voice. I look to Jeanine and shrug. "Unfortunately it didn't."

"He'll come around," she reassures me, but I don't need the reassurance. Right now I'm too angry with Nathan to even consider fighting for his friendship. "What did he say?"

"Not much. Did you know he was going to move all of my things out?"

She shakes her head. "He told me he had some family business to deal with and needed the house free, so I told him I'd invite you round for the morning."

I want to be mad at her betrayal but I can't; she was just looking out for someone she's known since he was a child. I can't blame her for her loyalty to him and not to me.

"If I'd known that he would do this, I would have told you." Her eyes hold sincerity and I believe her words. It brings me a small amount of relief. "What are you going to do now?"

I blow out a breath, which accidentally catches Dillan in the face and makes him jerk around with fluttering eyelids. Giggling, I take him into the room and lay him on the play mat. He stares up at the flashing lights that hover over his head and kicks his chunky little legs. "I'll call my mum or Sasha and see if one of them can pick me up."

"Well, if they can't, I will take you."

I shake my head. "I know how much you hate driving for long periods of time. We'll be fine."

"Where's your necklace?" She asks and I wince in response. "Oh dear."

"I had a moment of anger," I whisper, feeling ashamed of myself. My fingers seek out the necklace which is no longer there. "I'll be back. I'm going to make a few calls."

Unfortunately Sasha can't get me until tomorrow and my mum's car is in for repair. That leaves me with no options. Maybe I should just accept that ride from Nathan.

It would give us a chance to talk.

Burying my pride, I pick up my phone, having to lean over the couch as the cord for my charger isn't long enough to reach and if I unplug it it'll just die on me again.

Nathan answers after a few rings. "Forget something?"

Yes. You.

"No... umm... Nobody can collect me until tomorrow," I admit and chew on the inside of my cheek. "I'd go tomorrow, Jeanine has offered for me to stay, but I only have enough nappies to last me until tonight." I'm still breastfeeding so food isn't a problem. "And he doesn't have any pyjamas or even a place to sleep."

He doesn't speak for a long moment. "I'll take you but it won't be until later. I'm actually on my way to deal with a few things."

"I also still have your house keys," I tell him and pat my pocket for confirmation.

"I'll pick them up when I pick you up." He pauses for a moment. "I am sorry it has come to this, Guinevere."

What do I say to that? "Me too."

The longer I sit and think about my actions from earlier today, the more ashamed I become. My neck feels bare and I want more than anything to have my necklace back and erase the pain that flitted through Nathan's eyes when I ripped it from my neck.

I acted unreasonably and, despite my need to be angry and my need to yell, I can't. He's going through something and I'm not sure whether he's trying to protect me or himself.

Indecision clouds my brain. I want to fight for him, more than anything. I can't bear the thought of losing him but I also can't stand to be on the receiving end of his anger whenever something gets tough.

Also is this person, who is clearly holding something over him, dangerous? This concerns me. I don't just have myself to think about, I have Dillan now. Maybe I just have to put my faith in Nathan and trust that he's dealt with it.

Or maybe I should panic and call the Police, but what would I tell them?

I finally make a decision. It's not a huge one and it won't change much, but it will help my conscience ease a little. "Can you watch Dillan for me again?" I ask Jeanine, hoping I'm not pushing my luck.

She throws me her car keys and waves me away. Great.

CHAPTER TWENTY-FIVE

THE HOUSE IS DARK and empty when I arrive. The only car in the driveway is my beast of a BMW. I slide out from Jeanine's car and pull out my
keys.

All I want is my necklace back. I should never have ripped it off and the niggling in my mind is driving me crazy. Once I have it, I'll repair it and send it back to him. Or I'll keep it. I haven't decided yet.

I tiptoe up the stairs, feeling like a criminal and praying that Nathan didn't think to lock his bedroom door.

He didn't. Thank god.

I don't flick on the light. The room is dim but I can see where I'm going.

Using the camera flash as a torch, I drop down onto my knees in his closet and seek out the gold pendent.

Almost immediately, in the far corner, the tiny red jewel sparkles at me. I smile and shuffle forward, grasping it with one hand. I pick it up but the chain gets stuck on something, causing me to drop it. Must be a loose nail it has snagged on. There are clothes above making it pitch black and I feel for the end of the chain with difficulty.

I use my phone again and purse my lips when I see the chain is stuck between the skirting board and the floor. What are the odds?

I give it another tug but don't get anywhere. I'm starting to worry that I'll break the chain further.

Sliding onto my belly, I pray that there are no spiders and lean my phone against a shoe so it shines directly where the chain is stuck. I give it another tug. Nothing.

Damn it.

It is really stuck in there. I think the clasp has slid through and has twisted.

I head back into Nathan's room and pull open the top drawer of the desk by the bed. I've seen him grab pens and things from in here, so I'm hoping there'll be something I can use.

What the hell? When...? Oh my god.

I grab the photo and blink in astonishment. It's of me and Nathan on the Ferris wheel. I'm pregnant, my head is resting against his shoulder and his chin is on top of my head.

The memory surfaces and it suddenly dawns on me that this is what he must have been buying when I went to the toilet that night at the fair. My mouth stretches into a soft smile. I touch the picture with the tip of my finger affectionately and place it back in the drawer.

I think Nathan feels more for me than I realised. How else do I explain this secret photo? He clearly doesn't want me to know that he has it or it would be on display. Either that or he would have at least shown me.

So how long has he felt this way? I thought he disliked me back then.

My mind goes back to my necklace. I grab a ruler (why the hell he has a ruler upstairs I have no idea) and get back to work on loosening the necklace from the skirting board.

The corner of the plastic measuring device slips between the floor and board at the corner. I slide it along the crack until I'm a few centimetres away from my jewellery.

Click. Uh-oh. The skirting board just fell away from the wall. That's not good.

My attention is on the small dark space and I'm sure I can see something in its depths, like a box of sorts. Using the light from my phone, I shine it into the hole, scared I'll find any number of creatures. Instead I find a very small and clean space filled with DVD cases perfectly lined up.

What are these?

Nathan's porn stash? I can't help it, my curiosity won't let me leave them behind. If it's porn or possibly even Nathan doing naughty things, I'll just put them back.

I'm so lucky. Caleb always said I was lucky and he was right. It feels like I was meant to find this. What are the odds that this would happen because I threw my necklace?

I run my finger over the plain black cases with labels along the narrow edge. My eyes instantly zoom on one that seems separate from all of the others. It's the only one that's labelled.

First Time
(Inc---Stephan)

Isn't that Mr Weston's name? I'm sure it is.

I pull out three of the unlabelled DVDs and the labelled one and walk back into Nathan's room. I should have taken better note as to where everything was. He'll most likely notice that I've moved things, being the perfectionist that he is.

I wish I had my own TV in my room, less chance of getting caught, but I know he won't be back for a while. It still makes my hands shake at the thought though.

When I open the DVD the title baffles me.

I don't hesitate to place the disk into the attached DVD player behind the TV and turn it on.

He Knew

What kind of title is that for a homemade porno? That's assuming it is a porno.

I pop the DVD in the player and sit back on my knees. The screen is fuzzy for a few minutes with white noise. The quality isn't great either. Huh, seems to be some kind of... oh my god. That's here, I'd recognize that front door anywhere.

"Where is he?" A man I don't recognize speaks from behind the camera. "Where's my big boy today?"

Oh, it's some kind of home video.

"Here, Grandpa, here!" I let out a startled laugh as a dark haired boy who can't be older than six comes rushing through the archway and vanishes from sight as he no doubt hugs his grandpa. Wait... I've seen this boy before. The picture I found. It's Caleb!

My heart soars.

"Look what Grandpa has, Nathan."

Wow. It's Nathan? Is he sure? He must be, he's their grandfather. The resemblance is uncanny.

"Cool." The video wobbles a lot and crackles as the boy's grandfather shows him the camera.

Nathan is now back in view, his face only seeming to be a few inches away from the camera. Oh my god. I know those eyes and those lips and those freckles. That's Nathan. It is Nathan! Now that I'm getting a closer look I can tell that it's him.

"And how old you are now?" Grandpa asks as he takes the camera back from the happy little boy. So carefree, so happy. It's odd seeing Nathan this way.

The boy smiles and the smile is so easy, it reminds me so much of Caleb. "I turned six yesterday!"

"I'm guessing you'll be wanting a present?"

The little boy bounces on the spot, his tight white shirt and cute little blue bow tie the only thing in view as he goes up. He can jump pretty high for a kid of his age. "Pwease, pwease, pwease." Aww, he said pwease. He's so adorable.

"Come on then." Grandpa leads him outside. "To the barn."

"Yes!" Nathan hollers, his little fist pumping the air. "To the barn!" He says this like a superhero and flies forward through the long grass. I can't stifle my smile at his playful behaviour.

Ah, I get to see the barn which has been burned to the ground.

My suspicions are soon confirmed when they manage to make it to the huge white barn, almost as big as the house. I see Grandpa's slightly aged hand unlatch a door around the side and push it open. This camera movement is making me feel a little bit nauseous.

"Where is it? Where is it?" Nathan bounces up and down excitedly on the spot just inside of the doorway. The light flicks on, showing how terrible the quality of the video camera from eighteen years ago really was. And this video camera is probably one of the best of its time. Whoever made these videos must have gone to a lot of trouble to convert them onto a DVD.

"You'll see, but first," I hear the door shut and lock, "I need to tell you a secret. Can you keep a secret?" The camera focuses on the boy's face, which suddenly gets serious as he nods eagerly. Why am I suddenly feeling uneasy? Where are the animals in this barn? "Good. You're very special to me, Nathan. You're my eldest Grandson. That means when I die, all of this will be yours."

"All of what?" Nathan asks, his cute nose crinkling.

"My house, this barn, my cars." Cars? I haven't seen any cars. Maybe Nathan sold them.

"Cool! Can I have my present now?"

They enter another room. I don't know much about barns, but I know they're supposed to have more space than this. This room is a bit bigger than the last and I'm wondering why there's a bed in the corner. Maybe it's where the farm hands would rest or stay. There's a sink too but it doesn't look to be in very good condition.

Grandpa switches on another light but it's not very good. I can barely make out Nathan's face but I can see his white suit perfectly. He looks like a little sailor.

Grandpa moves around and stands by the bed, the camera still pointing at a curious Nathan.

"Ready for your present?" Grandpa asks Nathan, who beams. "You'll get it on one condition."

"What?"

Oh my god.

My hand flies to my mouth and tears burn my eyes. I watch but I don't. I scream but I don't. I sob but I don't. I can't look away and before it's even over I race to the toilet and vomit.

"Why is your pee pee out Grandpa?"

Oh my god. My body won't stop shaking.

"Well, to get your present you have to be a very good boy. We're going to play a very fun game."
"What game?"
"I need you to do something for me."

"I don't think I want to."

My stomach heaves again but my mind won't move to something else.

My body is in shock I just know it. Oh. That poor boy. That poor, poor boy.

"Stop! Stop! It hurts! Please stop! DADDY! MUMMY!"

The screams, the cries, the begging. Bile rises again.

I see... everything. I want to look away but I need to see, so I can absorb his pain. Make it so he never felt it.

"CATCH!"

I race into the bedroom and hastily take the DVD from the TV. It feels like fire in my hands. I place it back into the DVD case and tuck it into my coat. I don't know what I'm going to do with it, but I do know that I can't just not do anything.

Oh my god. Tears spill, my vision blurs. I can't believe this.

Nathan.

Oh god. Nathan. I'm so sorry this happened to you.

I shouldn't do it... I shouldn't, but I need to know if there's more. Are all of these DVDs recordings of abuse?

I check the few I have, one by one, only glimpsing at each one to confirm.

It takes me a few minutes but I manage to get through the entire stack of them that were hidden behind the skirting board. Only glancing at a few and sobbing when I realise that the last one is of Nathan when he looks to be about eleven.

Vomit comes up again and I barely make it to the toilet this time. The sound of the awfulness coming from TV only makes me feel worse.

My breathing is out of control. My mind wants to shut down and block this out. The things I've just witnessed are too painful to bear. How does Nathan live with this? Why has he never said anything?

How can he stay here after experiencing that?

I rinse my mouth out after brushing my teeth with a spare toothbrush from under the sink and stare at my reflection in the mirror. Nathan. Oh my god. Nathan.

Poor Nathan.

This explains everything. Oh god.

Sob.

My face burns from my salty tears; they won't stop.

"CATCH!"

This is why Nathan has an issue with his hands... isn't it? What am I going to do?

"What the fuck did you do?" I spin, my back hitting the sink as my eyes land on a furious Nathan, his hands gripping the doorframe as if anchoring him. "WHAT DID YOU DO?"

"Nathan," I attempt but it's cut off when he lunges for me, his hand fisting in my hair. It's not painful, not in the slightest, but it could be if he just pulled a little bit harder. Fear mingles with the overwhelming sorrow and my already weak body begins to shake. "I..."

The usual gold tone of his skin is now red, a vein throbbing angrily in his forehead. "I told you to stay out of my room!"

"I..."

I'm dragged into the hall and slammed roughly against the wall. Again, it doesn't hurt but it puts the fear of god into me. My bones rattle and my fear rises. "I TOLD YOU!"

"I know... I didn't mean..." I scream and cover my face when his fist comes up; it doesn't hit me but it hits the wall beside my head. My flight instinct kicks in, I duck under his arm and try to escape.

I don't make it three steps before an arm wraps around my midsection, slamming me back into his chest. "Let go!" I beg, my tears now of fear. What's he going to do? "Please, Nathan, let me explain."

I thrash, trying to tug my arms free, but he has hold of my wrists, pinning them across each other and to my breasts. "Where did you find them?"

"In... in the closet," I stammer and let out a sob. "I came back for my necklace but it got stuck. When I tried to get it out, the skirting board came off." His heavy breathing hits my ear; he sounds like he's about to hyperventilate. "I thought it was a home video. I swear... But then... I only checked the others."

I whimper when he spins me in his arms and forces me against the wall. His hands grip my neck as he moves his face to my ear. "If you ever tell anyone about this..."

"I..."

He squeezes the back of my neck, effectively shutting me up. "I will *end* you." The way he says this is so menacing, so cold, I barely recognise the Nathan I thought I knew.

My eyes widen with fear and my body trembles even more than before. "Nathan." I slide my hand up his arm and touch his cheek but he looks away, shame clouding his features. What does he have to be ashamed of? "I'm so sorry this happened to you."

His body tightens, his muscles now cement beneath his skin. "Get out." He pulls away from me and glares with an anger so potent, I back up a space. My coat is flung at me. "Don't come back, Gwen."

"Nathan..." I try, my brow furrowed with sympathy and concern. "I..."

"I said get out!" He bellows and grips my arm. I'm pulled down the stairs, stumbling slightly as my sluggish legs try to keep up with his quick and powerful strides.

"Please, don't..."

"No." He shakes his head and clamps a hand over my mouth. "I never want to see you again. I never want to hear from you again." I'm led down the last set of stairs, tears burning my cheeks.

"Nathan, please."

"Shut up!" He snarls, dragging me towards the door. I stumble but his grip doesn't loosen. "I mean it, Guinevere." The door opens and I'm shoved outside into the cold. Cold, emotionless brown eyes attack my greys. "You're dead to me." The door slams shut, leaving me petrified on the spot.

"Oh my god," I murmur, my teeth chattering. Tears that were falling before now rush from my eyes in two endless streams. I hold my coat tight to my body and race towards Jeanine's car. We have to leave and we have to leave now. Whatever demons Nathan's holding aren't something I want to address. He clearly doesn't want to share them and I don't blame him. I can only imagine what it's like having a secret that powerful.

I'll give him his wish.

I try not to break down when I get to Jeanine's.

I do. I break down so badly I can't even sob as I cry.

Jeanine instantly kneels beside me and pulls me into her arms. She tries to reassure me that everything will be okay. It's not like I don't know that it'll be okay. Of course it will be okay. If there's one thing I've learned over these past few months since losing Caleb, it's that life goes on. I'll be okay but I'll never be the same.

Not after what I've just seen.

Nathan... my poor Nathan. How do I deal with this? I want to take away his pain but I don't think he wants it taking away.

Another Weston male came into my life, made me feel alive and then left without looking back. For Caleb this was nature taking him from his body, for Nathan this was his nature taking him from me. Different types of nature that was forced on both of them. Caleb's was a natural nature, Nathan's was a nature so unnatural, it scares me to even think of it.

I'm going to vomit again.

Nathan would never be this way if not for his grandfather. If the man were still alive, I'd probably kill him myself, prison sentence be damned.

Was Caleb abused too? No... something tells me that this never happened to Caleb.

But why?

Will I ever know the answers? Do I even want to know?

No. I don't think I do. I want to take my son and get far away from here. So that's what I'll do. It's what I have to do.

It just hurts so bad, knowing that he's hurting...

TO BE CONTINUED...

SNEAK PEAK INTO THE FUTURE

I HOLD THE BROWN bottle in my hand and bring it to my mouth. My chest and throat burn after I swig the spirit. I welcome the burn, I deserve it. I deserve the pain and the torture. I'm no better than he was.

Her hands bang against the glass, she can see me. She's looking right at me. Screams of fright and anguish can be heard over the crackling and roaring flames that have engulfed the house. They lick at the sky, creating a huge cloud of thick, grey smoke that lingers over the trees.

She doesn't deserve to die this way, I didn't even know she was here, but she knows too much. This is a means to an end. She's seen it, she's heard it and she knows it so she must die with it.

I only pray that her end is swift. For the pain in her eyes troubles me, it must be scorching hot in there now. The room she's standing in has begun to glow orange. The flames have finally reached her. She's too high up to jump out of the window and there's clearly no other way out.

I take another swig and lean back against the tree behind me. Watching her long black hair fall from its hair tie as she frantically beats at the window.

My own sorrow for my sins overwhelms me and I cry silently as she falls from view, the smoke too thick for her lungs. At least darkness will claim her before she burns alive.

"I'm so sorry, Guinevere," I mutter and stand. "I'm so sorry." Sirens can be heard in the distance, so I take my bottle and vanish into the night.

ACKNOWLEDGMENTS

This journey has been an interesting one and I seem to have picked up many people on the way. First off there's Helen, honestly, you rock. I never thought I'd meet a woman as strange as myself. Thank you for all of your help, with my books and with life.

Nora, an amazing woman who has helped me so much. Sometimes words just aren't enough. Right now is one of those times.

Kids, please be quiet, Mummy is working. I love you very much.

Ali, I don't know where your socks are, I haven't done the laundry yet.

Loryn, you're crazy, but it's why we love you.

Ramya, my friend from across the sea, thank you for being honest with me.

Elisia Goodman and Rivka, without you these paperbacks wouldn't be possible. Thank you so much for putting up with my demanding ways.

David Lane, thanks for having me on SHCR. You rock.

There are a lot of people I'd like to thank but not enough space. To me you're all awesome and I hope you know that I love you.

ABOUT THE AUTHOR

A. E. Murphy is the queen of sarcasm and satire, she likes long walks in the park, as much as ice cubes like to chill in a roasting oven. She's efortlessly independent and so good at adulting it's unfair on the rest of the world. She only napped twice today and has only avoided the dishes for three days before making the child slaves do them this morning. Winning! (Kidding, she has a dishwasher now.)
Her favourite hobby is writing, her worst hobby is reading through that writing. Also, she has four cats that carry toys to the top of the stairs and drop them down so they can chase them. They do this repeatedly in the middle of the night. Who cares if she has work the next morning? Not the cats, that's for sure. And if it's not the cats doing the waking, it's the ridiculous amount of children and bonus children she has constantly asking for a snack, or the fiancé being a needy bear. This is likely why she is so happy all the freaking time, but not without coffee and chocolate.
P.S. Please leave feedback, if not on the book then on this ridiculous bio she wrote herself. It's the least you can do seeing as she'll forever talk in the third person now.
Alex loves her readers. Alex says thank you. Alex smiles.

CONTACT

Facebook
www.facebook.com/a.e.murphy.author
Email
a.e.murphy@hotmail.com
Instagram
aemurphyauthor
TikTok
@authorxelaknight
@authoraemurphy

ALSO BY

Standalone Novels
Masked Definitions
HIS FATHER
STEPDORK
NAKED OR DEAD
DANCE OR DIE
Becoming His Mistress
VICIOUS

Seas of Seduction
Seizing Rain
Freeing Calder

The Little Bits Series
A Little Bit of Crazy
A Little Bit of Us
A Little Bit of Trouble
A Little Bit of Truth
A Little Bit of Guilt

The Distraction Trilogy
Distraction, Destruction, Distinction
The Broken Trilogy
Broken Connected Forever

A Broken Story Disconnected (Dillan)
Sweet Demands Trilogy
Lockhart Lockdown Unlocked

Colouring Books
NAKED OR DEAD colouring book edition
Laurie's Life Lessons a colouring book novella (Becoming His Mistress
Spin-of)
VICIOUS colouring book edition
Audiobooks
NAKED OR DEAD
HIS FATHER
BECOMING HIS MISTRESS

XELA KNIGHT
(Paranormal Books)
Syphon 1A, Syphon 2A, Syphon 3A

Printed in Great Britain
by Amazon

40535944R00205